Praise for Mario D
Forbidden R

"**I absolutely loved following each man's story,** background, and bias as situations arose with members of the church and their student groups. **It was heartbreaking and tender, packed with real and raw emotion** that just pulled at your heartstrings and gave the reader a lot to think about. **Such an inspired story that I couldn't put down!**" – Ash Knight, author

"**I absolutely devoured this story!** It provides an inside look at a group of young seminarians trying to navigate through the duplicity, corruption, hypocrisy, and traumatic experiences of the religious systems perpetuated by the Catholic Church. **I loved** the different points of view of the characters during the 1980s and their insights on love, self-identity, and self-realization… the struggle between good and evil is revealed within the delusion perpetrated by the powerful men of the Vatican City… **a must-read!**" – Lali A. Love, award-winning best-selling author

"Dell'Olio flawlessly details the conflict of being gay and Catholic in an intolerant time. He opens a window into priesthood, Church politics, and corruption. **This book is perfect for anyone dreaming of something more**, finding the strength to believe in yourself, or searching for where you belong. **One of the easiest five stars I've ever given**." – Halo Scot, author

"A complex journey of immersive self-discovery between faith and identity. **A great read, talented author.**" – Rory Michaelson, author

About Mario Dell'Olio

Mario Dell'Olio lives in White Plains, New York. Dell'Olio's books are about finding one's value and worth in the world, coming to accept who you are, and loving yourself. Regardless of the story, this message rings through each book.

New Men: Bonds of Brotherhood, is a romantic journey of self-discovery inspired by true stories. It is filled with romance, hope, and desire.

Forbidden Rome is a complex and timeless journey of beautiful self-discovery between faith and identity, full of passion, prejudice, and ambition.

Mario's mission is to teach kindness and love to those around him. "Using my life experiences, I hope to communicate that we are all one human family and that we will all benefit by working with each other for the greater good."

Go to 5310publishing.com/author/mariodellolio to learn more about LGBTQ+ fiction author Mario Dell'Olio. Get exclusive updates, discounts, and news about Mario Dell'Olio and all his books!

Point your phone's camera at this page to learn more.

FORBIDDEN ROME

Passion. Prejudice. Ambition.

Mario Dell'Olio

Passion. Prejudice. Ambition.

FORBIDDEN
ROME

"A complex journey of
immersive self-discovery
between faith and identity."
—Rory Michaelson, author

"An addictive, perennial,
and timeless journey of
beautiful self-discovery."
—Halo Scot, author

"I absolutely devoured
this story! A must-read!"
—Lali A. Love, author

"Such an inspired story
that I couldn't put down!"
—Ash Knight, author

MARIO DELL'OLIO

Published by
5310 Publishing Company
5310publishing.com

Our books may be purchased in bulk for promotional, educational, or business use. Please contact your local bookseller or 5310 Publishing at sales@5310publishing.com.

FORBIDDEN ROME - First Edition ISBNs:

6" x 9" Paperback:	978-1-990158-46-9
Ebook / Kindle:	978-1-990158-47-6
Large Print Edition:	978-1-990158-55-1
Hardcover:	978-1-990158-56-8

Author: Mario Dell'Olio
Editor: Eric Williams
Cover design: Eric Williams

First edition released in June 2022.

SCAN ME

"We have to find a way to help that father or that mother to stand by their [LGBTQ] son or daughter." –Pope Francis

To all who struggle to love themselves because of who they love. –Mario Dell'Olio

Chapter One
The Departure

The New Men slowly gathered at the TWA international terminal at the John F. Kennedy Airport in New York. Each diocese across the United States chose from numerous graduate seminaries around the country. In 1982, many men attended undergraduate programs in philosophy at one of the college seminaries close to their home dioceses. But it was becoming more common for men to enroll at regular universities for their undergraduate work before entering the Theologate (graduate studies in theology.)

For a select number of young theologians, an appointment to the North American College in Rome was a coveted prize. Only the brightest and the best were sent to Rome, or so they were told.

The TWA terminal glowed with natural light from the floor-to-ceiling windows that looked out onto the tarmac. Dotting the red carpets, a group of young men in their early twenties gathered at the gate in eager anticipation.

It wasn't unusual to have some priests or religious sisters or brothers on flights to Rome. However, having nearly fifty young seminarians on one airplane created quite a spectacle. Most of the men wore black suits with white shirts and black ties. It was the end of August, and the New York City temperatures had reached 90 degrees with 68% humidity. It was oppressive, and most other travelers sported casual attire, including short-sleeved shirts and jeans.

The flock of young men dressed in black stood out in more ways than one. There seemed to be an air of self-importance among them – almost as if they were above the ordinary travelers. They spoke in quiet tones and were very formal with one another. It was obvious that there was a lot of posturing as they met one another.

When Anthony Rossi arrived with his entourage in tow, no one took note. The men headed for the North American College simply assumed that he was traveling on vacation. His bright pink Izod and docksider shoes told a story of who Anthony might be, but it certainly did not scream *seminarian*.

Once at the gate at JFK, his usual ebullient personality transformed into one of reserved. When he saw the gaggle of men dressed in black, Anthony knew precisely who they were, and he wasn't all that keen on joining them. *What have I gotten myself into?* he thought. They seemed so pious and judgmental. The clerical scene before him was not what Anthony expected.

***

Two hours earlier, he was loading up the car with his luggage. Anthony's family gathered in the driveway of their raised ranch house. So as not to prolong a painful goodbye, Mrs. Rossi decided not to travel to the airport to see him off. There, in their front yard, his siblings expected a tearful scene to erupt at any moment. However, Anthony's mother would have none of that. She had never cried in front of her children, and she didn't want to start now.

The course of study was four to five years in length, but what made it difficult was the rule that the new men were not allowed to return home for two years. It would be painful enough for him to leave the family for such an extended period. She was not about to make it even more unpleasant for her youngest son by crying. He was her baby, and the need to protect him poured out of her very being. Although she didn't have favorites, she shared a special relationship with Anthony. Out in front of their house, the car was packed with his luggage and his two sisters.

His brother, Joe, eager to get on the road, was in the driver's seat drumming his fingers on the steering wheel. Anthony turned to his father, hugged him tightly, and said, "I love you, Papa."

Then he looked at his mother and teared up. "*Vieni, Caro*. Come here, Anthony. Just look at the man you've become," she said as she pulled him into her loving embrace. She held him a bit longer than usual, then pushed him away. "Now go, go to Rome and follow your dreams. We are so proud of you." Anthony couldn't respond, knowing that if he tried to speak, he would burst into tears.

He squeezed into the car with his siblings and waved goodbye. They were not even a block away when he turned to look back at his parents. His father, who rarely showed any affection, had his arm around his wife holding her while she cried. That was all he needed to see—the tears were streaming down his face. His sister, Rosa, put her arm around him silently. His brother, Joe, looked at him through the rear-view mirror and noticed him crying.

"Knock it off! We haven't even turned off our street. What are you going to do for two years if you can't handle a goodbye to mom?"

"Leave him alone, Joe," Rosa chided. "How would you know what he's going through? You're twenty-six years old, and you still haven't left home." That broke the tension, and they all laughed.

"Why should I waste all that money on rent? Besides, what would I do without mom's cooking?" Joe finally said.

Before long, they were sitting in New York traffic with hundreds of other cars heading to Kennedy Airport. When they arrived, Joe pulled up to the curb and helped his brother unload his bags. Anthony looked up at the TWA terminal in awe. It was something out of a science fiction movie – the building looked like a space station. It had a wing-shaped roof made of white concrete and tall windows where passengers could watch the planes taking off.

The terminal was beautiful and modern. They wandered into the crowded lobby and got in line. After he had checked in, the four siblings headed over to the waiting area where there was a sea of young men chatting quietly. "I believe we've found your new buddies, Anthony," Joe said sarcastically.

"Stop that, they look nice," Rosa said. "Anthony, go over and introduce yourself."

Anthony had no desire to join the other seminarians, not only because of their clerical demeanor but because he wanted to spend as much time as possible with his brother and sisters. He knew they would be apart for two whole years.

"No thanks, I'll be with them for the next four years," he said to Rosa. "I think I'll just stay here with you guys. I'm going to miss you all so much – well, except for Joe."

His brother punched his shoulder and pulled him in for a rough hug. "Oh, you'll miss me more than the rest. You know I'm your favorite brother."

"You're his *only* brother," Rosa clarified.

Just then, his high school friend, Chris, spotted Anthony and came over. He and Chris had gone to the same university but had different circles of friends. Even so, it was good to have at least one person that he'd known in Rome.

"Hi, Anthony, you finally made it, and with the Italian mafia in tow!" Chris joked.

"You know I don't travel without my entourage, Chris. You remember my brother and sisters."

"Hi, everyone. How did the farewell scene with mom and dad go? Was it full of Italian drama?" he asked.

"Actually, it was pretty tame," Rosa answered. "We were all pretty impressed with mom's tearless goodbye."

"Yeah, until the car started moving. We weren't a block away when the spigot was turned on, and the tears flowed freely," he added.

"Anthony, why don't you come to meet some of the other guys? There are men from all over the country in our class. It's really kind of cool." Chris invited Anthony with a smile.

"I'll be right back," Anthony said to his siblings, and off he went with Chris. When the boarding call was announced, Anthony hugged his sisters and brother as he said goodbye. Then he picked up his guitar case and made his way to the gate.

The space-age architecture of the TWA terminal was even more pronounced as he entered the long tube that would bring him to the plane. It was shaped like an arch with red carpet and rounded walls. He gave one last glance toward his family and entered the tube that led to his new life. He slowly began walking with the rest of the passengers and was surprised by the intensity of feelings welling up within him. The gravity of the moment hit Anthony hard.

When he reached the apex of the tube, he paused. *How can I leave my family for two years? What am I doing?* he thought. Chris, who was just a few steps behind him, took note.

"Keep moving, Anthony. If you look back at them, you'll feel worse. You can do this," he said without breaking his stride. His confident voice snapped him out of it. Anthony took a deep breath and started to move toward the gate once again. This is what he had always dreamed of; he couldn't turn back now.

Once he was settled in his seat, he began to feel better. There was a buzz of excitement from the other guys, and Anthony was swept up in their enthusiasm. He was off to the Vatican to study for the priesthood. *How cool is that?* he thought. As the flight took off, Anthony knew that he would be just fine.

Chapter Two
The Arrival

After his emotionally wrenching departure from New York, Anthony was grateful for his newly discovered exuberance. As soon as the plane landed in Rome, he was like a new man. Anthony was finally living his dream of becoming a priest.

It all begins now, he thought. All the drama from his first relationship with a guy in college was long behind him. It didn't matter that they were deeply in love at the time – he was called to be a priest. He rested in the knowledge that, even though he was gay, he had no need to be in a romantic relationship. His year with Thomas had awakened his sexual awareness. If he chose to stay with him, his dream of becoming a priest would never come to pass. Entering the diocesan formation program that year reinforced his desire to become a priest. Now, he was finally doing it. He was in Rome, on his way to his new address: *Collegio Americano del Nord,* Vatican City State.

Now that he had arrived in Rome, his fears seemed far behind him. Oversized bags trickled out of the conveyor belt as Anthony waited for much too long. He was eager to get out of the airport and on their way.

Eventually, he spotted his luggage and pulled the overstuffed bag off the conveyor belt. Anthony didn't know what came over him back in New York – he was almost shy, dreading the painful goodbye with his family. But now that he was in Rome, Anthony couldn't contain his excitement.

He made the rounds, introducing himself to his classmates as they found their way to the coach. Many of them were jet-lagged and only half-heartedly returned his greetings. He boarded the bus and, in the first row, spotted a very handsome guy with his head leaning against the window. He was attracted to him immediately and knew he had to sit beside him. "Hi there, I'm Anthony," he said.

"Kevin. How could you possibly be so energetic after eight and a half hours in flight?" he asked after taking the seat next to him.

"Are you kidding? We're in Rome! How cool is that? I am so excited to be here. There'll be plenty of time to sleep later on," Anthony responded, excited.

"Yeah, I suppose you're right. But, seriously, you can bring it down a few notches, can't you?" Kevin said, only half-jokingly. Anthony couldn't help but notice the glint in his eyes and the slight smile on Kevin's lips.

"Not a morning person, eh? No worries, I'll do all the talking. Where are you from?"

"Connecticut, Archdiocese of Hartford. You?"

"The Bronx, Archdiocese of New York. We're almost neighbors." Anthony's optimism could not be dampened. Even when the bus broke down on the way from Fiumicino Airport to the North American College, Anthony used the opportunity to get to know everyone. There were nearly fifty guys on the bus, sleep-deprived and jet-lagged after the eight-and-a-half-hour flight from New York.

A broken-down bus was not the greatest of welcomes to their new life, but Anthony found it amusing. *That's Italy for you!* he chuckled to himself. Anthony had fallen in love with Italy when his parents brought him to meet his family many years before. He loved the food, the language, and the people. Being stuck on the roadside did little to dampen his enthusiasm.

A number of the guys got off the bus because the scorching sun was heating the coach. However, there was little relief outside. It was late August in Rome, and the soaring temperatures were only beginning to bake the countryside. Thirty minutes turned to an hour, which turned into two hours. Regardless of the discomfort of the predicament, Anthony's spirit would not be tarnished. He scanned the crew of guys to see if there was anybody he missed.

He spotted a tall guy with broad shoulders who had an amused smile on his face as he watched Anthony make the rounds chatting with his classmates. Anthony noticed his gaze, went directly up to him, and stuck out his hand. "Hi there, my name is Anthony. I'm from New York. Where are you from?"

"I'm Miguel, from Dallas, Texas. Where did you go to college seminary, Anthony?" he asked.

"Oh, I didn't go to college seminary. I went to a Jesuit school and entered the diocesan program during my junior year," he replied.

"I see. Well, you might be in for quite a shock," Miguel said teasingly. "We're not in Kansas anymore."

"What do you mean? Everyone is just wonderful! We are in Rome, and we'll be living in Vatican City State. How could it possibly get better than that?" Anthony answered with blinding optimism.

Miguel rolled his eyes. *"This guy is in for a rude awakening,"* Anthony heard him say under his breath. Bad news turned to worse when the driver informed them that the repairs were more extensive than he suspected. They would have to wait until another coach arrived. Undeterred, Anthony decided to take a walk. There was a convenience store a short distance from where the bus was parked. He was eager to start speaking Italian – he needed the practice.

"Hey, Kevin, let's wander up to that store over there. We can go practice speaking Italian. What do you say?"

"I have nothing to practice; I've never taken Italian. Besides, it's way too hot for a walk," Kevin replied.

"Aw, come on. I'll do the talking. We can get something to drink or a gelato."

"Now you're talking! I could go for a gelato. You can be my translator," Kevin said.

***

When the replacement bus arrived, the new seminarians pulled all the luggage from underneath the original bus and reloaded it onto the new one. The men in their formerly crisp black suits found themselves in wrinkled clothes and drenched in sweat.

Once settled on the new coach, everyone was more than a little cranky. But Anthony remained optimistic as he spoke to Kevin. He regaled him with stories about his relatives in southern Italy: aunts, uncles, and a whole slew of cousins. Anthony promised he would bring Kevin there to meet them all. By the time they arrived at the seminary, Anthony had stolen Kevin's heart. As they neared the ancient city, Kevin looked around in awe at the Roman ruins dotting every corner. It was his first time in Italy – he was at the epicenter of the Catholic Church, but rather than imagining his life as a priest, Kevin's thoughts were consumed with his guileless new friend.

Things are looking up, Kevin thought. *Perhaps this won't be a dessert of human interaction.*

Kevin looked over at his new friend. Anthony wasn't traditionally handsome, but Kevin was taken with him from the start. His Roman nose and ethnic look allowed him to blend right in among his compatriots in Italy. He had hazel eyes and chestnut brown hair that shimmered when the light hit it just right. He was small in stature but didn't have an ounce of extra fat on him. It was clear he worked out because the outline of his pecs underneath his polo and his defined biceps could not be ignored. To top it all off, Anthony was gregarious and full of life.

With a smile on his face, Kevin recalled the moment they first met. As he pondered the sweet images, it surprised him that he hadn't noticed him before at JFK in New York. Kevin was half asleep when he boarded the coach bus at the Fiumicino airport in Rome. It had been a long flight from New York.

After an uncomfortably restrained goodbye with his parents, all Kevin wanted to do was sleep to escape his emotional unrest. However, sitting in the middle seat, he could do nothing more than doze. Eight and a half hours later, after gathering his luggage and boarding the coach, he plopped himself down in the first seat he could find, leaned his head against the window, and closed his eyes. All at once, Kevin was startled from his drowsing by a very energetic voice climbing aboard the bus.

"Oh, my God! I can't believe we're here. We're in Rome!" Anthony said to no one in particular. Kevin lifted his head in annoyance and made eye contact with Anthony for the first time. A big grin spread across his face. He stuck out his hand.

"Hi, I'm Anthony. Is this seat taken?" he said as he sat right beside him without waiting for a response. His enthusiastic patter continued throughout the interminable bus ride to the Vatican. Although he was heavy with jetlag, this incredibly innocent but beautiful, young seminarian delighted Kevin. There was no need for Kevin to contribute to the conversation. Simply nodding his head or agreeing now and again encouraged Anthony to continue.

In his pink Izod polo and matching blue and pink belt, Anthony's tanned biceps flexed invitingly. Kevin couldn't stop staring at him, but Anthony barely noticed. Kevin knew he had to be careful not to show too much interest. Beginning his new life as a seminarian in Rome, there couldn't be any hint of his attraction to other men. However, there was certainly no harm in admiring God's beautiful creation.

Kevin was startled out of his reverie by the vice-rector's voice. "On your right is the Vatican wall," Father Connick announced. "Just inside those walls rests the chair of St. Peter and his successor, Pope John Paul II. Gentlemen, you are almost home."

At that statement, the weary seminarians burst into applause, and their conversations became animated with excitement.

***

As the Bernini colonnade came into focus, his mouth dropped. For the first time that morning, Anthony was speechless. Although he'd been to visit before, this time was different. Seeing St. Peter's with fresh eyes, the reality of his new life struck him. He would be living in Vatican City State. He was no longer a tourist – this was his new home. Just beyond the Vatican walls, the bus began ascending a steep hill toward the North American College. The metal gates slowly opened, and as they passed through the portal, he could hear the peeling of bells singing their welcome.

When he stepped off the bus, he looked up at the white marble façade of the chapel that shone in the afternoon sunshine. It was carved with a powerful image of Mary, the Mother of God, encircled by angels. The upperclassmen and faculty lined the stairs to the grand bronze doors, applauding as they ascended the staircase. *What magnificent world have I just entered?* Anthony thought. Their broad, welcoming smiles invited the new men into their exclusive community of seminarians.

At the top of the staircase, Anthony paused and turned back to glance at the welcoming committee. Just over a bank of umbrella pines, Michelangelo's majestic dome stood proudly in his view. Anthony's breath caught, and he could feel his eyes well up. His classmates urged him on, and he followed them indoors.

The massive doors opened into the darkened chapel. Anthony's eyes had difficulty adjusting from the bright sun – the pipes of the grand organ blasted their welcome as the men processed into the invitingly cool space.

The scent of incense filled the air, giving it a sweet yet solemn atmosphere. It was unlike anything Anthony had ever experienced. The opening prayer service was a blur to him. His senses were filled with sounds of joyous music and the aroma of incense. The grand mosaic behind the main altar glittered in the light. A floor-to-ceiling image of Mary watched over as all these young men joined in their first prayer as seminarians at the North American College.

This was a completely foreign world for Anthony, and he was in awe. As he exited the chapel, Kevin was right by his side. "What happened to you, Anthony? I know we've just met, but I can't believe you're so quiet. You hadn't stopped talking since you got on the bus at the airport, and now you're quiet as a church mouse."

"It's all so wonderful. The bells, the organ, the chapel—it's all so wonderful," Anthony replied dreamily.

"Lord of Lords! You look like you've had a beatific vision," Kevin said as he chuckled. "At least now I know how to shut you up."

***

Leaving the chapel, the new men made their way to the refectory and waited for the orientation tour. A massive portrait of Pope John Paul II with his arms outstretched before him was prominently displayed in the center of the room. One of the men on the orientations committee noticed Anthony looking up at it. "We call that the portrait of the pope catching a beach ball."

Anthony burst into laughter. "No, you don't. Really?" Then he spotted the piano immediately and glided over to it. "Does anyone play the piano?" he asked. "Look, there's a collection of Broadway songs. Anyone want to sing?"

There was a murmur in the room, but no one volunteered to sing. However, Seth quietly sat on the piano bench beside Anthony as he flipped through the sheet music.

I'll play," he said. "I was a church organist at home. There are some cool books here. I'm sure we can find something to perform." They were animatedly engaged in their new project while the rest of the guys were milling around chatting with one another. *"What I Did for Love,* from A Chorus Line. Let's do this one."

"Interesting choice," Seth said noncommittally.

"I love this song," Anthony exclaimed.

He stood as Seth played the introduction, looked out over the seminarians gathered, and sang. He was utterly oblivious to the strained reactions he received from his classmates. However, Kevin looked on with an amused smile. *He has no idea how inappropriate this song is amid a crew of seminarians,* he thought. Kevin laughed to himself and was determined to get to know him better.

As Anthony continued to sing with confidence, Kevin was drawn to this guileless young man. After finishing the first chorus, Anthony finally realized that no one had gathered around the piano as they used to do in college. He knew something was wrong and sensed that the energy in the room had changed. Something was definitely off. In fact, the guys were looking away; some seemed to laugh. *Did I do something funny?* he thought. He motioned for Seth to stop playing.

"I think that's enough for that song. Why don't you play something by yourself? Do you know any classical pieces?" Seth graciously complied, taking the attention away from Anthony.

Relieved, he sat beside Seth on the piano bench and got lost in the music. Anthony was still trying to understand what had gone wrong. For some reason, he felt ashamed for having sung. But Anthony couldn't figure out why – it made little sense to him. What strange world had he gotten himself into?

Kevin made his way over to the piano but hung back until Fr. Connick entered the room. He announced they would be divided into five groups and be given a tour. By then, they would place their luggage in their rooms, and they could take a bit of a break before *pranzo* – the main meal of the day.

The new men rose from their seats and followed their guides. Kevin seized the opportunity to talk to Anthony once again. He fell in step with him as they exited the refectory.

"Wow, Anthony, you have a beautiful voice."

"Thanks, Kev, but I don't think they received it very well," he said with an embarrassed laugh. "I guess our classmates disagree with your assessment of my talent."

"Well, your choice of repertoire was a little awkward in this room of celibate men. Don't you think?" Kevin had a wry smile on his face. "What I did for love—*we did what we had to do*," he said, quoting the lyrics of the song.

"Oh my God, that never even occurred to me." Anthony laughed, and without skipping a beat, said, "But who knows what they did to get here!"

"You're too much, Anthony," Kevin said as he bumped his shoulder against him as they broke into laughter. "I have a feeling we're going to be good friends."

"I hope so. This place is full of stiffs," Anthony replied, feeling better already. "It's good to know that I can be myself around you."

Chapter Three
Appropriate Behavior

O n week three of orientation, the new men gathered in the auditorium. By that point, the guys were feeling a bit more comfortable with one another, revealing bits of their actual personalities. In such a short time, affinity groups had formed: the pious, the ambitious, and the irreverent. The irreverent group had already started to meet for drinks and held impromptu gatherings on the roof deck of the seminary. The roof was affectionately known as the NAC beach because it was often filled with young seminarians sporting 80s speedos and working on their tans. The newly formed club laughed easily and enjoyed poking fun at the strange new world in which they found themselves. The priesthood was clearly in their future, so the slightly off-color humor regarding life at NAC was never meant to be disrespectful. It was their way of processing the many oddities of life in a Roman seminary.

Word had gotten out that the meeting later that day would address appropriate behavior for NAC seminarians. Miguel, a gregarious seminarian from Texas, hosted a pre-meeting gathering on the roof. It was BYOB, and there was no shortage of beverages to share. They joked about what may have prompted such a meeting and the behaviors that might be banned. It wasn't long before someone mentioned the dangers of having "particular friendships."

The group roared with laughter, and it wasn't difficult to detect the gay subtext to the conversation. "Oh, they were quite anxious about fraternization between seminarians at Trinity in Dallas," Miguel offered. "In fact, they made us change rooms every semester, lest we get too comfortable with our neighbors."

"No way," said Anthony. "That's so juvenile. How did they get away with treating you like children?"

"Ah, young grasshopper," Miguel responded, putting his arm around Anthony, "you have much to learn about seminary life and the lack of autonomy."

The guys laughed in agreement, but the very idea disturbed Anthony. *We are adults. Shouldn't we be treated as such?* he thought. The guys were well lubricated when the time came for their meeting. Any excuse for a cocktail party was welcome.

Stumbling down the grand marble staircase, they chanted: *"New Men, New Men."* Their high spirits and laughter could be heard throughout the building. As they rounded the corner toward the auditorium, the new men donned a suitable look of gravity and quietly took their seats. When Father Connick strode to the podium, the festive atmosphere took a turn.

It was as if the air was sucked out of the room. Stern and intimidating, Connick began his assault on the new men. "New men, you have been specially chosen to be here. Your presence at the North American College carries with it much responsibility. You are no longer ordinary men following your baser instincts. Yours is a higher calling with great demands. Be careful not to over imbibe in alcohol. In Italy, wine is cheaper than soda. Maintaining a respectful level of decorum is expected. When in public, drunken or boisterous behavior is never appropriate."

"What are we, sixteen years old?" Miguel whispered to no one in particular.

"And of course," Father Connick continued, "there should be no overt homosexual behavior."

That he used the word 'overt' in his directive did not escape anyone's attention. One could hear everyone shifting in their seats, and nervous coughs floated throughout the auditorium. "Then I guess we'll have to keep our homosexual behavior in the shadows," Anthony quipped.

There was an audible twitter from the audience, and Father Connick paused as he looked up to see where the laughter was coming from. The seminarians immediately put on the face of solemn agreement. That's when Miguel took note of Anthony. *This guy's got balls, and he's funny,* he thought. Miguel didn't suffer fools easily. When they had first met on the way from Fiumicino Airport, Miguel assumed Anthony was superficial and naïve. However, Anthony's candor displayed his authenticity–precisely what Miguel looked for in his friends. It also happened to be a rarity in seminaries.

Kevin, in contrast, was not amused by Anthony's impropriety. Joking around like that in a forum such as this could spell trouble for him. He was determined to make him understand that NAC was not like college life. "That was a close one, Anthony. You need to be more careful," Kevin whispered sharply into his ear, and without skipping a beat, his head turned back toward the podium.

Anthony could feel the burn of Kevin's reprimand. He was only kidding, just like the other guys. What was so wrong with his harmless comment? He could feel that familiar ache in his belly. It screamed, 'You are a bad little boy.' Anthony always sought to do the right thing, but his playful personality often got him in trouble. It dawned on him that although the other guys were free with their off-color remarks in private, they maintained a greater sense of propriety in these public forums. Formality seemed to be the rule at NAC. For the free-spirited Anthony, this was almost stifling. There was so much for him to learn about seminary culture, and he was having trouble reading the cues.

Then Father Connick listed off all the places in Rome that were forbidden. "The Roman circus is infamous for its lewd and perverted activities, as well as the area around the Colosseum, and Villa Borghese. These are places of grave danger to your souls. Beware of your human lustfulness and never give in to temptation. You must be vigilant with your chastity and avoid these locations, especially at night."

"Is anyone writing all these down?" Miguel asked, holding back his laughter. Anthony was bursting to respond, but after his previous comment, he held it in. After a glance over at Kevin, Anthony caught Miguel's eye and winked.

Later that evening, they found themselves on the roof deck, laughing about the speech that Father Connick delivered. They mocked him along with his false air of gravity. Then they rattled off the names of forbidden locations.

"He might as well have listed the seediest pickup joints in Rome," Andy from San Francisco said. "Better yet, he should have just told us where all the gay bars are!"

"All right, which shall we go to first?" Miguel asked. It was clear that he loved to stir up trouble.

"We should make this our Roman bucket list," Anthony added.

"Our goal should be to hit them all before the end of our first year," Andy replied.

"First-year? That's for neophytes!" Miguel said. "We can check these off by the end of the first semester." Kevin was a bit uncomfortable with how open they were with the conversation. His time at St. Thomas Seminary had taught him that there was a fine line between the unspoken tolerance for homosexuality and the open celebration of it. If anyone overheard them or reported their banter, they'd all be screwed. He found himself on the periphery of the scene, being careful to remain unobtrusive. They had only been there for three days. Regardless of how friendly this crew was, there was no way to know if they could be trusted.

As the party dwindled and people wandered off to bed, Kevin pulled Anthony aside and voiced his concerns.

"Look, Anthony, I know we're all having fun here. But we have to be more discreet. We don't know these guys well enough to joke so openly about this. Some of them may not even be gay. The seminary environment is very different from college, and there are lots of guys that can be very deceptive, even conniving."

"Oh, come on. We're just joking around. Why would any of us have to be careful?" Anthony replied. "Besides, they're all gay. It's as clear as day."

"You may be right, but I'm not so sure about Miguel. He doesn't give me that vibe at all."

"Come on, Kev, he was the first one to comment about hitting all the spots on the forbidden list."

"Miguel was in college seminary for four years. This kind of banter is ubiquitous. Most of the guys join in. That does not mean that he is gay," Kevin replied.

"Well, even if he's not, he's obviously okay with it. What's the harm in playing along?"

"Maybe there *is* no harm, Anthony, but we're in Rome. The tenor of that meeting today was more than apparent. They will not tolerate any overt gay behavior or activity. I am quite sure that here, in the shadow of St. Peter's Basilica, they mean it. We can't assume that anyone will be sympathetic to gay seminarians. Please, Anthony, promise me you'll think before you say anything off-color."

"Yeah, okay," he replied as he stared blankly at the glowing white dome of the basilica. "I know you're just looking out for me. A lot of these gatherings seem incredibly gay. I've never been in a community where it's discussed so openly. I just figured it meant that they were all gay. The openness is new to me, and I am much too easy to express my feelings. I'll work on that."

Kevin's warning was not without merit. The seminary culture was rife with landmines. Gathering young men at the height of their sexual prime in a singular enclosed environment was asking for trouble. The sexual tension between all of them, straight or gay, permeated every interaction. Then there was the never-ending self-evaluation during the process of discernment.

Seminarians are regularly asked to delve deeper into their hearts and to be in touch with their emotions. The spiritual journey they experience brings out each insecurity as they move forward with self-doubt. In-depth discussions about their unworthiness concerning ordination prompted an intimacy between friends that could quickly transform a relationship. Sharing turned into comforting, comforting to affection, and many times, tenderness turned to sexual expression. Making matters even more dangerous was the ever-present culture of drinking. Wine with meals, after-dinner drinks, and cocktails lowered inhibitions. It was fertile ground for sexual activity.

The constant navel-gazing fostered intense self-centeredness. Each struggle or doubt became an emotional crisis, and perhaps a vocational crisis. The level of self-immersion led to loneliness and isolation. And it was from that place of desolation that their need flowed. The only relief from the constant emotional anguish was a personal connection with others who could understand the process. They turned to one another for counsel and comfort. Of course, not all friendships turned into sexual expression. Combine the intensity of their emotional needs, self-doubt, and ever-present use of alcohol; the premier seminary in Rome was a pressure cooker just moments from exploding.

Chapter Four
Golden Boy

K evin grew up in a small town in suburban Connecticut. There were only sixty students in his graduating class in high school, and his classmates were into everybody's business. The drama about who was dating who or the latest breakup was rampant. No one could escape the school gossip mill. Keeping a low profile was his only hope of maintaining his privacy.

Kevin was well-liked for his even and approachable personality. He was friendly with kids from every clique, and his success on the track team earned him automatic respect. As the captain during his senior year, he demonstrated natural leadership abilities while exercising care and compassion for his less athletic teammates.

Track was one of those sports that attracted all kinds, regardless of skill, and Kevin felt a responsibility to support and encourage the less successful guys. He was especially incensed when others would pick on them and bully them mercilessly. He had no tolerance for that kind of behavior, even though it was merely a part of being a high school kid.

The hazing seemed to intensify at the beginning of each season. "Hey, fag, are you actually gonna make it across the finish line in under thirty minutes today?"

"Yeah, Bruce. Maybe I should just carry you over it. You'd like that, wouldn't you? You dream about having a real man hold you in his arms."

Kevin was stretching and overheard the encounter. He rose and walked over to them. The taunting was getting worse, and he could tell that Bruce was barely holding back his tears.

"Knock it off, guys. What the hell is wrong with you? It's not like you were a superstar during your freshman year, Dave. Didn't you finish last at our first meet?"

The guys grew immediately silent. Sharp words from Kevin were uncommon and were always taken seriously. They knew they had crossed the line.

"Sorry, Kev, we're just joking around."

"It's not me you should apologize to. Now cut the crap and finish stretching. Let's focus on winning today."

Kevin led the team in a few warm-up exercises, and they were off and running. But he kept an eye on Bruce for the next few weeks. He had a sense that he might be gay and tried to protect him from the usual taunts that would come his way. Coming to terms with being gay in the late 70s took a long time and could be torture.

His process had been private and quiet. There was no big revelation or major event; Kevin understood himself and knew that he had to keep it to himself. He always found other guys attractive but made sure not to let on. Kevin dated girls and acted as if he were just like every other straight boy in school. He focused his energy on track and cross-country and excelled at them both. The more athletic he was, the less likely anyone would suspect he was gay. He planned to attend a bigger school for college and hoped that would mitigate his fears of being discovered.

At the University of Hartford, he'd be able to fade into the thousands of students on campus. No one would care whether he was dating girls or not. As a philosophy major, Kevin found himself in a community of quirky students, and that suited him well. From the start, Kevin made no secret of his intention to become a priest. He actively took part in his local parish and had begun the vocational preparations at the Archdiocese of Hartford.

He was ready and felt sure of his vocation. Kevin met regularly with the vocation director during his first semester at Hartford. His path toward the priesthood seemed all but certain. "How do you like the University of Hartford, Kevin?" Father Devin asked.

"It's fine. The courses are challenging enough, but most of the students aren't very serious about philosophy."

"I imagine they aren't. Most of them are not planning to pursue seminary studies."

"It's true. Most of the time, I'm the only one who speaks up in class. Sometimes, I wish someone would challenge me or that we'd have a spirited debate."

"Perhaps we can find an environment that can provide that experience for you, Kevin."

"What do you mean, Father?"

"St. Thomas Seminary would give you a solid foundation in philosophy while preparing you for your graduate work in Theology. Besides, they give a great deal of attention to spiritual growth."

"That sounds great, Father Devlin, but I'm sure my parents can't afford the tuition. They gave me a generous financial aid package from U of H. I don't see how I can give that up."

"Kevin, once you formally enroll with the archdiocese of Hartford, they pay your tuition – all of it," Father Devlin emphasized. "So, what do you say? Are you interested?"

"I don't know what to say, Father. Thank you. I mean, of course, I'm interested." By January, he settled into St. Thomas and felt right at home. Kevin adjusted seamlessly to the structure of seminary life; it suited him well. Expectations were clearly delineated, and the daily routines gave him the discipline he craved to focus on his goals. Kevin didn't buy into the gossip or the ubiquitous seminary drama. Having gone to such a small high school, he was accustomed to the complexities of a small community. He was courteous and friendly but kept his own counsel. His personal demons regarding his sexuality were nobody's business but his own. However, he was surprised by the prevalence of gay culture and the ever-present homoerotic banter among the guys. Although he was sure to avoid participating, in many ways, it made him feel more comfortable with his own sexuality.

By his senior year at St. Thomas, Kevin was considered the perfect seminarian. He was well respected and incredibly intelligent. With a 4.0 GPA, he could argue and engage in philosophical debates better than some of his professors. His success at St. Thomas did not go unnoticed by the archbishop of Hartford. When it came time to discuss his graduate studies, the archbishop was effusive in his praise. But Kevin was utterly taken aback when the bishop informed him that he was appointed to the North American College in Rome. The NAC was the most prestigious of American seminaries. The men selected received their graduate degrees from one of two respected pontifical universities: the Gregorian or the Angelicum.

"You're ranked at the top of your class, Kevin, and you've shown great promise during your time at St. Thomas. Your service within the archdiocese over the past four years has been exemplary. I believe that you will be quite successful at the North American College," the archbishop declared. Kevin was feeling honored and surprised. "You should know that there have been numerous popes who have studied at the Pontifical Gregorian University. You'll be in good company. Simply pray for their guidance."

"Thank you, your Eminence. I am honored by the appointment and your faith in my abilities, but I don't speak Italian. I studied Latin and Greek in college," Kevin offered.

"Why, that's even better. You will be a step ahead of the others. With a strong base in Latin, you'll be speaking Italian in no time. If you like, you can take an introductory language course during your final semester at St. Thomas. But don't you worry, there will be a language immersion program when you get to Rome in August. All the new men will be enrolled."

Kevin was shell-shocked. He had never considered the possibility of studying in Rome. Kevin hoped to be assigned to Theological College in Washington, D.C. It was on the campus of Catholic University, and he thought it would be fun to live in his nation's capital. The possibility of studying in Rome had never entered his mind, and this new development intrigued him. He came from a family with modest means. His father worked as a mechanic at the Hartford airport, and his mom stayed at home. They were Irish immigrants who worked hard to make a life for Kevin and his sisters. He knew they would be proud of him, and he couldn't wait to tell them the good news.

As devout Catholics, Kevin's parents viewed his appointment as a great blessing. Their only son would be one step closer to God. Having their youngest become a priest was a great honor for them. The fact that he'd be studying at the Vatican was the icing on the cake.

Being the only boy, Kevin got special treatment throughout his life. Being a Roman seminarian could only make it better. His oldest sister, Mary, called him the little prince because he got away with everything. When asked to clear the table or take out the trash, he would reply, "These hands were made for chalices, not callouses!" To which Mary would roll her eyes and slap him playfully on the head as she handed him the trash can. As it turned out, he was right. Not one callous would blemish Kevin's smooth hands while studying Theology at the North American College in Rome.

Chapter Five
The Ranch

Miguel was gregarious and sharp as a whip. Texas had a long tradition of Mexican ranch owners from the many years before becoming a state.

Coming from a wealthy family of cattle ranchers in Texas, Miguel lived a life of privilege. Since it was family-owned, he had been exposed to the ins and outs of running a business. Miguel also had firsthand knowledge of the back-breaking work on the ranch. His work ethic was strong, and he believed that the wealthy had a responsibility to care for those who were less fortunate.

He grew up on the farm where his father hired many undocumented immigrants who labored through long days. His father's demeanor toward his employees left a lasting impression on Miguel. Mr. Perez always treated them with the same respect as his business partners. There was no caste system at the Perez Cattle Ranch, and Mr. Perez was sure to emphasize his belief in the dignity of his workers. He not only led by example, but he made a point to tell his son why.

"Miguel, my boy, you are no better than anyone here on this ranch, and neither am I. Do you understand?"

"I think so, dad."

"I mean it, son," Mr. Perez continued. "Without these hard-working men, we would be nowhere. They help put food on our table and a roof over our heads. They deserve as much respect as your teachers at school or the priests at church. Remember, we are all in this together."

"Yes, sir."

"Being Hispanic in Texas, our family has experienced our share of prejudice. We are some of the lucky ones, though. People treat us differently because we have money. We could just as easily be on the streets looking for work as many of these men. You've seen how people treat them, don't you?"

"Yes, dad. They spew all sorts of hateful names at them – and sometimes at me as well."

"That's right. If people don't know who you are, they treat you just as bad. That's why we are going to make a difference in their lives. We're going to give them a hand up," said Mr. Perez.

The Perez ranch boasted over five-hundred acres with approximately five-thousand cows. Miguel enjoyed wandering the pastures and the freedom they provided.

He was not afraid of getting his hands dirty when he accompanied his father on his rounds. His parents had a farmer's mentality where everyone in the family worked as soon as they were able. When Miguel grew a little older, he was assigned his own chores, one of which was to provide the feed for the cows in winter.

After the first frost, the grass didn't grow enough to provide adequate food, so they used cottonseed as feed because it was a substantial source of protein. Once a year, the men would round up the cattle and sift through them. They sold the older cows and vaccinated the calves.

They had to sell a few older calves to make sure the cow could nurse her newborn. It was hard work, but he loved every minute.

After being in the family for several generations, Mr. Perez's ranch was stable and wildly successful. There was no need for him to be actively involved with the day-to-day operations, but he could not tear himself away from it. That is how he started the business, and he never wanted Miguel to forget their humble beginnings.

Mr. Perez believed in the diligent pursuit of his goals and instilled that work ethic in his son. As Miguel grew older, everyone simply expected him to follow in his father's footsteps and take over the business when Mr. Perez retired. Miguel never thought twice about it. He loved the ranch, but more than that, he relished working right beside his father.

Raising cattle was a family business, and this was the only life he knew. As children, Miguel and his siblings took every opportunity to horse around in barns and the pastures. None of them thought beyond their children's games and the rich experience they shared growing up on the ranch. They simply assumed it would always be a part of their lives.

Miguel's family were regular churchgoers who took part in the missionary work of their parish. Mr. Perez often hired men and women from the congregation to work at the ranch, many of whom were undocumented. It was not uncommon for many of the ranchers and farmers in border states to hire undocumented help.

If not for the migrant workers, Mr. Perez would have trouble finding people to fill their seasonal positions. More than that, Perez believed in the church's social mission and saw it as his duty to give a hand up for people in need, especially his workers. None of this was lost on Miguel, and he participated fully.

It was because of his parents that he maintained such a firm foundation for his faith. It was sometime during his junior year in high school that Miguel first thought about the priesthood. He was helping the pastor with some errands when Father Lopez got a call. A parishioner from the barrio had gotten injured while working on a local cattle ranch. During the yearly round-up, the men rode to each of the pastures, bringing the cattle in. Juan had been riding behind a particularly stubborn bull when a gunshot rang out. Startled, the bull turned and charged. Juan's horse reared back as it approached, knocking him to the ground. In fear, the horse retreated, trampling over Juan's legs. He could feel his bones being crushed by the sheer weight of the animal and its iron horseshoes. He shouted in agony as he was being stomped on, then he blacked out.

"I have to go. Juan Martinez is seriously hurt. Can you finish up here, Miguel?"

"Sure, Father, but I'd rather come with you. I love that family. I've taught religious education classes to three of their kids. Maybe I could help."

"All right then, let's go. Just be prepared, I believe Juan is in awful shape," Father Lopez warned.

"I'll be okay, Father. Thanks."

***

They pulled up to the emergency room entrance of St. Vincent's Hospital. They could see Juan lying on a stretcher, moaning in pain. Father Lopez spotted his wife, Lupe, trying to comfort him while tending to her frightened children. Miguel took them from her immediately and set about distracting them.

"Why is he still out here in the waiting room?" Martinez asked.

"We don't have insurance, Father. They won't treat him," Lupe cried to Father.

"That's ridiculous! They're required to treat everyone." Seething with anger, Father Lopez flew to the registration desk and demanded answers.

"This man needs immediate attention. Can't you see that he's in excruciating pain? A horse ran him over."

"Yes, Father, of course. As you can see, we have a full room of patients ahead of him. He'll just have to wait."

"You can't be serious. Surely you treat people with serious injuries first. How can you leave him in such pain? There may be internal bleeding or worse."

"I understand, Father. I will alert the doctors. In the meantime, perhaps you can help fill out the registration form. They don't have medical insurance."

"So that's what this is all about. If Mr. Lopez had insurance, he would've already been with the doctor. Let me speak to your supervisor." She looked at him in shock. It was a Catholic hospital, and it wouldn't look good if she ignored a priest. She quickly stood and fetched her boss. Father Lopez could see the tense interaction as she informed her of the altercation and Mr. Martinez's condition.

Father Lopez was furious. They treated undocumented and migrant workers as if they weren't even human. There was little regard for their well-being, even in hospitals. He scolded the supervisor and indicated that he would inform the local bishop. The supervisor tried to explain that they were only following protocol, and that there was no hint of mistreatment or prejudicial behavior among his staff. That's when Father Lopez threatened to call the press. The scene played out so that everyone in the ER could hear. His threat had the desired effect. The supervisor summoned the orderlies immediately, and they wheeled Juan into the ER to be treated.

His injuries were extensive: the horse had broken both his legs in multiple locations, he had several broken ribs and internal bleeding. His lengthy stay in the waiting room caused some of his bones to repair themselves incorrectly, and they needed to be broken again and reset. The hospital's negligence caused his injuries to worsen while he was left to suffer on his stretcher.

Miguel spent over five hours in the waiting room with Mrs. Martinez and their children. He tried to keep them occupied, distracting them with silly games and stories. All the while, Miguel watched Father Lopez taking charge. He was their fiercest advocate and guardian when they needed it most. This kind of prejudice was ubiquitous throughout Texas. Miguel was struck by the fact that Father Lopez could combat the hateful behavior, even though he was Hispanic. Wearing the Roman collar gave him automatic authority. Strength radiated from this man, and Miguel wanted to be just like him. He wanted to be there for people in the hour of their greatest need, to guide them through and assure them of God's love and care. In those long hours in the ER, Miguel wondered what it would be like to become a priest. That day was a turning point for Miguel. It was then that he knew he had a calling.

Although his father was disappointed that his first-born son would not follow in his footsteps, he was proud to have a son studying to be a priest. He never had a second thought about the ranch when Miguel broke the news about his graduate studies. His boy was one of the chosen few to be sent off to Rome, and he couldn't be prouder.

Chapter Six
The Awakening

Kevin had been serving Mass at St. Thomas Aquinas church throughout high school and college. The church was conveniently located close to the seminary and the University of Hartford campus.

Though sparsely attended, the daily Mass provided him a time to put his worries into perspective. He could center himself and focus on his ultimate goal of becoming a priest. Father Bill, a junior associate at St. Thomas, had only been ordained for a few years. He was thirty years old and was well-liked by the parishioners, especially high school and college students.

Father Bill was a good-looking man with curly black hair and deep brown eyes. His gregarious personality was like a magnet drawing parishioners to him. After Sunday Mass, he could always be spotted with a crowd of young people gathered around him. With a keen sense of humor, he always seemed to hit the nail on the head during his homilies. He knew how to relate to the younger crowd and enchanted his audience. All the young girls had a crush on Father Bill. He and Kevin had struck up an easy friendship over his years as an undergrad. Now in his senior year, with an appointment to Rome looming before him, he and Bill became even closer. Besides serving Mass regularly, Kevin was the youth minister at the parish.

He worked on the maintenance staff during the summers and lived at the rectory whenever school was not in session. Saturday evening dinners were often followed by hours of discussion in Father Bill's suite. Kevin enjoyed debating current Church topics with him and could share his concerns about priesthood and seminary. Kevin felt he could always speak freely with Father Bill. During his last semester of college, their friendship deepened, and they treated each other more like contemporaries.

Kevin found Bill attractive from the first moment they met, and there was always a spark between them. There was an unspoken sexual tension between the two men, but neither acknowledged it. Their banter often included double entendres or sexual innuendos. Kevin wasn't at all unnerved by their apparent sexual attraction. He had been interested in other men before, but never felt the need to act upon his desires.

Although Kevin had taken no vows, he reasoned that both he and Bill had nothing to worry about since they were both celibate. Neither of them had ever discussed their sexuality, but he always wondered. He couldn't tell if Father Bill was gay or straight, and Kevin certainly didn't share any information regarding his own sexuality. Discussing personal issues was not part of Kevin's custom, and he was never one to share his feelings. It certainly wasn't part of growing up in an Irish family. Kevin had never come out to anyone as gay. Why should he? He was going to be a priest, so it would never be an issue. The weekend before commencement, Bill took Kevin out for a celebratory dinner. He chose an expensive steakhouse befitting Kevin's accomplishment, and the wine flowed freely. By the time they returned to the rectory, they were both feeling no pain. Kevin took his usual spot on the couch while Bill excused himself to use the restroom. When he returned, Kevin thought he smelled the distinctive aroma of Listerine on Bill's breath. Rather than sit in his recliner, Bill took his place right beside Kevin.

"I can't believe that you are graduating," Bill said as he ruffled Kevin's hair.

"Hey, anything but the hair!" Kevin reacted as Bill pulled him closer. "Yeah, soon I won't be just up the street at the seminary," Kevin said. "I guess I'll have to find more excuses to hang out with you," Kevin added.

"You know you don't need an excuse, Kev. Besides, we're going to be brother priests. We'll be seeing each other all the time."

"Brother priests. That sounds so cool," Kevin said as he laid his head back to rest against Bill's arm. The physical intimacy was new, but Kevin liked it.

"But we're more than that, aren't we?" Bill said.

Kevin wasn't sure how to respond, so he remained silent. The energy in the room changed. They could feel it. *What is happening?* Kevin thought. He could feel his body flush with heat, and Kevin found it difficult to hide his arousal – he was afraid Father Bill would be put off if he noticed. Kevin moved his arm, draping it over his lap, trying to cover himself. "What do you mean?" Kevin finally asked as Father Bill pulled his hand from around him and placed it on his neck, squeezing it affectionately.

"You know, it's rare to have a connection as tight as ours, Kevin. We have a special bond, wouldn't you say?" Father Bill asked.

"Yeah, I guess we do. I feel really close to you," Kevin managed to say as his breathing quickened with excitement.

Kevin had come to terms with being gay, but until this very moment, identifying as gay didn't seem to matter because he was going to become a priest. He wouldn't be having sex with anybody, man or woman. *So, what is happening to me right now? I really want to touch him.* Before he knew it, Bill pulled Kevin's face closer and kissed him gently. Bill let his lips linger, barely touching Kevin's for a moment longer, then finally moved his face away to gauge his reaction. Kevin's eyes slowly opened and returned his gaze without trepidation. He seemed receptive, so Father Bill went in for more. Soon they were making out like teenagers.

Bill had wanted this from the first moment they had met, but he was never really sure if Kevin was gay. Once Father Bill's inhibitions were unleashed, he let himself go and took the lead. Lifting the polo over Kevin's head, he found a receptive neophyte as he raised his arms so Bill could easily remove it.

Bill admired the lean but muscular body before him, "Nice," he exclaimed, then he took off his own shirt as they continued to caress and kiss each other with a newfound passion. Kevin was in heaven. He had never kissed another man before, and his desire was almost overwhelming. He was startled from his fervor when Bill broke their kiss and pulled away. "Hey, let's go to the bedroom. I'm sure we will be more comfortable there."

As Father Bill stood, Kevin couldn't help but notice the ample bulge in his pants and reached out to touch him, but Bill turned too quickly. Momentarily frustrated, Kevin straightened himself out and eagerly followed Bill to his bed.

That evening, a whole new world opened up to him. Although he had fantasized about men over the years, nothing could compare to the real thing. Kevin was consumed with desire as years of pent up sexual tension exploded from his body – finally expressing every hidden desire. "Slow down, Kevin. I'm not going anywhere. Let's just take our time, okay?"

"Sure, yeah, sorry. I can't help it – it's just so hot."

"Don't be sorry. Just enjoy the process and don't finish too soon – let's make it last. We have all the time in the world," Bill assured him. His counsel had to be repeated several times throughout the evening, and although he was a bit frustrated, Kevin gave into Bill's wishes.

It was all worth it in the end. By the time they let themselves go, Kevin felt utterly out of control – he had never experienced such intense ecstasy. When it was over, they lay languorously on Father Bill's bed, lost in their post-coital haze. The dreamy melody of Elton John's *Goodbye Yellow Brick Road* washed over them. Bill looked over at Kevin, concerned that he might feel awkward now that their passion had subsided.

"Hey there, Kev. What are you thinking about?"

"Nothing, really. Just getting lost in the music," Kevin responded quietly.

"Are you okay?" Father Bill asked. "I mean – did what just happen between us upset you?" Kevin propped himself up on his elbow and looked at Bill.

"Why, should it? Are you upset?" Kevin replied, feeling his insecurity creep in.

"No, no, not at all. I was just checking in with you. You know – you're not the most expressive guy I know when it comes to sharing feelings."

"That's certainly true, but I feel really great. To be honest, that's the first time I've ever had sex. I'm just trying to process it all," Kevin said.

"Oh, my God! Seriously, you were a virgin? What have I done?" Father Bill responded.

"You corrupted me, Father Bill. I was an innocent child until you seduced me," Kevin said.

Father Bill stood up. "I'm sorry, Kevin. I didn't know. I thought you and I were on the same page. I would have never..."

Fear was all over his face.

"Easy there, Bill, I'm just kidding. I was a willing participant. Besides, I'm twenty-two years old. I can make my own decisions. Come back to bed."

Father Bill freaked out. The last thing he needed was to be accused of seducing a young seminarian. Kevin talked him down, and eventually, his reassurance eased Bill's mind. They spent the rest of the evening chatting and laughing at how the two of them had danced around their mutual attraction for years.

"I remember the first time I spotted you. You were showing a layup for the youth basketball game. As you went up for the shot, your t-shirt lifted, and all I could see was that washboard stomach of yours. I could barely breathe after that."

"I remember that night," Kevin replied. "Father D'Ortenzio introduced you as the new associate. No one believed that someone as good looking as you could be a priest. The girls were fawning all over you, and I wanted to be right there with them."

"Well, you were fantastic at keeping your cards close to your chest. It was ages before I got an inkling that you might be gay."

"What? I'm not gay," Kevin replied with mock indignation. "How dare you assume? Are you gay, Bill?"

"What a silly question. Priests can't be gay, Kevin." Then they burst into laughter and playfully wrestled on the bed. However, Kevin's over-analytical mind took over as he mulled over the implications of their evening together. *How many other priests are gay?* he questioned. Given that they had sex throughout the night, he wondered how many other priests disregarded their vow of celibacy. Father Bill was eight years older than Kevin, but somehow it didn't seem to matter. He was breaking his vow of celibacy. For the first time, he wondered if the requirement of celibacy was a ridiculous requirement for priests. The Episcopal Church allowed married clergy, and it doesn't detract from their ministry. He began to think the Catholic Church was way out of step with the modern world.

Chapter Seven
First Love

"Why is Uncle Joe at the table all by himself?" three-year-old Anthony shouted. The packed church was in silent prayer during the consecration at Father Joe's first Mass – Anthony's high-pitched voice echoed throughout the grand space. The toddler was mesmerized by the incense and pageantry of the celebration. The booming organ grabbed his attention immediately as he turned to see where the sound was coming from. The colorful vestments and the golden vessels shimmered in the candlelight. His earliest memories were of attending Mass with his large Italian family.

Their weekly routine rarely varied. Every Sunday morning, they would dress in their finest clothes – the girls in dresses and the boys in jackets and ties. Anthony could picture the white mantilla draped over Mrs. Rossi's head as she genuflected and took her place in the pew. He thought she looked like a bride with her white veil dripping onto her shoulders.

He had always dreamed of becoming a priest. Anthony grew up in an Italian neighborhood in the Bronx. He was just a few blocks from the famous Arthur Avenue, where customers came from all over to shop for fresh seafood, fresh Italian cheeses, and pastries. Italian culture and traditions were a central element in his life. His mother had the most considerable influence on Anthony instilling a deep and abiding faith in him.

As the youngest child, he spent a great deal of time with her as she regaled him with tales of her life growing up in Italy. One of the most poignant stories she shared with him was of her parents. She was only ten years old when she lost her mother and father. Her only solace as an orphaned child was attending daily Mass, and she described it in great detail. Kneeling at the Marian altar, she spoke as a child speaks to her mother. She asked for advice and prayed for guidance. In his heart, Anthony could almost feel the devotion she had to Mary, and he carried it with him throughout his life. As he grew older, his faith deepened as did his certainty of becoming a priest.

Anthony was active in his parish youth group throughout high school. He played guitar, sang at mass, and was a lector. By his senior year in college, Anthony had entered the formation program for men discerning their vocation to the priesthood.

His spiritual director was the head of the campus ministry at Fordham University, run by the Jesuits. He helped advise him on his spiritual journey and guided Anthony through some troubling relationship issues. Before Anthony entered the formation program at the Archdiocese of New York, he wondered what it would be like to become a Jesuit. He always thought he'd become a teacher, and the Jesuits were a teaching order of priests. Anthony was quite active in the Campus Ministry department at Fordham. He played guitar and sang at Mass, attended countless retreats, and was a Eucharistic Minister. Anthony even went to visit the novitiate for the Jesuits and felt very much at home with them. But the idea of waiting eight or nine years to be ordained turned him off. Besides, his uncle would be so disappointed if he didn't become a priest in New York.

During his senior year, Anthony began attending the daily Mass at noon each day. With only ten or twelve people in attendance, the chapel was pretty empty. It was the same crew every day, so when it came time for the sign of peace, each of them would leave their pews to shake hands. A few weeks in, he noticed someone new. A flash of blond hair and prominent V-shaped lats was standing several rows in front of him. Anthony's curiosity was more than piqued.

At the sign of peace, a set of white teeth smiled broadly and extended his hand. Anthony became catatonic as he stood there, saying nothing. The Adonis before him had beautiful blue eyes and blond hair. He sported a light blue Izod polo that outlined the muscles in his broad chest. "Peace be with you," he said to Anthony, startling him from his reverie.

"Oh, yeah, peace be with you," he finally responded, taking hold of his hand. Anthony was distracted throughout the rest of the Mass. *Who is this guy? I've never seen him on campus.* After the final blessing, everyone waved goodbye and went off to lunch or class. It was the same routine every day, except that Anthony and the mystery man sat closer and closer together. By the end of the week, they were only one pew apart. When Mass was over, Anthony turned and introduced himself.

"Hi, I'm Anthony. Seems foolish not to chat with you since we see each other every day."

"I'm Thomas. I know who you are. I see you singing every Sunday," he said.

"Are you heading to lunch?" Thus began another daily ritual. Thomas and Anthony attended Mass each day, followed by lunch in the cafeteria. The pair couldn't be more different. Anthony was artsy, a musician, and an actor. Thomas was on the swim team and very athletic. As their friendship deepened, they started working out together at the RecPlex. Their mutual attraction only intensified at the gym.

"Hey Thomas, can you spot me here?" Anthony asked, laying on his back for his chest presses. Thomas stood just above his head to make sure he didn't drop the weights on his chest. But Anthony couldn't take it; Thomas's crotch was almost touching his face. Anthony turned bright red and sat up.

"What's up?" Thomas asked.

"Me, actually—I'm sorry, but that is quite a view from down there. I couldn't concentrate."

"Well then, perhaps you need a shower," Thomas suggested with a mischievous grin.

"Not in my present condition," Anthony replied, covering himself. And so, their playful relationship began. It was the early 80s, so they had to be careful not to be discovered, especially at a Catholic university. Since Anthony commuted from home, Thomas's dorm room became their regular hangout.

His relationship with Thomas was a first for Anthony. Before long, they were inseparable, and by the end of the first semester, they were in love. Anthony knew being in love was incongruous with his desire to become a priest, but he buried his concerns deep in his psyche. He'd never been in love before and certainly never had sex. That it was with another man didn't seem to bother him. He had always followed his heart.

Communication with the Archdiocese was infrequent, but he couldn't ignore it completely. Compartmentalizing these two dichotomous desires was more comfortable than he thought. When thoughts of seminary rose to the surface, he pushed them away.

I can't think about that now. Who knows what will happen between now and next September? Anthony chose to focus on Thomas, the first man he'd ever fallen in love with.

***

Thomas sat in Anthony's bedroom, taking in so many of his childhood memories. Photos of his first Communion, Boy Scouts, and school plays. He was lost in his sweet fantasy of little Anthony. Running his fingers over the books on his shelf, he gathered more knowledge of who he had fallen in love with. He noticed a Separate Peace, Huckleberry Finn, and Giovanni's Room by James Baldwin. Anthony's free spirit and profound heart were on full display in his choices. Laying in a pile on his desk was an envelope from the office of the Cardinal, Archdiocese of New York. His curiosity piqued, Thomas pulled out the letter and read.

"Congratulations on your appointment to the North American College in Vatican City State. You are among the select few whose priestly formation will take place at the prestigious seminary in Rome."

Thomas read the letter several times, not believing his eyes. This can't be real, he thought. Anthony would never do this to me – to us. He was still staring at the letter in disbelief when Anthony came bouncing into the room.

"Hey there, I'm finally ready. Let's go," he said, not realizing what Thomas had just read.

"What is this, Anthony?" he asked without lifting his eyes from the letter.

"Huh? What?" Then it dawned on him. *Shit!*

"This letter from the Cardinal, what does it mean?"

"Nothing, look, I started that process before we met. I…"

"You want to become a priest? And they're sending you to Rome?" Thomas asked. "That's not nothing!"

"You're right, it's crazy – and amazing, and confusing," Anthony said, not knowing what to say.

"We've been together for six months now. How could you keep this from me?"

"I, I didn't know how to tell you. It wasn't such a big deal at first, you know?"

"No, I don't know. Enlighten me, Anthony. How is this not a big deal?"

"I'm sorry. I didn't realize we were going to fall in love. I thought we were just having fun. And then we just got closer and closer. I put the priesthood thing out of my mind, honestly. But then I got that letter."

"And?"

"And… I couldn't find the right time to bring it up. I know we have to discuss this, but I was afraid."

"I don't get it. What's there to discuss? You're either going into the seminary, or you're not. And what exactly are you afraid of?" Thomas's simmering anger was boiling over.

"Of you, of losing you," Anthony said, closing the gap between them. "I love you, Thomas."

"But?"

"But nothing. I needed to process this, talk to you about it," Anthony replied.

"So, this is what I understand right now. You've always wanted to become a priest. You fell in love with me, but never mentioned that you had applied, or whatever one does to become a priest. The Cardinal of New York wants to send you to the Vatican, the center of the Catholic Church. Did I leave anything out?"

"Yes, I haven't decided what to do yet. That's why I want to talk about it."

"How do you say no to an offer like that, Anthony? There's no way I can compete with this."

"It's not a competition. You're everything to me. I've never been in love before. You've transformed my life," he said honestly.

"You left out the part about deceiving me for all these months. How am I supposed to trust you after this?"

"Please, Thomas, please try to understand. I don't want to lose you," Anthony replied.

"Can you honestly tell me you no longer want to become a priest? And that this prestigious appointment means nothing to you?" Thomas asked.

Anthony looked down at his feet and said nothing. A heavy sigh escaped Anthony's lungs as he sat on the edge of his bed. *This is not how I expected this conversation to go. What do I do?* Thomas stood and walked to the door, Anthony's pleading eyes following his every step.

"I need some time to think. I'll see you later."

"Wait, where are you going?" Anthony asked. Aren't we having dinner at Mario's Pizza? Come on, Thomas. Can't we just talk about this?"

"Not now. I can't even look at you right now. I'll call you," Anthony stared at the door that just closed behind his boyfriend.

What just happened?

***

During the following week, Anthony tried in vain to contact Thomas. His roommate said that he hadn't spoken with him – he was out early in the mornings and came in after he had gone to bed.

Anthony went to the gym during their usual workout time, but nothing. *He'll be at the Noon Mass, for sure.* But Thomas did not attend the entire week. Anthony was beside himself. He just wanted to talk it through.

A week later, he was sitting at a study carrel in the library when he felt a tap on his shoulder.

"Hey, can we talk?"

"Thomas, it's you! Where have you been?" Anthony asked in desperation.

"I needed time to think," he said cryptically.

It was a crisp winter's day. The sun was shining brightly as they strolled through campus in silence. Finally, Anthony couldn't take it any longer.

"Thomas, let me explain."

Thomas cut him off. "Don't, Anthony. Let me share some of my thoughts. I have done a lot of soul-searching this week, and I needed every minute of it. I thought back on how we met. What joined us was our mutual faith. On a campus of thousands of students, we are among ten or fifteen people who made a commitment to going to Mass – *every day*. We found in each other kindred spirits. Discovering that we are gay and attracted to one another was a phenomenal gift. I wouldn't give up the months that we had together... I love you, Anthony," Thomas said.

"I love you, too," Anthony replied before getting cut off again.

"Please, let me finish," Thomas said, holding up his hand. "I love you, and I know you. Although you never mentioned your desire to become a priest, as you should have, I see it in you every day. You wear your ministry in everything you do. You are compassionate and kind, even to the assholes on campus who'd bash you into a wall if they discovered you are gay. You're generous with your time and care for each of our friends, and you are the ear we all go to when we have a problem. You *are* a priest, Anthony. I know you love me, but I am your first and only romantic relationship, and I am so grateful to hold that place in your heart. But I can't compete with God. This desire you have for the priesthood goes way deeper. It's probably always been there, and I won't stand in your way."

"Can I talk now?" Anthony asked. Thomas nodded. "I love you. You know that. And I'm sorry. I should never have kept this from you. When we first got together, I thought we were just having fun. I had no clue that I'd fall in love with you. Then it was too late. I was afraid of losing you."

"But that's just it, Anthony. You can't have both. It's either the priesthood or me, and whether you know it or not. You've already made your choice."

"How can you know that? I am still working through it. But you're right – I want both the priesthood and you."

"And that's just not possible, Anthony. They're going to send you to Rome. Who gets to do that? From the letter I read, it sounds like that is a tremendous honor. You can't pass that up," Thomas said.

"It's pretty incredible. I've read it over and over."

"So, here's the hard part. We have to stop seeing each other," Thomas said as Anthony protested. "Let's not argue. You are going to be a priest. My heart can't bear losing you again when you leave. It's best to make a clean break." Anthony hung his head.

"You're right. I hate that I put you through this, but I don't want this to end."

"Neither do I, but it's the only solution. I love you, Anthony. You are going to be an outstanding priest someday."

Chapter Eight
An Affair to Remember

Kevin spent the first weeks of summer with Bill and found himself falling head over heels in love with the priest. And although he knew that Bill was breaking his vow of celibacy, it didn't bother him. Deep in his heart, Kevin believed that the church was utterly wrong in its teaching against homosexuality. He did not think of himself or Bill as depraved. They were simply ordinary men who fell in love with each other. If the church was wrong about something as significant as that, perhaps they were incorrect about celibacy as well. The relationship he and Bill shared was a loving one. How could that make Father Bill a bad priest? He fully believed that he should follow his conscience regarding his sexuality, and he was certainly not in any position to judge Father Bill.

Ultimately, Kevin felt everyone had to make their own moral decisions. But while Kevin was enjoying the infatuation with first loving relationship, Bill felt smothered. There was an eight-year age gap between them, which doesn't necessarily matter as one gets older. But at 22, Kevin's inexperience and youth were showing. He wanted to spend every free moment alone together. He was often disappointed when Bill invited some of his priest friends to join them for dinner or drinks. They were gay as well and knew of the budding relationship between the two men. Naturally, the guys teased Kevin about his "daddy" complex or his exuberant affection toward Bill, and he became increasingly defensive, which caused him to cling to Bill even more.

Bill had invited several other priests to rent a cottage in Madison, a beach community on the Connecticut shoreline. Bill and several of his buddies from out of state made their beach house get-away an annual event. He hoped that having new people in the mix would change the dynamic and distract Kevin from his infatuation.

Kevin was very excited – it would be the first time that he and Bill could spend the night together without fear of being discovered. During his drive down to the coast, he had romantic visions of waking up and making love before sleep had fully left them. There would be romantic walks on the beach and lazy afternoons lying in the sun. Upon his arrival, Kevin pulled into the driveway, grabbed his gear, and sprinted up the path. Bill greeted him at the door and hugged him.

"Come on, handsome, I'll show you to our room. It's the best one in the house," Bill said affectionately. He wasn't exaggerating. The master bedroom on the second floor had an extensive terrace that overlooked Long Island Sound. He could hear the surf gently lapping on the shore as they entered the room.

"Wow! This is stunning, Bill. I can't believe we have an entire week together in paradise. I don't think we will ever leave this room."

"Hold on there, buddy. There are other guests in the house, and they've heard a lot about you. I'm sure that they'll all want some time with our Roman seminarian."

Kevin put his arms around Bill and gave him a sensual kiss. "Of course, my love. But you know I only have eyes for you. I'm like Yahweh, the faithful one," he said, paraphrasing a contemporary hymn. Rather than laugh at his pun, Bill rolled his eyes and backed away from his embrace.

"Listen, let's make this perfectly clear. We are not married, and we don't want to make the other guys uncomfortable by hanging all over each other like love-sick teenagers. So, let's stop with the lovey-dovey stuff."

Eyes frozen in surprise, Kevin was stung by his harsh reprimand. He was confused by the change in Bill's behavior toward him. "Bill, I'm sorry. It's just that I thought we were a couple, you know that we're together."

"That's the problem. I'm a priest – we can't be like a married couple. Besides, I'm the first man you've ever slept with. You're only 22 – you should be out there having fun."

"So, all that talk of having something special was just a rouse to get into my pants?"

"What if it was? We're men who like to have sex. There's nothing wrong with that. You can't equate us with straight people. The same rules don't apply," Bill said.

"That makes no sense. Why wouldn't gay people have the same types of feelings or commitments that straights do?" Kevin said.

"Because we're not allowed. In most states, we can get arrested or fired from jobs just for being gay. We should be grateful that we can even find other guys to hook up with. Gay folk have to live by their own set of rules. Now, enough with this," Bill said as he pulled Kevin into a kiss. "You are special to me, Kevin. Let's not get carried away, OK?"

Kevin had a sinking feeling – none of this made sense to him. His heart ached, and he was hurt by what Bill had just said. Already self-conscious as the youngest, he resolved not to let his feelings show. By late afternoon, the rest of the guys had arrived and settled in. The banter at the dinner table was lively and openly campy – not what Kevin had ever expected from a group of priests.

There were countless sexual innuendos and physical displays of affection among the new men. Their interaction was so intimate that Kevin wondered if Bill had slept with any of the other priests, and he felt a pang of jealousy. Kevin attempted to reinforce the fact that Bill and he were a couple, but each time he reached out to hold his hand, he was rebuffed. In fact, Bill barely made eye contact with him that whole evening. As he returned from using the restroom, Kevin overheard Bill joking with his friends.

"Thank God he's going off to Rome in August. The kid is infatuated with me. A bit of distance will be good for him – give him some perspective. I can't say I'm not enjoying our triste, but I'm not interested in an exclusive long-term relationship with this young seminarian." Kevin was devastated and questioned his clingy behavior. *Maybe he's right. Perhaps I need to lay off a bit.*

Later that night, as everyone headed to bed, Bill stumbled up the stairs with Kevin in tow. The fresh ocean air blew through the balcony doors – the sheer curtains billowed in the wind. With the sound of gentle waves lapping on the shore, they made love. But something had changed. Bill had had a lot to drink throughout the day and was not as tender as usual. There was no kissing or caressing, and, although their sex was sometimes energetic, that night, it was downright rough. Bill never looked into his eyes and seemed lost in his own pleasure. He almost barked out commands during sex.

Kevin wondered if Bill was angry with him. To make matters worse, after it was over, Bill rolled over without even saying goodnight. Kevin felt used. *What have I done to upset him?* Kevin wondered. Bill's behavior was entirely out of character. Tossing and turning, Kevin barely slept that night.

Dawn was on the horizon before he finally fell asleep and barely stirred when Bill got up. He was out of bed and showered well before Kevin awoke. With sandpaper eyelids, Kevin forced himself to get up. He couldn't believe that it was nearly eleven.

Rubbing his eyes, Kevin sleepily made his way down the stairs and into the kitchen. He desperately needed coffee. "You look like hell. Rough night riding the bull?" Ned asked.

"You could say that," Kevin replied tersely. He liked Ned, but he was in no mood to be teased. Ned was from Wisconsin and had that Midwestern charm. It didn't hurt that he was incredibly handsome, lean with a runner's body and clearly defined muscles.

"Here, let me get you some coffee, stud. It's painful watching you try to move around the kitchen. Black? Cream and sugar?"

"Cream and sugar, please," Kevin replied, running his hands through his messy hair. "Where is everybody? Where's Bill?"

"They're all at the beach getting a heavy dose of vitamin D."

"Why aren't you down there with them?"

"I was, but I got bored, and I went for a quick run. I just got out of the shower. I'll go for a swim after lunch," Ned replied. "Do you mind the company?"

"No, of course not. I just need to follow my morning routine. I start my day slowly – I'm not really coherent until I finish my morning coffee," Kevin explained.

"No worries. I can regale you with tales from the Wisconsin countryside."

"Are you sure your stories won't put me back to sleep?" Kevin said with a smirk.

"Funny guy, and that's before you've finished your first cup. Impressive," Ned replied. They ended up hitting it off and chatted the rest of the morning away.

Sometime after noon, the others came in for lunch to discover Kevin and Ned laughing and carrying on. Bill noted how comfortable they were together and felt a pang of jealousy. It made little sense. This was precisely what he had hoped for.

Kevin was enjoying Ned's company and had left him alone for the entire morning. Mission accomplished. But there was something about their interaction that bothered him. It was almost as if they were flirting with each other. He knew he should feel relieved, but he became resentful.

He brushed right by Kevin on the way to the kitchen without saying a word, and it didn't go unnoticed. "Hey, Bill, how was your morning?" Kevin asked as he passed by.

"The beach was beautiful, but of course, you wouldn't know. What time did you finally get up, noon?" he asked sarcastically.

"Meow!" Ned said, mimicking a cat scratching at an enemy.

"I had trouble falling asleep last night. I just slept in a bit. Ned has been keeping me entertained for the last hour," Kevin explained.

"I'm sure he has," Bill sniped. "Ned can be very amusing when he wants." The rest of the day went on like that. Kevin was thrown entirely off balance. He avoided Bill until dinnertime, but once again, Bill continued his assault. He couldn't seem to do anything right. So, when dinner was over, Kevin excused himself and found a comfortable chair outside on the deck. With the sound of the tide coming in and the warm breeze caressing his face, Kevin was lost in his thoughts when Ned found his way out to him.

"Hey, what's got you down, Kev?"

"Isn't it obvious? Bill is treating me like shit."

"Yeah, he can be a real dick sometimes. You just learn to deal with his mood swings after a while. Don't take it personally."

"Hard not to. I'm dreading going up to bed later."

"I have an idea. You're a track star, right? Let's go for a run on the beach. Maybe that'll clear your head. Now that the sun has set, there's a pleasant breeze."

"Didn't you already go for a run today? That's probably pushing it," Kevin responded.

"Nah, I've been running forever. Besides, this morning's workout was brief. What you say, Kev?"

"I'm definitely down for that. The exercise might help work out my frustrations," Kevin responded enthusiastically. A few minutes later, he and Ned were stretching on the beach. Bill and the guys found their way onto the deck and were sharing another bottle of wine. He watched Ned and Kevin as he downed his drink and glared at them. His jealousy at their familiar rapport intensified.

"Well, those two certainly seem to be hitting it off," one of the priests said.

"Yeah, you better be careful, Bill. Ned may make off with your boy-toy," the other teased.

"Fuck you!" Bill responded playfully, but he was seething inside. Ned and Kevin took a leisurely jog on the shore, savoring the last glimmers of light on the horizon. Barely speaking at all, they reveled in the quiet time that it afforded them. It was a beautiful night, and they ran for over an hour. Their conversation on the walk back to the cottage, however, was animated and intimate.

As they strolled along the shore, their bodies naturally bumped into each other. Kevin could feel the heat and sensed their mutual attraction. He turned toward Ned and took a chance. "So, I know we've just met, but I'd really like to get to know you better."

"Get to know me better? Seriously, Kevin? You mean you want to have sex with me?" Ned said.

"No, it's not like that," Kevin responded defensively.

"So, you don't want to have sex?" Ned said seductively.

"No, I mean, yes, I do want to sleep with you." Kevin was embarrassed.

"Wow, you *are* new to this, aren't you? You know it's okay if you just want to have sex?"

"Well, yeah, I suppose so. But Bill is the only person I've ever had sex with," Kevin confessed.

"Well then, let me be the second," Ned said as he pulled him in for a deep, sensual kiss. Kevin could feel synapses in his body firing as their tongues intertwined. His body tingled. He felt the fabric of his running shorts tighten with his arousal. He didn't want it to end.

"Come on by the jetty where we can find a spot that's hidden from view. It helps that it's pretty dark out here on the beach – no moon tonight," Ned said as he took off his t-shirt and laid it on the sand. "Here, give me yours. We can lie on these so we don't get sand where it shouldn't be."

With that, they lay down together and had sex, no strings attached. No emotional baggage. Just an expression of mutual attraction. It was tender and sensual, then raw and passionate. It was a novel experience for Kevin, and it felt good to be with someone other than Bill. Ned was masculine in a way that was different from Bill. He had a sense of confidence that made Kevin burn with desire. He reveled in caressing his buff body and his rippled stomach. In turn, Ned loved being worshiped by this young stag. Every touch and caress aroused him.

When it was over, they brushed the sand off of themselves and walked toward the cottage. Kevin felt oddly content. There was not a twinge of guilt afterward, and he had Ned to thank for that – sex didn't have to bring emotional baggage with it.

As they neared the cottage, it was only around 11 p.m., but the house was strangely quiet. When Kevin tried turning the doorknob, he discovered it was locked. *That's weird.* They walked around to the front door, and it was locked as well.

"That's strange, they knew we were out. Why would they lock the doors?" Kevin wondered.

"Not they – Bill. *Bill* locked the doors. He has a real jealous streak," Ned said.

"Wow, that's just so petty. First, he ignores me, then treats me like shit, and then the asshole gets mad at me for hanging out with you. That's pretty screwed up."

"He's a complicated guy – a great friend, but he's always had tumultuous relationships."

"But Bill lectured me this morning about not being monogamous, that I should be out there having fun. Why the hell would he get jealous of us?" Kevin asked.

"Welcome to the world of relationships with priests. We all have arrested development. Bill has it worse than most," Ned explained.

They ended up curling up on lounge chairs on the back deck. To keep warm, they covered themselves with the towels that were left out to dry and settled in for the night. Aside from the occasional mosquito, they slept undisturbed.

When Bill opened the door the following morning, he had a mischievous grin on his face. Ned looked up and said, "You outdid yourself, you nasty old queen."

"Why, thank you, Gladys. Did you two enjoy your sleeping arrangements? I hope you didn't catch a chill out here," Bill said. Kevin got up without saying a word.

Kevin hopped in the shower and was out the door within the hour. During his long drive home, he seethed with anger. He was done with Bill. This was not what he had bargained for.

It was good that he was leaving for Rome in a few short weeks. A change in scenery was just what he needed.

After his brief affair with Father Bill, Kevin's eyes were opened. He never entertained the idea that he might be an attractive guy, much less the idea that other men might seek him out. While the way Bill treated him hurt, Kevin wondered if he might be right. He should play the field, especially since he'd be taking a vow of celibacy in a few years. Kevin realized that he quite liked his newfound sexual freedom, and he wanted more.

Sleeping with Ned with no strings attached was a breath of fresh air. He never even considered having sex just for fun. He had been quite guarded concerning his sexuality at St. Thomas Seminary. In fear of being discovered, he kept his distance from the more flamboyant seminarians and was careful not to engage in gossip. He knew it was dangerous to even chat about being gay.

But after his weekend, he realized there was a very active gay subculture among priests, and being invited to the party was a given if you looked like Kevin. He just had to be prudent with his behavior and not to be too obvious.

Chapter Nine
New Friends

The new men had settled into a comfortable routine during their first month in Rome. There were daily Masses and morning prayer to attend, as well as regular meetings with their spiritual directors. Italian language classes took place each morning from 9:00 to 12:00 noon throughout September. Most of the new men were taking introductory courses at the North American College. Since Anthony had studied the language throughout college, they sent him and two other guys for advanced classes. Anthony was thrilled to discover that they were held at a language school near the Pantheon. Anthony looked forward to his daily stroll to the language school. It was a twenty-minute walk along which he passed through Campo de Fiori, Piazza Navona, and several iconic Roman churches.

Just on the far side of the Pantheon, Anthony discovered his favorite café, *Tazza D'oro*, the cup of gold – and it deserved its name. It was the best cappuccino he had ever tasted. Anthony was a creature of habit, so his daily routine included a stop at Tazza D'oro for a cappuccino and a *cornetto*, an Italian croissant.

He loved the independence these walks afforded him. Seminary life offered very little freedom and even fewer opportunities to make one's own decisions or schedule.

It seemed that every other moment of the day belonged to someone else. However, the weeks of language classes were boring for him. Anthony spoke and read Italian quite well, and he felt there was no point in attending classes. Kevin was in the introductory course, so they didn't get to see each other until after *pranzo,* the main meal of the day, at 1:15. But because they discouraged particular friendships, the seminarians had assigned tables and were rotated each week. They didn't even get to sit with their friends at lunch. Anthony hated all these adolescent rules from the very start. His college experience differed vastly from most of the other guys at NAC.

Living on campus where no one cared when you woke up or got in at night, Anthony got used to being responsible for himself and his actions. He was an adult. Anthony couldn't understand how NAC could justify treating all these grown men as children?

Despite the structured days, there were some routines that Anthony truly enjoyed. P*ranzo* was a three-course meal, starting with an incredible pasta dish, then a meat or fish course, followed by dessert. He couldn't be happier with the food, and the leisurely way it was served at NAC. *Pranzo* easily lasted two hours, and he thoroughly enjoyed it. Afterward, the guys would take a *giro,* a spin, around the soccer field, to work off the heavy meal. Many in-depth discussions occurred during those walks, and meaningful bonds of friendship were formed. A distinctly Italian tradition followed the *giro.* Everyone would disappear into their rooms as people settled in for their afternoon naps. In the courtyard, one could hear the echoes of food, the window shades sliding down.

One afternoon, Anthony had barely laid his head down on the pillow when he heard a light knock on his door. He got up and opened it. There was a sweaty man, dressed in running shorts and a t-shirt standing before him. Kevin looked enticingly sexy with the smooth shine of sweat gleaming off his muscular legs. *Stop it, Anthony!* He told himself.

You're in Rome. You can't go jumping into bed with every hot seminarian. At the same time, he reasoned, there was no harm in enjoying the view, and Kevin was one of the best he'd seen since his arrival. It didn't hurt that the two of them had settled into a flirty banter whenever they were alone. Anthony wasn't sure if he was reading him wrong, but he got a charge out of the game.

"Ciao, bello," Anthony said, enthused. "What? No nap today?"

"No, I had to work off all that pasta I've been eating. It's not in my Irish blood like you Italians. I could feel the inches adding to my belly," Kevin replied.

"I don't know. Your stomach looks pretty flat to me," Anthony said with a wink. "Did you have a good run?"

"Yeah, but man, it's hot out there. I had no idea that Rome was so humid," Kevin replied breathlessly.

"Yeah, well, that's why I don't do anything athletic. Why should I submit myself to such torture?"

"Because it's almost a natural high, and when you're finished, it feels really great," he said.

"So, I should torture myself so that I'll feel better when I stop? No thanks," Anthony exclaimed. Kevin shook his head and laughed.

"I could use some water," Kevin said as he walked over to the sink. "Can I use your glass?"

"Help yourself," Anthony said. As Kevin turned away, Anthony savored the vision of his butt outlined in his sweaty running shorts. "Are you sure you don't want some Baileys instead?"

"No thanks, I'm completely dehydrated, maybe later."

With that, Kevin gulped down a couple of glasses of water and collapsed onto the bed right beside Anthony. Then he picked up a familiar book from the nightstand. "What're you reading?"

"Actually, before my eyes got heavy with sleep, I was trying to read the book on spirituality the rector assigned. I can't believe he gave us homework before classes have even started."

"Yeah, it really sucks. But I'm pretty far into it. If you want, I can walk you through it," Kevin offered.

He scooted himself up, sitting right next to Anthony on the narrow twin bed. Their arms and legs were touching, with Anthony almost pinned against the wall. Kevin opened the book and held it between them so that Anthony had to lean into him to see it.

"Give me that highlighter," Kevin said as he went page by page, marking relevant passages. "See, this way, you'll get the main ideas without reading the entire text."

"Thanks, Kev. You're the best. How can I thank you for this?"

"Don't you worry, I'll figure out some way for you to make it up to me," he said, putting down the book and squeezing Anthony's thigh. "Let's finish the rest later. I need to close my eyes for a minute – and I definitely need a shower," Kevin said.

"I'm a little tired myself. I was just drifting off before you came in," Anthony replied.

"Want some company?" Kevin asked as he raised his eyebrows suggestively.

"Do you snore?" Anthony asked.

"I don't know. There's only one way to find out," Kevin said as he slid down onto the bed and lay his head back on Anthony's pillow. "What do you say we take a nap together?" Kevin asked, smiling.

"That's the best offer I've gotten since we've arrived in Rome," Anthony responded tentatively. He wasn't sure if this was an actual invitation or only their playful banter. The seminary code was so difficult to decipher. He scooted himself so that his head was on the pillow right beside Kevin's.

They were quiet for a moment, and the silence was ripe with possibility. Anthony could hear Kevin's breathing regulate and relax. He could feel the heat emanating from his body and was flush with desire.

As Kevin's arm rested at his side, his index finger made gentle circles on Anthony's thigh. It was a simple, affectionate movement, but the atmosphere was charged with sexual tension. Anthony could feel his heart rate quicken as he began to get aroused. Through his thin nylon shorts, he could see that Kevin was getting hard, but he was afraid to move. The silence seemed to last forever. He knew that he probably shouldn't, but he was finally overcome by his hunger and took a chance. Anthony said nothing as he turned his face toward Kevin and gently kissed him.

Kevin felt himself give into the warmth of Anthony's full lips upon his own. The attraction was clearly mutual, and their lust simmered just below the surface. Kevin had wanted this from the moment they met that first day. Everything about him screamed sensuality, and he wasn't merely taken with his sexy body. Kevin fancied everything about Anthony. And Anthony suddenly felt as if he wasn't not alone as a gay seminarian in Rome.

"I was hoping you would do that," said Kevin with a big smile on his face.

"Well, I wasn't really sure if you were interested," Anthony responded shyly.

"You know, Anthony, you can be pretty dense. I've basically been howling outside your door every night. Seriously, I've been trying to get your attention since day one," Kevin said.

"Well, now you have it. Now, shut up and kiss me again." Their shorts and t-shirts were swiftly thrown onto the floor, and they pressed their sweaty bodies together. Their hands moved with urgency as they explored the objects of their desire. Neither of them held back. Having both been in relationships before, they asserted themselves and made their preferences clear. They were good at communicating what they liked or didn't like.

The excitement between them continued to build. Anthony pulled away and kissed Kevin on his neck and down to his navel. Beads of sweat slowly trickled down toward his upper thighs.

Anthony let his tongue catch one, and he was startled by the acrid musk that lingered on his tongue. He looked up at Kevin and said, "Your sweat is so bitter!" Anthony said with his face scrunched up. "Next time, let's take showers before we do this."

"That's real man musk, sexy, eh? Just don't stop. The anticipation is driving me crazy."

It was a languorous September afternoon, and the fact that they were making love in the Vatican didn't escape either of them. As they caressed each other tenderly, Anthony spoke to Kevin in Italian, and that made their union even more romantic. Soon they were reaching the intensity that they both longed for, but both realized they couldn't make any noise. Although all the window shades were down, the courtyard below acted as an echo chamber. It was strangely unnatural to be silent during their orgasms, but it seemed to heighten their excitement. As they let their heartbeats return to normal, they laughed about their muted moaning and silent orgasms. From then on, they called their silent encounters "seminary sex."

***

They were an unlikely pair, but from that moment, they were inseparable. Anthony was passionate and wore his heart on his sleeve. He responded to everything with heartfelt emotion. In contrast, Kevin was intellectual and reserved. One never knew what he was thinking. Kevin loved to debate theological or philosophical topics, and he would win most times, especially with Anthony, who would get frustrated while trying to organize his thoughts. But that was what Kevin loved best about him. As Anthony would passionately expound upon the human toll of some issue, Kevin would smile inwardly and think, *I wish I could kiss him right now, in front of all these people.*

Anthony had a profound impact on Kevin as well. He brought the playful side out of him. Together, they would make fun of everything and laugh constantly.

One evening during orientation, the New Men were invited to the Casa Santa Maria, the house of graduate studies for American priests. The *Casa* is located in the heart of ancient Rome, a short walk from the Trevi Fountain and the Gregorian University, where many seminarians took their classes.

Upon arrival, the rector of the house greeted the new men. First on the agenda was a tour of the historic building. There were approximately fifty members of their class and only one tour guide, so it was easy to become distracted. Kevin and Anthony ended up near the tail end of the line. They weren't paying attention any longer and were totally absorbed with each other – a touch here or there, a caress, or pat on the butt. They enjoyed flirting with the danger of being caught. At one point, Kevin pulled Anthony into a dark room and kissed him deeply. Anthony responded in kind and put his hand down Kevin's pants and grabbed him. At his touch, Kevin moaned a bit too loudly. They immediately froze, listening to see if they had been overheard.

"We better knock it off before we get caught," Kevin said, snickering.

"Okay, I'll join the group first, so we don't raise suspicions. You can follow a few minutes later. Just say you were looking for a bathroom," Anthony replied.

"Good. That'll give me some time to calm down, if you know what I mean."

"Don't worry, Kevin, your giant erection isn't *that* obvious!" After dinner, the seminarians dispersed on their own as they made their way through the city back up the Janiculum Hill to the NAC. Kevin and Anthony enjoyed their wine throughout dinner and felt its effects as they wandered through the cobblestone streets.

They walked by the Trevi fountain, which was just a block or two from the Casa. The echo of the splashing water bounced against the Roman architecture, and the exuberant voices of the crowd gave it a festive atmosphere. It was packed with tourists and vendors trying to hock their wares: postcards, toys, candy. The two of them were laughing so hard when Kevin shouted at Anthony.

"Watch out! You're about to step into a pile of dog shit."

"Oh, shit!"

"That's what I'm saying."

In fact, it was a gag gift a vendor was selling, and it looked uninvitingly real. "We have to buy one," Anthony declared. "We can put it right outside Miguel's door. It'll be hilarious."

"He's going to kill you. Besides, there's no way that I'm buying *that*."

"No worries, Kevin. I got this one." Anthony turned to the vendor and said in a perfect Italian accent, "*Quanto costa questa merda?*" How much does this shit cost?

The two seminarians, who received odd looks from the vendor, broke into side-splitting laughter. A few moments later, he completed the transaction, and they continued on their journey home, laughing the entire way.

The following weeks were delightful. Both young men had found a lifeline amid the clerical world of Rome. For Anthony, it helped distract him from being homesick. He missed his family and his close circle of friends back home. Finding Kevin gave him someone to fill that void; through their mutual infatuation, both felt energized. Kevin was thrilled to have what he considered a genuine romantic relationship with someone his own age.

He and Anthony were going through this strange and wonderful transition to NAC together. Kevin connected with him like no other person he had ever met. Anthony consumed his thoughts and emotions in a way that rattled his intellectual mind. Considering both he and Anthony were preparing for the priesthood, everything that was happening between the two of them made little sense to Kevin. But he found Anthony to be a titillating companion on this strange Roman journey. Anthony's innocence was intoxicating, and Kevin knew it could spell trouble in the seminary. Having been at St. Thomas during his college years, Kevin could help Anthony navigate the unfamiliar political climate at NAC. Anthony could be a loose cannon sometimes. He would speak what was on his mind, often calling out the unspoken words with an off-color joke. He had difficulty understanding that he could not be as free with his thoughts and opinions as he had once been.

But no matter what new drama they faced each day, they knew they had an anchor to keep them grounded. Each night, after the cavernous marble halls had grown quiet, Kevin would sneak up to the fourth floor and knock almost imperceptibly on Anthony's door. He'd slip in before he could be seen, and they would make love silently. Together, they explored each other's bodies and tested uncharted waters; as they came to understand what it meant to pleasure their partner unselfishly. They joked about how smooth their skin would be after using so much Nivea skin cream as lubricant.

They laughed at their ingenuity – it was the only thing they could find. Kevin and Anthony fell into a comfortable routine and with each other, finding great comfort from their loneliness.

For Anthony, Kevin filled the void that Thomas had left. He believed he would never love anyone as much as he loved Thomas. Their breakup, though necessary, broke his heart. His loneliness consumed him, but he believed he was meant to be alone. Kevin changed all that. Kevin got a kick out of his silliness, his naïveté, and his ubiquitous emotional responses. He would simply smile and shake his head, and if they were alone, Kevin would pull him close and kiss him playfully. Kevin relished every new experience with Anthony. Expressing his sexuality was a novel concept for him, and he approached each encounter with wonder.

In contrast, Anthony was as free with his sexuality as with expressing his emotions. He approached their coupling playfully, and whatever they did together was simply a spirited expression of affection. There was no embarrassment or discomfort at communicating what each of them desired or preferred. Kevin never felt pressure to be or act a certain way. During sex, he felt free to experiment and to laugh if something just didn't work. Anthony often spoke in Italian throughout their lovemaking, and Kevin joked about his sexy Italian lessons.

"How is this going to help me? It's not like I can use any of this while ordering pasta in a restaurant."

"Well, if you do, you might get more than you bargained for," Anthony replied. Those first few weeks together were a glorious adventure. No matter what the challenges of adjusting to a new culture and new city, Kevin and Anthony viewed them through the lens of their infatuation.

It was a time of new beginnings for them both.

Chapter Ten
Lessons Learned

B y the last week of orientation, Anthony was bored – as with so many language programs, his lessons couldn't be less challenging. They never covered the advanced grammar that he sorely needed. Conversational Italian was rudimentary, and he hoped to be challenged. His classes ended up being a source of frustration rather than a vehicle toward fluency. However, Anthony experienced a deep sense of loss – he missed his old friends in New York. Although he had met some great people, he longed for the comfort of long-time friends he left behind.

There is nothing like being with friends who have known you for years. There's no need to explain things; they understand your fears and dreams – they know your history, Anthony thought. After sharing his frustration with and loneliness with Kevin and Miguel, Anthony felt a little better. Each of them was experiencing his own brand of homesickness. After four weeks, the glow of all things new had dulled. They commiserated but acknowledged that they were fortunate to have each other.

"What we need is an adventure," Kevin announced.

"Yeah, something to get us out of funk," he agreed.

"Have you heard about the old NAC cassocks?" asked Miguel. "The ones with the blue piping and red sash."

"Seriously, red, white, and blue?" Kevin asked. "Was that the plan?" He wondered.

"I think so," Miguel said. "They call us the West Point of seminaries."

"How patriotic," Anthony said sarcastically.

"So, I have an idea," Miguel said. "The nuns who do the laundry still have them. They might let us borrow them if we say we're doing something official at the basilica."

"Why would we want to borrow them? It's not like we want to promote that clerical culture," Kevin said.

"Hear me out," Miguel said. "We could don the NAC cassocks and parade around St. Peter's Square. It would be such a goof to see the reactions of the tourists."

"Get out," Anthony exclaimed. "That would be crazy fun! We could take pictures and send them to our friends back home." Kevin was a bit wary of the whole idea, but eventually got swept up in the excitement. In the blink of an eye, the cassocks were acquired, and the three seminarians were posing in the *piazza* with curious onlookers taking photos of them. With their red sashes, they looked like young monsignors. Anthony staged them in front of the grand obelisk, the twin fountains, and kneeling at the basilica altars. It was wholly inappropriate and irreverent, but the three new men were having the time of their lives laughing at their audacity.

Anthony truly felt that he had found kindred spirits in Kevin and Miguel. And although they had met a mere four weeks before, he believed he had found his tribe. Even so, Anthony longed for his best friends back home and, of course, his family.

The excitement of his infatuation with Kevin helped ease some of his loneliness. The companionship comforted him, but Anthony felt guilty that they were sleeping with each other. He knew that falling in love and having sex was incompatible with celibacy and the priesthood.

Although he rarely went to confession, he hoped it might do him some good. Just getting his worries and fears off his chest would provide relief. But Anthony knew he could never confess his sexual relationship to any of the priests at NAC. He couldn't divulge anything that might create an impediment to his vocational pursuits. Even though it would be technically under the confessional's seal, his confessor would know who he was. Some way or another, the NAC faculty would make his life miserable.

What if he requires me to inform the rector as part of my penance? I just couldn't do that. He was already talking himself out of going to confession at all when he had an idea. St. Peter's Basilica had priests manning their confessionals at all hours of the day. At the basilica, he could indeed be anonymous. While the rest of NAC rested in the stillness of their afternoon siestas, Anthony noiselessly slipped out the door and down the hill to St. Peter's. Anthony knelt at the *prie dieu* before St. Joseph's altar and did his examination of conscience.

There was so much to cover, not the least of which was his relationship with Kevin. His first weeks at NAC had given Anthony a new perspective on himself. His eyes were opened to the fact that he was willful and narrow-minded. He had trouble giving in or compromising if he was in the wrong. Anthony had begun to believe the rhetoric stating that the new men were the chosen ones and destined to be bishops or cardinals. He had to confess so much, but the most egregious of sins was having sex with Kevin.

Looking up at the altar, Anthony was consumed with self-doubt as he tried to work up the courage to confess his sins. Finally, he went to an Italian-speaking priest. At least then, it wouldn't feel as bad. Somehow, admitting that he had sex with another man didn't sound as bad in Italian. He laughed at himself for his ridiculous reasoning. But it worked.

While in the confessional, he poured his heart out as he listed his many transgressions. After a momentary pause, the priest counseled him on the gravity of his sins and instructed him to go to daily Mass.

Anthony lost in his relief at having confessed, then volunteered some sensitive information about himself.

"Oh, that won't be a problem, *Padre*. I'm a seminarian; they require us to attend daily Mass."

"Is that so? And do you go to confession before each Mass?" the priest asked.

"No, I don't. I figured the penitential rite of the Mass covered that."

"For sins as grave as yours, you should go to confession before you receive holy communion. Have you received the Eucharist without confessing your sins?"

"Well, yes, *Padre*. But that is why I am here today. To receive absolution," Anthony replied.

"I cannot absolve you for your sins if you don't go to confession regularly."

"But I am in confession now. That is why I am here seeking the sacrament of reconciliation?"

"As a seminarian, you should know better. Go, I will not absolve you of your sins."

"You can't be serious, *Padre*. This makes no sense."

"I am sorry. I will not forgive your sins. Go."

Anthony was shocked. *Wasn't that the purpose of confession?* So, because he didn't go to confession before receiving communion, he can't absolve him now. What kind of logic is that? As he trudged up the steep Janiculum hill, he marveled at how irrational the priest was. Clearly, the guy missed the whole point of reconciliation. He was disheartened by his dismissal from the confessional. But then it dawned on Anthony that the priest's real reason for withholding absolution was that he was sleeping with a man. And although he knew the Church preached about the evils of homosexuality, it had never hit him so hard.

His revelation proved to be a significant blow to his image of the Church. It reinforced every fear he had about the priests at NAC. He could never discuss his sexuality with anyone in power. Anthony always had a well-established moral compass, not that he didn't falter, but he realized that he would have to create his moral code and follow his own conscience.

With all the bizarre experiences during his first weeks in Rome, Anthony felt the need to get away. The latest confrontation with the priest at the basilica rocked his faith in the Church. It did not seem to be the same Church that he grew up in. Love, compassion, and mercy appeared to take a back seat in the pursuit of power and the teachings against sexual sins. The Church of Rome was more dogmatic than he ever imagined. His questioning of Church authority eroded his foundation. He needed the security of his family – he missed them terribly. Anthony thought spending time with his cousins in Sorrento would help fill that void and give him some much-needed perspective. He decided he would take a train south to Sorrento for a weekend visit. Anthony knew his aunt and uncle would be thrilled to see him. So, he checked the train schedule and phoned his cousin Gino telling him of his plans.

Relief washed over him immediately. But when he told Kevin of his idea, Anthony's bubble was popped. "Did you ask permission from Monsignor O'Connor?" Kevin asked.

"No, why would I need permission to visit my family?" he asked innocently. "The academic year hasn't even started yet."

"Because you're in the seminary now. Anything we do that's out of the ordinary needs to be approved by the rector," Kevin replied.

"But we have nothing planned this weekend, and I am bored to tears with my Italian classes. I'll learn so much more speaking with my cousins," Anthony responded.

"Noted, but your life is not your own anymore. Did you ever hear of obedience?" Kevin said sarcastically.

"Seriously? I'm an adult. I can make my own decisions," Anthony said defiantly.

"Just the same, you should ask the rector's permission before you leave the seminary. Be careful to pick your battles, Anthony. I'm not sure this is the hill to die on."

As it turned out, Monsignor O'Connor disapproved of his trip to Sorrento. "Anthony, you are just beginning your formation here at the

North American College. Your lack of seminary experience during your undergraduate years puts you at a slight disadvantage. I realize that the structure and some rules are new to you and perhaps annoying. But everything is in place to give you a sense of discipline and order. Your priority at this moment is to continue developing the bonds that you have begun with your classmates. Try to acclimate to the routines of morning and evening prayer, daily Mass, and especially your spiritual direction," Monsignor O'Connor said.

"I understand, monsignor, but I am bored out of my mind with my Italian classes, and I am terribly homesick. I hoped that a visit with my family would help," he pleaded.

"Homesickness is unavoidable, Anthony. It will pass. I promise you. Take the time this weekend to meditate on your journey. Visit some of the many significant churches in Rome and ask God for guidance and healing. Sorrento is not in the cards for you, Anthony. I hope you understand." Anthony was furious.

I am not a child. How dare he patronize me like that?

His rebellious nature prompted him to wonder what would happen if he were to get on the train, regardless of what the monsignor instructed. But he knew better than to challenge authority so soon. Kevin's advice about picking one's battles echoed in his mind.

Anthony thought that obedience would likely be his greatest challenge concerning seminary and priesthood. It had never occurred to him before; his powerful will would have to be stilled. It was too soon for him to be having a vocational crisis. He needed to calm down and put this into perspective.

Chapter Eleven
A Blessed Encounter

Kevin had overslept. He had to get to the showers before the hot water was shut off. There was a two-hour window of hot water each morning and evening. If you took a shower at any other time, the water was cold – ice-cold.

There were only ten minutes left before it was shut off. Kevin flew out of his room and nearly ran over Carlos, whose towel was loosely wrapped around his waist. It almost fell completely off. Carlos caught it just in time, but not before Kevin got a glimpse of his perfectly rounded butt. Kevin was beyond flustered, only inches away from a washboard stomach that glistened with stray drops of water.

"So sorry, I, I didn't see you," Kevin stammered. "Trying to get in before the water goes cold."

"It's cool. I think there's plenty left. I'm Carlos," he said as he held out his hand. His towel draped just a little lower, revealing his pubic hair. Kevin's eyes couldn't help but follow its descent. When he looked back up, Carlos was looking directly into his eyes. He knew that he'd been caught checking him out. How could he be so careless?

"I, I'm Kevin. I am so sorry. I better run," he said, nervously.

"Hey, no worries. We'll have a proper introduction after we're both fully clothed," Carlos said, with a wink.

What a fool I am, thought Kevin. *But my God, he is beautiful.*

***

It was the end of September, and the upperclassmen had all returned. There were many gatherings at which the faculty encouraged them to befriend the new men. Two doors down from Kevin's room was a second Theology student from San Antonio, Texas. Carlos had thick black hair and caramel-colored skin. His eyes were wide and as dark as his hair. Being from Hartford, Connecticut, Kevin had never met anyone as exotically beautiful as Carlos. His Mexican good looks were only out shown by his gentle and loving personality. While their sudden collision unnerved Kevin to no end, Carlos seemed amused by it all. It was undeniable that this new man was checking him out, and he quite enjoyed watching him squirm when he was caught. He was determined to have a little fun with it. So, at *pranzo* later that day, Carlos stopped by Kevin's table.

"*Ciao, bello.* Why don't we take a *giro* after we eat? Perhaps we can start fresh. *Va bene?*" he said with a wink.

"Oh, hi, Carlos. That would be great," Kevin stammered, his heart pounding in his chest. He could feel his face flushing red as he turned back to his table to find Anthony staring directly at him. As Carlos walked away, Anthony had to ask.

"Who's that?"

"Carlos. His room is a couple of doors down from mine. I literally ran into him this morning when he was coming out of the showers," Kevin replied.

"Is that so?" Anthony saw Kevin was blushing bright red. He could tell that there was more to the story, but he couldn't ask him in front of the others.

"We're going for a walk around the soccer field after lunch. You're welcome to join us if you like," Kevin replied half-heartedly.

"No, that's okay. I don't want to interrupt anything," Anthony said curtly and began chatting with the guy sitting beside him. Kevin knew Anthony was upset, but his excited anticipation of time with Carlos obscured any sympathy he might have had toward Anthony. Once the refectory cleared out, Carlos made his way to Kevin.

"*Andiamo, Kevino*. Let's go."

Not long into their walk around the field, Carlos broke the tension, teasing him about his inappropriate behavior earlier that morning. And Kevin took it on the chin. He was caught red-handed. "What can I say, Carlos? You caught me off-guard. How could I resist gazing at a subject more perfect than Michelangelo's David?"

"Is that so?" Carlos replied to Kevin with a grin. "You really *are* full of it, aren't you?"

Their good-natured banter had the desired effect, and Kevin's embarrassment all but abated. They walked around the field at least ten times, and the conversation never stopped. They couldn't have been more different; one dark and exotic, the other fair and blue-eyed. Kevin grew up in a lower-middle-class white neighborhood in Hartford's suburbs, while Carlos had lived in the barrio in San Antonio. But the two of them spoke with ease about their calling to the priesthood and their complicated family lives. When Kevin was speaking, Carlos made him feel he was the most important person in the world. He looked at him with his beautifully expressive dark eyes. He had a subtle way of flirting that made Kevin wonder if he was misreading the signals. Kevin was entranced by Carlos.

By the time they made their last round, they were the only two on the pathway and made their way up to their rooms. They climbed the stairs to the second floor and stopped outside of Kevin's room. "It was wonderful to chat with you, Kevin. You seemed more comfortable than this morning," Carlos said as he winked again.

"Hey, now you're making me self-conscious again. Besides, you were only wearing a towel around your waist. It was scandalous."

"Oh, I see. So, your depraved ogling of my ass was my fault?" He paused for dramatic effect. "In the future, I'll be sure to cover myself up appropriately when passing by your room."

"Well, now, I wouldn't take that too far, my sexy friend," Kevin ventured.

Carlos moved in for a hug and gently ruffled Kevin's hair. "You are a bold one, aren't you?"

"Not usually. But I've had a few glasses of wine, and there's something about you that I just can't resist, Carlos."

Carlos ignored Kevin's last remark. The last thing he needed was to deal with a crush from one of the new men, even if he was handsome. On the other hand, Carlos was thoroughly enjoying the attention.

"Have a good nap, *caro,*" Carlos said and walked on to his own room. Kevin didn't know what to make of their entire encounter. He was no closer to finding out if he was gay or not. But Carlos didn't seem put off by the many sexual innuendos, so perhaps he was. And while he was fully involved with Anthony, Kevin's infatuation with Carlos continued to intensify. Kevin's latent sexual awaking was only months old, and there was so much time to make up for. Why limit himself to one guy?

That evening, after dinner, Anthony approached Kevin. "Let's go for a walk. I need to talk to you." They exited the main gates and walked down the Janiculum hill towards St. Peter's Square.

"What's up, Anthony? You've been very quiet since we left NAC. Are you all right?" Kevin asked, though he knew exactly what was bothering Anthony.

"I guess I should ask you that?"

"What do you mean? I'm fine. Let's stop the guessing game and tell me what's on your mind."

Kevin wanted Anthony to bring up the topic on his own. He knew he was torturing him, but he couldn't help himself.

"So, I don't want to sound like a jilted girlfriend – but what's the deal with you and Carlos?"

"What? Nothing, really. We're just getting to know one another. We took a *giro* around the soccer fields after lunch. That's all," Kevin said.

"A *giro*, you mean he took you for a spin? Look, I saw your face flush red when he came to the table at *pranzo* today. You are completely smitten."

"No, Anthony, it's not like that. I almost knocked him down this morning when I was running into the shower. I nearly knocked off his towel. I was embarrassed," Kevin said, obfuscating the intense attraction felt for him.

"Come on, he's hot, and you're into him. It's plain as day. Did you guys *nap* together after your walk?" Anthony asked bitterly.

"No, honestly, no. I don't even know if Carlos is gay."

"But if he were, you'd want to sleep with him, right?"

"He *is* beautiful. I don't know, yes, maybe. But I have you, and we are together. I don't want to do anything to jeopardize that."

Anthony was struck by Kevin's candor. He didn't deny his attraction to Carlos, and he affirmed their relationship as something special. And although Anthony was jealous and annoyed, he understood the seminary was full of attractive gay men who hungered for affection.

This was a new reality, and as difficult as it would be, he needed to get used to it. "Okay, Kevin. I get it. But please be honest with me—about him—or anyone else that might come along. I don't want to be blind-sided and get my heartbroken. Can you at least promise me that?"

"Of course, Anthony. You mean so much to me. Without you in my life for the last five weeks, I'd be lost. Nothing will change how much you mean to me. I promise, really, I do." Kevin genuinely meant what he said. Anthony had become the most important person in his life, and he truly loved him. He didn't want to risk losing him just because he was tempted by a sexy man in a towel, although that was easier said than done. Kevin resolved to work harder at being faithful to Anthony. Regardless of his sexual appetite, Kevin knew he couldn't do anything to jeopardize their relationship. But even with his firm resolve, there was a stirring in his loins whenever he pictured Carlos with drops of water trickling down his nearly naked body. Kevin had let the genie out of the bottle when he first had sex with Father Bill. Any attempt to stuff it back in proved futile; his sexual appetite seemed to drive the bus. He had to snap out of it – there was no use in obsessing over Carlos or any of the other sexy men at NAC – not if he wanted to safeguard his relationship with Anthony.

Chapter Twelve
Destined for Greatness

Carlos had worked hard to get to where he was. When he was a child back in Texas, he was bullied for being a bookworm. While his friends and siblings were out playing or causing trouble, Carlos could be found reading or doing homework. He excelled in his studies, and the teachers at his small Catholic elementary school delighted in his curiosity and well-mannered comportment.

One day, the mother superior pulled him out of class unexpectedly. Sitting in her office, across her carved mahogany desk, Carlos was both happy and disappointed when she recommended he go to St. Mary's Hall. It was an elite independent school with an excellent college-prep program. Carlos knew his parents could never afford the costly tuition. He promised the mother superior that he would talk it over with his parents, but he never even mentioned it to them. Why rub their noses in what they couldn't provide?

It would make them feel inadequate that they couldn't send him to an elite school. His parents had already sacrificed so much by sending him to a Catholic school. He couldn't imagine asking them to do more.

A week or two later, he returned from school late in the afternoon. He stayed after school, spending hours working on a project about the Spanish Missions in Texas. It was nearly 5:00 p.m. when he opened the kitchen door to find his parents sitting at the kitchen table. He immediately knew something was wrong. There was no sign of dinner, and his siblings were nowhere to be found. "Mom, dad, what's wrong? Did something happen?" Carlos asked.

"Nothing is wrong, Carlos," his mother replied.

"Why do you look so serious? Where is everyone?"

"We sent them out to play. Dinner is going to be a little late tonight," his mother said.

"I don't understand. Am I in trouble?"

"Sit down, *mijo,* don't worry. We want to speak with you about something important."

Then his father, who generally let his mother do the talking, joined in. "We got a phone call from the mother superior today. She says that you are the top student in your class," he said.

"But that's good news, isn't it?" Carlos said, still trying to figure out what this was all about.

"Yes," his mother replied. "But she also mentioned that they want you to apply to St. Mary's Hall."

"I know, but that's just silly. We could never afford that."

"So, you knew about this. Mother said she spoke to you about this, but we thought she was mistaken."

"St. Mary's is for rich kids. I knew there was no way I could go there," Carlos said.

"Is that why you didn't mention it to us?"

"I guess so. I mean, why discuss it at all if it's not even a possibility?" he replied.

"*Mijo,* that is not your decision to make. You should always talk to us about important matters. We will let you know if something is possible or not."

"I'm sorry, mom. But it sounded so ridiculous. I never gave it a second thought."

"Okay, so here is the good news. There is a scholarship available, and if you do well on the entrance exam, you could get a full ride. That means all four years of high school would cost less than what we are paying now."

"Are you kidding? That would be amazing! But what if I don't do well on the test?"

"Carlos, you are an excellent student. Of course, you will do well," his father said and slapped him on the back.

During the weeks leading up to the testing date, Carlos studied and studied. Now he had to do well. His parents were counting on him, and there was no way he could disappoint them. The pressure was on. When the day of the test arrived, Carlos was sick to his stomach. He lay in bed with the covers pulled up to his chin. "Mom, I don't think I can take the test. I feel really sick," he whined.

She gave him a sympathetic smile and felt his forehead. "Carlos, you don't have a fever. You're fine," she said. "I'm sure it's just nerves. Come, let's get you some breakfast." Carlos was miserable as he dragged himself out of bed and shuffled to the kitchen.

He knew his mother was right, but he couldn't snap out of it. His father's pickup truck looked oddly out of place as it passed through St. Mary's majestic entry gates. Beautifully manicured lawns and colorful plantings lined the driveway, and tall palm trees framed the stately main building. Carlos pulled open the heavy wooden doors and found his way to the classroom. A sea of faces looked up at him as he entered, and he felt as if he were facing a death squad. He stood immobile; his ashen face was so alarming that the proctor stopped him to ask if he was alright.

As it turned out, his excessive worrying was for nothing. In fact, Carlos had scored in the top 1% of the candidates. When he received his letter of acceptance and a full scholarship, he was floating on a cloud. His time at St. Mary's Hall had a profound effect upon Carlos. It was during his high school years thoughts of becoming a priest arose. By his senior year, he believed he had a calling and entered St. Mary Queen of the Angels Seminary in Los Angeles. It surprised no one when the bishop appointed him to the North American College after his graduation. Everyone thought he was destined for greatness.

***

Carlos's first year in Rome was filled with new experiences and fruitful friendships. He found that the faculty and his closest friends were supportive of his journey toward the priesthood. The theme of his first year at NAC was that of encounter—meeting your brothers along the way to Christ. The rector encouraged them to reach out and spend time with one another to get to know each other on a deeper level. Carlos had meaningful and fulfilling relationships with his classmates. Although he was fascinated with one or two of the guys along the way, there was never any thought of carrying it any further.

They were seminarians who would eventually take a vow of celibacy. Learning to develop healthy, intimate relationships without sex was part of his formation.

However, the dynamic completely changed during his second year. The new men at NAC seemed to be a different breed. There always seemed to be some drama brewing among them. The guys were incredibly forward with their desires and sexual preferences. They called out hypocrisy, or any perceived injustice that may have occurred. Carlos and his classmates were at once intrigued and fearful. Something was enticing about their guileless love of life. They seemed to live their journey with tremendous passion, and with that came much drama and conflict. Carlos was not equipped to handle the volatility that came with this batch of new men. He resolved to give them a wide berth. That was until he met Kevin. There was something about him that drew him in. It wasn't merely that he was handsome and fit. He presented himself with a combination of innocence and intellectual wisdom. His confidence was wrapped in a charming personality, and his blue eyes flickered with good-natured mischief.

Kevin had literally bumped into him as Carlos returned from the shower early one morning. Nearly falling, they stumbled to regain their footing as Carlos barely prevented his towel from falling off. He could recall the warm scent of sleep radiating from him. Kevin was athletic and masculine, and his pheromones were screaming out to him. Carlos was taken aback by how blatant Kevin was about checking him out, his eyes scanning his bare chest and lingering on the line of hair leading below his towel.

That alone piqued his curiosity, and he was determined to get to know him. Carlos boldly invited Kevin to join him in the ritual *giro* around the soccer field. When they took their walk together, he approached Kevin with the idea of an encounter. Regardless of their mutual attraction, they could bond over their collective journey toward the priesthood. To ignore their chemistry was fool-hearted; better to name it and move beyond it.

Carlos hoped they could become friends who would support each other in ministry. Their pleasant conversation and mutual attraction captivated them.

He and Kevin seemed to connect on a deeper level almost immediately, and Carlos longed for this kind of intimacy. When they stood outside Kevin's door, however, he realized Kevin was expecting more. Although he was extremely attracted to him, Carlos was not ready for that. In fact, he had thought they had remained in safe territory as they shared some of their personal stories.

This encounter had gone in an entirely unexpected direction. During his first year in Rome, there were several times when he became infatuated, but neither party was ever as forward as Kevin had been. He had practically propositioned him as they stood outside his door.

No, this needs to stop now, Carlos thought. But the stirring in his loins indicated he didn't have as much control as he had thought. It was the last thing he needed. Carlos had always been focused on his goals and aimed to keep it that way. His focus and drive led him to Rome – he had no intention of letting a handsome new man distract him. During his childhood, his brothers were continually picking on him for being so diligent in his studies. Worse yet was that he was not athletic at all. On the rare occasion that he was forced onto the soccer field, he was taunted mercilessly. Inevitably, he'd miss the ball or get smashed in the face rather than hitting the ball with his head.

He had never had any interest in girls, which further caused his brothers to taunt him. From an early age, he found the other boys attractive. College seminary had presented many opportunities to sleep with his classmates, and occasionally, he found some comfort there. But he was determined not to give in to his baser instincts at NAC. During his first year in Rome, he met Sean.

The two friends hit it off immediately, and their mutual attraction was clear from the start. They would often find themselves hugging and eventually kissing, but then they would launch into a conversation about celibacy.

"This is nice," Sean would say to Carlos after they kissed. "I feel so close to you."

"It *is* nice, but you know we can't go any further."

"I know, and I'm fine with that, really," Sean replied.

Carlos lifted the hand that covered his crotch. "Are you, really?" he asked with an ironic smile.

Sean was embarrassed at his apparent state of arousal.

"We can do this, Carlos. All we've heard about this year is the need for a healthy intimacy; that it's the only way we can survive our vow of celibacy. We'll never make it if we don't develop intimate relationships."

"I agree, but we have to be careful, Sean. Both of us would take this further if we could. I fear that we've gotten too close to the edge on too many occasions."

"I have to confess that I've had a lot of fantasies about us having sex together."

"Don't, Sean. We can't even entertain that. If we do, it will call our priesthood into question." That scenario and the ensuing discussion were re-enacted many times over. Sean and Carlos had developed an affectionate friendship over that year. They struggled to keep their sexual desires in check, and it worked. By the end of the year, the cuddling and kissing ceased, and they felt solidarity as they supported each other on their journey toward celibacy.

Carlos believed that if he could master his sexual feelings toward Sean, that celibacy would not be as much of a burden. Then Kevin entered his world and rocked the foundation.

Chapter Thirteen

Sexual Awakening

K evin found that his newly awakened sexual awareness had very few limits. Although he loved Anthony and was falling in love with Carlos, he couldn't help being attracted other men at NAC. It seemed that there was no end to the number of second and third-year men that vied for his attention. Even some ordained deacons and priests overtly flirted with him, and the attention exhilarated him. The game would always begin the same way.

A philosophical topic would arise during *pranzo*, and everyone at the table was well lubricated with the ever-present bottles of wine. Kevin would become immediately engaged in debate and was quite adept at defending his position and challenging any opposing opinions – he held his own with the upperclassmen. Following a heated discussion, they would often ask him to take a *giro,* a walk around the soccer field after the meal. Only later did he come to understand that going for a *giro* had a double meaning. It was apparent that several upperclassmen were hoping to take a spin with Kevin.

He found himself deep in discussion with each new suitor as they made their rounds on the field. As each turn would come upon them, they would wordlessly agree to go another round. Shoulders would bump, and arms and fingers would occasionally brush against each other during their walk. By the end of the *giro,* the energy between them changed. Inevitably, they made their way into the building and up into the upperclassman's room.

"How about a *digestivo?"* Kevin's debate partner would routinely ask, offering him an after-dinner drink.

"Sure, why not?" Kevin always responded as he continued to discuss whatever point he was trying to make passionately.

Once in his room, Kevin downed the first drink and was offered a second without pausing his philosophical argument. Each time his partner would return with another shot, he would sit closer to Kevin; legs were touching, a hand on his knee, and by then, it was clear that the discussion was over. Kevin stopped talking and let the seminarian kiss him as his hand slid up his thigh and hardened sex.

Clothes were hastily shed, and soon the pair would continue their debate in another language. There was never anything romantic about these encounters. It was just sex. Most times, it was desperate, lustful sex. It seemed as if the older guys were starved for affection, and Kevin was more than happy to oblige. Kevin didn't exactly feel guilty about each new sexual partner, but he wanted to talk about his latest sexual experiences to someone who might understand.

That *someone* was always Anthony.

Somehow, even though Anthony's feelings for him ran deep, he was never judgmental, and he never seemed hurt by Kevin's constant infidelity. At least, he expressed no jealousy or hurt feelings. Anthony was much more in love with him than Kevin knew. While Kevin considered Anthony to be his primary relationship, he couldn't stop himself from exploring his sexuality – he never gave it a second thought. His attraction to all these young seminarians surprised and excited him.

During high school and college, Kevin never gave in to his sexual desires. His rigidity regarding Church law and ethical behavior allowed for no gray area. Actions were either right or wrong – they did not depend on the circumstances and certainly not upon one's emotional state. His first taste of sexual expression with Father Bill burst the dam, and he was not willing to hold back any longer. He now knew what he was missing.

Time after time, he could be found knocking on Anthony's door. After each one of his sexual exploits, he would seek Anthony. "Ciao, *bello*. Were you sleeping? Sorry. You'll never guess what just happened," Kevin would begin, oblivious to Anthony's true feelings.

"Again, Kevin? Be careful, or you'll get the reputation as the whore of Babylon."

"You mean the whore of NAC, don't you?"

They laughed as Kevin recounted the entire experience, giving every exciting detail.

"Kevin, I feel as if I'm your confessor. It's too bad I'm not ordained yet. I could give you absolution for all of your sins."

"Perhaps, but that would require me to repent and be sorry for them," Kevin replied.

"True, and it doesn't seem like you are the least bit sorry," Anthony said with an indistinguishable touch of bitterness to his tone.

"I don't know about you, Anthony, but this is the most sex I have ever had in my entire life. I love it here!"

"Seriously, Kevin? I don't think this is what anyone imagined our first year of Theology would be like. Don't you think you should cool it a bit? Maybe we should concentrate more on our studies."

"Are you kidding? I am learning so much by debating with these guys. They say you learn so much more when you interact with more educated people than yourself."

"That's true, and I'm sure they are teaching you a thing or two about sex as well."

"An added bonus – maybe I can show you what I just learned," Kevin said, raising his eyebrows suggestively.

"That's an attractive offer, Kev. But I'm really not in the mood after your confession – and certainly not until you've thoroughly showered.

You need to rid yourself of the remnants of your last sexual venture before I come near that hunky body of yours."

"Ah, there it is. You still love me, don't you? – even after I wander into someone else's bed." He reached over and caressed Anthony's upper thigh. "Do we *have* to wait until I shower?"

"Gross! Yes, get out of here and let me finish my nap, you horny leprechaun," Anthony exclaimed as he slapped his hand away.

Anthony stared at the door as it closed behind Kevin. His mind was still, but he could not focus. He played the scene repeatedly. Kevin's sexual escapades bothered him, but not enough to end their relationship. Mulling over the many seminarians Kevin had been with, Anthony realized that something disturbed him. *Was everyone in the seminary having sex?* he wondered. Being new to the seminary scene, the culture and practices at NAC continually surprised Anthony. But he never expected the ubiquitous sexual tension that boiled just beneath the surface of every interaction.

Although it wasn't openly spoken about, it seemed that both seminarians and priests were sexually active. Did the vow of celibacy mean nothing? What would people think if they really knew what was going on behind closed doors? Strangely, it made sense. Gathered in this grand edifice were men in their early twenties, all of whom were told to refrain from physical intimacy. That primal need was barely simmering under the surface of each of the men. Add the prodigious consumption of alcohol before, during, and after every meal, it was no wonder that one's inhibitions all but disappeared.

Anthony was also amazed at the gay subculture at NAC. He had never been around so many gay men in his life. The fear of being exposed that Anthony experienced in college seemed a world away. Back then, Anthony believed he was alone – that he would never find anyone to love him. The isolation chipped away at his ego and his relationship with God. There were so many moments when he felt unworthy or sinful because of his attraction to men.

Strangely, here in Rome, it seemed that most of the seminarians were gay, or at least accepting of it. However, the straight guys flirted and went out with women too. It was a unique environment – one that did not yet make sense to him.

Back in his room, Kevin pulled out his journal. He had started to write a prayer journal during his time at St. Thomas Seminary in Hartford and was pretty faithful about keeping up to date. Now that he was in Rome, there were so many new experiences, and he wanted to note each of his unique struggles and reflections.

Although Kevin worried his journal would fall into the wrong hands and that they would read all his inner secrets. But his sexual encounters were so new to him, and he didn't want to leave out the details. So, he locked up his journal so that he could include his many hook-ups at NAC.

He pulled out his pen and dated the page, and then he lifted his head and stared out the window toward the dome of St. Peter's. *How did I end up here?* he thought. He was such a different person just six months ago. Kevin was the guy with the level head who everyone would go to for advice. He was the guy who protected the kids who were bullied, counseled his classmates, or helped resolve conflicts. Kevin's emotions were always in check, and his life goals were clear. Long before he admitted it to anyone else, he knew that he would become a priest. With that in mind, he had no interest in pursuing an intimate relationship with anybody, boy or girl.

But something changed.

Kevin wasn't sure if it had started with his failed relationship with Father Bill. Since then, however, he felt that something kept locked deep inside was finally set free. Still, he never expected that he would have to keep his physical desires in check. They had never ruled his behavior before, why was it such an issue now. It wasn't that he couldn't control his sexual appetite; he just didn't want to.

The dichotomy of his circumstances stared him directly in the face as he gazed out upon St. Peter's Basilica, the heart of Roman Catholicism. In a place where gay sex was even more taboo, he seemed to find no end to his opportunities. *How can this be? I live in Vatican City State.* He wrote about today's encounter with a fourth-year guy, Dan.

Tuesday, 11 p.m.

Dan was just ordained a deacon last June; he had taken his vow of celibacy, and he still put the moves on me. For some reason, hooking up with men here in Rome is more straightforward than it ever was in Connecticut.

It's so strange that each time I run into one of the seminarians I had sex with, they carry on as if nothing happened. I always thought that it might be awkward, or at least uncomfortable. But it's the exact opposite. There seemed to be an unspoken understanding that everyone is fair game, or that everyone is in on the secret—as long as nobody names it. In fact, there have been many repeat customers. I'm not sure why none of this fazes me.

How can this be? I have always been so strict in following my ethical code. Why aren't I bothered by this? I know that St. Thomas Aquinas wrote that same-sex behavior was against natural law. Philosophically, it makes perfect sense. If it is natural for beings to procreate to propagate the species, then any act counter to that is considered unnatural. But St. Thomas also wrote that one must use human reason in all ethical dilemmas.

What if we are born gay? What if there is no choice in the matter? Wouldn't I merely be acting according to my nature? Perhaps it is perfectly natural to express one's love to a member of the same sex?

Kevin found himself thinking in circles. If anyone had told him he would come to question the Church's teaching on sexuality, he'd have thought they were crazy. However, the world inside the priesthood and the Roman seminary was a completely alien world to him. It clearly made its own set of rules. There was one set for laypeople, those in the pews, and quite another for the clergy. Kevin never dreamed that so many priests ignored the vow of celibacy.

What was even more striking was the fact that the official teaching against homosexuality was quite clear.

Homosexual acts were sinful, yet he was surrounded by scores of gay seminarians and priests. This dichotomy was staring him right in the face – in Vatican City.

He wrestled with the blatant hypocrisy he witnessed every day at NAC. Kevin wondered if it was easier to ignore a vow made to an institution rather than to another person. He couldn't imagine his parents breaking their vows of fidelity to each other.

Somehow knowing that you would cause your partner great pain seemed onerous. Admittedly, that guilt alone would make it more challenging to break your vow. And although one could argue that the vow of celibacy is made to God, not the institution of the Church, breaking it doesn't seem as severe. Who is hurt by breaking the vow of celibacy? It was a faceless institution that had gotten a significant number of things wrong in its history. The teaching regarding gay people was a perfect example of how official education could be detrimental to the faithful. What made it even more problematic was the Church's archaic rule that any physical expression of sexuality between people of the same sex was evil.

It required them to live a life of celibacy. In Kevin's eyes, the Church had abandoned her gay children. Also, the Church actively worked to deny their rights. How could one respect such an unenlightened teaching? The moral authority of the Church was deteriorating all around him.

Ultimately, he came to believe everyone had to wrestle with their sexuality in their own way. He wasn't ready to judge himself harshly for his recently discovered sexuality. He was an intelligent young man and knew that homosexuality was no longer considered a mental illness. From his personal experience, he knew this to be true. He was being true to himself, a little trashy, but true. He chuckled. He often got a kick out of himself when he was caught in a philosophical loop.

For now, he decided it was his time to explore. Besides, when he was a teenager, while all his straight friends were figuring this out, he was busy being celibate. Now it was his turn to let loose.

Chapter Fourteen
Inseparable Friends

Kevin, Anthony, and Miguel were rarely apart and were seen having heated debates, laughing a bit too loudly at some inside joke, or wandering into Rome for an evening meal. They were never exclusive; others with an irreverent bent similar to their own were always welcome. From the second year of Theology, Carlos and Sean joined the trio, enjoying their playful banter or helping to quell their ever-mounting dissatisfaction with NAC. They were each dealing with a powerful sense of loneliness and homesickness. But more importantly, they were keenly aware that their dreams and visions of life as Roman seminarians bore little resemblance to their lived reality.

Not attending a college seminary, Anthony wasn't the only one shocked by the microscope under which they all were living. The etiquette at the North American was more complicated than seminaries back in the states. The formality carried with it an undercurrent of privilege, and with that, a heavy burden of responsibility. They were expected to act as envoys to every foreign visitor and to visitors from the United States. They watched the upperclassmen put on entirely distinct airs when walking on the main seminary floor, the *rapresentanza*.

The *rapresentanza* was the stage for the North American College. One had to be ready to be an ambassador at any given moment, as guests were commonplace at the NAC. But it wasn't simply putting on a friendly face and representing NAC with professionalism.

It smacked of clericalism, and all three of them had had enough of it. Many of their classmates, who seemed reasonable enough during the initial weeks of orientation, transformed into militant traditionalists. Contrary to their misguided notions, none of them was better than any of the laypeople who entered those doors.

Many of the guys bought into the idea that Roman seminarians were the future princes of the Church. And as the year wore on, the chasm within their class became wider. Arguments and disagreements would flare in the common rooms or while at *pranzo*. The different camps had clear delineations. It was almost as if you had to choose your friends based upon which side you fell. Any fraternization between the groups was noticed and cause for suspicion.

The three friends resented their false piety and the message it seemed to communicate. Kevin, Anthony, and Miguel clung to each other for support. But even more so, they watched out for one other. If they detected anything negative aimed at them from that faction of the class, they would deflect it. Being the most even-tempered, Kevin seemed to have a finger on the pulse of the class politics.

Not long into their first semester in Rome, the newly elected and charismatic Pope John Paul II began to show his traditional leanings. Although he helped to fight against Communism in Poland and contributed significantly to bringing down the Berlin Wall, John Paul was very conservative in his social teachings. For him, clerics were a symbol of activism against the Communist regime. Merely wearing clerical garb placed the priest at odds with the government as they became witnesses to their faith and a threat to communism. Clerics were the radical leaders of the community and stood apart from the corruption of evil governments.

For most people in democratic countries, this was not their experience of the Church. During the 1960s and 70s, priests and nuns shed their religious garb to show solidarity with the people they served. It was an act against clericalism. They believed that there should be no separation between the minister and his people. Many viewed religious garb as symbols of power and abuse, holding priests and religious (nuns and brothers) above laypeople. This was especially true of the Church in the United States, where the sexual revolution and social upheaval witnessed the crumbling foundations of many influential institutions.

When John Paul II changed the directive of his predecessor, Pope Paul VI, all hell broke loose at NAC.

According to the teaching of Pope Paul VI, seminarians were not to don clerical garb until after they were ordained as deacons.

With a dramatic move in a conservative direction, the new document stated that the seminarian should wear religious clothing to give witness to their faith and commitment to the Church from the moment one entered formation. This was the beginning of a broader conflict that would permanently divide their class. The tensions brewing during the first months now had a cause that manifested a foundational division in the Church's philosophy.

One faction followed the teachings of the Second Vatican Council, which sought to bridge the gap between the laity and the clergy. The council taught that priests were no longer held up on pedestals; they were flawed humans who struggled to follow God's will just as the people in the pews. Ordained ministers had a unique role in leading the flock but were to do so among the people.

Vatican II sought to bring the laity into active ministry by reading, serving, and ministering hand in hand with the clergy. Its teachings were more inclusive and used common language that was more familiar to ordinary people's lived experiences.

Many priests and nuns stopped wearing habits or clerical garb that set them apart from the rest of the Church. The change in dress was meant to be a symbol of the shared journey toward communion with Christ. By contrast, the more conservative wing of the Church longed for a return to tradition and structure. They believed that the teachings of Vatican II removed the mystery and grandeur of the Church.

They resented the loss of ritual and symbols of other-worldliness. Not only did they want priests and nuns to wear habits, but they also sought a return to cassocks and birettas for priests and veils that covered the sisters' hair. They believed that clergy and religious sisters should be set apart from laypeople. They disdained dialogue and preached rigorous adherence to Church law and custom.

Any diversion from strict compliance to authoritative directives was considered disloyal to the pope. One was never to express an opinion counter to the pope or any Church teaching. When the command regarding clerical garb came down, the two camps immediately took to their corners. The very next day, several seminarians were dressed in cassocks or clerical shirts. However, the North American College did not issue an official policy immediately.

The rector and the faculty at NAC held meetings to discuss the new directive. Together, they hoped to reach a consensus as to how they would follow the orders. The goal was to gather the community, bringing various voices together to discuss and decide the best course of action. This was taken directly from the teachings of Vatican II, where the world's bishops would gather to address the issues at hand and advise the pope accordingly.

However, the faculty underestimated the level of tension that was brewing, especially among the new men. The once spirited class that showed so much promise at the *Possibility Show* would channel that lively nature into a cause that revealed a great deal of animosity. Decorum quickly deteriorated as the discussion became a contentious debate with Anthony, Miguel, and Kevin as some of the most outspoken men opposing the clerical dress.

"So, are we saying that the teachings of Pope Paul VI are less important than that of John Paul II?" Anthony asked.

"No, it's not that at all. Church teachings evolve over time," Father Connick replied carefully. "Guidance from the Magisterium addresses additional concerns as they arise in our contemporary world."

"To be sure," said Seth was from the same diocese as Miguel. He spoke from the opposing camp. "This is a good example of the Holy Spirit trying to correct errors from the past decade."

"Exactly what errors are you speaking of, Seth?" Miguel asked.

"The diluting of the sacredness of ordained ministry. Priests are ontologically changed by ordination – they differ in essence from all others. They should be set apart from the laity because they are no longer on the same level. They have been raised up," Seth replied as he took the bait and caused the tension to escalate. He named the unspoken philosophical bone of contention.

"Ah, so that's it," Anthony interrupted. "You think we are better than the people in the pews because we're seminarians."

"That's not what I said, but if we don't give witness to the greatness of the Church, how will people respect us and follow as we try to lead?" Seth clarified.

"Respect should be earned by what you do, not from what you wear," Anthony added.

"There you go, Anthony. Once again, you think you're the moral authority for our class," Arnold said, joining the fray. "Thank you for your socially conscious words of wisdom."

"Seriously?" Kevin responded. "Now we're launching into personal attacks? Make your arguments based on the issues at hand. Let's not devolve into adolescent bickering."

"Well stated, Kevin," Father Connick interjected. "Let's be civil with one another as we continue this conversation."

"We simply want to comply with the directives given to us by the Vatican. We should be witnesses to our faith and our ministry," Arnold said.

"Agreed," added Seth. "Many of us have cassocks from our college seminaries. I think we should be uniform in our adherence to the rule. Cassocks would make a bold statement of obedience to the pope."

"Oh, you've got to be kidding," Miguel burst out. He had been tolerating Seth's self-righteousness for years. "So now you want to take us back to the 1950s, before Vatican two? Come on. No one wears cassocks anymore."

"Vatican two was simply a pastoral council. It was never meant to change the Church as it did," Arnold added. "It wasn't supposed to affect the ritual of the mass or the significance of the priesthood."

"He's right," said Seth. "All you Vatican II people have had your way for years. It's over. Now it's our turn. The winds have changed, and you can't fight it."

"This is ridiculous! You just want the smells and bells back, and all the frilly vestments. If that isn't indicative of repressed homosexuality, nothing is," Anthony shouted.

At that point, all hell broke loose. Both sides were shouting at one another. This was no longer an argument over clerical garb – it was indicative of a more significant divide within the Church.

One camp sought progress, the other remained entrenched in the days of old. Monsignor Connick's attempts to calm the argument were in vain. The faculty left the room when it was clear that the discussion had devolved beyond repair. They were disconcerted with the new men's behavior, and although both sides had provoked the other, Anthony's last comment was the match that lit the flame. If he weren't careful, he'd be marked as a rabble-rouser.

Kevin tried to calm everyone down after the faculty left, but he had little success. This argument could do nothing but hurt their already fractured class. He feared Anthony had gone too far and worried that the faculty would target him.

"Hey, Anthony, let's get out of here," Kevin said.

"Now? We're finally getting into it, and I have a few things I want to get off my chest."

"Just let it go, Anthony. This is a volatile situation. The best we can do is let tempers calm a bit. Please, let's go," Kevin pleaded. Back in Kevin's room, the discussion continued. Carlos and Sean had joined them and were rehashing the meeting.

"This was inevitable," Sean said. "The only reason they brought us into the discussion was so we would feel as if we had a say. They've already made their decision."

"That can't be true," Anthony argued. "This isn't a dictatorship. They genuinely wanted our input, and we can make a difference."

"Don't be so naïve, Anthony," Miguel said. "The Church is not a democracy, especially under John Paul II. Any whiff of dissent is anathema."

"He's right," added Kevin. "Anthony, you have to be way more careful with what you say. You let your emotions get the best of you in there."

"Oh, now it's my fault? Am I too emotional? What the hell? Expressing my frustration doesn't nullify my point. Those closet cases in our class are self-loathing hypocrites. I can't even stand to look at them," Anthony said.

"Hey, calm down. I'm not the enemy here," Kevin said, holding up his hand in defense. "I'm just trying to explain how you came across. I don't want you to have a target on your back," Kevin said.

"He's right, you know," Carlos calmly said as he put his arm around Anthony's shoulders. "You can't let them get to you. Even if you're right, you diminish your point if they think you're a loose cannon. You've got to watch what you say. We all do, especially in front of the faculty."

Reality began to sink in. Anthony could see that they were right, but he was still so angry. He lowered his head in defeat. He couldn't even make eye contact with Kevin.

"So, we just let them get away with dragging the Church back into the dark ages? Let them spout their pious bullshit and wear their dresses?"

"No, Anthony. We just have to choose our battles," Miguel said wisely. "Look, I'm with you. This whole discussion is crap. We have to find a way to express our dissent without looking like rabble-rousers."

From that point on, Miguel became the voice of the opposition. His even temperament did not raise hackles like Anthony's emotional and passionate arguments. He used reason and quoted Vatican documents that spoke of social justice and the importance of the laity. Miguel took every opportunity to gather support for his cause. As one of the few people of color at the seminary, he made it a point to speak up. Since he was erudite and eloquent, his very presence flew in the face of their prejudice. Miguel garnered a great deal of support from at least half of his class.

Miguel began a study group dedicated to the teachings of Vatican II. During the first few weeks, there were only a handful of men in attendance. But word got out, and by the following month, Miguel was facilitating a seminar with over twenty seminarians each week. His efforts did not go unnoticed. Although his style was less of a flash point than Anthony's, the faculty considered him even more dangerous. He was reasonable and well-spoken. He used Church documents and writings from respected theologians to make his arguments. The faculty could chalk up Anthony's emotional outburst to inexperience; however, Miguel's approach could quickly become a movement contrary to their official position.

Week after week, Miguel selected a reading to be discussed. He began with *Lumen Gentium* from Vatican II, which states that the hierarchy of the Church is placed in the service of the people of God. He stressed that the authority of the pope and bishops is to be done in a collegial manner.

The laity is supposed to take part in the mission of the Church entirely. His seminar studied *Gaudium et Spes,* which clearly states that the Church must read the signs of the times and should be part of the world, not apart from it. In and of themselves, his choice of documents and topics did not challenge Church teaching.

They *were* Church teaching. However, given the move to the right, it was seen as a direct challenge to Pope John Paul II and the NAC faculty. Miguel believed that this was the proper way to approach the conflicts between the traditionalists and the progressives. Passionate arguments did nothing but escalate the conflict. Both sides would become entrenched, and there would be no useful dialogue. He believed he had created a safe place for that dialogue. He was determined to get Anthony to change his approach when arguing. In one of many discussions, he knew how to affirm him while challenging him to redirect.

"Listen, buddy," Miguel said gently. "Your heart is always in the right place. But you have to approach your arguments without emotion."

"I know, I know," Anthony conceded. "I just get carried away. I'm Italian, you know."

"Don't I know it," Miguel said with a chuckle. "The key is to use reason. You can back up every stand you hold with solid Church teaching. That takes the wind out of their sails, AND makes you look cleverer than they are."

"But I'm at a disadvantage. You and Kevin have four years of philosophy and theology under your belts. I'm a neophyte," Anthony said.

"Look, amigo, you are just as intelligent as anyone else at NAC, perhaps more so," Miguel replied. "But you don't believe in yourself. The way you pick up information in class is remarkable. What I'm suggesting is just taking it a step further."

"Sounds like you know me better than I know myself. I have to admit, I've always relied upon making a passionate case for my beliefs. I was always able to sway opinion," Anthony replied.

"That's the problem, Anthony. Passion doesn't work here – reason does. When you present with passion, they dismiss you as emotional, and they miss your point."

"This is like a paradigm shift for me. This might take some time," Anthony said with a nervous laugh.

"You know that Kevin and I can help you with that," Miguel said. "The politics of seminary life are complicated, especially in Rome," he added.

"That's an understatement. You do know that I value your sage counsel. It's just hard to take sometimes."

"So many things at NAC *are*, Anthony."

Chapter Fifteen
Winds of Change

The faculty at NAC needed time to read and process the original document written by the Vatican. After the disastrous meeting with the seminarians, the rector was deeply disturbed. Monsignor O'Connor had always been moderate concerning Church politics and sought to smooth over disagreements – he wanted unity among his seminarians. But this seemingly trivial matter of whether to wear clerical garb was indicative of a profound chasm within the Church. The tension between the conservative and the progressive wings of the Church had been brewing since the 1960s. With Pope John Paul II, people had high hopes for continued reform. However, he had taken a sharp turn to the right and ruled with absolute authority. The warring factions of the Church were playing themselves out within his very walls. O'Connor's approach to conflict was based on communication and building relationships with God, fellow priests, and seminarians. The outburst at the meeting prompted a visceral reaction. It disturbed the rector deeply. Interpersonal conflicts as heated as those he witnessed could have lasting effects. He had high hopes for Anthony and Miguel. He realized that Anthony was rough around the edges. His lack of experience in seminary life put him at a distinct disadvantage.

He wore his heart on his sleeve, and although that was refreshing, sometimes, it was plainly inappropriate. His candor at the meeting was a perfect example.

In some ways, O'Connor agreed with Anthony, and he had a soft spot for the young seminarian. His innocence and sincere approach to his faith were inspiring. In contrast, many of the new men were enamored by the trappings of the old Church. They were using the new guidelines to reclaim the pageantry and status of the pre-Vatican II church.

For many, the priesthood was not about service to others. Instead, it was a way to command respect, hold power, and authority. But when Anthony named it for what it was, the entire room exploded. He had to be reprimanded in a way that would teach him new ways to approach such a conflict. O'Connor was sure that his years at NAC could help Anthony grow into his priesthood.

Miguel, although measured in his response, was just as disruptive. He had learned that he was lobbying his classmates and encouraging them to speak out against the new guidelines. Miguel was actively organizing a counter-attack. O'Connor perceived this as much more dangerous and resolved to keep a watchful eye on him. Regardless of his personal stance on the issue, he would not tolerate any subversive activity at the NAC.

After several days of deliberation, the faculty settled on a reasonable response to the rules. Requiring cassocks, as some seminarians had lobbied for, would incite more division within the ranks. Instead, they settled on the clerical shirt and black or gray slacks. They required all the seminarians to be dressed accordingly by Monday of the following week. The practical repercussions were that everyone had to go out and buy new clothes. Adding to the frustration, there were only two official Church suppliers of priestly clothing in Rome, and they were incredibly costly. Given the new directive, the owners took the opportunity to gouge the young seminarians – clerical shirts cost twice that of an ordinary dress shirt.

That Saturday, Kevin, Anthony, and Miguel decided to mark their last day wearing laymen's clothes. As good seminarians, they ritualized the event. They put on neckties, argyle sweaters, and dress shoes; they looked like Harvard law students. Following their busy morning of classes, they skipped *pranzo* at the NAC and went to their favorite restaurant near the Greg. Its name was *Abbruzzi,* but the seminarians affectionately called it *"i dodici,"* referring to the Church of the 12 Apostles that was across from it. The *Abbruzzi* was famous for having the best *rigatoni carbonara* in Rome.

The wine went down smoothly, and when the complimentary *digestivi* appeared on the table after dessert, they nearly drank the entire bottle. They were feeling no pain as they climbed up the Janiculum Hill to NAC. Miguel was so drunk, he could barely make it up the stairs, longing for his afternoon nap, but Anthony followed Kevin to his room. Once inside, he locked the door, turned, and leaned against it with a hungry look. Kevin gave Anthony a quizzical look. *What is he up to?* he wondered.

"Okay, you sexy Irishman, it seems that everyone is getting a piece of that hot body of yours except me. You don't want me to feel neglected now, do you? After all, I was your first here in Rome," Anthony said as he pulled Kevin's tie from around his neck and pushed him down onto the bed. "Lie down and don't say a word," he commanded.

"Wow, I like it when you take charge, Anthony. I am at your mercy."

"Yes, you are. Now shut up already and let me work my magic."

Anthony slowly unbuttoned Kevin's shirt and ran his tongue from around his neck down to his chest, lingering on his nipples. After a muffled moan, he continued the fine line of hair to his belt buckle and unfastened his pants. He paused for a moment and looked up at Kevin, teasing him with his fingers. Before long, they were writhing in ecstasy, trying to make as little noise as possible. Anthony straddled Kevin and kissed him passionately as they made love and spoke in Italian.

"Ti amo, caro mio. Tu sei il mio amante." I love you, my dear one. You are my love.

"Ti amo, Anthony, ti amo," Kevin whispered as they pressed their hungry lips together. After their energetic love-making, they rested in the remnants of alcohol-induced buzz from *pranzo*. Kevin flipped onto his side on the narrow bed and turned Anthony's face toward him. "Anthony, you know I meant what I said, don't you? I love you. I really do. All those other guys are nothing to me."

"Yeah, I know." Anthony paused, trying to work up the courage to say what he truly felt. "But you have to understand that even though I don't make a big deal about it – it hurts. Sometimes I wonder why I am not enough for you." Kevin was silent. He knew Anthony was right but didn't know what to say.

"Look, Kevin, as much as I accepted that you're sleeping around, it bothers me. I get that monogamy doesn't fit with the priesthood. Hell, we shouldn't be doing this at all. But here we are."

"None of this makes sense, Anthony. When I was sleeping with Father Bill last summer, it became clear that the whole crew was having frequent sex. Yet, none we're in loving relationships."

"But that's just it, Kevin. I love you."

"I love you too," Kevin confessed. "I'm just not ready to be your husband."

"You suck, you know that?" Anthony said, punching his shoulder playfully.

"And I do it quite well, don't I?" He said, raising his eyebrows.

"Listen, I can live with that – for now. But I need you to come back home to me. I don't want to be your confessor or your priest – *I* want to be the love of your life. Got it?"

"Of course you are, and I am yours. I just get lost sometimes. To be honest, I don't know how you put up with me – but I promise you I will always come back to you."

Kevin cupped Anthony's face in his hands and kissed him tenderly. They closed their eyes and drifted off to sleep.

Anthony tolerated the fact that Kevin was having sex with other guys. It wasn't ideal, and he wished it wasn't so often. But as long as Kevin's heart was with him, he could put up with his sexual infidelity.

Defining what they had together was much too complicated. He knew that he'd have to deal with that before ordination. He just couldn't face it at the moment. Anthony expected that Kevin's wanderings would dwindle as time wore on.

Kevin was just having fun, and why not? As long as he didn't fall in love with any of them. Anthony knew that all too soon, they would take a vow of celibacy. He might as well get it out of his system now. Anthony wondered how he would manage this relationship after ordination. Not being able to make love to Kevin would be agony. He hoped the idea of celibacy would get more comfortable with time.

***

By the following Monday, all the American seminarians were dressed in black. It was a parade of young clerics marching down the Janiculum hill toward the university. They would often run into the same shopkeepers or people going off to work on their daily commute to school. As they neared Piazza Navona, a group of young women was just coming out of their portal.

Miguel, who loved to flirt with everyone, had hit it off with one of the women the previous month. They had exchanged nothing more than pleasantries, but there was a definite spark between the two. When she spotted him in his priestly garb, she screamed and ran back into the apartment. The guys burst out, laughing at her dramatic display.

"You've done it now, Miguel," Kevin remarked. "She thinks she's going to hell for flirting with a priest."

"I'm not a priest yet," Miguel said, raising his eyebrows mischievously.

"But she doesn't know that – you evil tempter," Kevin joked.

"Poor woman," Anthony chimed in. "How could you lead her down the road to ruin only to break her heart?"

They laughed the entire way to the Greg, but it was clear that the world around them would now treat them differently. They were no longer ordinary students wandering in the city. Roman seminarians and priests received a different reaction from the locals. Some responded with deference, others with disdain. In either case, the response was rarely neutral. They would have to learn how to navigate this unfamiliar landscape of clericalism in the eternal city.

Once they arrived at the Greg, they were surprised to see that all the other seminarians were still dressed in civilian clothes. The new directive had been given, and as rule-following Americans, they toed the line. Of all the international colleges in Rome, the North American College was the only one that took the directive literally.

This only heightened the frustration among the liberal crew. Tensions at NAC were exacerbated by the latest conflict between the Church's conservative wing and the progressives. More and more, the three friends found themselves on the outside looking in. As a whole, the Church was moving to the right. They could either quietly play along or continue to fight and be ostracized.

That evening they gathered on the NAC roof along with Carlos and Sean. As had become their routine, Carlos passed the pipe around. "Nothing like a little *weed* to calm the tensions of a tough day," Carlos said.

"Couldn't agree more. Give that to me, I need another hit," Miguel said.

"This just sucks," Anthony began. "This is not the church I grew up in."

"Me neither," Sean added. "But you had better get used to it. John Paul II is very conservative. His charisma has blinded people; it just masks his true intentions. He's bringing us back into the nineteen-fifties."

"Come on, Sean. He can't be that bad," Kevin said.

"Believe it, guys. Cardinal Ratzinger heads the Congregation for the Doctrine of the Faith, the former office of the Inquisition. He couldn't be more of a right-wing traditionalist."

The guys groaned. Little did they know that Ratzinger would eventually be John Paul II's successor and become pope. The move to the right had only just begun.

"I just don't know if I can do this anymore," Kevin broke the silence. "It feels like a foreign power has taken over our church."

"It has, and there won't be an end to it anytime soon. John Paul is only about sixty-two years old and as strong as a bull. He's got a long papacy ahead of him," Sean said.

Gazing over the eternal city, they were disheartened as the silence enveloped them. Thoughts of their future in the Church of John Paul II and Cardinal Ratzinger tampered with their high.

Chapter Sixteen
Kevin, Carlos, & Sean

A mid the political and philosophical conflicts at NAC, the seminarians continued to grapple with their interpersonal challenges. They were actors in a soap opera of their lives–it seemed almost unreal. Kevin was falling in love with Carlos while simultaneously carrying on his relationship with Anthony. For some reason, Carlos rocked Kevin's foundation. He was not like all the other guys he had slept with while at the NAC. Kevin longed to be with him, to touch him, and to hold him. His conversations with Carlos dove beneath the surface and got to the heart of whatever topic they discussed.

Except for Carlos, no one other than Anthony could get Kevin to express his feelings. Carlos drew him in just as Anthony had. But the two of them could not be more dissimilar. Anthony's open vibrancy thrilled and titillated Kevin. He yearned to drink in his energy. He could sit endlessly and watch Anthony spin during a debate; or even more entertaining, as he worked a room full of stodgy seminarians. Anthony was a force to be reckoned with, whereas Carlos was the opposite. He had a peaceful air about him that exuded tenderness. His dark eyes widened as he listened attentively, taking in the whole person as if inviting him into his heart. Just being with him made Kevin feel more comfortable with his inner demons.

As their friendship deepened, their physical expressiveness grew more intimate. Kevin was not much taller than Carlos, but his chest was broader.

Often, they would sit on Carlos's bed with their legs and arms touching, and soon Carlos would lean in and lay his head against Kevin. He wondered if Carlos could feel his heart rapidly beating as he rested his beautiful head of black, shiny hair on his chest.

He couldn't remember when it had turned romantic. At some point, Kevin recalled looking deeply into his eyes as they moved closer together; then their lips finally touched. They were moist and soft – almost like velvet.

Their kisses were tender and loving. Unlike Kevin's routine hook-ups with the upperclassmen, there was no urgency or lust. His kisses were enticingly warm and inviting. With Carlos in his arms, Kevin felt safe and secure. With rooms only two doors apart, they met regularly before turning in at night. On many occasions, the two climbed the stairs to the roof to share a pipe as they wound down from their stressful days. Inevitably they would discuss the priesthood, their vocations, and the impossibility of living a life of celibacy.

Before heading to bed, Kevin and Carlos would spend thirty minutes or so kissing and cuddling. This had been going on for weeks with no hint of going any further. Each time they were together, Carlos pulled away before it got too heated. If Kevin's hands wandered south, he'd firmly redirected them. Kevin got frustrated and longed for more. He was afraid to be too forward with Carlos for fear of scaring him off. But Kevin was becoming exasperated; cuddling went only so far. He had to find out if this was going anywhere. So, one day after *pranzo,* Kevin knocked on Carlos's door.

"Hey, Carlos. Feel like having some company?"

"Ciao, bello. Sure, come on in. I was just about to close my eyes a bit. Come join me," Carlos replied.

They began kissing slowly, gently. Then Kevin decided to take a risk. As he lay beside him on the bed, Kevin let his hands caress Carlos's muscular body. Feeling his well-defined pecs and his rippling abs, Kevin wanted more. He squeezed his nipples as they continued kissing, and he heard Carlos moan with approval, so he became more assertive and moved his hand down. He allowed it to rest just above his belt to make sure he wasn't advancing too quickly.

After a minute or so, Kevin took a chance. He slipped his hand under the waistband of Carlos's briefs and felt the beginnings of his pubic hair. He was almost there, and Carlos had not stopped him yet. They broke from their kissing, and Carlos looked into Kevin's eyes.

"*Te quiero*, Kevino." I want you, he said in Spanish.

Encouraged by his declaration, Kevin used his other hand to unzip his pants and reached in to grab hold of him. That was the moment Carlos sat up.

"Hey, Kev, stop. We can't do this."

"Aw, come on, Carlos, we both want it. We've been dancing around this for weeks."

"I know, and I shouldn't have let it go this far. I'm sorry," Carlos said.

"Why not? It's more than just sex for me, I really love you," Kevin admitted.

"I know. That's the problem," Carlos said.

"Wait, what do you mean by *problem*?"

"Look, Kevin, we can't fall in love. That just doesn't work with the priesthood. We have to be celibate."

"Carlos, we are both years from ordination and our vows of celibacy. Why can't we enjoy it while we can? Celibacy will come soon enough," Kevin argued.

"Don't you understand? It's not about the vow. It's a life choice. If we can't get ourselves mentally and physically prepared for this now, it will be that much harder later on."

"I'm sorry, Carlos. I just can't help myself with you. You're like a drug for me. When I'm with you, I just want to touch you."

"That's why we have to stop. We've got to find some way to make our friendship work without sex."

Kevin was exasperated and sexually frustrated. He understood what Carlos was saying – in principle, he actually agreed. But it didn't mesh with his own carnal desires, and those seemed to trump Carlos's logic.

"You're right, as usual, Carlos. But I don't like it. Look, I'm sorry for pushing it. I didn't mean to upset you."

"No, don't worry about it – I wanted it too. But we have to stop. We're just teasing each other like this."

"I don't want to lose you, Carlos. I won't do that again," Kevin said, getting upset.

"You won't lose me, Kevin. But we need to cool it for a while. No more nighttime rendezvous, okay? We're just torturing each other."

Kevin's advances tormented Carlos. He sincerely sought to live a chaste life within the priesthood. Although Carlos had fallen in love with Sean the previous year, he had worked through their sexual attraction. They had struggled to create a healthy and intimate relationship without sex. That's what they taught in seminaries; priests needed intimacy but could not express it sexually.

Of course, they were not supposed to have particular friendships, either. Throughout their formation for the priesthood, this healthy intimacy was talked about but never explained. Seminarians were left wondering how to maintain an effective support system with no emotional attachments. What made the situation with Sean more challenging was that they were in love with each other, and chaste intimacy was not supposed to have a romantic element. Carlos knew he had failed at that, but he was only human. At least he and Sean would not be breaking the vow of celibacy once they were ordained.

Now Carlos had Kevin to contend with, and he was wildly attracted to him. Who wouldn't be? Kevin was handsome, and his relentless pursuit was like a drug. It had been a long time since a man actively sought his affections. Although he enjoyed spending time with Kevin, their connection was missing the emotional depth he shared with Sean. Carlos knew he had to extricate himself from this physical relationship with Kevin. Other than the sexual energy in their budding friendship, there was little beyond infatuation. He could tell that Kevin was determined to sleep with him; perhaps he was falling in love. But Carlos would not let it go there, and he had to make that clear to him. They hugged each other goodbye, and Kevin silently slipped out of his room.

Sean was just coming down to the second floor when he spotted Kevin sneaking out of Carlos's room. He paused and watched as he silently closed the door and tip-toed back into his own room. Most of the seminarians were still deep into nap time – the crisp click of the door latch broke the heavy silence echoing down the hall. What was he doing in there with Carlos? Had they spent the last two hours in bed together? Sean could feel his anger surging to the surface. How could Carlos do this to him? After all the relationship struggles during their first year, he thought they had come to a workable solution to their mutual attraction.

Sean loved Carlos and wanted nothing more than to sleep with him. He would have done so months ago had Carlos not denied him. Although Carlos sought to follow the Church laws regarding a celibate priesthood, Sean wasn't so sure. The Church didn't even recognize that most of their clergy were gay. The teaching that love between two men was evil made his blood boil.

The Church's hypocrisy on this and so many other issues allowed Sean to develop his own moral code. Some of the Church's teaching seemed illogical and archaic. Sean believed that a celibate priesthood was one of those. There were endless discussions regarding the importance of celibacy and the need to forge relationships of chaste intimacy. *What did that really mean? It was just another platitude to justify a practice that was never meant to be. What would be so wrong with a married clergy? What is so bad about having gay clergy?* Sean raised these questions often, but Carlos would not entertain them. There was no use debating something that wasn't likely to change. Carlos believed that if they did nothing more physical than a hug, the temptation would not lead them further. Any thought of sex would simply complicate their lives and lead them away from their vocations to the priesthood. For Sean, it was a constant struggle.

He longed to be with Carlos, touch him, kiss him, and make love to him. Each time they hugged, he would breathe in his scent and imagine what it would be like to hold him throughout the night. He took every opportunity that arose to be physically near him or to touch him. But he was always careful to make it look as innocent as possible. He knew that his fellow seminarians had eyes like hawks. They were always looking for some sign of those forbidden particular friendships. He was just as careful when he and Carlos were alone. He didn't want Carlos to have any excuse to put distance between them for fear of his sexual desires.

Maybe I've been too aloof; taken the platonic friendship act a little too far, he thought. I may have inadvertently left the door open for Kevin. Regardless, at that moment, he was just angry. He couldn't imagine any other reason for Kevin to be with Carlos during the siesta, and if his sneaky behavior was indicative of anything, it was of his guilt. Sean didn't know what to do next. If he knocked on Carlos's door now, he'd likely suspect that he saw Kevin. Sean couldn't pretend that he saw nothing – he'd be deceiving himself. He turned to head back to his own room when he felt a flash of anger well up within him.

No, Sean needed to confront Carlos now – give him the chance to explain or defend himself. He turned back and marched with determination. He knocked more forcefully than he had intended, and it echoed down the marble hall.

Carlos opened the door with a look of fear on his face. *Had someone seen Kevin slip out of his room?* He was relieved to see his good friend, Sean, staring back at him.

"Sean, thank God. What's wrong? You seem upset."

"Mind if I come in?" Not waiting for a response, he walked past him. He scanned the room, and his eyes landed on the rumpled bedcovers. He looked at Carlos with a mixture of pain and anger. "I saw Kevin leave your room a few minutes ago. What's going with you two? Did the sexy new man seduce you?"

"What? No. I... listen, Sean. Nothing happened between us," Carlos said. He was taken aback by the accusation, but felt the pang of guilt creep in.

The tone of Sean's voice startled him – he had never seen him this angry. "Are you really going to lie right to my face? I saw him, acting as guilty as sin. And look at your bed."

"Come on, Sean. Stop this. Sit down and let's talk, okay?" Carlos pleaded.

"I think I'll just stand. Thank you very much. So tell me, what *is* really going on between you and Kevin?"

"Sean, believe me, we did not have sex. We were just talking and, well –"

"Well, what? Did you kiss him?"

"Yes. We kissed, but nothing more. I promise."

"But you wanted to, didn't you? I can tell by how you look at him. You practically have to wipe the drool from your chin."

"I'm sorry," Carlos replied. "Kevin is totally infatuated with me, and yes, he's a stud. And even if I wanted to sleep with him, I wouldn't do that to you."

"No? Come on, how could you resist him? He's incredibly sexy, *and* he wants you."

"Sean, please sit down." Sean reluctantly moved to the bed and sat facing Carlos. His anger was waning, but sadness was in its stead. He was hurt.

"I thought you and I had something here – that we were more than friends," Sean admitted.

"We *are* more than friends, Sean. You know I love you, don't you?"

"I do, Carlos. But when I see you and Kevin together, it rattles me – causes me to doubt everything."

"Sean, there will always be guys in our lives that we find attractive, guys we want to have sex with. That doesn't mean we have to act on it. You are my touchstone, and I love you," Carlos said.

"I love you too, Carlos." They fell into each other's arms and held on. It was like coming home. Soon they were caressing, then kissing. They hadn't let themselves touch each other in nearly a year. "Carlos?"

"Si, caro."

"I don't think I can do this. I can't keep all these feelings pent up inside me."

"What do you mean?" Carlos asked.

"I want to make love to you. I want to touch you and feel you. I want to lie next to you afterward and talk about our dreams. What we are doing now is just not enough for me," Sean told Carlos.

"Sean, you know we can't do that."

"Why not? Half of the guys here are sleeping with each other. Why are we so different?"

"I don't know. I am struggling with that, as well. This is exactly why I wanted us to stop teasing each other. But I have to admit, I miss this too," Carlos said as he kissed Sean gently on the lips.

"So, we're back to this again, are we?" Sean asked.

"Why not? As you said, everyone else seems to be doing it. We just have to stop before we go too far," Carlos said. Sean let out a sarcastic laugh and shook his head.

"You know, just because we stop right before orgasm, doesn't mean we're not having sex."

"I realize that, but somehow, going all the way seems worse. I'm sorry," Carlos said with a heavy sigh. He was losing both his resolve and his willpower. Sean's reasoning was sound. They had been breaking the vow of chastity in their hearts for over a year; carrying it to the next step was simply a technicality.

Carlos was having a crisis of conscience. He buried his face between Sean's neck and shoulder. His musky scent was enticing, and he tenderly kissed his bare skin. All at once, his heart flooded with feelings of guilt.

"This is not right. I'm sorry, Sean, really, I am. But I can't do this."

"What? You are giving me whiplash. Yes, no? Make up your mind, but whatever you decide, stop teasing me," Sean said, his frustration showing.

"You're right. This is not fair to either of us. This must stop. I want to be a good priest someday, one who lives with integrity. I don't want to be a guy who simply breaks his vows at the sight of the first beautiful man or woman. I love you, Sean, but we can't be lovers. Do you understand what I'm saying?"

"Yeah, sure. But, Carlos, I can't take this cat-and-mouse game. I need some space. Being together like this drives me crazy."

"I know, and I'm sorry for my waffling. I promise to be a better friend."

Later that night, Carlos made his way to the chapel. Opening the heavy door, he let his eyes adjust to the darkness. The faint smell of incense assaulted his senses as the tabernacle candle's red glow came into focus. Finding his way to the altar, he knelt in prayer. Carlos resolved to live a life of celibacy. That is what the priesthood required, so that is what he would do.

"Dear God, please forgive my human frailty. Help me bear this cross with humility and strength. I know I am weak, but I resolve to do your will," he prayed.

Carlos leaned his head on the pew as a single tear rolled down his cheek. There was nothing he wanted more than to become a good priest.

Chapter Seventeen
A Visitor from Paris

Miguel was getting more and more frustrated with his classes and with the clerical atmosphere at the NAC. If not for Kevin and Anthony as his best friends, he'd be lost. But as the months passed, he realized that the two of them were more than just friends. The way they were always hanging of each other made it pretty clear that they were in love, or at least infatuated with each other. They had never spoken openly about whether they were gay, but he'd been in seminary long enough to read the signs. Not that he was uncomfortable with it. No, he believed everyone had the right to love whoever they wanted. His thinking was way more progressive than many people he knew back in Texas. His open-mindedness was because of his father. Mr. Perez had welcomed everyone into the fold.

As accepting as Miguel was, sometimes he felt like the third wheel. Kevin and Anthony attempted to include him in every gathering or dinner out in the city. However, as the months passed, he could see them becoming more intimate with each other. Witnessing the intensity of their relationship and the closeness of their bond punctuated how lonely he really was.

The other seminarian at NAC from Dallas was Seth. Miguel and Seth had known each other for years. Although they got along well enough, Miguel found him frustrating. You could never tell what he was thinking or feeling because he was so dichotomous. When Seth engaged in pertinent conversations or debates with his classmates, he came across as self-righteous and combative. When married clergy or celibacy would come up, he quoted the most conservative texts he could find.

However, Seth was also friendly and gregarious. He was the first to offer to help classmates struggling with their studies or waiting on the tables during *pranzo*. That's what made his traditionalist leanings confusing – Seth always seemed to have an ulterior motive. Miguel didn't trust him – he viewed him as the class tattle-tale. There was no way he could strike up a genuine friendship with him.

But there was more to Miguel's dissatisfaction with his vocational studies. For the first time in years, he questioned whether he was cut out for a life of celibacy. It wasn't merely about sex. In fact, the lack of sex was only a small part of it. Miguel yearned for companionship, intimacy, and someone with whom he could share his fears and dreams. The more time he spent with each of the navel-gazing seminarians at the NAC, the more his need gnawed at him. Everyone around him was turned inward, analyzing every thought or feeling. It was all about discerning the will of God in their lives. Miguel was sick of the self-absorption and wanted to look outward. *Wasn't ministry to the people of God about meeting them in the real world?* He wondered if he'd be better suited to marriage – having someone to share his life with.

In November, Anthony's friend Maria traveled from Paris to spend a long weekend with him. She was doing her junior year abroad and was as animated and expressive as Anthony. Miguel was immediately attracted to her. He pictured her getting from the bus after a 27-hour ride from Paris. Most people would be exhausted and cranky, but not Maria. She squealed with delight when she spotted Anthony. She came running at them and engulfed Anthony in the biggest hug while babbling on with her high-pitched voice.

"And who are these two handsome men? Are they here to escort me during my visit?" Maria crooned as she pulled Miguel into a hug, ignoring his outstretched hand. She didn't even acknowledge it – a handshake was simply out of the question. Her exuberance was infectious, and although they had never met before, both he and Kevin joined in on the joyous reunion.

"You've obviously met Miguel," Anthony interrupted. "Now, if you can pull yourself away from him for a moment, let me introduce you to Kevin."

"Hi, boys! I am so happy to meet you. Can you believe it? I'm in Rome!"

"We can believe it," Miguel said with a sarcastic smile on his face. He was immediately enchanted by her.

"Let's get you out of this station," Kevin directed. "I'm sure you're hungry. How about authentic Italian food?"

"Oh, I was hoping for Chinese," Maria responded, not skipping a beat.

"Great! Our favorite Chinese restaurant is in Trastevere. It's a bit of a hike, but let's go," Miguel said.

"What? Oh, wait, you're serious, aren't you?" Maria asked as she looked blankly at him.

"No, he's not," Anthony jumped in. "I mean, he's right. There is a Chinese restaurant in Trastevere, but we've never eaten there."

"You're such a jerk," Maria said as she punched Miguel in the arm.

"You're a spirited gal, aren't you? I can tell this is going to be an exciting visit," Miguel said.

"You'll learn not to mess with me, mister. Or should I address you as Father?" she said with her arms crossed over her chest. Then she winked at him and broke into a wide grin. Their fate was sealed at that moment. The spark between them continued to grow throughout her stay in Rome.

"You guys have no idea what you're in for with Maria," Anthony said, noticing the connection. "Right, honey?" he said as he pulled Maria in for a hug.

Throughout dinner, Anthony and Maria never stopped chatting. They told stories of their days at Fordham University and laughed loudly at their own jokes. Afterward, the three seminarians walked Maria back towards NAC. Along the way, there was a long staircase that scaled a good portion of the Janiculum hill. It was a shortcut that the guys often took. The marble steps were completely overgrown with weeds. There was litter strewn all about, and graffiti decorated the walls.

"Maria, I don't know you've heard about these steps," Miguel said. "They're quite famous."

"No, really? Are these the…" Her voice trailed off, and her jaw dropped.

"Yes, indeed," Miguel continued. "These are the beautiful Spanish Steps."

"Oh, my God! I can't believe it."

"Beautiful, aren't they?" Kevin said, playing along.

"Anthony, honey, they're amazing. It's just that they looked so much prettier in pictures."

"Yeah, they always touch up those postcards. Reality is often far grittier," Miguel responded.

"Well, they are still beautiful," Maria said with conviction. "There must be over a hundred steps."

Then they all burst into a fit of laughter. Maria finally caught on and joined in the joke.

"You guys are such assholes! I thought seminarians were supposed to be nice," she said with indignation. "I expect you to bring me to the real Spanish Steps before I leave. That means you, Miguel."

"It would be my selfish pleasure," he responded as he offered her his arm.

Back at the NAC, they gathered in Anthony's room. Having gone to college together, Anthony and Maria were used to hanging out in each other's quarters. But Miguel thought it was odd to have a girl in the dormitory section of the seminary.

"Not to be a killjoy, but does anybody know if Maria is allowed to be in our rooms?"

"Why wouldn't she be?" Anthony asked. "We're seminarians. Why wouldn't they trust us?"

"Actually, Miguel's got a point," Kevin interjected.

"They would have never allowed women past the public areas at St. Thomas Seminary."

"But I've seen other female visitors here. No one seems to bat an eye," Anthony said.

"True, I suppose it's easier to beg forgiveness than to ask permission," Miguel said.

"Now you sound like a Jesuit educated man," Maria chimed in.

They burst out laughing and didn't give it a second thought. The happy quartet could be heard carrying on throughout the rest of the evening.

When it was time for lights out, Miguel and Kevin joined Anthony as they walked Maria to her *pensione*, which was just beside St. Peter's Basilica. On their return to NAC, Anthony was feeling nostalgic. "Guys, I just want to thank you for making Maria feel so welcome here. It means a lot to me," he said.

"Of course, Anthony. She's great, so funny and full of life. It's nice to hang out with someone other than NAC guys," Kevin offered.

"And she's adorable. Who knew you'd have such cute girlfriends?" Miguel joked.

"Yeah, she *is* pretty cute. She's pretty popular at Fordham back in New York. She's like the college cruise director, organizing parties, getting people involved, and making sure that everyone is having fun."

"Hey Anthony, do you realize that Maria is the female version of you – only hotter?"

"You know – you're right, Miguel. They're like the same person," Kevin added.

"I always knew you were hot for me, Miguel," Anthony joked.

"You've found me out, Anthony. But now that you've introduced me to Maria, I'm afraid that you're off the hook."

"See how you are, Miguel. Another pretty girl comes along, and you drop me, just like that." They all enjoyed a good laugh, but Miguel was only half-kidding. He liked Maria – a lot. He wasn't sure how to deal with his budding infatuation, but he had to address it. The gang planned to spend the week of New Year's in Paris with Maria, and without the ever-present authorities at the NAC looking over his shoulder, who knows what might happen. If he was about to take a vow of celibacy someday, he needed to explore his feelings for her.

*****

Maria created quite a stir at NAC during her visit. Just like Anthony, she didn't quite get the formality of the seminary. Its restrictive behavioral norms were utterly foreign to her. She was her usual lively self who squealed in delight at every new experience, and she freely expressed her affection to the seminarians who flocked to be near her.

There were numerous visits to local trattorias and plenty of wine to accompany the exquisite food. Their boisterous laughter could be heard over the din in each restaurant. Anthony noticed that Miguel and Maria were quite intrigued by each other. Their attraction was mutual, and he watched with amusement, wondering if anything would come of it. When classes began the following Monday, Anthony was concerned that Maria would have little to keep her busy. He didn't have to worry about the morning–Maria was sure to sleep until noon. But he had his Greek class later that afternoon.

"I don't know what to suggest for Maria today," he mentioned to Kevin and Miguel. "After *pranzo,* I have to go back to Greek class. I won't be home until after eight. Then I need to do my homework. I have done nothing all weekend."

"She's an independent woman," Kevin said. "She'll wander around and be perfectly happy."

"I'm free, Anthony," Miguel offered. "I'll keep her entertained while you guys are in class."

"How generous of you, Miguel. You're such a giver; generous to a fault," Kevin said with a wry smile.

"What do you mean? I'm free. Why wouldn't I show her around?" Miguel replied more defensively than was necessary.

"Don't listen to Kevin. He's just a dick," Anthony said. "Listen, I'm glad that you two have hit it off. I'm sure she'll be in good hands. Thanks, Miguel."

"The question remains, how handsy will Miguel be?" Kevin joked.

Miguel punched Kevin as hard as he could. "You really *are* a dick!" They got a good laugh out of it and went on with their busy day. It thrilled Maria to have a private escort around Rome. The first stop on her tour was the Spanish Steps – the real Spanish Steps. It was a packed afternoon that included the Colosseum, the Pantheon, and his favorite coffee shop – Caffe S. Eustachio, whose claim to fame was that roasting of the beans was blended with water from ancient aqueducts. Their conversation was natural and animated. Maria was not shy, and soon she peppered him with personal questions.

"So, I've known Anthony for a few years now. I think I understand his desire to become a priest. But I'm curious. What motivates you, Miguel?" she asked. "How did you end up here?"

"Good question," Miguel said, taking a moment to reflect. "I guess I just wanted to do something more, give back to the world. I've led an extraordinarily privileged life. My parents own a cattle ranch, and I've always had more than I need. I suppose I feel responsible for making life a little better for those who don't have as much as me."

"That's pretty cool. But couldn't you do that without becoming a priest?"

"Yes, I really could. My father has done that his entire life. The thing is, I have always admired priests. They are present during both the happiest and most difficult times in a person's life. They give advice, console, and celebrate. I'd love to connect with people during their most meaningful moments, on a more profound level, you know?"

"Yeah, that sounds pretty great. Again – there are professions other than priesthood that would allow you to connect in a meaningful way.

And what about getting married? Won't you miss having a family – children of your own?"

"Man, you ask tough questions, Maria. Anthony didn't warn me about that."

"I call 'em as I see 'em," she said with a grin.

"All right. So, that is one of the most troublesome issues I am dealing with. I wrestle with the lack of intimacy more often. To be honest, since I've been in Rome, I have been pretty lonely."

"I can't imagine what it must be like to look forward to a life without a husband or wife. It seems sad to face life knowing that you'll always be alone," Maria said candidly.

"I can't say I disagree. This has been the greatest struggle of my discernment process. I don't expect it to get any easier, either."

"Well, you know, you can always talk to me about it. Paris is only a phone call away."

"You know, I've never been so open about this with anyone, not even the guys."

"I meant what I said, Miguel. Let's keep in touch."

Miguel and Maria recognized that their conversation had grown more intimate. Their previous banter, though stimulating and amusing, paled by comparison. As the rest of the evening unfolded, Maria and Miguel learned more about what made each of them tick. Maria described her wanderlust and the need to be independent. She spoke of her search for meaning and purpose.

"I'm always looking for something more. But the answers to my big philosophical questions always seem just beyond my grasp," Maria confessed.

"I know what you mean. Every time I reach a goal, it never seems to be enough. In no time, I'm wondering what's next." Maria looked at Miguel directly and placed her hand on top of his.

"It seems that we are kindred spirits. I'm so glad that we had this evening alone. Thank you for being so open with me."

"You make it easy for me, Maria. Perhaps too easy," he said as he leaned over and kissed her on the cheek. *What am I doing?* he thought.

Maria was not surprised by Miguel's display of affection. It seemed completely natural, and although she knew he was a seminarian, she hoped for more.

Chapter Eighteen
Italian Thanksgiving

I t was Thanksgiving Day, and Giovanni, the seminary chef, prepared a special American meal in honor of the holiday. Turkey, stuffing, and mashed potatoes, along with many other traditional side dishes. The American priests from the Casa Santa Maria joined the men at NAC for their communal celebration of Thanksgiving.

Their participation in the party added an exciting dynamic. The ordained priests didn't have to be careful or worried about what they said or whether they acted inappropriately. They had no one looking over their shoulders, and as the day wore on, the abundance of alcohol took its toll. They were lewd and loud, which just fueled the fire for the young seminarians. Even the faculty at NAC seemed to let loose during the festivities.

After *pranzo,* a committee of seminarians put on a special presentation in the auditorium to commemorate Thanksgiving. It highlighted the many traditions from different parts of the country and included the religious aspects of the holiday and being grateful for all the gifts they, as Roman seminarians, had been given. To their credit, they did everything possible to ward off any homesickness the new men might be feeling.

After the show, groups of guys splintered off into various common areas. Some of the guys remained in the refectory and others to their rooms. That's when Miguel noticed Seth was schmoozing with the priests from the Casa. Before long, he was in an animated discussion with a newly ordained priest from Louisiana.

Many of the guys ended up on the roof deck drinking until late in the evening. Miguel wondered what his fellow Texan was up to and kept an eye on him. Father Jeff and Seth were getting very friendly, and Jeff put his arm around a tipsy Seth. Then the two of them made their way to the stairwell–Seth visibly staggering. Miguel had a feeling that they were becoming more than friends.

***

Anthony did his best not to think about the grand family celebration taking place back in New York. His mother always went all out for Thanksgiving.

She fully embraced this genuinely American holiday as her own. After all, this was her home now, and she was an American citizen. However, the meal reflected her immigrant roots and included Italian antipasto, ziti with a simple marinara sauce, followed by the roasted turkey, green beans with tomato sauce, and stuffing.

No one left the table hungry. Everyone was full by the time the turkey was served. Anthony was lounging in his room after a full day of NAC festivities. He jumped when he heard the phone ringing out in the hallway. With the six-hour time difference, Anthony knew that the family dinner was just finishing up. He flew out of his room and got to the phone by the third ring.

"*Pronto.*"

"Is that you, Anthony?" his mother sang.

"*Sì*, mom, Happy Thanksgiving!"

"Oh, how I miss you, Anthony! Have you eaten yet?"

"It's 10 p.m., mom. We ate hours ago."

"Oh, that's right. I always forget. How was your day, *caro*?" she asked.

"It was great. Giovanni went out of his way to roast a turkey and make an authentically American Thanksgiving feast. It's been an enjoyable day, but I miss being home with all of you."

"We miss you too. It's just not the same without you here." Mrs. Rossi passed the phone around the table to each member of the family.

Anthony's heart was so full of love and nostalgia. The call transformed the entire day, and he couldn't have been happier. When Mrs. Rossi got back on the line, Anthony told her how meaningful it was to speak with each of them. Then he asked about his noticeably absent uncle. "Have you spoken to Father Joe today? He usually joins us on Thanksgiving," Anthony asked.

"Yes, he called earlier to tell us he wasn't feeling well, some flu or something that he can't get rid of," she explained.

"That's weird. Father Joe never gets sick."

"Well, since they made him monsignor, he never has a free moment. I'm sure that he's just run down."

"You're probably right, mom. Tell him to call me when you talk to him again. I miss hearing his voice."

Anthony found it odd that Uncle Joe was missing. He never missed a holiday with the family. But his mom was probably right. He was installed as a monsignor at the end of October, and Anthony had not spoken to him since. He was so proud of his uncle that he went to the clerical clothing store to buy him something. Anthony thought it funny that the color of a monsignor's cassock was a bright magenta. Knowing that Uncle Joe was not into all the fancy vestments, he wanted to get him something over the top, something very Roman. However, he was shocked by the prices. Anthony could barely afford the new clerical shirts he was required to buy, let alone the monsignor's garb. *Clothes must get more expensive as you climb the ecclesiastical ladder,* he thought.

In the end, he settled on a pair of magenta socks. It was an odd gift, but he knew that Uncle Joe would get a kick out of them. Joe phoned him just before the installation Mass. "Uncle Joe, oh, sorry, I meant Monsignor Joe," he said sarcastically. "It's so great to hear your voice."

"You ought to remember that and address me with my proper title from now on, young man."

"Yes, Monsignor. I will be sure to do that," Anthony replied with mock deference.

"So, *caro,* I want to thank you for the lovely socks," Joe said. "I'm sure that I'll be the talk of the archdiocese."

"Yeah, I knew you'd find them amusing. I wanted to get you something fancier, but as you know, I'm just a poor seminarian."

"Thank God you didn't. I will don the magenta cassock – and your lovely socks for the installment Mass. But I doubt I will wear them ever again. I hate the smell of clericalism."

"Amen to that. I have so much to tell you regarding what's going on here at NAC. There's a great divide in our class." Anthony explained the rift between the traditional camp versus the progressives. He knew that Uncle Joe would understand his frustration. By the end of the conversation, Anthony felt his concerns had been validated by someone he admired and respected.

Uncle Joe continued to be his most significant mentor, both as a priest and a human being. It had been nearly two months since they had spoken. They rarely let so much time lapse between phone calls.

The fact that Joe wasn't with Anthony's mother and father for dinner on Thanksgiving set off alarm bells. Why did he feel like something was wrong? It was probably just the flu, as his mother said. Anthony resolved to give his uncle a call over the weekend.

Chapter Nineteen
The Holidays

Christmas break was quickly approaching, and Anthony felt the pain of being far from his family. He was thrilled that his aunt and uncle in Naples invited him to celebrate Christmas with them. At least he would be with family and feel a bit like home. But Kevin and Miguel were disappointed. They hoped the three of them could travel somewhere together; go on some sort of adventure before heading to Paris for New Year's week. It would be the first opportunity to get away from NAC for an extended period, and they all needed the break. They persuaded Anthony to join them the day after Christmas. He would still have an entire week with his family. Since Maria would also spend the holidays far from home, this was the perfect opportunity to support each other and ease their homesickness.

Kevin was thrilled that Carlos had also joined them on their Parisian vacation. They planned to meet Anthony at *Gare du Nord,* the central train station in Paris. Then they would head to the Sulpician religious community to connect with Carlos, who had gotten there a few days earlier. Religious houses often hosted seminarians traveling through

Europe. Plus, they provided affordable housing near city centers. The accommodations were modest, but the dorm was ideally located – close to the Latin quarter. That evening they met Maria for dinner, and she played tour guide to her new friends from Rome. The roles were reversed, and Miguel loved seeing her take charge. The four seminarians followed Maria as she walked them throughout the city. Now and again, they were allowed to take the Metro. Miguel loved hearing her speak French. To his ear, it was flawless as she sang all of her phrases. *Allons-y,* let's go, she intoned, and they dutifully followed like ducklings.

Later that evening, when Anthony began having stomach cramps, he assumed it was just nerves. But they intensified throughout the night, and he felt nauseated. Soon he was lying on the bathroom floor, writhing in pain. The cramps led to diarrhea, which led to vomiting and more diarrhea. By morning, he was spent. It was their first full day in Paris – his first time in that beautiful city, and he couldn't wait to explore. But Anthony was down for the count – he could barely move from his bed to answer the door. "You look like shit," Miguel said when he and Kevin entered the room.

"Damn, what is that smell?" Kevin exclaimed.

"Don't ask. I've been sick all night."

"Well, stay away from me. I don't want to catch anything," Miguel said, holding his hand up.

"Don't worry, Miguel. I think it was food poisoning. The mussels tasted a bit off last night."

"That's why I don't eat anything from the sea. You should have had the steak frites," Miguel said.

"Spoken like a true cattle rancher," Kevin said as he clapped him on the shoulder. "By the way, you can get food poisoning from beef too."

"Not from the beef from the Perez Ranch. It's the best in the world," he bragged.

Maria and Carlos arrived soon after. They doted on Anthony and called the sisters at the infirmary. Before long, a nun dressing in a white habit appeared with a bowl of hot broth. She felt his head and fluffed his pillows. The crew mocked him good-naturedly as Sister pulled up a chair and sat right beside his bed.

"I can't believe I'm going to miss my first day in Paris. Maybe I can join you later," Anthony whimpered.

"You shouldn't risk it, Anthony," Kevin said. "We have an entire week here. Just stay in bed and rest."

"Don't worry, honey. I'll take good care of your Roman friends. You have to get better in time for New Year's Eve," Maria said.

Maria toured them all over Paris. They visited the Louvre, the Arc de Triomphe, and she walked them through countless quaint neighborhoods. That afternoon they checked in with Anthony, who felt much better but had little an appetite. He resigned himself to the fact that he had better play it safe and not have dinner with them.

Kevin was secretly hoping to spend some time alone with Carlos. They hadn't spoken about their relationship after Carlos had rebuffed his advances. Many weeks had passed, and his feelings for him had not yet abated. He continued to yearn for his touch and fantasized about sleeping with him.

He was clearly still infatuated with him. After the initial discomfort following his rejection, their rapport seemed to be back to normal. Although Carlos had warmed up to him again, Kevin needed to chat with him away from prying seminarians.

"Hey guys, do you mind if Carlos and I grab dinner alone tonight? I just need an older and wiser seminarian to help me discern my vocation."

"Awe, that's so sweet," Miguel joked. "Of course, you two haven't had a one-on-one date in months."

"Don't be so mean, Miguel," Maria chided. "You just wish you had a date tonight."

"I do, don't I? You're not going to abandon me in this big city all by myself, are you? I might lose my way."

"That depends."

"On what, exactly?"

"On how nasty you are to Kevin and Carlos."

Miguel turned to them with his hands folded over his heart and said, "Love you, boys, lots. Now run off and have fun together."

"You're a piece of work, Miguel," Carlos said, smacking him lightly on the head.

"But you love me anyway?"

"Hmm, I'm not really sure about that," Carlos replied with a smile. And with that, the two couples went their separate ways; they were delighted to have time with their respective dates. Anthony was a little resentful and jealous of Kevin and Carlos, but he didn't have the energy to deal with it. He rolled over and drifted off to sleep. Once out the door and on their own, Maria looked at Miguel and flashed him an enormous smile.

"What do you feel like eating tonight?" Maria asked.

"I don't really care, but can we go someplace quiet, away from the tourist areas?"

"You're a mind-reader. I know just the place."

***

Maria and Miguel had written to each other several times during the months they were apart, and it was clear to both of them that their affection for one another had continued to grow. His first letter was a profound description of the internal struggle Miguel was battling. His written words conveyed a level of clarity that he could only hint at during their discussions. Writing allowed him to communicate the depth of his feelings for Maria while also explaining his intense attraction to the priesthood.

Maria was blown away by the beauty of his prose. It was pure poetry. She had never been with anyone like Miguel. The boys she had dated in the past were party guys that enjoyed drinking and carrying on. She never expected anything serious from them, nor did she care to dive deeper into her own heart. Maria enjoyed dating enough, but she found most guys tiresome, too many games, and very little depth. Relationships with them never seemed to have substance. For that, she looked to her girlfriends or college roommates. Miguel was beyond different. He treated her with respect – as an intellectual equal.

Though she knew he was attracted to her, she never felt objectified. Unlike her other boyfriends, sleeping together wasn't the ultimate goal. The playful banter they shared was witty and amusing. But the ease with which they transitioned into intimate conversations was startling.

She found herself challenging him and asking personal questions that most guys would never entertain, and Miguel responded willingly. Maria's vibrant personality often attracted guys that just wanted to have a good time. Most never took the time to get to know her. She found herself in unfamiliar territory with Miguel, and Maria barely understood how it all began.

Before she knew it, she was emotionally attached to this Roman seminarian. *What the hell?* she thought. *How did this happen so quickly?* She was also quite aware of how complicated their budding relationship was. Miguel was unavailable – he was a seminarian, for god-sake!

She wasn't sure when it happened, but Maria was quite taken with him. Miguel's letters tapped her reflective instincts. Maria thought intensely about the meaning of her life and her goals. While many of her classmates knew the career path to take after college, Maria did not. She believed she would figure that out as her life unfolded. In her journal, she wrote about the many adventures she had while trying to make sense of her struggles. Maria had always searched for a deeper meaning in life. Her gregarious personality didn't reveal her true depth. Only Maria's dearest friends were given a glimpse. Miguel's letters, so eloquently written, frightened her. In some ways, she was entirely out of her depth – she felt a little intimidated. Miguel was two years older and seemed so wise. Strangely, she never felt that way when they were together. But somehow, his written word had tapped into her core.

When Miguel even called her on Thanksgiving Day, Maria's fears swiftly dissolved. Merely hearing his voice made her realize he was real, that what they shared was mutual. They launched into an animated conversation about their New Year's plans and laughed about all the crazy personalities at NAC. They seamlessly transitioned into their own struggles – being away from home on Thanksgiving and their loneliness. They chatted for nearly an hour, which was exorbitantly expensive.

"Hey, handsome, I love that you called me, but we've been on the phone forever. This is going to cost you a fortune," Maria finally said. She did not know the breadth of his family's wealth.

"You're worth it, Maria. I mean it," Miguel replied.

"How are you so wonderful? I mean, I've never met anyone quite like you."

"You make it easy, Maria. I can't wait to see you next month," Miguel said.

"Yeah, me too."

***

Being in a group for the first day and a half tortured both of them. They were finally alone, thanks to Anthony's stomach virus. The irony didn't escape either of them. It took his illness to give them an evening alone, and he was the one who brought them together.

After a short walk, they had arrived at a cozy little restaurant in the neighborhood where she lived.

"Voilà," she sang with a sweep of her arm.

Once again, Miguel was under her spell. Rather than sit across from her in the booth, Miguel took his place beside her. The intimacy that had begun during her visit to Rome came right back, and by dessert, Miguel had his arm around her. Maria leaned into him, and her shoulder fit comfortably under his wing. As he walked her home, they held hands like high school sweethearts.

"So, what are we doing here, Miguel?"

"I really don't know. But I do know that I like you," Miguel said.

"And the priesthood?"

"Yeah, I guess I have some decisions to make."

"I guess you do."

He leaned down and kissed her tenderly. She gave into him, and before long, they were kissing like teenagers leaning against the wrought iron fence outside of her building. When they broke for air, he looked up at her apartment and said, "I guess I can't come up, huh?"

"No, not unless you want to tangle with Madamme Beaulieu. She's very protective of her girls."

"Then I'll see you tomorrow?"

"Yes, my dear, we'll have the whole day together."

She kissed him, then playfully pinched his cheek.

"You're adorable, you know."

She disappeared into the apartment as Miguel stood motionless, staring after her.

***

Even though he was in a rush, Miguel walked around a nearby park. He needed time to think, and the cold Paris winter was the perfect company for his conflicting thoughts. Miguel had been with girls before, but it had been years before. He had been so young when he last dated. This was obviously different – Maria was a woman. She didn't play childish games and didn't let him get away with anything. Her questions were direct, and she challenged him when he avoided giving answers. He had been more himself with her during the last few hours than he had been with anyone before. Not even Anthony and Kevin knew the depth of his internal battle. Miguel dreamed about making love to her–he was in dangerous waters.

Physically shaking his head as he walked, it looked as if he were arguing with a friend. They had only known each other for a few months, and she was still in college, not to mention that he was a seminarian. How could this possibly work?

She is unlike anyone I have ever known. If I don't seize this moment, it may never happen again. But surely, she can't be ready for such a serious relationship, can she? It doesn't matter; I must be with her, he thought. But somewhere inside, he still had that nagging desire to become a priest. *Damn it! Enough of this. Perhaps it's time for a new direction.* He was dead tired when he lay his head down on his pillow, but sleep evaded him.

***

The days leading up to New Year's Eve were like a dream. Each of them seemed to let go of their worries and enjoyed the holiday festivities. Anthony noticed how affectionate Maria and Miguel were, and he knew her well enough to know that she was smitten. He saw they had passed the flirting stage. A comfortable intimacy had replaced the superficial banter. Anthony watched their conversations delve into more substantial topics. They discussed celibacy, Church corruption, and the desire to have children. They bickered good-naturedly and seemed entirely content in each other's company. He was happy for the two of them but wondered what that meant for Miguel.

How would he reconcile this new relationship with NAC and the priesthood? Then again, Anthony questioned his own future there as well. Maria filled their days with visits to museums and quaint cafes or restaurants beyond the city center. Each night, after everyone had gone off to bed, Miguel would walk Maria to her residence.

The ritual was the same each night–they'd kiss and giggle, then he'd stroll back to his room. His reflections were filled with *what if?* scenarios. There were so many possibilities. Why not explore them?

On New Year's Eve, the merry seminarians, led by Maria, basked in the holiday festivities. They enjoyed a sumptuous meal, watched a fire eater entertain the crowd outside of their restaurant, and wandered around Paris with the many other revelers. As midnight approached, they strolled down the Champs de Lyse. They were entranced by the grand display of fireworks above the Arc de Triomphe when the clock struck the final hour of 1982. Their troubles seemed so far away, and they rejoiced in the celebration of a new year to come and new beginnings for each of them.

Chapter Twenty
The Inquisitor

Candidacy is the first official step toward the priesthood. Upon return from Christmas vacation, NAC was a flurry of activity to prepare for the big day. The formation team met with the new men countless times. After two weeks away, Anthony returned with a renewed commitment to his vocation. It had done a world of good to get a little distance from the petty drama within his class. He was floating on a cloud after a productive meeting with his new spiritual director at the *Casa*. Father Garcia was an amazing man who was pursuing a doctoral degree in spirituality. Anthony had begun informal spiritual direction with Garcia back in November, but he was afraid to ask the rector for an official switch from Father Connick.

He knew it was unethical to deceive him, especially when he barely shared any meaningful spiritual or emotional information with Connick during their sessions. Anthony believed their meetings were useless. He needed to process the many complex emotions he was experiencing, and he just didn't feel comfortable with him. During one of their appointments, Father Connick asked him directly.

"Anthony, you have been meeting with Father Garcia quite often, haven't you?"

"Yes, he's a terrific person, and he's helped me through some of my struggles with homesickness."

"Does he act as a spiritual director as well?"

Anthony knew this was a trap. He had to navigate it very carefully. "No, not really. It wouldn't be right to have two spiritual directors."

"You are correct. But it seems that our conversations remain safely on the surface. Why do you think that is?"

"Well, to be quite honest with you, Father, I am more than a little intimidated by you. I am afraid to be as vulnerable with you as I should."

"But that is what I'm here for. The faculty is here to guide you as you discern God's will. Being vulnerable is a necessary step in that process."

"I understand, Father. But as vice-rector, you are also an authority at NAC. It's difficult for me to get beyond that."

"My son, how can we move forward if you are not honest with me?" Father asked.

"But I am honest with you. When we were asked to choose a spiritual director, we were told we could select someone outside of the NAC faculty as long as it was approved. I have been happy to have you guide me until now, but I feel like it may be time to change."

"I see. Do you think it's wise to make a change of such great importance in the middle of the academic year? Perhaps we can discuss this in June."

"I understand, Father. I will defer to your authority."

"That seems a bit cold. I would like to know what you truly think, Anthony."

Anthony took a deep breath and looked away. He felt trapped and wasn't sure if he should lie to save face.

"Father, my spiritual journey is the most significant component of my life. It should be a priority for each of us," he said, building up his courage. "I honestly feel that I should make that change now, especially with candidacy coming up in three weeks. I hope you understand that it is not about respecting you less. It's about finding a connection."

There, he said it. He had acted with integrity and spoke the truth to an authority figure. It was in God's hands now. "All right, Anthony. Father Garcia is highly respected among the faculty. I am certain this will be approved. I just wish you had been more forthright with me."

"Thank you, Father. There is still so much for me to learn here," Anthony responded with a mixture of humility and irony.

"That you do, Anthony," Father Connick replied.

***

Kevin and Anthony had noticed that Miguel was cagey about candidacy. While everyone else was getting swept up into the excitement, Miguel seemed distant. He wasn't one to share his feelings, so they gave him space. However, they realized he was simply going through the motions. In actuality, Miguel was wrestling with this first official step toward the priesthood. He had just returned from the most amazing vacation with an incredible woman. Maria consumed his thoughts, both night and day.

They had spoken on the phone several times since their time together in Paris. However, it was difficult to talk candidly about their feelings. The phone was on a shelf in the center of the hallway. There was absolutely no privacy to be had.

Before being accepted into candidacy, each of the new men had to be interviewed by an ordained priest. These men were chosen from various Pontifical Universities and the Casa Santa Maria, the American house of graduate studies. The priest selected for each seminarian was a crapshoot. Miguel woke up the morning of his interview and dressed in civilian clothes, a blue button-down shirt, and khakis. He gave himself a once over in the mirror and decided that he was presentable.

After the thirty-minute walk to the Angelicum, he entered the anteroom for his interview. Before his eyes was a sea of black – everyone else was in their clerical garb. They turned and looked at him with astonishment. *How dare he wear his civvies?* Rather than get upset, he smiled and said, "I guess I didn't get the memo." No one laughed.

There were three offices in which priests gave interviews, and they opened to a single waiting room. In one of the offices was the infamous *Inquisitor*. He was known to be a *hard ass*. With beads of sweat dripping down their temples, the men coming from his office looked as if they had just been tortured. The seminarians sat anxiously, waiting for one of the doors to open. Most of the other men exited their interviews with smiles on their faces. However, when Miguel's turn came, the entrance to the Inquisitor's office opened. At first, he stalled to see if another interview might become available, but then realized he had no choice.

Father Inquisitor looked up from his desk and frowned. "This is how you dress?"

"Sorry, Father, I…"

"Sit down," he interrupted, and with a thick German accent, he continued.

"Tell me the ten impediments to the priesthood?"

Miguel had no idea what he was asking.

Are there specific things that would prevent a man from becoming a priest? Is this in an official document that I'm supposed to have read?

"Well, I suppose marriage would be an impediment and maybe having sex." Miguel stumbled through several more fabricated impediments before the Inquisitor slammed his hand on the desk.

"No, no. How can you expect to become a priest if you do not know the answer to such a simple question?" Miguel, usually never at a loss for words, sat there stunned.

"Come with me," the Inquisitor demanded.

He walked out into the waiting area and knocked loudly on one of the office doors and opened it without waiting for a response. He had no qualms about interrupting the interview his colleague was conducting. Standing at the door with Miguel just behind him, the Inquisitor could be heard by everyone in the vicinity.

"Father, this young man cannot tell me the ten impediments to the priesthood. I cannot, in good conscience, recommend him for candidacy. He is completely unprepared."

A hushed silence swept the room, and everyone's eyes were locked on Miguel. He was shocked by his harsh treatment, which only served to alienate him more. The Inquisitor turned on his heels and flew back to his office – his cassock flapping like a cape in his wake. Miguel was a pillar of salt, frozen in his tracks. Knowing his colleague's infamous reputation, the priest graciously dismissed the other seminarian and looked up at Miguel.

"What's your name, my son?" he asked kindly.

"Miguel Perez."

"Sit down, Miguel. Take a deep breath and calm yourself. Now, tell me why you want to be a priest."

As his adrenaline subsided, Miguel was able to put his thoughts together. Still reeling from being publicly shamed, he wasn't convinced that his answers were coherent. After a few minutes, the kindly priest shook his hand and told him he would be happy to recommend him for candidacy. Miguel left the room in a daze. He had to get away from his classmates and their judgmental stares. He needed to clear his head. A long walk along the Tiber would be perfect. He descended the stairs from the street level and strolled along the river's edge. The coffee-colored water rushed angrily past – occasionally, bits of trash sailed by. Miguel felt the chill of the January winter through his coat as he relived the last few hours. Everything about his experience here was surreal.

How did it all go wrong? he wondered. Word got back to the seminary in a flash, and it had spread like wildfire. When Miguel entered the main doors of NAC, the vice-rector stood, waiting for him.

"Let's have a chat, Miguel," Father Connick said, motioning to a door nearby.

They entered the receiving room, and Connick closed the door behind him. "First of all, how could you think it was appropriate to dress this way for your interview?"

"I didn't know there was a dress-code, Father. It is not a class day," Miguel replied.

"You should have known better, but that's the problem with you, Miguel, isn't it? You don't know better, or was this another attempt to make a statement about clerical attire?" His fierce attack shocked Miguel. Indeed, dressing in Khakis was not a mortal sin.

"You just can't seem to follow protocol here, and it disturbs me. I heard that your first interview did not go well. Thankfully, Father Laterno took pity on you."

"I apologize for my lack of insight concerning my dress, and you are right; I should have figured this out on my own. But, Father, this experience today has reinforced some of my doubts about the priesthood."

"I see, and what, exactly, does that mean?"

"I suppose it means that I would rather not commit to candidacy at this moment."

"Is that so? Well, that *is* quite disappointing. You realize that is the whole point of being here, don't you?"

"Yes, Father. I also know that we are in the process of discerning God's will. Someone who chooses candidacy should be certain of their vocation. I'm just not sure that I'm there yet," Miguel responded honestly.

"I see. A word of warning, Miguel – you ought to tread very carefully. You are on thin ice here at the North American College." All at once, Father rose and left the room. Miguel sat in shock. Mulling over all that had transpired during the last few hours, he thought, *this place is positively bizarre*. Miguel understood that his tenure at NAC was far from certain. But he genuinely believed that he was authentic to the discernment process. The worst thing one could do was to go through the motions mindlessly. No, if he was to choose the priesthood, he had to be sure. Miguel needed more time to reflect on it.

Chapter Twenty-One
Candidacy

The day before the ceremony, the doorman phoned Anthony to tell him he had a guest. *That's odd,* he thought; he wasn't expecting anyone. On the other hand, there had been many unannounced visitors during the months he'd been in Rome. Anthony bounded out of the building and across the driveway. When he opened the door to reception, his jaw dropped.

"Maria, what are you doing here?" Anthony howled as he wrapped Maria in his arms.

"It's candidacy tomorrow, isn't it? How could I possibly miss such an important milestone for my boys?"

"Oh, we're your boys now, are we?"

"Of course you are. You look wonderful. How are you, honey?"

"I'm doing great now that you're here! This is the best gift ever! Wait until the guys see you! Come on upstairs."

They noisily burst into Kevin's room with laughter and excitement. Miguel was lying back on the bed with a glass of Baileys in his hand. As soon as he heard her voice, he froze. A flurry of emotions flooded his heart.

"Maria!" Kevin sang in a high-pitched voice. "What are you doing here?" he said as he wrapped her in his arms. "I guess you missed us."

"I'm here for your big day!" Maria turned her head and addressed Miguel. "Hey gorgeous, what? No hug?"

"I, I'm just stunned," he said as he slowly stood.

"Come here, handsome." She kissed him on the cheek and turned to the others. "So, you're actually surprised? No one let it slip?"

"Who did you plan this with?" Anthony asked as it gradually dawned on him. "Carlos! He has been incredibly tight-lipped. He never said a word."

"Well, that's nothing new," Kevin said under his breath. The two of them had cooled off considerably after their time in Paris. Hearing the commotion, Carlos entered the room to more shouts of joy. They passed around the Baileys and made dinner plans.

To celebrate, they chose an upscale restaurant in Trastevere called Romolo. The seminarians loved to tell the local lore, and Romolo had a great story. Legend has it that Raphael, the Renaissance painter, used to meet his paramour in that building. The evening was filled with laughter and good food. The guys splurged, having both primo and secondo dishes, the pasta and the meat course.

The wine was plentiful as usual, and of course, they polished off the complimentary *digestivi* left on the table at the end of the meal. Miguel and Maria sat beside one another with their legs pressed together. They had written and spoken several times since their time in Paris, and Miguel had been honest about his confusion.

Maria didn't understand why he was vacillating so much. In her limited experience, she knew Miguel was the best man she had ever been with. At the same time, however, Maria was only a junior in college.

She was certainly not ready for a life-long commitment and didn't want him to make his decision solely based on their relationship. The festive party continued as they walked along the Tiber back toward NAC. Stories of their recent vacation in Paris came alive in their alcohol-induced haze. It was a crisp cold evening with stars in the sky and lights reflecting off the river – the water almost looked clean. As they reached the bottom of the Janiculum hill, Miguel turned to Maria.

"Are you staying at the same *pensione* as last time, near the Vatican?"

"The very same."

"Let me walk you home," he said as he offered her his arm. No one questioned it when they peeled off from the group and waved goodbye. They were quiet for a few minutes when finally, they both spoke at once.

"Maria, let me explain..."

"Miguel, it's okay, I..."

"I know this doesn't make sense. Honestly, I get it. I'm fucked up," Miguel said.

"Look, Miguel, this is an impossible situation," Maria continued. "You've dreamed about becoming a priest your whole life, and then I come flying in and turn your world upside down. I never expected you to give everything up for me," She said.

"Hey, I still might want to – I mean – give everything up for you," Miguel responded.

"Seriously, Miguel, we hardly know each other. But, honestly, I've never met anyone quite like you."

"I can certainly say the same about you. The fact that you have had such a huge effect on me after so little time together means something. Clearly, I have some important decisions to make."

"I'm sorry. I didn't come here to upend your world, honey. I really just wanted to celebrate with my boys."

"Your boys?" he said with a smile. "I believe you, Maria. But seeing you now is making my head hurt."

"So, I give you a headache?" she joked.

"No, I mean – I need more time to figure this out, Maria. I'm just not ready yet."

"Hey, Miguel," she stopped and turned him to face her. "No pressure. This is your life we are talking about. We have all the time in the world to figure out if there is something real between us. In the meantime, can't you just enjoy this moment?"

"I'm not sure, Maria. Tomorrow night is the first step toward priesthood. It's when the Church officially accepts us as candidates for the priesthood. It's a big deal."

"But it's not a vow, is it?"

"No, but," his voice trailed off. He hadn't told Maria yet. "Listen, the guys don't know this yet, but I'm not going through with candidacy."

"What? Are you serious?"

"Totally. I am still not sure about you and me, or my vocation to the priesthood. But I do know that I have to act with integrity. If I go through with candidacy tomorrow, I'd be lying to everyone there, lying to God and myself. I can't live with that," Miguel replied.

"You see, this is why I'm so enchanted by you. Who else talks like that? Who else cares about integrity as deeply as you?" she said.

"So, I enchant you?" He bent his head and kissed her.

"Yeah, you do," she said breathlessly.

They continued their walk and chatted more about the meaning of his decision and about the repercussions that would inevitably ensue. The more he spoke to Maria, the more secure Miguel became in his decision.

"Here we are, honey," she said as they stood at the pensione's door. Are you going to be alright?"

"Yeah, sure. I'm glad you're here, Maria."

"Me too. Get some sleep. You have a big day tomorrow, probably more so now that you are not going through the ceremony."

She got on her toes and kissed him gently on the lips. Miguel wanted more but knew he couldn't go there. Even though his relationship with Maria was a part of his decision, it was only one factor in his great dilemma. He couldn't let himself get distracted. As he gazed into her open and trusting eyes, he was amazed by Maria's simple acceptance of his continuing struggle. But he could tell that she was hoping for their relationship to develop further, and so was he.

The following day, Miguel snuck out of NAC before breakfast and ran down to *Campo de Fiori*. The chilly January air caused him to see his breath as he jogged down the hill. Throughout the narrow alleyways, he zig-zagged toward the *piazza*. Even though it was early in the morning, the market was bustling with activity. He made a bee-line to the first flower stall he spotted and chose the most beautiful bouquet to give to Maria. He hoped they would show her how much he still cared about her. He needed her to know that he didn't take her patience with his indecision for granted. Feeling content, Miguel was lost in his thoughts as he made his way back toward NAC.

Unfortunately, at the bottom of the Janiculum hill, he ran into the vice-rector. "Hello, Miguel. What are you doing out so early today?" Father Connick asked.

"I just woke up early and needed to get some fresh air," Miguel responded to the vice-rector.

"It's a beautiful morning for a walk. That's a beautiful bouquet, red roses too... Who are they for?" Father Connick asked.

He couldn't lie. All of his talk about integrity would mean nothing if he did. "They are for Anthony's college friend, Maria. She surprised us for candidacy."

"Ah, that seems awfully romantic for a friend of a friend..." There was a pregnant pause and then, "Do you have feelings for her?" Father asked.

"Yes, I do. But we're not dating or anything. We've just become close." Technically, that was not a lie, but he was undoubtedly obfuscating the truth.

"Close enough to give her red roses? Miguel, what are you doing? I believe you are making things more difficult for yourself. You're simply adding to your confusion by tugging at your heart this way. How can you discern your vocation if you are constantly being distracted?"

"I'm sorry, Father Connick. I realize that I'm a bit of a mess right now. I'm not quite sure where any of this is going. But believe me when I say that I am still committed to my discernment process. I haven't let go of my desire to become a priest. I just need a bit more time."

"Miguel, I believe you. But this is not a discussion to be had at the foot of the Janiculum. We will speak at length during our next appointment."

Miguel watched Father Connick continue on his way and shook his head. He just couldn't get a break. It was just his luck to be caught buying flowers for a girl on the day of candidacy. He knew that this would get around to the rest of the faculty before the day was over.

***

The chandeliers twinkled along the chapel's nave, the ten-foot candles on the main altar were lit, and the fragrance of incense filled the air.

The grand organ sounded its fanfare before the choir of men's voices filled the sacred space inviting the long procession of candidates to come forward.

The ceremony was one of the most beautiful that Maria had ever seen. She and Anthony had been actively involved in campus ministry back at Fordham University, so she had taken part in some great liturgies. But this was at a completely different level. The awe-inspiring solemnity of it overwhelmed her. It wasn't just any liturgy.

This one looked toward the future of each of these men as ordained priests. The men before her would preside over Mass in the not so distant future. She gazed at each one of her boys, as she affectionately referred to them. They were all handsomely dressed in their black suits, French cuffs, and formal clerical collars. They had an air of holiness that she had never seen before.

One by one, they were called by name and ascended the steps to face the archbishop. Individually, each stood before him as he accepted them as candidates for holy orders, blessed them, and embraced them. Maria cried as she watched her dear Anthony enter the next phase in his life. Then Kevin went up, and she glanced at Miguel's expressionless face. He sat like a statue as he watched his best friends move on toward the priesthood.

She wasn't sure what her tears meant, but her heart ached for Miguel and what might be. The party afterward could only be put on by NAC.

The refectory was transformed. Tables were set with delicate linen cloths, silverware bearing the crest of the North American College, and a prominent spray of red roses as the centerpiece. It was a lavish affair with an elegant dinner, including five courses paired with fine wines. After all the drama leading up to their candidacy, they let loose and partied, including Maria.

As the evening turned to early morning, some of them began dancing and singing along with the music. All of their quarrels with the Church, NAC, and each other were forgotten for one festive evening. And they were all grateful for it. That was until they had all gone off to bed.

Miguel was dead tired and more than a little drunk when he got to his room. He was emotionally drained and wanted nothing more than to close his eyes. After his clothes were shed and piled at the foot of the bed, Miguel got under the covers. He drifted off to sleep as soon as his head hit the pillow.

Not long after, he awoke to hear a faint knock on the door. He thought he was imagining things and turned toward the wall to get comfortable again. He heard it again and could see the light from the hall brighten his room as the door opened. *Who the hell can that be?*

"Miguel, are you awake?" a drunken voice asked as he sat beside him on the bed.

"I am now," he said with annoyance. Miguel rolled over and saw that it was Father Connick. He moved closer to the wall to put more space between them. "What are you doing in my room, Father?"

"I was watching you all evening, and I know you are going through an emotional time right now," he said, placing his hand on Miguel's thigh. "I just want you to know that you have a friend in me."

"Father, this is not okay. You need to get out of my room." Miguel said.

"Look, Miguel, you can trust me. I can smooth things over for you. I can be your advocate during the evaluation process," Father Connick said as he rubbed Miguel's thigh. Miguel bolted upright and spoke with a low measured voice.

"Stop touching me and get out of my room, or you'll be sorry. I mean it, Connick – Now!" Connick was startled by the tone in his voice. He stood abruptly and had to regain his balance. *This was a foolish mistake. Miguel was a lost cause*, he thought as he quickly exited the room.

But from that moment on, Miguel's future at NAC was all but sealed. The faculty were compiling a file on him and were just waiting for him to stumble once again. He knew that this was his last chance to turn the tides. However, Miguel would never let that happen. If he were anybody else, he would have allowed Connick to have what he wanted. But just thinking about it turned his stomach. Beyond the fact that he was coming on to a straight guy, Connick used his authority to get what he wanted. It was a clear case of sexual harassment – a blatant abuse of power. His body trembled with anger as it sunk in, his fists in balls. *"Goddammit! This place is really fucked up."*

Chapter Twenty-Two
Final Exams

Finals followed shortly after candidacy, and a thick fog of worry covered the NAC. Having no idea what to expect, the new men were incredibly anxious. Each of them had meetings with the academic dean to make sure that they were studying and knew the gravity of their exams.

Unlike the American system, the pontifical universities had no papers or midterms. There was only one shot at passing a course. At the Greg, students had to take one-third of the tests in written form, one-third orally, and the final third was of their choosing.

The oral exams were only thirty minutes long, and the professor could ask anything from the entire semester.

Even though Anthony had done well as an undergraduate, his academic insecurity reared its ugly head. He was surrounded by some of the brightest students he'd ever encountered. When discussions and debates arose, he felt totally inadequate. His classmates could pull names and dates out of nowhere. They were adept at parsing philosophical theories and applying them to the issue at hand. Anthony was better at writing thoughtful responses, but had difficulty keeping up when heated debates would erupt. He believed that the faculty at NAC did not consider him a serious student. It was true that he often let his emotions get in the way of a well-reasoned argument. Throughout the first semester, Monsignor Connick, from Anthony's home diocese, met with him to gauge his progress. He asked how many hours he studied a day and if he had study partners. Connick regularly checked to see if Anthony had done all the reading. Although Connick was trying to be supportive, Anthony believed he was being treated like a child, and he resented the attention.

February 1st arrived in a blink of an eye. Exams had begun, and Anthony was beside himself with worry. The constant blows to his intellectual ego had chipped away at his confidence. He never believed he was an intellectual giant, but knew he was smart. He found himself at a loss during the many study groups that took place during the last few weeks of January. What made him feel worse was that both Kevin and Miguel seemed to run circles around him. They could explain abstract moral theories and systematic theology as if they were ordering off a menu. And although Anthony understood the material, he found it difficult to summon the correct terminology to explain it.

His familiarity with the notes from each class should have eased his anxiety, but he wasn't confident that he had done enough. Anthony had been negligent with the hundreds of pages of reading. And while he could quote his notes from memory, he was woefully behind in the text.

He just hoped that the professors concentrated on their lectures rather than their books. He hadn't slept at all the night before his first exam. He tossed and turned, got up for water, and shuffled down the cavernous hall to the restrooms. Meditation didn't calm his nerves, nor did listening to meditative instrumental music. By 6:00 a.m., he got up, showered, and quietly made his way to the refectory to pour himself a cup of coffee. Sitting by the far window, he gazed out on the beautiful umbrella pines lining the property, the dome of St. Peter's Basilica standing proudly above them. *This may be the end of my NAC career,* he thought. *If I don't do well this week, I'll be out of here.*

Alone, Anthony walked down to the Greg. He didn't want company or idle chat. Lost in his thoughts and self-doubt, Anthony made his way across the Tiber, through the narrow streets to *Piazza Navona*. The city hadn't woken up yet, and the *piazza* was empty.

Not a single person disturbed the peaceful scene. The black cobblestones washed clean from daybreak showers, shined in the early morning sun. Anthony paused as he reached the center fountain and did a loop around it, gazing at the representations of the four major rivers of the old world. The strength and determination carved into the faces of the statues continued to awe him. Then he walked on to the *Piazza del Pantheon*, sitting regally in its own square.

Since it was early yet, he decided to treat himself to a cappuccino at *Tazza D'Oro*. Standing at the counter, he closed his eyes as he took his first sip. It was like a balm to the soul. The creamy foam coated his mouth, and the slight taste of chocolate caressed his tongue as the rich espresso soothed his throat. He reveled in the pure pleasure of a good cappuccino. Less than ten minutes later, he was at the Greg and made his way up to the exam room. Anthony found a wooden bench and sat just outside Father Vittorio's office.

When it was time, Anthony took his place in line and let out a heavy sigh. Not long after, Kevin and Miguel showed up.

"*Ciao*, Anthony! We were looking for you this morning. What time did you get here?" Miguel asked.

"Maybe a half-hour ago, but I left NAC really early. I couldn't sleep," Anthony replied.

"Tell me about it. I was up half the night studying," said Kevin. That only made Anthony feel worse. He scolded himself for not using his sleepless night more wisely. They chatted a while longer and then fell into restless silence as they waited for their turn for the oral exam. Anthony looked back at Kevin, who winked at him when the door opened and gave him a reassuring smile. *Here goes nothing,* he thought.

"Antonioooo! *Buon Giorno!*" Father Vittorio sang as he greeted him. As Anthony made his way through the door, Kevin and Miguel exchanged a look of disbelief.

"Are you kidding me? He dreaded the final exam, and that's how the professor greets him?" said Miguel with wide eyes.

"Yeah, we were told that the professors barely speak during exams," Kevin replied.

"Only Anthony could elicit that kind of response!" said Miguel with a touch of admiration in his tone.

"He's one of a kind," Kevin agreed.

Anthony was immediately relieved after hearing the warm welcome from Father Vittorio. He took his seat facing his professor, and the questioning began. Once started, Anthony was confident that he could express himself in Italian, but although he'd become adept at taking notes, when he spoke, he would often stumble, and the English word would come to mind instead. He began to get frustrated, and Father Vittorio interrupted him.

"*Piano, piano*, Anthony. Slow down, don't get so worried."

"*Sì, Padre*. But sometimes, the only words that come to mind are in English."

"Then speak in English. The most important part is to communicate your understanding. English or Italian – it doesn't make a difference to me," Father Vittorio said.

"If it's okay with you, may I speak in both languages. That's how I take my notes."

"*Perfetto*, Anthony, let's continue."

When it was over, Anthony said a warm goodbye to Father Vittorio, opened the door, and exited the room. As the door closed for the next exam, he joined Kevin and Miguel in line. Anthony was euphoric. "I did it, guys. I didn't freeze or stammer. I think I did well," he blurted out.

"Bravo, *caro!*" Kevin said with his arm around him.

"Seriously, Anthony? The way Father Vittorio called out your name when he saw you. I'm surprised he has time for the rest of us."

"What do you mean?" Anthony asked.

"Nothing, just that your daily question-and-answer sessions after each class paid off."

"Oh, so you think I did well because I'm a brown-noser?" Anthony asked them.

"No, Anthony. Lighten up," Miguel said. "Obviously, this shows that you are smarter than all of us. You didn't understand something, and you didn't let the local custom stop you. You just went up and asked for an explanation. That's not a brown-noser. That's a genius."

"Thanks, I guess. Hey, I'm going to head back to NAC. I need a nap after my sleepless night. Let's meet for lunch. Good luck, guys, though I'm sure you won't need it."

Anthony took the long way back to the college. He wandered through *Campo de Fiori* and marveled at the beautiful open market. Crowds were bustling about visiting stall after stall as they examined the fresh products laid out before them. Anthony looked up above the crowd and noted the statue of Giordano Bruno sitting proudly in the center of the square. He had been burned at the stake for his cosmology theories, which proposed that stars were distant suns surrounded by their own planets. He had a fleeting thought that the Church was still, albeit figuratively, burning dissenters at the stake, including gay people. The image of the solemn-faced friar stood in stark contrast to the modern market's hustle and bustle. There were colorful vegetables, cheeses, and loaves of bread on display. Women in kerchiefs filled baskets with the freshest of foods for the day's meal. Anthony lingered wherever his attention drew him. One of the flower stalls caught his eye, and he inhaled the sweet fragrance of the various blossoms.

Without hesitation, Anthony chose the most beautiful bouquet to bring back to his room. Crossing the Tiber river, he stopped to look at the rushing water pass under the bridge. The coffee-colored waves poured through the steep stone walls that encased the river many feet below the street level. He looked up the hill toward NAC. Over to the right, he glimpsed the cross above the basilica and smiled. Anthony gave a silent prayer of thanks. After days of stress, he was genuinely happy.

Chapter Twenty-Three
The Fiddler's Elbow

B y the second semester, the new men were feeling much more comfortable in Rome. Routines were set, and given the excellent results from their exams, they let go of their rigorous study schedule. Classes were not held on Thursdays, and rather than spending the day studying, Anthony persuaded Kevin to explore beyond the city of Rome. On Thursday mornings, before most of the seminarians had gotten up, they would head to *Stazione Termini* and look up at the list of departing trains.

"Have you ever heard of Nettuno?" Anthony asked.

"Nope, but it looks like a short train ride. Let's go," Kevin replied. Just over an hour-long train ride from Rome, Nettuno is a seaside town that featured prominently in World War II. The *Santuario Santa Maria Goretti* sits right on the coastline, and its gracious square is framed by arches and covered walkways. Across the street is an expansive beach overlooking the Tyrrhenian Sea. Anthony and Kevin strolled along the secluded seashore. The aquamarine water lapped peacefully upon the sandy beach. A summer resort town, only the locals could be seen running errands and working in little shops around the main *piazza*.

Each week they chose a different destination and spent the day exploring. As was their routine, they found a quaint trattoria and settled in for a leisurely meal. Following their feast, they walked off the calories visiting tourist attractions until it was time to catch the late afternoon train. They were always back by night prayer, so no one ever questioned where they went on their weekly travels.

It was during these weekly expeditions that Kevin and Anthony cemented their heartfelt commitment to each other. Thursdays offered rare opportunities for them to be alone, away from prying eyes or NAC authorities.

During those days spent together, they began to feel like a couple. Their interactions were ordinary yet intimate, and Kevin gained a sharper understanding of how Anthony approached his world, and the same was true for Anthony. They were magical days that opened windows into the hearts of these dear friends and lovers. Because of those intimate Thursdays, their lives were inextricably woven together.

***

Another exciting addition to their second semester in Rome was discovering a bar called the Fiddler's Elbow. It was not far from the Colosseum and the grand Basilica of Santa Maria Maggiore. Kevin's nostalgia for home manifested itself through his quest for an authentic Irish bar. He was determined to find a place to celebrate St. Patrick's Day before March rolled around. Back home, every weekend leading up to the big day, Kevin and his cousins would gather to sing old Irish tunes. When he walked into the bar, he was transported to another world.

It seemed to be the perfect antidote to the constant grind at NAC. Some familiar surroundings, a few Irish songs to tug at his heart, and he'd be right as rain.

Kevin's enthusiasm was infectious, and he gathered a willing crew to accompany him on his Irish night out. The following Saturday, Kevin, Anthony, and Miguel took a taxi to the bar and settled in for the evening. There was live music, and the crowd was spirited. What made it even better was that they served American-style hamburgers. After all the pasta they had eaten over the last months, a juicy cheeseburger hit the spot. They were in heaven.

Kevin chatted up the bartender from County Cork, the same area from whence his parents hailed, and soon, Kevin's English developed a distinctive lilt. Trading stories of the old country, he became more in touch with his Irish roots. Kevin still had family in Cork, so he and the bartender bonded over the familiar pubs and landmarks they had visited. The Guinness on tap was like balm to the soul, and the guys were singing along with the familiar Irish songs in no time. Kevin's smile broadened when he looked over at Anthony, who knew every song.

"Look at him," Kevin said to Miguel. "You would never know he wasn't an Irishman!"

"Yeah, he's a regular Paddy with a Roman nose!" Miguel said, laughing along with Kevin.

This began yet another one of their NAC rituals. When things at the college got too intense, they made a pilgrimage to the Fiddler's Elbow and pretended to be ordinary ex-pats studying in Rome. They flirted with the women at the bar, and Anthony learned to drink beer like a genuine Irishman – well, almost.

The bartender loved his tenor voice and coaxed him into singing with the band occasionally. "Where did you get that sweet voice of yours, Anthony?" he asked. "You know the words to all of our songs – you must have sung in an Irish band back in the states."

"Yeah, that's our Tony Mac Rossi," Kevin blurted out as they joined in the laughter.

"Come on now, lad, get up there and sing for us," the bartender pressed Anthony.

"All right, my friend, but just one song. I've had too much beer to sing in tune," Anthony said as he relented.

As he launched into the Unicorn, The Wild Rover, and his favorite, Seven Old Ladies, their troubles were quickly forgotten. *Oh dear, what can the matter be? Seven old ladies are stuck in the lavatory…*

On and on, he sang. It was a night to remember. The last call came upon them without warning, and before they knew it, the boys were wandering the alleys searching for a taxi. Sadly, it was past 2:00 a.m., and there were none to be found near the Fiddler's Elbow. They walked towards the immense Basilica of Santa Maria Maggiore.

They staggered around the piazza, looking for a taxi-stand. When an empty cab finally slowed to pick them up, they poured themselves into the backseat. The driver didn't blink when Anthony gave him the seminary address. He was used to inebriated clerics in the holy city of Rome. Alcohol and sex were two of the ways they coped with the loneliness.

Upon their return to the seminary, Kevin was in rare form. "Hey, let's see if they have any Irish whiskey in the faculty lounge."

He walked right in and turned on the lamps. "We can't go in there," Anthony added. "You really *are* drunk."

"Have a seat, gents," Kevin said, ignoring their protests. "What's your pleasure? We have Baileys, Amaretto, and look, Jameson!"

"This is crazy, Kevin. What if we get caught?" Anthony asked nervously.

"What are they going to do, kick us out for drinking some of their liquor?" Kevin replied. "Take a load off your feet and relax. After your performance tonight, Anthony, you deserve a nightcap!"

After they were done, Miguel looked for a place to wash their glasses. "Hey, where's the sink in here? I'll wash them out." He asked.

"No, don't turn on the water! You know how much noise the old plumbing makes," Anthony cautioned him.

"Then what do we do with the glasses?"

"I have an idea," Kevin said with a mischievous look in his eyes. "Make sure they're empty and give them to me." Then he moved all the glasses in the cabinet forward and carefully placed the used ones in the back. "By the time they get to these, they won't even know they've been used."

"You're a genius, Kevin," Miguel said. "An evil genius!" The three of them ended up in Anthony's room, sprawled out on the bed, listening to Fleetwood Mac. They were pretty drunk; Kevin and

Anthony were less careful than usual with their affection towards each other. Anthony leaned his head on Kevin's chest while Miguel dozed at the other corner of the bed.

"God, that was fun," Kevin said.

"We should go there every weekend," Miguel replied.

"I'm not sure I can handle that much alcohol," said Anthony. "It gives me a headache."

"Well, it certainly didn't seem to bother you much when you joined the band singing Seven Old Ladies!" Miguel remarked.

"No kidding. If I didn't know better, I'd think you were a fellow Irishman," Kevin said and kissed the top of Anthony's head.

"Tone it down guys, or get a room," Miguel said when he noticed their overt affection.

"This *is* my room," Anthony said, snickering.

"You know what I mean. You're going to get your asses kicked out of here if you're not careful."

"He's right," Kevin added. "Sorry, Miguel."

"No need to be sorry, just don't be so obvious about it. It's not cool." Despite Kevin's initial thoughts about Miguel, Anthony had just assumed he was gay. He never seemed to mind the gay innuendos and horseplay. It was merely a part of seminary culture; there was always some sexual undercurrent in their interactions.

After Miguel went off to bed, Kevin and Anthony talked about their conversation with him. "That made me so uncomfortable," Anthony said.

"Yeah, I didn't think we had to worry about Miguel. But he was pissed. We do need to be more careful."

"Until tonight, he's never blinked an eye at all the stuff we say," Anthony said.

"Look, he was at Trinity Seminary in Dallas. I'm sure our banter is nothing new to him. But kissing you in front of him was over the line."

"So, is he homophobic? How angry is he with us?"

"I don't think so. Miguel's probably cool with the gay thing, but that doesn't mean he's okay with us having a romantic relationship. I'm sure he takes the idea of celibacy very seriously."

"Yeah, that makes sense. It looks like I missed out on a lot by not going to seminary for college."

"Well, you're certainly making up for it now!" Kevin replied to Anthony and kissed him as he unbuttoned his shirt. Their overconsumption of alcohol didn't seem to affect their lovemaking one bit. Anthony quickly launched into Italian, which, after a night of drinking, seemed fluent. Kevin thought it was the most romantic thing in the world and joined in without embarrassment.

Chapter Twenty-Four
The Limousine

He was not sure when it happened, but sometime during his months in Rome, Anthony had become disillusioned with the Church. Gone were those exclamations of *Wonderful! And Beautiful!* He was no longer enchanted by the peeling of church bells each day, nor the gleaming white dome of St. Peter's Basilica on those evenings getting high on the roof of NAC. Anthony started taking solitary walks throughout the ancient city to clear his head. Often, he found himself at the Vatican, where he meandered through the magnificent St. Peter's Square.

Gazing up at the façade, Anthony marveled at his good fortune. He never dreamed that he would be standing in St. Peter's Square as a Roman seminarian. Beauty and history surrounded him as he slowly turned to take in the sites. There were nearly three-hundred white marble columns that comprised the Bernini colonnade, which stretched like arms in front of St. Peter's Basilica, protecting all within their grasp. On top were a hundred and forty statues of saints that stood like sentinels defending Holy Mother Church. Anthony was in awe of the grandeur before him. The power and reach of the Catholic Church were on full display. *He was studying to be a priest right here in Vatican City.*

He thought back to his first weeks in Rome. He truly believed that his appointment to the North American College was a dream come true. He had been in this very spot when it all changed. Anthony recalled the tolling bells had roused him from his reverie; he realized he was running late. Evening prayer at the North American College was about to begin. Passing through the columns, he glanced at the Swiss guards dressed in bright red, blue, and gold stripes that were stationed at the official entrance to Vatican City State.

As he began to cross the street, a limousine stopped directly in front of him, blocking his way. The back window slid down to reveal the probing eyes of a distinguished cleric. At first, he didn't recognize the man as he greeted Anthony by name. The priest seemed very familiar, but he couldn't place him. Slowly it dawned on him; it was the Pope's personal secretary who he had met a week before at the papal audience. Now, as he stood just outside St. Peter's Square, Monsignor Kowalski sat right before him, smiling at Anthony from his beautiful stretch limo. *"Ciao, Anthony. Che fai qui alla piazza?"* What are you doing here in the piazza? the Monsignor asked.

"Hello, Monsignor. It's good to see you again. I am just on my way back to the college for evening prayer."

"Well, this is a wonderful coincidence. I am on my way to say Mass for the sisters at the *Monasterium S. Luciae in Silice.* Have you been to the cloisters there?"

"No, I haven't. I imagine it's beautiful."

"They are beautiful, indeed. Why don't you come along? It would be a rare opportunity for you to see the private cloisters, and I would be grateful for the company," Monsignor Kowalski offered.

"I would love to, Monsignor, but I shouldn't miss evening prayer. I've only been here for three weeks, and I don't want the rector to get the wrong impression of me. Besides, I am hardly dressed for Mass," Anthony replied.

"Oh, don't you worry, Anthony. I can contact Monsignor O'Connor to tell him that you served at Mass with me. And as far as your attire is concerned," the Monsignor said as he blatantly looked him up and down, "no one will know what you have on under your cassock—well—except for me." For the first time, Anthony was embarrassed by his dress. The sun was still up, and the temperatures in Rome were soaring, as was typical during late August.

Anthony had known that it wasn't customary for adults to wear short pants in Rome. Only little children wore them, but it was hot, and he didn't much care what anyone thought of him. The Roman heat and humidity were stifling; why should Anthony follow local customs rather than ease his suffering? He was an American in Rome, an adult, and he would dress as he pleased. Wearing the standard preppy uniform – a brightly colored Izod polo, a pair of white *Ocean Pacific* shorts, and docksiders without socks, Anthony knew he stood out in the sea of Italians dressed in dark colors, as well as the many Roman clerics in black cassocks rushing about the neighborhoods surrounding St. Peter's Square. However, it was evident that Monsignor Kowalski took notice of his inappropriate outfit.

"I'm sorry, Monsignor. I didn't expect to run into anyone I knew today. I probably should have worn long pants, but it's just so hot," Anthony replied to Monsignor Kowalski.

"The Roman summers *are* certainly oppressive, but I'm sure that showing off your legs like that has garnered a great deal of attention in our holy city. Rest assured, I am not offended in the least. Now, get in the limousine, and we'll be on our way." *How could Anthony refuse?* It was an incredible opportunity to serve Mass with Pope John Paul's personal secretary. He'd be crazy to turn him down.

As Anthony slid into the luxurious car, the cool leather caressed his bare thighs. It felt so good after being out in the hot, humid weather. He let go of his worries and thought back to when he first met Monsignor Kowalski. All the new men at the North American College seminary had been in attendance. St. Peter's square was packed with faithful Catholics from all over the world, waiting to catch a glimpse of the charismatic Pope

John Paul II. Their seats had been prominently positioned right up front. Just behind them, a row of Spanish nuns had greeted them amicably as they took their seats. Dressed in their black suits and black ties in the hot August sun, the new seminarians had suffered through the Pope's greetings in many languages. After his introductory remarks, there was a reading from scripture followed by a sermon.

Including the wait time, the audience was over three hours long. Even still, Anthony was enthralled; he was oblivious to any discomfort as he gazed upon the stage that was lined with cardinals dressed in bright red and bishops in brilliant magenta. Behind the dais rose the façade of St. Peter's Basilica, topped by its gleaming white cupola. He could hardly believe that he was only steps from the Vicar of Christ, the head of the Roman Catholic Church.

When it came time for the Pope to step down from the papal throne, Anthony felt the adrenaline rushing through his veins. As was the custom, the Pope walked along the guardrails to greet the faithful and give them his blessing. The crowd rushed toward the barriers for an opportunity to shake his hand. Being short and quick, Anthony was adept at weaving through crowds, under people's arms, and through any opening, where he soon found himself squarely in front, directly against the barricade. The hordes were pushing from all sides, but he found his spot and held his ground against the demanding crowd. As the Pope neared, he could feel the excitement mount. The lovely Spanish nuns that were seated just behind the seminarians at the start of the audience became frantic and climbed onto his shoulders in hopes of touching the Pope. It was suffocating as he felt the masses push in on him from all sides – he could feel the wooden barrier pressing uncomfortably into his stomach and ribs.

Anthony kicked into survival mode and flexed his muscular arms, elbowing anyone who tried to press in on him. It was comical that everyone around him, and perhaps he too, was losing their composure, becoming like little children desperate for attention.

Slowly, Pope John Paul II made his way toward the seminarians of the North American College. He appeared bigger than life. John Paul was robust and healthy, and his smile was as broad as his shoulders. When he shook Anthony's hand, he placed his other hand upon his upper arm. Knowing that the seminarians from the North American College were in attendance, he asked his name and what diocese he was from.

The Pope encouraged him, "Anthony, listen to the Holy Spirit as you continue on your path toward ordination. If you place your trust in God, you will never falter." Anthony felt like he had just seen the face of God and that he received a direct message.

Later, on the walk back to the seminary, the other guys ribbed him good-naturedly, laughing about his sprint to the guardrail. Still awestruck from his brief encounter with the Pope, Anthony realized someone was addressing him. Following directly behind the Pope was his personal secretary, who John Paul had brought with him from Poland. Anthony was still speechless when he greeted him.

The secretary had taken note of his name during his brief conversation with the Pope and spoke to him personally, engaging Anthony in a more extended discussion. "*Ciao*, Anthony, it is good to meet you. My name is Monsignor Kowalski. I am the personal secretary to His Holiness. You and your classmates have just recently arrived from the States. Tell me, how are you adjusting to Rome?"

"*Buon giorno*, Monsignor. Being at the heart of the Catholic Church is a great privilege," Anthony replied earnestly. "I can hardly believe that the North American College is only steps away from St. Peter's Basilica. I can't wait to explore this beautiful and ancient city."

"That's wonderful, Anthony. Perhaps I can help. I would be happy to show you around."

The Monsignor handed Anthony his card and extended an invitation to contact him directly at his private number. He then moved on to speak with the other seminarians. Anthony placed the card in his wallet. Still walking on clouds from his post papal contact, he fully planned on contacting the Monsignor in the coming weeks. *What an incredible coincidence to have run into him today,* Anthony thought.

Initially, their conversation was formal, but the Monsignor did his best to put him at ease. He asked questions about what brought him to

NAC, and Anthony entertained him with opinions on moral theology and expounded upon the philosophy of St. Thomas Aquinas and his theory of natural law. He spoke for the entire drive to the *Monasterium.* Everything about Rome enchanted him: the cobblestone streets, the grand churches, and beautiful fountains. Anthony had always wanted to become a priest, but he never imagined that his studies would take him to the heart of the Catholic Church. He marveled at the Church's history, which revealed itself at every turn. Even his address at the North American College stated that he was living in the Vatican City State.

Anthony could see a look of mild amusement on Monsignor Kowalski's face. He seemed to be enchanted by his idealism, and Anthony was more than willing to oblige.

Once in the sacristy, Anthony donned the black cassock and surplice and served Mass with the Monsignor. Enthralled with the solemnity of the convent, he passed into another realm as the sacrifice of the Mass revealed its sacred mystery. Holding the patent under the chin of each nun, it felt as if he were serving at the right hand of God. The entire scene was beyond his imaginings; the barrel-vaulted ceiling and frescos glowed in the candlelight. Incense filled the sanctuary, and the chanting voices of the nuns echoed in the ancient space. It was as if he were a character in a Fellini film. He could barely believe this was merely the beginning of his stay in the eternal city.

Back in the sacristy after Mass, Monsignor Kowalski took off his vestments, revealing his ample potbelly. He was feeling more brazen and placed his arm around Anthony's shoulder. "Now wasn't that worth missing evening prayer at the North American College?"

"It was beautiful, Monsignor." Anthony replied. "Thank you so much for this opportunity."

"All right then, what do you say we find a nice little trattoria? I could use something to eat," Kowalski offered.

"Well, I am always up for pasta. Why not?" he agreed. Anthony was more reflective at dinner than he had been during the drive to the cloister. Serving Mass in its historic chapel made him feel as if he had been in the presence of true holiness. He was struck by the realization of how unique his seminary experience would be.

Throughout dinner, Kowalski peppered him with questions. Where did he go to school? How many siblings did Anthony have? Did he ever have a girlfriend? Had he ever been in love? - Anthony thought nothing of it and answered each question without guile. Only later he realized that Kowalski was sizing him up, leading him to share even more personal details.

After dinner, the limousine driver opened the door, and Anthony scooted in after the Monsignor. Once in the car, their conversation became more personal as the driver took them in the direction of St. Peter's Basilica.

The Monsignor usually waited until their second or third meeting, but Kowalski decided that he had discovered enough about Anthony to take a chance.

"This has been a lovely evening, Anthony. I am not ready for it to end," he said as his eyes blatantly scanned at Anthony's biceps, broad chest, and rested on his crotch. "You know, there aren't many joys in my administrative, clerical life at the Vatican. But I'm often delight by you shiny new men from the North American College." Anthony was caught off guard by his remark. He wasn't sure what he meant, but he suddenly felt uncomfortable. "Why don't you come to my suite for an after-dinner drink?" Kowalski continued. "There is a lovely view of the Basilica from my apartment. Perhaps we can continue getting to know one another?"

"That sounds wonderful, Monsignor, but it's getting late. I should get back to the seminary."

"It's only nine o'clock—come for one drink, and I promise to get you home at a reasonable hour."

"Honestly, Monsignor, I can't. I have so much homework to do for Italian class tomorrow. But I would love to get together with you again soon. I hope you understand."

"Well, of course, Anthony," he said as he placed his hand on Anthony's thigh and squeezed. "Are you sure I can't persuade you to join me for just one drink?"

With the feel of Kowalski's hand on his thigh, Anthony's eyes were opened. This was no friendly mentor taking him under his wing. Kowalski was making a pass at him. Anthony could feel his heart beating rapidly within his chest. He didn't know how to handle it, but he knew he had to get out of the car immediately. He looked past the Monsignor out the window; they were just crossing the Tiber river, heading toward the Vatican. There in the distance, the imposing dome of St. Peter's Basilica glowed against the darkening sky. The irony of his present circumstance was not lost on him. Then Anthony shifted in his seat so that Kowalski's hand fell from his leg.

"Oh, Monsignor, it was incredibly generous of you to treat me to dinner, and I have so enjoyed our evening together, but I must get back to the seminary. I am sure that they will be wondering where I am after all this time. We are so close to NAC; I can get out right here. It's right up the hill, and I could use a walk after such a big meal."

"No, no, we will drive you to the gates. There is no need to walk," Kowalski said, showing a slight annoyance.

"Anthony, my son, there will be many doors opened to you should you make the correct choices during your time here in Rome. Keep your sights on the prize and what you envision for your career. Look for people who might help in achieving those goals." The Monsignor said, looking at Anthony. "In my position, I can be the gatekeeper to many unimaginable opportunities for you."

"Yes, Monsignor, I truly appreciate your guidance. This evening has opened my eyes," he said honestly.

"You have my card. I hope to hear from you soon, Anthony. You will call me, yes?" he asked.

"Of course, Monsignor. Thank you again for dinner; I really enjoyed talking with you." The limousine pulled up beside the cast iron gate of the North American College, and Anthony hopped out as quickly as he could. With a disingenuous smile, he turned back and gave Kowalski a wave as he dashed through the doors.

Once in his room, he sat on his bed and held his head in his hands. *What just happened? It started so innocently. Was he actually trying to get into my pants? That's absurd.* The more he thought about his encounter with Kowalski, the angrier Anthony became. His eyes had been opened, all right. The guy was a chicken hawk who preyed upon powerless young seminarians.

He began to accept the fact that there was nothing innocent about Kowalski's intentions. The Monsignor obviously saw Anthony as an easy target and lured him into a false sense of security. Anthony had felt honored, special. The Pope's secretary remembered him and wanted to spend time with him. Kowalski was one step away from the Pope. It was clear that Anthony had misunderstood his intentions. *How could I have been so naïve?* he thought. *The signs were all there, so why didn't I see it coming?*

He had been here before; the seduction and the manipulation were all so familiar. He thought that he had put all of it behind him, but memories of a similar encounter flooded Anthony's mind.

Chapter Twenty-Five
Misplaced Trust

Anthony could picture every detail of that night. The day before, he had gotten into a car accident while driving to a high school party. Working a full-time summer job at a local department store, Anthony was assigned to the closing shift that Friday. By the time he got his department in order and got on the road, it was already past 11:00. It had been a long day, and Anthony was tired, but there was no way he was going to miss out on the party. He had been working forty hours a week all summer long, including Fridays and Saturdays. He rarely saw his friends, so he was determined to have some fun. Drew's house was on the north side of town, where all the rich people lived. Grand colonial houses were perched on vast lawns with tree-lined driveways. Drew's parents had a luxurious pool and an expansive game room. It promised to be a great party.

Though he'd been to Drew's house before, he never paid much attention to the directions. Not being in the driver's seat, there was no need. Anthony had gotten his driver's license only three months before and was still unsure of the roads.

As he entered the neighborhood, he was having trouble remembering where to turn. He could picture it in mind, but the streets all looked the same to him. Anthony just needed to keep his eyes peeled for his landmark–if he passed the little fountain, he had gone too far. Grand maple and oak trees obscured the streetlamps, which made it difficult to read the signs.

As he passed by a familiar street on the left, Anthony craned his head to read the street sign. *Yes, that was it, h*is mind registered just as the sound of crashing metal and skidding tires resonated through his ears. He felt the initial impact when his head hit the steering wheel and snapped backward. Then the car spun around, and when it finally came to a halt, his entire body was shaking. Anthony had drifted over the double yellow line into oncoming traffic. Luckily, his front end had smashed into the rear door of a car traveling in the opposite direction. Had his Ford Maverick drifted a moment sooner, it would have been a head-on collision.

After a few minutes of stunned confusion, he focused his eyes and reached for the handle of the car door. He put his feet on the asphalt and rose slowly, but his legs were shaking so much that he fell back into his seat. Anthony looked up to see a man walking over from the car he hit. He was waving his arms and cursing at him. "What the hell were you thinking, you dumb ass? You drove right into me!"

"I, I'm s-sorry, sir. It's all my fault. I lost my way, and…" Anthony stuttered.

"You're damned right, it's your fault. Give me your insurance card and your license."

"Yes, Sir. I am so sorry. Here it is."

"How old are you? You look like you're thirteen. Was this your first time out?"

"No, I'm sixteen years old. I'm sorry, I didn't see you," Anthony responded pathetically. His parents were going to kill him. How were they going to pay for this? His dad had been out of work for months and was struggling to get by. This was the last thing his parents needed. By the time they had exchanged information, the police had arrived.

Since nobody was hurt and they had established the fault, they simply took statements from both drivers and let them go. Anthony was a wreck. *How can I tell mom that I crashed her car?* he thought. *How is she going to get to work on Monday?*

The following day unfolded as he expected. His parents didn't yell or punish him. They knew he hadn't been drinking and that he was a responsible son who was working throughout the summer to help with expenses. Still, they were distraught. Insurance would pay for most of the damage, but the deductible would have to be paid out of pocket. With Anthony's dad laid off from work, every penny counted. To make matters worse, it would leave them with only one car for weeks while the repairs were being done. Since it was a Saturday, Anthony and his parents kept to their routine and went to the 5:00 Mass. Afterward, they walked down the aisle and out to the car.

Anthony gathered his courage and asked his dad. "Do you mind if I drive you guys home? I want to come back to see if Father Smith is around."

"That's a good idea, son. I am sure that a good talk with Father will do you good. Just drop us off," his mother responded as she gently placed her hand on his shoulder.

***

Not long after, Anthony stood at the door of St. Andrew's rectory. He had to talk to Father Smith about how he ruined his parents' lives. That was dramatic, but he couldn't help but feel that way. His parents were always worried about finances, and the car accident had made everything worse. When the receptionist answered the door, she greeted him warmly.

"Hi, Anthony, what are you doing here on a Saturday night? Don't you have plans with Paul this evening? You two are always together," she said.

"No, not tonight. I've had a rough couple of days. Is Father Smith around? I just need a shoulder to lean on."

"I think so. Come on in and have a seat. I'll buzz his room." Moments later, Father Smith appeared. He had heard about the car accident and approached him with open arms.

"Anthony, how are you? You look like you're carrying the weight of the world on those broad shoulders."

"It sure feels like it right now. Do you have some time to talk?" Anthony asked.

"Sure, come up to my suite. You know the way," Father Smith said with a gentle smile.

Fr. Smith had a spacious suite of rooms on the second floor of the rectory. There was a bedroom with a private bath off to the side, and a spacious living room with a couch, chairs, and a cherry wood desk facing the window. This was not the first time Anthony had been in Father Smith's suite. He and his buddy, Paul, would often hang out there after their weekly youth group meetings. There were always snacks, and although they were under the drinking age of eighteen, Fr. Smith would always offer them wine or beer.

"Have a seat. How about a beer? It looks like you could use one," Father Smith offered.

"Yeah, sure. Thanks, Father."

"So, tell me, Anthony," Father Smith said as he sat on the couch beside him and handed him the beer. "What's on your mind?" Not wanting to show his emotions, Anthony was startled as his eyes brimmed with tears.

He took a huge swig of the beer hoping to ward them off. Although he was close to Father Smith, he didn't want to cry in front of him. But his efforts were useless. As soon as he began to share the jumbled thoughts and fears within him, tears poured from his eyes. Soon he was sobbing, and Father Smith pulled him into his arms. He was uncomfortable with Smith's physical display, but he let go and allowed the priest to console him.

"It was all my fault," he cried. "I should have kept my eyes on the road. mom has no way to get to work, and dad has no job. I should have gone straight home after my long shift at the store. I was already exhausted. But no, I had to go to the party. I can't believe how irresponsible I was."

"Come on, now, Anthony. You made a mistake. You had a car accident. It happens to everyone."

"No, Father, I just made everything harder for them. They work so hard, and I just screwed it all up," he said as he shook his head, trying to regain his composure.

"Anthony, your parents are going to be fine. I know it hurts, but believe me, this will all work itself out. They'll be fine, and so will you," Father Smith comforted him as he rubbed his back.

Anthony cried in his arms for several more minutes. The tears were abating, and he let his forehead rest on Father Smith's shoulder. That was when he noticed Smith's hands. He draped his left arm over his shoulder, massaging his neck, while his right hand was rubbing Anthony's thigh. It seemed odd, and perhaps inappropriate, but it felt good. Little by little, Smith's hand inched upward toward his crotch, and Anthony could feel himself becoming aroused. It was as if there was a tempest brewing within his body. *Why am I getting excited?* he thought. *Oh, God, that feels good.* No one had ever touched him down there. Somewhere in the back of his mind, he knew he should make him stop, but he was losing control. Gradually, Father Smith became bolder as his hand engulfed and squeezed Anthony's hardening sex. Giving in to his feelings, Anthony let out a weak moan.

"You like that, don't you?" Smith said seductively. Anthony didn't know how to respond; he was so confused. *What is happening?*

"Ughhh," he groaned, "yeah, I think so."

"Well, if you're not sure if you like it, just look down here," Smith said as he unzipped Anthony's pants and pulled out his erect penis, beginning to stroke it.

Anthony closed his eyes, let out a gasp, and savored these new sensations. Father Smith's hand was rough on his smooth skin, and it felt good. His ministrations became more urgent as he tugged and pulled. Anthony couldn't hold back any longer. He felt his body tighten and shake.

"That's it, just let it go, Anthony. Give in to it," Father Smith encouraged, his breathe becoming ragged as his own climax built.

All at once, it was over. Anthony's body shook when he realized what had just happened and attempted to cover himself up. He was deeply ashamed and wanted nothing more than to run right out of that room. But Fr. Smith hugged him tightly and brought his face close to his. Before he understood what was happening, Smith's lips touched his and forced his tongue into his mouth. The stale taste of alcohol on his foul breath repulsed Anthony.

Repulsed, he pulled away and ran to the bathroom. "I, I'm sorry. I have to pee," Anthony said as he escaped his grip. Father Smith sat on the couch, reveling in the afterglow of their encounter.

In the bathroom, Anthony cleaned himself up and leaned his head against the mirror. A whole series of thoughts swam through his mind in rapid succession. None of them were good. *What had he done? How could he have let that happen? How can I face Fr. Smith again?* Anthony blamed himself for what had just transpired.

Did this mean he was gay? If he hadn't had all these impure thoughts about other guys, none of this would have happened. He was ashamed of himself and could barely look at his reflection in the mirror. After gathering up his courage, he took a deep breath and walked back into the sitting room. Father Smith was sitting in the same spot, sipping his scotch. He hadn't moved.

Anthony walked over and took a seat a couple of feet away. From there, he could see the wet spot on the front of Smith's tan polyester slacks. He was immediately sickened by the sight of him. *He didn't even bother to change!* He thought.

All he wanted to do at that moment was get out of there. But Anthony couldn't figure a way to exit gracefully. He was a priest, after all – Anthony had to show him respect. But Anthony was so ashamed of himself, and he longed to be alone. Anthony raised his eyes to look at Father Smith, who returned his gaze with a satisfied grin.

He was going on about something completely pointless. When Anthony couldn't take it any longer, he stood abruptly. "Thank you so much for letting me cry on your shoulder, Father Smith. Sorry to leave so quickly, but I really have to go. My parents are expecting me, and right now, they are stranded at home without a car."

"Of course, of course. You are welcome to visit me anytime. Are you sure you're okay to drive?" Father Smith asked perfunctorily as he rose to kiss him goodbye.

Anthony felt his revulsion build and backed away from Father Smith's embrace, turning his head away from the kiss. "Yeah, I only had one beer, Father. I'll be fine. Thanks again," Anthony said as he quickly opened the door and fled.

"Call me if you need to talk again, Anthony," he called down the corridor. "You know where to find me."

Anthony was already down the hall and waved back at Smith as he spoke. Once in the car, he leaned his head against the steering wheel, unable to move.

What was I thinking? How could I let that happen? He's a priest, for God's sake! Once again, thoughts were swirling in his head. He'd been struggling with his same-sex attraction for a while now. He knew it was sinful, but he thought he had control over his desires. Clearly, what just happened with Fr. Smith showed it was getting out of hand. He had fantasized about other guys before but never dreamed of acting on it. If he hadn't had all those sexual thoughts about other guys, nothing would have happened.

It's all my fault! He would never have done that if I wasn't gay. But I can't be gay, I just can't! His self-loathing had begun in earnest; never mind that Anthony was a minor, whereas Father Smith was a 40-year-old man.

It was a clear abuse of trust and power, but Anthony couldn't see beyond his own guilt. *Nothing would have happened if I was a normal teenager. Why can't I be attracted to girls?* he thought. When he walked into the house, his mother smiled and asked, "How is Father Smith? Did you have a pleasant talk?"

"Yeah, he's, he's good," Anthony said with his head hanging as he swiftly made his way to his bedroom.

He needed to be alone. Once inside, he curled up into the fetal position on his twin bed and cried. Thank God his brothers weren't home – at least he had a moment of privacy. Images of his encounter with Father Smith continued to reappear as he sobbed into his pillow. He felt worse than he had before. Seeking his comfort was a mistake.

When he pictured Father Smith's hand creeping up his thigh, and onto his hardening penis, Anthony became aroused once again. His desire for the touch of another guy surged through him. It seemed stronger than his aversion for what had just happened with his parish priest. *What is wrong with me?* he thought. *I'm disgusting!*

Chapter Twenty-Six
Self-loathing & Confusion

Days went by, bringing further feelings of self-hatred. Anthony could not concentrate on anything at work in the department store. Handling the automotive section, they relied on him to find the correct parts for the various cars the customers owned. Time and again, Anthony pulled the incorrect part, and angry customers would complain to the manager when they returned. The manager chided him about his absent-mindedness several times during the week that followed.

"Anthony, what's wrong with you? This is the third time that you've pulled the incorrect part for a customer. You're better than this. Pull it together," he admonished.

"Sorry, Mr. Stanton, I haven't been sleeping all that well. I'll do better," Anthony replied.

"You had better — unless you'd like to go back to working in the stockroom." His distraction was getting out of hand. Anthony knew he had to talk this out.

Father Smith and his family had a long-standing relationship, and he knew he could trust him. Smith had attended many family dinners — he and his father always ended up drinking together. Anthony resolved to make another appointment with Father Smith to apologize and confess his sins. He had to figure out a way to rid himself of his impure thoughts and be absolved of his evil actions. He was sure that Father Smith would understand.

It was Saturday evening — Father Smith had just finished saying the 5:00 Mass and suggested that he and Anthony grab dinner at a nearby steakhouse. The Peppermill was an upscale restaurant only a few miles north of St. Andrew's, and they welcomed Father Smith warmly. Anthony was not accustomed to fancy restaurants. He came from a working-class family that lived paycheck to paycheck.

Anthony's father had never taken the family out to dinner — mom's cooking was better than anything you could get in a restaurant, anyway. But Father Smith had taken Anthony and his best friend, Paul, out to dinner frequently. He taught them which fork to use, how to order, and to place the cloth napkin on your lap.

Father Smith was animated throughout dinner — he rambled on about his recent vacation to Vermont, the beautiful mountains, and the peaceful lakes. All the while, the server kept him supplied with his favorite drink — vodka gimlet. The more he drank, the happier he got. Father Smith always ordered wine or beer for Anthony and Paul when they were out together. The wait-staff never questioned him about whether they were of legal drinking age. They were with Father, so it must have been okay.

As the meal drew to a close, Anthony, having drunk enough wine, gathered his courage to bring up his feelings about their encounter the previous weekend.

"Father Smith, can we talk about last week? I don't understand what it all means and…"

"Not here, Anthony. Let's go back to the rectory, and we can discuss it in private." His words came out more sharply than expected, and Anthony could feel himself flush red. His shame washed over him like icy water, and he lowered his eyes to stare at the napkin in his lap. *I AM disgusting. He won't even talk to me about it.*

It was quiet at the rectory as the two of them made their way to Smith's rooms. Father Smith walked over to his liquor cabinet and poured himself another drink.

"Would you like a beer, Anthony?"

"No, I think I've had enough. Maybe a glass of water." Once again, Anthony found himself on the couch with Father Smith. But he made sure that they were sitting a foot or two away from each other.

"Now then, what's going on in that head of yours, Anthony? You seem upset."

"Father, I just don't understand what is happening with me. I keep thinking about what happened last weekend, and I feel really awful," Anthony said.

"You mean the car accident? Look, your parents are going to be fine. You made a mistake. Their insurance will pay for the repairs. These things happen all the time."

"No, not that. What happened here, on the couch. You know, when I came to talk to you. I keep playing that scene over in my mind, and I just don't understand."

"Oh, I see. Well, let me ask you. What do you feel when you think back on it?"

"I don't know, I feel dirty. I picture it, and I know it's wrong..." Anthony's voice trailed off as he lowered his head.

"But what? What do you feel when you remember?"

"This is really difficult to say aloud."

"Try, Anthony. You can trust me. How do you feel when you think about what we did?"

"I get excited again, I know I shouldn't, but I do."

"Come here, closer. You know you are safe with me, right?" Anthony nodded his head, and although he knew he shouldn't, he moved next to him on the couch. Smith put his drink down on the table and put his arm around Anthony. Smith drew him in so that their bodies were touching.

"So, you liked it when I touched you?"

"I guess so, it's just that — I don't know." He couldn't seem to articulate his shame and confusion.

"You're excited right now, aren't you?" Smith asked as he placed his hand on Anthony's crotch and squeezed his hardening cock. Anthony let out a muffled cry, and his body grew rigid. *What was happening? Why was he letting this happen again?* He resolved to stop it, but Smith was relentless. In a flash, he unbuttoned Anthony's jeans, unzipped them, and pulled out his cock.

"Feels good, doesn't it?"

"Ughhh, yeah," Anthony moaned as he pushed his pelvis into Father Smith's hand. All thoughts of sinfulness or self-loathing were gone from his mind. All he could think about were all the new sensations he was experiencing.

Before their first encounter, no one had ever sexually touched him, and he was lost in his lust. Then Father Smith grabbed Anthony's hand and placed it on his own hardening penis. "Go ahead, touch it. Yeah, that's it. Pull it out of my pants." Anthony did as he was told, and when he touched Father Smith's bare flesh, he felt his stomach turn. It was small and ugly, so he looked away. This was not right. Why is this happening again? Just then, Father Smith pulled at him with force, and Anthony could feel his orgasm building. He couldn't hold back, and his body spasmed with orgasm. Just then, Smith ejaculated all over Anthony's hand. In disgust, Anthony looked down to see the sticky semen dripping from his fingers.

He jumped up and ran to the bathroom to wash it all off. He could barely stomach the sight of his own, let alone Father Smith's. This just sent him over the edge; it was way more than he could handle. Under the scalding water, he rubbed and rubbed his hands as hard as he could. Though the semen had been washed off long before, Anthony rubbed harder. He could feel the tears building behind his eyes and was at once disgusted and excited. It felt good when Father Smith touched him, but as soon as it was over, he regretted having let it happen. "Are you all right in there?" he heard Smith ask.

"Yeah, yeah, I'll be right out," Anthony said, trying to make his voice sound even. He opened the bathroom door and headed back to the couch. Father Smith had zipped up his own pants and patted the seat next to him. "Come here, Anthony. What's wrong? Talk to me."

"I'm sorry, Father. I just couldn't help it. Your hand felt so good." Anthony said.

"Why are you sorry? It felt good to me, too."

"But isn't this wrong? Everything the Church has taught me tells me that what just happened is a sin."

"Look, Anthony, I can't say, 'If it feels good, do it,' but you and I are close, right? We were just expressing our affection for each other. There's nothing wrong with that, is there?"

"I guess not... But I still feel bad, like I did something dirty."

"Hey, it's okay. You liked it. It felt good. Trust me, Anthony, you are not going to hell just because we shared something special." Anthony lowered his head in shame once again. "Look at me, Anthony. Why would I lie to you? We have a connection. It's going to be okay. Trust me."

"But Father, none of this makes any sense to me," Anthony replied. "I'm sorry."

"I believe that you've been hiding from yourself for years now. I've seen how you worship your best buddy, Paul. Don't you think you might be in love with him?"

"What? In love with Paul? That's just crazy!" Anthony said defensively.

"Maybe, but I do see you checking out all the boys in the youth group, and you haven't had a significant relationship with any of the girls. What do you think that means?" Father Smith asked.

"I don't know. I have always admired guys who are more athletic than me. That doesn't mean anything."

"Alright, then. Hear me out. I think you may be gay, and there is nothing wrong with that. But the world makes us feel that we are evil. Did you know that during the time of Socrates, teachers often had young boys as companions? There was nothing wrong with it then, and there is nothing wrong with it now."

Anthony sat, staring out the window into the night. He was incredibly uncomfortable with the conversation. Perhaps being gay was fine during the time of ancient Greece, but that was literally ancient history. Besides, Smith was at least twenty years older than him. Even if he was gay, he wouldn't want to be with someone that old. As much as Anthony looked up to Father Smith, he knew the guy drank way too much. He had always been a little too "handsy," but he never gave it much thought.

"Are you with me here, Anthony?"

"Yeah, yeah, I was just thinking," he responded, startled from his catatonic state.

"Anthony, what I'm saying is that I can help you come to terms with your sexuality. I can be the older and wiser teacher that ushers you through it, and we can have a little fun at the same time," Father Smith said, raising his eyebrows suggestively at Anthony.

"I don't know, Father. It just doesn't feel right."

"Well, your body certainly liked the way if felt. You got hard because you were excited. If you weren't gay, nothing would have happened. Come on now. Our little encounters have been a bright respite from my lonely days, Anthony. You mean a great deal to me."

Anthony didn't know how to respond to Father Smith. He wanted it to stop, but the struggle with his sexuality made him doubt himself. Somehow, Smith's words made him feel responsible for it all. Once again, he felt his shame wash over him.

In the weeks that followed, they had gotten together a couple more times. Anthony tried to talk to Father Smith about what they were doing, but he was rebuffed or ignored.

Every time they got together, Anthony was determined to keep his distance so that they could talk. Smith, however, became more aggressive, and sixteen-year-old Anthony gave into his confusion. The boy felt worse after each encounter, and his guilt continued to heighten. His revulsion for Father Smith grew more intense along with his own self-loathing. Before the end of that summer, Anthony missed many planned dates with Father Smith.

His buddy, Paul, started ragging on him for being late for every youth group event that Smith led. But Anthony didn't care. He knew he could not take the chance of being alone with Father Smith, because when they were, he seemed to have no power to stop the inevitable sexual encounter. Anthony needed to avoid him altogether. He stopped attending the parish youth group and made sure that he only went to Mass said by the other priests. All the while, Anthony blamed himself for every indiscretion.

If he didn't have these feelings for other guys, none of this would have happened. Somehow, he had to overcome his attraction to guys. Being gay was not an option. Besides, he had nothing in common with the images of gay men he saw on TV. He repressed any sexual thought of other boys. Anthony convinced himself that he was straight. He was going to be a typical straight teenager if it killed him. By the time his senior year of high school began, Anthony resolved to change his behavior. He had always had comfortable friendships with girls – a little flirting came naturally to him. Although he never had sex with his dates, Anthony enjoyed the initial period of infatuation and excitement. But he would inevitably get bored and move on.

His numerous girlfriends became a running joke with his friends. When he was with the guys, his best friend would go on about him. "Anthony is a stud," Paul would joke.

"He's always got a new girlfriend and a flock of them trailing him around." Turning to Anthony, he'd say, "You leave a wake of broken hearts, Anthony."

In his heart, Anthony knew that his newfound heterosexuality wouldn't last. However, his desire to become a priest would mitigate the need to carry his relationships very far. Once he took a vow of celibacy, it wouldn't matter who he was attracted to – problem solved.

Chapter Twenty-Seven
Consolation

Anthony had buried the memories of Father Smith deep in his psyche. Since his encounter with that priest back in high school, he had come to terms with his attraction for other men. But his experience with Father Smith continued to haunt him. He couldn't believe that here in Rome, where his dream of the priesthood was finally coming to fruition, he would encounter the same predatory behavior – from the Pope's secretary no less.

A familiar sense of shame washed over Anthony. It was too much to deal with it alone. During his first week in Rome, his friendship with Kevin developed rapidly.

Kevin was a regular guy and seemed to have a level head on his shoulders. Kevin also seemed protective of Anthony, since he was so new to seminary life. Anthony had to admit that he was more than a little naïve regarding acceptable behavior. He had already come to rely on Kevin. Even though Anthony felt ashamed by what had just happened with the Monsignor, he needed to talk to someone about it. By that time, they had already passed the superficial stage of friendship and were sharing their fears and dreams about the unique experiences at NAC. If there was anyone here that he could trust, it was Kevin.

Anthony pulled himself together, walked down the hallway, and climbed up the grand marble staircase to the fourth floor. It was still relatively early; he knew Kevin would always be up. He knocked quietly on his door so as not to create a disturbance throughout the echoing hallway. "Hey, buddy, where have you been all evening? I missed you at dinner," Kevin said with a big smile lighting his face.

"You wouldn't believe what happened to me tonight," Anthony said as he walked into the room and closed the door behind him. "Remember that monsignor who followed the pope at the audience last week?"

"Yeah, John Paul's personal secretary. What about him?" Kevin asked.

"Well, I was walking back from St. Peter Square this afternoon, and his limousine pulled up. He rolled down the window and asked me to take a ride with him. I thought it was so cool that the Pope's secretary invited me to serve Mass with him."

"Holy crap!" he shouted. "You didn't go with him, did you?"

"I told him that I had to get back for evening prayer, but he insisted. Plus, I thought it was really cool that he wanted to spend time with me. After all, he's John Paul's personal secretary. I felt honored."

"Don't you know his reputation?"

"Hold on, what do you mean? What reputation?"

"After your blessed encounter with the Pope last week, I overheard some of the older guys talking about his secretary – that he was a lecherous chicken hawk. Apparently, he was chatting up several new men."

In fact, Monsignor Kowalski's reputation was more than idle gossip. The gay subculture of Roman priests was alive and active. Kowalski was often seen at the *Angelo Azzuro,* a gay bar in the bohemian neighborhood of Rome. On the same side of the Tiber River and an easy walk from Vatican City was a neighborhood called *Trastevere.* Off the beaten path and far from touristic Rome, it was home to an artsy crowd. The young people of Rome flocked to the *piazza* to connect with their friends. Some Americans compared it to Greenwich Village in New York City. The *Angelo Azzuro* was a notorious gathering place for gay priests. Young and old frequented the bar to escape their loneliness and find comfort in random hookups, sometimes with other clerics, other times with men from the local community. Even a few bolder seminarians from NAC found their way into the bar.

Kevin's revelation shocked Anthony.

"No way! Why didn't you tell me?" Anthony asked.

"It didn't really seem to matter. I didn't realize that you had spoken to Kowalski."

"He followed directly behind John Paul and gave me his card. When his limo pulled up beside me tonight, I couldn't believe he remembered me," he said, earnestly.

"Yeah, well, there's a reason he remembered you," Kevin responded dryly.

"What do you mean? Why would he remember me?" Anthony asked innocently.

"Why would he remember you? Look at yourself. You're like an ad from a muscle magazine and wearing those shorts that show off those legs – I'm sure he couldn't resist you. The guys said he goes after all the young new men – he can't resist the fresh crop of seminarians."

Anthony blushed. He wasn't expecting Kevin's sexually charged compliments.

"Seriously? Who told you that?" Anthony asked. "Besides, he's the Pope's secretary. How can he get away with going after young guys? Wouldn't everybody notice?"

"Look, if I've learned one thing during our first few weeks, it's that everybody around here is doing something inappropriate," he replied. "I guess someone with that level power and influence can get away with almost anything."

"Listen to you being all-wise and knowing. I suppose your four years as a seminarian taught you more than philosophy," Anthony said. "I suppose I shouldn't be surprised. But all I did was get in the car with him to serve Mass at the monastery. By that time, it was too late to have dinner back here, we went out to a trattoria. Felt like a perfectly honorable thing to do. I thought nothing of it."

"Sounds innocent enough. So, what changed?" Kevin asked.

"I don't know, it's hard to describe. It just began to feel uncomfortable. Kowalski started asking a lot of personal questions like: Did I ever have a girlfriend? Did I ever get lonely? Had I ever had sex with a girl? It seemed as if he had nefarious intentions. At first, he wouldn't let me get out of the car. He kept inviting me for an after-dinner drink in his apartment. I told him I had to get back to NAC to study, but he wouldn't let it go." Anthony explained. "Then he put his hand on my thigh and began to rub it. When I continued to protest about my need to get back to NAC, he became more aggressive. His hand went all the way up to my crotch."

"Oh my God, Anthony, that's insane. What did you do?" Kevin asked, worried, wanting to know more.

"I moved over as far as I could toward the opposite window. His lecherous hand fell off, and I just told the perv I couldn't stay out any longer. He got really agitated and bitter," Anthony replied.

"Man, you dodged a bullet. But now he knows who you are. He'll definitely try to see you again. You probably shouldn't have any more contact with him."

"Obviously, but what do I do if he calls? He was relentless. He insisted I call him. What if he won't stop?"

"Hell, I don't know. This is uncharted territory for me, as well. He can't force you to see him, and I don't see how you could get in trouble by not responding to him. Who is he going to complain to?"

"You've got a point there. But, man, it creeped me out. I feel so dirty like it was my fault."

"Yeah, well, that's how it works, doesn't it? The victim always feels like it's their fault. One of these days, I'll tell you my story... But that requires a few glasses of wine first." At that revelation, Anthony looked directly into Kevin's eyes. He could tell there was some painful history there, and that he could relate.

"Look, I know it's difficult, but you have to get beyond blaming yourself and understand that he's the one at fault," Kevin continued. "The guy's a perverted fool who preys on men more than half his age."

Tears welled up in Anthony's eyes as he lowered his head and turned away from Kevin. He couldn't help it. All the repressed emotions from his abusive high school encounter were bubbling to the surface. He and Kevin had just become friends, and he didn't want him to think he was weak or immature. Anthony was already self-conscious regarding his apparent naïveté. As an experienced seminarian, Kevin frequently gave advice to Anthony about seminary life and its perils. Anthony felt like he was reinforcing his naïve or foolish image.

"Hey, Anthony, come here," Kevin said as he reached out his arms and pulled Anthony into a hug. "I'm sorry this happened to you. You have to believe that it's not your fault," he said.

"I don't know about that. I'm not a kid anymore," Anthony said. "I'm responsible for my own actions. To be honest, this isn't the first time something like this has happened to me. What is it about me that attracts pedophiles?"

"Come on, Anthony, look in the mirror. It's not that you attract predators; you attract everybody. You're handsome, gregarious, and you exude kindness. You're like an Italian gymnast wrapped in a preppy package. You're a sexy guy. Everyone is attracted to you, don't you see that?"

"Get out of here. People around here don't even notice me. It's not like when *you* enter a room. You command the audience," Anthony said.

"Yeah, that's right, there's nothing as attractive as a nerdy intellectual," Kevin scoffed. "But, seriously, Anthony, you're a handsome guy, and the fact that you don't realize that makes you even more attractive."

"Get out! Seriously, Kevin, I wish I could express myself the way you do. You run circles around everyone in our class, especially me," Anthony said.

"Like I said, people on the streets don't turn their heads for intellect. You, on the other hand, turn heads all the time, and you're completely unaware of it. In fact, that's what attracted me from the very first moment I saw you."

Anthony lifted his head, and once again looked in Kevin's eyes. *What is he saying? Is Kevin saying he's attracted to me?* He knew he shouldn't press him on it, but he had to know. "What do you mean, Kevin?"

"Nothing," Kevin said, back peddling. "I mean, I'm glad we've become friends. It's just that it can be very lonely so far away from home, and you've been by my side from the start. We're lucky to have connected so quickly," Kevin said, evading the genuine answer to his question.

"Yeah, I know what you mean. There is so much to get used to, and we've only been here for a couple of weeks." Although he knew he shouldn't be, Anthony was disappointed in Kevin's answer.

"I'm sure we'll be too busy to feel homesick once classes start," Kevin responded. After a moment of silence, he said, "Hey, it's getting late. We should probably get some sleep."

"Kevin," Anthony said, reaching out to touch his shoulder, "I already feel insecure here at NAC, but I needed to work through what happened to me tonight. You were the first person I thought of. I am so grateful to have a friend like you. Thank you." They embraced each other affectionately, and Anthony made his way down to his room.

As he laid in bed that night, his mind was swimming – scenes from his encounter with Kowalski played over and over again. Talking it through with Kevin had helped. His feelings of shame and guilt had abated somewhat, but in their place were thoughts of Kevin.

Chapter Twenty-Eight
Disillusionment

Thinking back to those first weeks with Kevin, Anthony understood that his candor and Kevin's compassion was what brought them together. They had both let down their guards and opened their hearts to one another. The intimacy that developed between them was natural and loving. Their relationship had been the one stable thing since coming to Rome. But he wasn't sure it was enough to keep him there. Anthony felt as if his dream of becoming a priest was slipping away.

The historical significance and grandeur of the Vatican didn't sparkle as it had back in September. The shine was tarnished with the reality of real life. His idealism was no match for the constant blows coming at him from within the Church. With all devastating memories flooding back, Anthony had little patience for the constant drama at NAC.

He had trouble getting past the gossip and the politics of life in the Vatican. The constant back-biting of both the faculty and seminarians was chipping away at his faith. Who really cared if seminarians wore clerical garb? And why are so many guys sleeping with each other?

Aren't they supposed to be preparing for a celibate life? What's the deal with Latin? Why would anyone want to return to the Latin Mass? No one pays attention at Mass *now*; how much worse would it be if it was said in a language no one understood? But the passionate arguments raged on all sides. What did any of it matter? And what did any of it have to do with the Gospels or priesthood – or God, for that matter?

In addition to the relentless arguing, Anthony couldn't seem to get beyond the pointless rules and regulations. He reasoned that he was an adult who could make rational decisions. Why should everything have to be approved by the rector? He felt belittled at the seminary – treated as if he were a child. Just a year ago, as a college student, he was hailed and respected as a leader, but at NAC, it seemed that they were not recognized as adults. Somehow, they were all reduced to their adolescent selves, continually seeking approval and permission. When the desired response was not forthcoming, they would rebel. Anthony hated being labeled as a rabble-rouser whenever he believed in fighting for a cause. Each time he spoke up, he could see eyes rolling as if to say, "There he goes again. What is it this time?" He felt infantilized and resented the faculty for putting him and the others in that position.

Anthony felt so distant from the experience of the Church back at Fordham University. The Jesuits there gave him a more familiar faith, one where he could be himself, without any of the trappings of clericalism.

The liturgies around the coffee table in the Campus Ministry house were intimate and personal. He missed the retreats where people could share their burdens without fear of judgment or reprisal. He missed having an ordinary relationship with God.

He used to dream of his ordination here in Rome and his first Mass at one of the chapels at St. Peter's Basilica. Visions of rising incense and pews filled with admiring friends and family permeated his imagination. There was invariably a sense of majesty and glory that encompassed his dreams. The new men were told from the very beginning that they were the chosen ones.

They were exceptional, the future princes of the Church. Now, as he knelt before the Blessed Sacrament in the dark chapel at NAC, he felt nothing. Gone were his dreams, gone were images of his priesthood, gone was his hope. In return for his prayers, there was silence. Where was the God to whom he had entrusted his life? Why did He give no counsel or comfort in this dark night of the soul?

Anthony felt numb. He was simply going through the motions, hoping that by doing so, his deep faith would return. He attended daily Mass, as well as morning and evening prayer. Anthony was diligent in his classes and studied every day. But he felt nothing, not even when he received the Holy Eucharist, which was supposed to be the most sacred of moments. How could he feel nothing when taking the actual body of Christ into his mouth? What had happened to him in such a short time?

Anthony had shed many tears over the last few months. He cried for his family when each birthday or holiday came – his heart ached for them. He cried for Kevin as they forged their way through their undefinable relationship. He cried for the Church and its archaic teaching regarding homosexuality. He lamented that he had to keep so much of himself hidden from his friends and faculty at NAC. How sad that, although he felt right with God about his sexuality, he could not be honest with his spiritual director or the faculty. Priestly formation should be completely honest and transparent. How else could they shepherd these men through their discernment process? Anthony understood enough to know that if he ever named the struggles with his sexual orientation, they would kick him out of the seminary. That would be the end of his dream of becoming a priest.

But on this day, on his knees before the tabernacle, there were no tears, there was no sadness, no anger. On this day, Anthony felt nothing.

After what seemed like hours, he stood, genuflected, and silently exited the chapel. Once in his room, he pulled out a sheet of NAC stationary with the coat of arms and the motto stamped across the top: *Firmum Est Cor Meum,* My Heart is Steadfast. He paused as he read those words in Latin. He never imagined a day when he would not feel steadfast in his faith. He felt the pang of that loss deep in his heart. He knew what he had to do. Even if he could not share his most intimate thoughts, indeed, the one person to whom he had entrusted his spiritual journey should know of this crisis of faith. Putting pen to paper, he began to write:

Dear Cardinal McGuire,

With a heavy heart, I seek your guidance. For as long as I can remember, I have heard the calling to become a priest. My deep faith has been the guiding force in my life during good times and bad. I was fortunate to have a family whose dedication to the Church and its ministry helped to form the man I am today. Further, Monsignor Joe Rossi, my uncle, has been my mentor and spiritual rock throughout my process of discernment.

However, during these months in Rome, I find myself in crisis. The foundation has dissolved beneath my feet as I stand before the altar of the Lord. The faith that was once rock-solid now feels like quicksand. I am drowning in gossip and fear as I sink deeper into the mud. All around me, I feel the darkness closing in on me. The bright light of my faith is nowhere to be found. At no time in my life have I ever felt that my soul was in mortal danger. Never would I have entertained the possibility of losing my faith. But I find myself facing that very fate.

I ask that you release me from my commitment to the North American College and allow me to return home. Perhaps with continued spiritual direction, I can pursue my studies at a seminary in the states. As my bishop and spiritual father, I seek your counsel and your help.

Yours in Christ,
Anthony Rossi

He folded the thin sheet and placed it into the airmail envelope. He licked the stamp bearing the image of the Vatican and affixed it on the feather-weight envelope. Then he walked down the Janiculum hill, toward St. Peter's Square. Standing in front of the mailboxes, Anthony paused to look up at the basilica with its beautiful dome.

The stately façade stood as a fortress of faith amid a sinful world. Its grandeur had always inspired him. Then he turned and gazed down to the grand colonnade topped with statues of the saints. They were arms that embraced the piazza and the people of God. But at that moment, Anthony felt no loving embrace. *What am I doing?* Anthony thought. *They're going to think I've lost my mind.* His heavy sigh was audible to those around him. A moment later, he inserted his letter into the mailbox and, in a cloud of uncertainty, walked back to NAC.

Chapter Twenty-Nine
One More Nail

By March, the second semester was in full swing. Anthony, Kevin, and Miguel had gotten into a productive rhythm with his classes. After his stellar achievement on his final exams, Anthony gained more respect from a number of his detractors. The buzz of wonderment swept through NAC when it came out that he earned three perfect ten scores. No one received tens. With such stellar results, the faculty and his classmates took a harder look at Anthony, and he gained more respect for his academic prowess. Miguel continued to lead seminars on Vatican II, with Anthony at his right hand. The elusive Seth, Miguel's fellow Texan, came to every meeting, but Miguel wasn't sure if he was supporting him or reporting him. Seth hung back one evening to chat. He hoped to get Miguel to listen to reason, but, he didn't want to implicate himself or appear to be sympathetic to his cause. Seth made sure to attend meetings, casual or formal, held by both camps.

"Seth, we haven't spent much time together since we've been here. Did you enjoy the discussion tonight?" Miguel asked directly.

"Your sessions are always thought-provoking. You certainly know your stuff," Seth replied noncommittally.

"Well, I know you avoid conflict, so I appreciate that you've been coming," Miguel said candidly.

"Sure, we're brother Texans. We have to stick together. I just wanted to say that you might want to be more careful," Seth replied to Miguel.

"Careful of what – stepping on toes?"

"Well, yes. You're getting a reputation here, and I don't want you to get hurt," Seth admitted honestly.

"Look, I get it. But that horse has already left the barn. I am who I am. Toning down my rhetoric now is not going to change anyone's opinion of me."

"I get that, but I worry for you, Miguel."

"Thanks, Seth. Really – I do appreciate that."

But Seth's warning did nothing to change Miguel's approach. The tension among the new men continued to grow. His seminars only served to punctuate the chasm between the two camps such that they were hardly even cordial to one another. Stoney silence filled the air as they passed each other in the hall or refectory. The only exception was when a faculty member was nearby, and even then, they showed only a modicum of respect.

Miguel needed to reconnect with what initially drew him to the priesthood. He was determined to improve the experience at NAC. Each time they had a class meeting, Miguel suggested ways to bring the class together. Despite their distinct philosophical differences, he wanted them to foster a sense of community and support.

Miguel believed NAC should not be a factory that spits out priests at the end of four years. He posed the question each time they met, "How can we make our formation more personal? How can we reach out to each individual as they discern God's will in their lives?"

Miguel was becoming bolder in his challenges to the Church leadership under John Paul II and Cardinal Ratzinger.

His seminars were the talk of the seminary, and it was apparent that he was the voice of opposition. Kevin was continually telling him to be more diplomatic in his attack. But Miguel was adamant and pushed back even harder.

"Miguel, don't you see you are alienating the faculty? They barely look at you when they pass by."

"To hell with those hypocrites. They know I'm right, that's why they can't look me in the eye. I'm only stating what they don't have the balls to."

"That may be so, but you are a marked man. If you don't back off, they'll come for you, and let's face it. There is no way you'll win," Kevin reasoned.

"Let them come after me. I don't need those pompous asses to tell me what's right. This is a matter of principle for me. If I don't continue to fight, I won't be able to look at myself in the mirror. I have to act with integrity." Anthony knew Kevin was right and tried to soften Miguel's more challenging statements.

But he agreed with Miguel. Anthony believed that the traditionalist approach to the Church was what led to his own crisis of faith. The only way he could survive was to look at it as an academic exercise. If he could argue the teachings of Vatican II, perhaps his sense of mission would return, and with that, his faith.

But that was not in the cards. Three and a half weeks after Anthony wrote the Cardinal regarding his crisis of faith, he received a response. It was from the vocation director whose economy of words was striking. The letter read:

Dear Anthony,

Thank you for your letter dated February 28, 1983. We appreciate your honesty in expressing your difficulties at the North American College. Please understand that you are one of the few chosen to attend such an esteemed institution. Yours was a singular appointment that carries great honor and weight. With this in mind, the Cardinal directs you to stay at the North American College for the remainder of your theological studies.

Yours in Christ,
Monsignor Ryan

Anthony was shocked at the coldness of the letter. His perception of the Cardinal and Monsignor Ryan had been so positive since he entered the formation program nearly two years before. They always seemed to have his best interest in mind and were supportive custodians of his journey. He had poured his heart out in his letter to them. It was more than homesickness or being unhappy with the seminary. Although he did have many issues with NAC, his plea to them centered on his loss of faith, his spiritual crisis. He could not understand how they could ignore such an essential part of one's vocation.

Anthony needed to share the letter with Miguel and Kevin. But first, he had to explain why he had written it at all. His crisis of faith would not be shocking to either of them. They each shared their spiritual struggles and discussed how much NAC had rocked the foundation of their faith, but leaving NAC was another story. The three men had become steadfast friends. Each was there to support and challenge one another.

Then there was his relationship with Kevin. He was confident that he would feel betrayed by even the slightest mention of leaving Rome. It would be as if Anthony had chosen to abandon him. In the end, Anthony decided to share only part of his request. He was so broken by the response he received that he simply couldn't face Kevin's hurt feelings as well. He needed Kevin to be on his side.

Letter in hand, Anthony went to Kevin's room for their post *pranzo* drinks. Miguel was just pouring himself a Baileys and looked up at him and said, "What's the matter with you? You look like you just lost your best friend."

"Listen, guys; I have to tell you something. It's pretty serious," Anthony began.

"We're all ears, buddy," Kevin replied.

"We've talked endlessly about how our faith doesn't fit with the clericalism of Rome. Everything that's happened here at NAC seems counter to the Church I was raised in. It's no secret that we are all struggling," Anthony began.

"That's why I'm trying to bring us back to the teachings of Vatican II," Miguel said.

"Well, about a month ago, I wrote a letter to the Cardinal. I told him I was losing my faith. I shared some of my concerns and explained that I was in crisis."

Anthony described his dark night of the soul and how he felt entirely incapable of dealing with something as foundational as a loss of faith. They had discussed similar struggles with each other during the last few months. Anthony knew they understood, but he left out the part about his request to leave NAC. He wasn't ready to share that yet. Instead, he told a white lie. "I asked to return to New York for the summer. I hoped that being back with my family might help build up my foundation."

"So, what did he say?" Miguel asked.

"See for yourself." Anthony handed Miguel the letter he had just received. "He didn't even have the courtesy of answering himself. He got the vocation director to do it. That bastard!" Anthony said bitterly.

"Let me see that, Miguel," Kevin said as he took the letter from his hand. "Wow, this really is cold."

"Not only did he not address your crisis of faith, but he slapped you on the hand. He's scolding you for questioning his judgment and authority," Miguel added.

"I thought that if I were honest about my spiritual journey, they would understand that it's not about being homesick," Anthony explained.

"That asshole doesn't give a damn about your spiritual well-being," Miguel continued. "It's all a matter of how it looks. God forbid one of the chosen ones leaves NAC. That would be a dark spot on the reputation of the diocese."

"Anthony, I am sorry. They completely missed the point. Your spiritual journey is the most important part of your formation. That has to take priority," said Kevin.

"Well, I guess I have to take care of my own spiritual life from now on. If the Cardinal made anything clear, it's that I can't entrust them with it."

"So, what are you going to do now, Anthony?" Miguel asked.

"I honestly don't know. It's like I'm stranded in the middle of the ocean without a life-vest." Kevin pulled him into his arms and hugged him tightly.

The hell with coming across as gay in front of Miguel. He'll just have to get over it. But Miguel extended his hand and placed it firmly on Anthony's shoulder. "Don't worry, Anthony. No matter what happens, you have Kevin and me at your side. No one is going to let you down."

That letter Anthony sent was just one more nail in the coffin for each of them. Miguel was infuriated and channeled his anger into ranting against the soulless church leadership. Anthony was sincerely questioning his beliefs and, even more so, the Catholic Church's validity as the ultimate authority in matters of doctrine and morality.

Kevin tried to be reasonable and encouraged Anthony to discuss it with his spiritual director, Father Garcia. Anthony felt as if he had suffered another blow and walked around as if in a fog. Although his sessions with Father Garcia were fruitful, he couldn't seem to regain his footing. Anthony was a lost soul. He wondered what this meant regarding his vocation and his future.

Chapter Thirty

Sacrae Eucharistiae

Anthony's parents arrived on the Saturday before Palm Sunday. The plan was to spend a week in Rome during Holy Week, followed by a second week in southern Italy with the family. They were full of gleeful anticipation as they waited for their luggage at Fiumicino airport. It was like a dream come true for the two Italian immigrants. To have their youngest child become a priest was a magnificent gift, but to have him studying in Rome, the seat of the Roman Catholic Church, was something they could never have imagined. NAC was positively amazing when the parents of seminarians visited. They rolled out the red carpet and treated them like royalty, and Anthony could not have been more grateful. He was still reeling from the heartless response he received from the Cardinal. With NAC's display of overt generosity and celebration, his parents couldn't have come at a better time. This visit was a balm to his aching spirit.

During the many letters exchanged and precious phone conversations, Anthony kept his parents in the dark. He knew he couldn't share what was truly going on. They wouldn't understand the mean-spirited conflicts that had marked his first year at NAC. It would rock their belief in the Catholic Church, and he wasn't willing to dissuade them from their steadfast dedication to the Church.

But what Anthony most feared was disappointing them. How could he let them down? They would be devastated if he were to leave Rome, even to study in a seminary in the states. They wore his appointment to the North American College as a badge of honor. He couldn't take that away from them. Concerning his recent battle with the Cardinal, questioning his authority and that of the Church would challenge everything they had ever taught him. No, he had to put on a good face, *la bella figura* – at least while they were visiting.

The Rossis were staying in a residence run by an order of sisters just on the backside of St. Peter's Basilica, and they relished the fact that their son was living in Vatican City State. They walked through the Bernini colonnade and across the grand *Piazza San Pietro* every day.

Knowing how religious his parents were, Anthony planned for them to spend Good Friday in Assisi. It was only a two-and-half-hour train ride from Rome. Ever since NAC had brought the new men to Assisi for their class retreat after their weeks of orientation back in October, he had always loved the medieval hilltop city. As a seminarian, it was imbued meaning because it was in a tiny church in the countryside that St. Francis heard his calling.

Anthony would escape to Assisi whenever he could. Several times he and Kevin took the train on their weekly Thursday rendezvous. It always centered him and led him back to why he wanted to become a priest.

Alone, Anthony would make the arduous trek up the steep hill toward the hermitage where St. Francis went to pray. He found solace in the peaceful paths leading into the wooded hillside. It continued to amaze him that doves still sat vigil on branches where the mendicant friar slept hundreds of years before. It was in Assisi that Anthony could actually feel the presence of God. Now, he was going to share this spiritual home with his parents.

The procession through the main square of Assisi was breathtaking. Scores of young men dressed in white robes carried life-size crosses over their shoulders, and the crowd of worshipers sang mournful hymns as they processed to the basilica. Anthony looked over at his mother and saw tears streaming down her cheeks as she recalled similar processions from her childhood. He knew he had made the right choice. Good Friday in Rome would have been grand, but not nearly as moving. In Assisi, they would experience a solemn and holy Good Friday, far from the Vatican, away from NAC, and far from all his worries.

The next day, they returned to Rome for the Easter Vigil Mass in the seminary chapel. Lasting three or more hours, it's the longest Mass of the liturgical year, but Anthony loved it just the same. From the lighting of the Easter fire to the many psalms sung before the Gospel, the ritual drama of salvation history was on full display. Anthony helped lead the music, and his parents couldn't have been prouder. Mrs. Rossi loved hearing Anthony's lyrical tenor voice echoing in the magnificent chapel. It was the thing she missed most about having her son so far away from home. Afterward, NAC hosted an elegant dinner, and Mr. and Mrs. Rossi were one of many visiting parents in attendance. The seminarians were dressed in their most acceptable clerics, with French cuffs and official NAC cufflinks. There were flowers on each table, and the meal marked the end of Lent with four courses of delicious food. After-dinner drinks were held in one of the guest parlors, with the rector as the host. It was a grand reception, and NAC never looked more elegant. That evening, Anthony looked over at his beaming expression on his parents' faces and was very proud to be a new man at the North American College.

It had been a full and exciting day, and the Rossis were dreamily recounting all they had done during the last few days. It was just past 10:00 p.m. as they crossed through St. Peter's Square. Kevin and Anthony were escorting the Rossis back to their *pensione* when they heard a loud swoosh from above. They looked up to see the majestic St. Peter's Basilica lit up for the vigil Mass which had just begun. The great bell of the basilica was moving. Of the six bells in the façade, it is the greatest – with a diameter and height of approximately two-and-a-half meters and a circumference of seven-and-a-half meters. Weighing eleven tons, one could distinctly hear it swaying as it came up to speed. All at once, the clapper struck with a thunderous clanging sound. Then, the other bells joined in the joyous song for the first time since the beginning of Lent.

"They must have just started the Gloria, mom. That's the first time they ring the bells announcing the Easter season. They only ring the big one for Christmas and Easter."

"*Madonna mia*, I have heard nothing as magnificent as this." Mrs. Rossi said.

"Yes, although we've heard it before, it always sounds spectacular. I hope we never get used to it," he added.

"You boys are so very fortunate to be here in this holy city," she said.

"Yes, mom, yes, we are," catching Kevin's eye.

The following morning was Easter Sunday, and the warm sun shined on the *Piazza San Pietro*. The rector had arranged for Anthony and his parents to attend Mass at St. Peter's Basilica, and as a special surprise, they were to receive communion from the Pope. Anthony didn't know how to thank him. He knew that this would be a highlight of their lives. But Anthony wanted to surprise them. Although he mentioned going to Mass at St. Peter's, he left the rest a secret. The proximity of their seats to the Pope astounded Anthony's parents.

The grand altar was set up on the grand staircase in front of the basilica. The expansive piazza was bursting with the faithful congregation. The beautiful Bernini colonnade was like two loving arms extended in an embrace. There were Vatican guards at numerous checkpoints directing the overflowing crowd. As they displayed their tickets, the ushers continued to wave them closer to the main altar.

"Anthony, what is this? How did you get seats right in front?" Mrs. Rossi asked.

"I know, isn't this great?" He was as excited as they were. "Mom, dad, there's another surprise for you."

"What do you mean? How could there be more than this? We are already in the front row?" Mrs. Rossi asked in disbelief. His father nodded in agreement. He rarely spoke unless he was telling a tale from his childhood. Otherwise, he sat quietly, observing each and every interaction, happy to let his wife take the lead.

"Take a closer look at your tickets. See that red print on the bottom? It says *Sacrae Eucharistiae*. It means Holy Eucharist in Latin."

"Yes, of course, my dear. The Mass was in Latin for most of our lives. We know what it means," she said, chiding him gently.

"So, that's the surprise. The three of us are going to receive communion from the Pope today!" Anthony said.

Mr. and Mrs. Rossi were beyond thrilled. Neither of them could contain their excitement throughout the Mass. When it was time to go up, Anthony had them go in front of him. He just had to witness this significant event. Tears welled up in his eyes as he watched his mom standing before the Pope, followed by his dad. Say what you will, but he knew he was in a most remarkable place. For all its issues, NAC had provided the highest of highs along with the most profound of lows. However, watching two of the most influential people in his life receive communion from the Pope would forever be etched in his mind. *Perhaps I've been approaching my life at NAC completely wrong,* he thought as he stood before Pope John Paul II. He prayerfully said Amen and opened his mouth to receive the Eucharist.

Chapter Thirty-One
The Fall

With each day that passed, Miguel found himself pinning over Maria. They had spoken over the phone every week after candidacy. However, the phone was in the middle of the hall. There was no booth around it, so there was no privacy. Several times a week, he walked to the phone office in the city to make private calls. All he had to do was put down some money and go to the individual booths to make his call. Maria was thrilled. "I am so glad you're rich, Miguel. Getting to chat with you so often is luxurious!"

"I kind of like it too," he said. "This certainly beats waiting for letters, which, by the way, you are terrible at."

"Who, me? Excuse me for not being as eloquent as you. The words don't flow from my pen as easily. It takes me forever to write them."

"Oh, come on, Maria. Just write to me. I don't care what you say or how you say it."

"But, honey, now that you call me so often, there's no need to write," Maria replied.

"I suppose you're right. How is it you seem to wrangle out of everything?"

"You miss me, don't you?"

"Understatement. I have a proposal for you," Miguel said, pausing to take a breath.

"It's a little too soon for that, sweet cheeks."

"You're so witty. I can hardly keep up," Miguel said dryly. "Seriously, do you think you can get away for a long weekend? I really want to see you."

"I'd love to come back to Rome, but I really can't swing it. I'm spending money like water lately. Can you come to Paris?" Maria asked.

"They'd never let me take time off. I've been under the microscope lately. The faculty has been watching my every move," Miguel said.

"If I were there, I'd watch your every move, too. You have such a cute butt," Maria said with a sly giggle.

"You finally noticed, eh? But seriously, I can get you a train ticket and a hotel room. This way, we could actually visit without prying eyes."

"Miguel, I can't accept that. It's too much," she protested half-heartedly.

"Yes, you can. If you can take a couple of days off, I will make the reservations. Please say yes."

"OK, twist my arm. How about the week after next?"

"Perfect! I can't wait to see you again!"

***

Miguel booked a room at the Hotel Columbus, an old Cardinal's palace right on the Via del Conciliazione, the major boulevard leading up to the Vatican. The area was bustling with tourists, so he'd be able to sneak in and out with little attention drawn to him. Miguel took a taxi to Stazione Termini late Wednesday evening.

It was perfect timing since he had no classes on Thursdays. When she spotted him at the end of the track, she nearly broke into a sprint until she collided with him. Her childlike laughter peeled through the station as she planted a big kiss on his lips. Usually, Miguel would be embarrassed by the scene, but he melted into her embrace. He finally felt like he was home. She never stopped chatting during the taxi ride to Columbus. But she was speechless when she laid eyes on the hotel. She had never stayed anywhere so lavish.

"Miguel, this is gorgeous! I can't believe I'll be staying here," she said.

"You deserve it, my love. Come on now, let's just drop off your stuff and grab a drink."

"You certainly know the way to my heart, Miguel. Let's go!" Miguel and Maria laughed and drank late into the evening. It was as if they had known each other for years.

Stumbling back to the hotel, they stood in the courtyard – the fountain masking their conversation. Miguel did not want to say goodbye. He'd waited so long to see her, and he desperately wanted to spend the night with her.

He promised himself that he would explore his feelings for Maria before committing to the priesthood. His heart and his body were alive for the first time in years. He took his hand and brushed a lock of hair from her eyes and kissed her tenderly.

"So, I had a wonderful time with you tonight, and I don't want it to end," he said.

"It was perfect, wasn't it?" she replied.

"I suppose it's too late for me to come up," he said.

"Late? I've only just begun. Do you need to get back to NAC?" she asked, noticing his expectation.

"Not really. I just don't want to assume anything."

"Monsieur, you have been a perfect gentleman this evening. You have nothing to worry about." With that, she stood on her toes and kissed him on the lips.

"You're driving me crazy, Maria," he confessed.

"*Oui, Monsieur*, that's my secret power. Now let's be quiet as church mice and sneak you in there," she said as she pulled him into a lingering kiss.

Once in her beautiful hotel room, Maria led Miguel to her bed. She stood in front of him and unbuttoned her blouse, still leaving it on. He reached up and placed his hands around her waist. Her skin was soft and warm to his touch.

"Come here," he said as he gently pulled her down to his lap and kissed her. His right hand slid up her back, and he adeptly unhooked her bra strap. Maria broke their kiss.

"Well now, Mr. Seminarian, it seems that you've had some practice at that," she said teasingly.

"Just a little, but obviously it was enough," he laughed self-consciously. When their clothes were finally shed, Miguel moved his body over hers. The touch of her warm flesh upon his made his entire body burn, yet he had no desire to rush. Her breasts were firm and soft to his touch, filling his hands as he gently caressed her. Tearing his lips away from hers, Miguel ran his tongue down her neck and teasingly kissed her nipples before making his way to her taut abdomen. Her skin tasted like wild honey. When neither of them could wait any longer – he entered her with reverence, feeling every pulsating sensation. His tenderness was unlike any other man Maria had been with, and she was lost in his lovemaking. Soon their kisses became impassioned as they let go of their uncertainty and fear. Each of them reveled in the fire that had been burning in them for weeks. Their time together became an explosion of pent-up fear and desire. They lay on her bed for hours, her head curled under his arm. Miguel twirled her hair between his fingers and rested in what they had just shared. It felt so right to be with her. Gone were his doubts or fears about NAC. For a brief moment, he was right with the world. Soon, his eyelids became heavy, and he drifted off to sleep.

Hours later, Maria woke with a start and glanced at the clock. It was already 4:00 a.m.

"Miguel, wake up, honey."

"Hey there, beautiful."

"You have to go. You have to get back to NAC before you get in trouble." Miguel sat upright immediately, with fear in his eyes.

"What time is it? Oh, my God. I have to get back before everyone gets up for morning prayer." He quickly dressed, then turned to her. He had to tell her how much their time together meant to him. "Maria, you are so beautiful. I am so…"

"I feel the same about you, Miguel," she said, interrupting him. "Now, *mon amour*. Go on your way, hurry," she said rushing him to go back to NAC.

***

Since Miguel had Thursday off, they took a train to Castel Gandolfo, the town of the Pope's summer palace. Exploring the tiny village, he and Maria held hands and shared some of their family histories. Miguel told her about the ranch and his family's history in the region.

She was entranced as she tried to imagine his life back in Texas. Then Maria explained that her family had been expelled from Cuba by Fidel Castro. His regime had seized their once profitable tobacco business. Once one of the wealthiest families in Cuba, Maria's parents arrived in the United States penniless. They worked endlessly to put her through school. Sending her to Paris to study was a once in a lifetime experience they didn't want her to miss. They sacrificed everything for their children. "Whenever they speak of their childhood in Cuba, there is such sadness in their eyes. They'll probably never be allowed back."

"I'm so sorry, Maria. I can't even imagine."

As the hours passed, they grew closer and fell more in love. They spent the next few days wandering around Rome as a couple. Miguel told no one that Maria was in town, not even Anthony. Maria felt terrible about deceiving her old friend, but she knew they could not discover her visit. But Kevin and Anthony were suspicious. Miguel was evasive when they pressed him regarding his whereabouts. If not for their own personal drama, they would have pushed harder.

On Saturday night, Miguel took Maria out to one of the fanciest restaurants in Rome. Cecelia Matella was located just near the ancient Appian Way. He had been there once before when his bishop was visiting from Texas. He had taken him and Seth out to dinner. It was an elegant meal, and the location was beautiful.

The maître d' showed them to a quiet table out in the courtyard. It felt luxuriously private, and he lavished her with fine wine and four courses. By the time the *digestivi* were placed on the table, they were both pretty drunk. Miguel excused himself and made his way to the restroom.

On his way back to the table, he thought he recognized a priest sitting a few tables away. He craned his head to see who it was and lost his footing. He staggered a few feet and tripped on the leg of a chair, landing flat on his face. Maria came running over to help him up.

"Oh, my God, Miguel. Are you alright, honey?" She helped him up and kissed him before he could stop her.

"I'm fine, Maria. I just tripped," he said as he struggled to stand. Maria's affectionate concern was on full display. When Miguel looked behind him, Father Connick was walking over. He had been having dinner with several other faculty members. Miguel knew he'd been caught.

Chapter Thirty-Two
The Perfect One is Tarnished

After Anthony spent a week with his parents visiting relatives in Sorrento, Mr. and Mrs. Rossi couldn't stop talking about all they had done in Rome and Assisi. Most of all, they bragged about their son, saying that nothing would have been possible if he had not been appointed to the prestigious Vatican seminary. It was becoming increasingly challenging to think about returning to the States for seminary. Back in Rome, Anthony returned to the reality of life at NAC. He and Kevin continued their relationship, and both realized that it had become the central focus of their lives.

One evening, they were sitting on the roof deck, smoking a bit of pot that Anthony's older brother sent him. "How did you get this?" Kevin asked, holding up the joint.

"I've told you how crazy my big brother is, right? He smashed up the pot, enclosed it in aluminum foil, and flattened it. Then he put it in a bulky Easter card and mailed it off to me," Anthony replied.

"I can't believe that the dogs didn't sniff it out!"

"Me neither. We would've both been screwed if they found it," Anthony said. That night on the roof, neither of them was up for a gut-wrenching discussion about their future. They chatted effortlessly about their travels and the ordinary goings-on at NAC. Soon they were gossiping about the cast of characters in their class.

"Hey, have you noticed Seth lately?" Anthony asked Kevin. "He's acting weird."

"He's always been weird. Everyone's favorite seminarian, but no one knows anything about him. He never shares anything personal."

"Yeah, the one thing I know is that he's very conservative. He keeps his distance from Miguel, especially since he refused candidacy."

"As I said," Kevin added. "He's an odd one. But one thing is for sure; he'll always cover his ass. Any association with the black sheep of his diocese would be a stain on his perfect record."

"I don't think he's all that perfect," Anthony said. "I think he's hiding something."

"Do tell."

"Haven't you seen him going into the *Casa* almost every day after classes at the Greg?"

"Yeah, he's been exceptionally chummy with that priest from Louisiana," Kevin said. "What's his name – oh, Jeff."

"That's right. I think something's going on between those two. I mean, he's not close with anyone at NAC. Having a relationship beyond our doors would certainly prevent the usual gossip," Anthony said.

"Now that you mention it, I *have* noticed that Seth spends a lot of time there. Damn, I thought he was asexual."

"Speaking of sex," Kevin continued, "what are we doing, Anthony? I mean about us."

"God knows none of this worked out the way I planned," Anthony said.

"Yeah, well, who would have thought that I, who was the model seminarian in Connecticut, would fall head over heels in love?" Kevin replied.

"You? I'm supposed to become a bishop, you know. At least that's what I've been told," Anthony said wryly.

"We've all been told that. But seriously, we came here for a reason, and the priesthood is important to both of us, not to mention that we're studying in Rome," Kevin said.

"I know. Seeing it all through the eyes of my parents made me stop and think. Maybe we've lost sight of what's trully important. Maybe we have to regain our wonder."

"Oh, Anthony, does that mean Mr. *'Everything is Wonderful'* is back?" Kevin joked. "I can still picture you coming out of the chapel on our first day. I thought that was the only word you knew."

"I was so innocent, wasn't I?"

"It was beautiful, Anthony. *You* were beautiful, and you still are," Kevin replied, smiling at Anthony.

"Do you think we'll ever make it until ordination? Can we get through three more years here?"

"I honestly don't know," Kevin said as they both looked out toward the dome of St. Peter's.

They were silent for a long while, lost in their thoughts. Then Kevin put his hand on Anthony's shoulder.

"We've talked about celibacy *ad nauseam*, but seriously, do you think we can still be together after we're ordained?"

"I don't know, Kevin. Vow or no vow, it seems that almost every priest we know is having sex. I don't see why we can't continue our relationship as priests. We don't live very far from one another, and we can always go on vacations together."

"It's funny. It never occurred to me that so many priests slept with each other or had clandestine sex until last summer. When I was at the beach with all those priests, it seemed as if they were all sexually active. It was like the worst kept secret," Kevin said.

"You know, I would have never considered breaking a vow of celibacy before I met you. Somehow, being with you has changed how I think. We can both be good priests and still love each other, can't we?" Anthony asked.

This conversation was played over and over again in the weeks that followed. They never came to a conclusion as to what was morally correct. They knew that the foundation of their reasoning was on shaky ground, but they couldn't take it to the next level. That they were madly in love with each other was a fog that clouded their judgment. Their sexual relationship had become the expression of that love. Neither could rationally argue for celibacy.

***

Seth had been cautious in his dealings with Miguel. He always appeared supportive and friendly to his fellow Texan, but Miguel knew he had no desire to be drawn into his cause. He knew Seth wanted to become a priest and climb the ladder. If the rules were changed along the way, so be it. He would do anything that the Church required of him. Therefore, his reputation could never be tarnished. Anthony's suspicions regarding Seth were spot on. Ever since that first encounter on Thanksgiving, he and Jeff had been meeting at the Casa regularly.

Anthony noticed Seth lingered at the Gregorian until his classmates had gone, then he walked across the square to the Casa. Anthony never knew who he was meeting, but could sense that Seth wanted no one at NAC to know. Miguel shared with Anthony and Kevin that Seth was always concerned about his reputation. He tested the political waters before saying anything. Seth was perpetually vigilant regarding how others perceived him. There could be no hint of his sexual orientation or that he might be sleeping with someone. That's why most of his classmates couldn't tell if Seth was gay or straight. He was guarded in everything he did. Miguel knew that having a sexual relationship with anyone from NAC was out of the question. The place was a rumor mill, filled with gossip mongers. No, Seth would never be that careless.

Recently, Anthony hung back, wondering what Seth was up to. As usual, he lingered at the café on the Greg's ground floor after their morning classes. Without subtlety, he looked around to make sure that his classmates had left the building. Then Seth walked over to the Casa.

Anthony and Kevin would often grab lunch at the *Abruzzi* restaurant, right near the Casa, and when weather permitted, they sat at a table outdoors. Time and again, as they were enjoying their meal, Anthony noticed Seth coming out of the Casa a half-hour later with a sense of urgency as he walked back to NAC for *pranzo*. One day, after his regular visit to the Casa, he altered the routine. It was a scorching day for early May, and no one relished the walk all the way back to NAC, up the steep Janiculum hill. Kevin and Anthony were already in the midst of their meal when Anthony noticed the waiter lead Seth and Jeff to a quiet table in the corner. It was apparent that they didn't want to be seen by passersby. Seth sat facing the wall, probably so that he wouldn't be recognized should there be any other seminarians around, Anthony thought. He nudged Kevin under the table.

"Look who just walked in – it's the happy couple."

"Well, they're looking very friendly. I think you may be right about those guys," Kevin replied.

"God, I wish Miguel was here to see this. Seth is such a thorn, always questioning his motives and criticizing him for not following the rules," said Anthony.

"Did you see that?" said Kevin. "Jeff just caressed his knee under the table. That is definitely not a platonic relationship."

"They do have that freshly fucked look, don't they?" Anthony joked, and they were reduced to giggling like teenagers. After they paid the bill, Kevin and Anthony made sure that Seth knew he had been seen. They walked over to his table to say goodbye. The look on his face was too good to pass up. "Seth, fancy seeing you here," Anthony said. "Couldn't resist the *rigatoni carbonara,* eh?"

"Anthony, Kevin, hi," Seth responded nervously. "You've got that right. It's the best in Rome. You remember Jeff from the Casa."

"Of course, hey Jeff," Kevin said, extending a hand.

"Skipping *pranzo* at NAC, all three of you are testing fate," Jeff said. "You know they're probably keeping a tally of your attendance."

"No doubt about that. I must confess that we are regular offenders. But I am surprised to see you here, Seth," Kevin said.

"Yeah, Seth," Anthony chimed in. "You're the model seminarian. This doesn't fit your image."

"Nothing wrong with following the rules," Seth responded indignantly. "You do realize that we will take a vow of obedience when we're ordained."

"True enough. Enjoy the *carbonara; we'll* see you back at NAC," Kevin said with a self-satisfied look.

Before they left, Anthony made his way to the restroom. It was just around the corner from where Seth and Jeff were sitting. He paused at the door and craned his neck to see if there was any further drama. He could see that Seth was a wreck after their brief encounter. His furrowed brow said it all. He had always been cautious with his public behavior. *He must wonder how long we had been in the restaurant or if we had seen anything that might incriminate him,* Anthony thought. And the answer was yes. Both Kevin and Anthony noticed their not-so-subtle touching, brushing hands, or pressing legs together under the table. They looked like a couple, not just friends. Anthony moved a little closer to listen to their conversation.

"Hey, Seth, I can see the gears turning in your head. What are you thinking?" Jeff asked.

"How long were they here? Did they see us come in?" Seth asked Jeff.

"Probably, since they finished before us. Why?"

"I don't know. I mean, you kind of had your hand on my back when we came in, then you rubbed my leg under the table. What if they saw that?"

"So what, don't you think they've been sleeping together? What's the big deal?"

"The big deal is that I don't want to be associated with that crowd. Anthony and Kevin spell trouble. Besides, I don't want to be just another seminarian who's sleeping around. I have a stellar reputation at NAC. I don't want to screw it up," Seth responded vehemently.

"Okay, calm down. There's nothing you can do about that now. Do you think they'll tell anyone?"

"I don't know. Gossip spreads like crazy there. Up until now, I've been able to stay above the fray."

"Look, if they tell anyone," Jeff said, "won't they be implicating themselves? Anyway, if they are together, why would they care about you?"

"I hope you're right, Jeff." Seth paused, thoughts racing through his mind. "Maybe we should cool off a bit, take some time apart."

"You'll get your wish soon enough, Seth. I'll be leaving Rome for good in a few weeks. We might as well make the best of the time we have left."

Kevin and Anthony felt vindicated as they left the restaurant. Anthony felt slightly guilty about eavesdropping, but he was glad he did. Neither of them suffered self-righteousness well, and Seth was one of the worst in their class. It was so satisfying to catch him in his duplicity. The only thing that would have made the revelation sweeter was if Miguel were with them. In any case, they gloated and laughed for the entire walk home. Seth was having an affair with an ordained priest. It didn't get better than that.

"Just goes to show that even those that appear to be perfect seminarians – or priests have something to hide. You never know what people are doing behind closed doors," Kevin said to Anthony.

"Is everybody at NAC having sex?" Once again, Anthony pondered the highly charged atmosphere at NAC. Although he had been in Rome for months, the pervasive sexual energy continued to shock him. Logically, Anthony knew that his dismay was hypocritical, given his romantic relationship with Kevin. However, he never imagined that there would be such an active sexual sub-culture in the Church, let alone at a Vatican seminary. His eyes were opened time and again throughout his NAC experience. Anthony wondered if he would ever get used to it.

Chapter Thirty-Three
Consequences

On Sunday morning, Miguel awoke with a massive hangover – the stale taste of sour wine lingered in his parched mouth. As he lifted his head off the pillow, the pounding in his head grew worse. Glancing over to his clock, Miguel realized that he had missed breakfast by hours – as well as the hot water in the showers. He grabbed his towel and headed to the restroom. *Perhaps a cold shower is just what I need,* he thought. Standing in the frigid water, images of the previous evening flashed through his mind. Falling flat on his face in the middle of the restaurant was one for the books. Every head turned at his spectacular face plant. Miguel lifted his hand and gently touched his forehead. A large scab had begun to form, but it was still tender to his touch. The confrontation with Connick wasn't as bad as he would have expected. Given that Maria came running to help him up, calling him honey, Miguel was sure Connick would explode. Instead, he seemed genuinely concerned.

"Are you alright, Miguel?" he asked.

"Yes, yes. I tripped, that's all. Thanks for helping me get up," Miguel replied.

"I think it's time for you to get back to NAC. Let me call you a taxi," he offered.

"Don't worry, I can manage," Miguel replied as Father Connick turned to Maria.

"Hello, I believe we've met before. You're Anthony's college friend, aren't you?" Connick asked.

"Yes, Father. I'm Maria," she replied.

"What brings you back to Rome, Maria?"

"I just love it here. I had some time off and decided on an impromptu visit."

"Well, it's lovely to see you again." Then Connick turned to Miguel. "Get some sleep, Miguel. We'll chat tomorrow." *Not sure why he was so lovely to me, but I'll take it,* he thought as he toweled himself dry, still shivering from the cold water. He padded down the hall to his room and noticed someone had slipped an envelope under the door. He sat on his bed and read the cryptic note.

Dear Miguel,
Please report to my office directly after dinner this evening.
Father Connick

Miguel tried not to read too much into the tone, but it was difficult to believe he was simply being called to a friendly meeting. Trying to recall the events of the last evening, he scanned his memory. *Were Maria and I too obvious? Did I say anything disrespectful?* He wracked his foggy brain but couldn't come up with anything concrete.

He'd just have to wait and see.

***

He dashed out to Maria's hotel. She was packed and ready to go. They took a taxi to *Stazione Termini*. Sunday mornings were delightfully clear of traffic, and they made it well before her departure. "Let's grab a cappuccino. I'm in dire need of one this morning," Miguel suggested.

"You do look pretty bad, my love."

"If I look as bad as I feel, then I'm in trouble."

"I'll miss you, Miguel."

"Me too. Listen, I know a lot happened this weekend, and I want you to know that I don't take it lightly," Miguel said earnestly to Maria.

"Neither do I. You have some decisions to make, Miguel. But let me be clear. I don't want to be the reason you leave the seminary. That puts way too much pressure on me and our relationship," she said.

"I know, I know. But I can honestly say that you've opened my eyes. I never thought I could feel this way for anyone. I just have to do this in my own way. Does that make sense?" Miguel replied.

"Of course, it does. We have plenty of time to figure this out. Just promise me you'll call soon. I've gotten quite used to being together," Maria said. They hugged and kissed goodbye, and she went on her way.

***

Dinner seemed interminable. All he could think about was his appointment with Father Connick. When he finished his meal, he excused himself and made his way to the office. Sundays at NAC were quiet. Many of the guys were ministering at local parishes, and the faculty were rarely in the building. Miguel knocked lightly on the door.

"*Avanti, come in!*" *Father Connick said.*

"*Good evening,* Father."

"Please have a seat, Miguel. Well, you certainly look better than you did last night."

"Sorry about that. I admit I drank too much wine," Miguel replied.

"From the looks of it, it was more than a bit. It seems that your over-drinking is becoming more frequent."

"I'm sorry, Father. But I know that I'm not the only one. It seems to be part of our NAC culture," Miguel said defensively.

"Be that as it may, your behavior in public last evening was not up to NAC standards. You made quite a spectacle of yourself."

"Once again, I'm sorry."

"It's not enough to be sorry. As a seminarian at NAC, you represent the American Church each time you leave these walls. To top it off, you had an intimate dinner with a young woman," Connick said.

"We're just friends, father," he lied. "Kevin, Anthony, and I spent New Year's in Paris with her."

"If you are just friends, then why weren't they with you at dinner? It seems odd that Anthony wouldn't have joined you." Miguel didn't know how to respond. He hadn't even told Anthony about her visit. Connick may have already checked with him today. *No, that's not possible*, he thought. *Anthony would have said something to me.* Miguel couldn't be sure, so he remained silent.

"*Basta.* Enough, let's stop the pretense. Isn't this the same girl you for whom you bought roses? You've had feelings for her for months. She was quite demonstrative in her affection after you fell. How many friends call each other, honey? Miguel, this is the last straw in a destructive pattern of behavior. You refused candidacy, you hold seminars counter to current Church teaching, and you were in a relationship with a woman... Have I left anything out?"

Miguel stared blankly ahead, his eyes brimming. What could he say?

"I'm sorry to say that this is your last day with us. You will go to your room, pack up your stuff, and be on the first flight to Dallas tomorrow morning."

Miguel was stunned. He couldn't believe what he was hearing. He knew he screwed up, and yes, he needed to sort out his romantic feeling for Maria. But had he done anything worse than many other guys — many of whom were sleeping with each other? His temper flared.

"You're a hypocrite, you know that?" Connick flinched. "You say that I have not represented NAC as I should, and perhaps that is true. But how about you? How many times have you been inebriated at local restaurants? And concerning sexual or romantic relationships, I recall in vivid detail your drunken visit back in January. Was that simply a social call? As you sat on my bed, stroking my thigh? How can you judge me for trying to honestly discern my vocation when you and so many others sneak around as if this were a brothel?"

"You're treading on dangerous ground, Miguel. How dare you accuse me? Remember your place."

"Oh, I'm just getting started. I demand to see the Rector. I am sure he'd be delighted to hear what I have to say about your behavior."

"You're not in a position to demand anything. The Rector is well aware of your behavior. Your file is thick with infractions. You will leave my office now. You are not to speak to anyone about your departure. Go pack."

"I will talk to Monsignor O'Connor about this. I am entitled to that—and who are you to tell me I can't speak to anyone? I am not leaving NAC without saying goodbye to Kevin and Anthony."

"Monsignor O'Connor asked me to handle this. About your friends, the Rector has taken them to Castel Gandolfo for the day. They won't be returning until very late. Now, my assistant will accompany you to your room. He'll make sure that you don't do anything stupid. Good day." With the wind taken out of his sails, Miguel was summarily dismissed. In a catatonic state, he gathered his belongings and packed them. *How did this spin out of control so quickly? What is going to happen to me now?*

Chapter Thirty-Four
He's Gone

"Anthony, wake up!" Kevin shouted, pounding on his door during siesta time. "Hurry, please."

"What the hell, Kev? What's got you all up in arms?" Anthony said as he wiped the sleep from his eyes.

"It's Miguel! He's gone."

"What do you mean, gone? He probably slept in this morning," Anthony replied, still wiping his eyes.

"That's what I thought too, but when he didn't show up for *pranzo,* I got worried. I just came from his room. It's empty," Kevin said.

"What? How? Why would it be empty?"

"I told you, he's gone! Packed up and gone!"

"You can't be serious. You must have gone to the wrong floor. You're always on the wrong wing or something," Anthony replied, not believing that Miguel had left.

"I'm not kidding, Anthony. Let's go to his room so you can see it for yourself," Kevin replied.

Once inside Miguel's room, Anthony's wide eyes gaped in disbelief. He just sat on the bare mattress and stared at the empty closet. *What is going on here?* He thought.

"This can't be happening. Miguel can't be gone. Maybe he just moved to another room."

"You know that's not possible. I think they kicked him out."

"Why? For speaking his mind? That's just crazy."

"Is it? You remember your meeting with Father Connick after the blow-up about the clerical garb. You were strongly reprimanded," Kevin replied.

"True, but I'm still here. I got the message and shut up," Anthony responded.

"But Miguel didn't. He's been a thorn in their sides ever since. He challenged any directive that smelled of clericalism. And we both know he had no time for anything he considered unjust."

"I know, but that's not against Church teaching or the Gospels."

"No, but it *was* in opposition to authority. I think you know how well that's received here."

"No, there must be another explanation. Did you see Miguel at all yesterday?" Anthony asked.

"No, of course not. We were with the rector all day in Castel Gandolfo. Miguel has been missing for days."

"This can't be happening. Is this a communist country where dissenters just disappear?"

"Might as well be – it's Holy Mother Church," Kevin said bitterly.

They checked around, but no one seemed to have any information. It wasn't long before the rumor mill spilled the information they sought. Miguel had indeed been asked to leave the NAC. After exams, they contacted his bishop to voice their concerns. But the final straw was the revelation that Miguel was in a romantic relationship with Maria. The Rector informed his bishop of the latest development, and his return ticket to Dallas was activated. They escorted Miguel to Fiumicino Airport and boarded a flight home. He couldn't believe that it was happening, and it devastated him. Miguel attempted to sneak off and make a phone call before his flight. He was desperate to say goodbye to Kevin and Anthony. But his escort would not leave his side.

Although he disagreed with their decision to expel him, Miguel knew that his relationship with Maria was forbidden. However, denying him proper closure with his best friends was downright cruel.

For Anthony and Kevin, the departure of their dearest friend and the third member of the unholy trinity rocked their worlds. The weeks that followed seemed to pass in a haze. Kevin chose not to think about it. Instead, he poured himself into his studies. Only through the abstract concepts and analysis of theology could he find relief from his inner turmoil. Poison pulsed through the veins of his vocation, yet he denied its existence and allowed it to fester. His bitterness toward the Church took a firm hold and lived just below the surface. It didn't go unnoticed that he said very little at community gatherings or meals. But he made up for it in his seminar in Systematic Theology, which Monsignor O'Connor taught. Kevin was eloquent and let his intellectual curiosity lead him. He resolved to appear as if nothing had changed; he couldn't show them how broken he was. And it worked.

The Rector was very impressed with Kevin. He felt that by extricating Miguel from their trio, he had saved both Kevin and Anthony. Anthony, try as he might, could not bury himself in his studies. He found it difficult to concentrate on his reading or the redaction of his notes from class. Anyone who witnessed the extreme change in his personality knew that he was grappling with something.

His once vibrant personality appeared sullen and introverted. He was never discourteous, and his interactions with others were still friendly, but his spark was gone. To fill the emptiness, he felt inside, Anthony committed himself to following a strict schedule. He needed the structure of his daily routine to keep him from falling deeper into despair.

Anthony's attendance at morning and evening prayer, though not required, was faithful. He could always be seen in the same pew for daily mass and was dutiful in his other responsibilities. While the rector and seminary faculty marveled at his magnificent metamorphosis, his friends knew better. Carlos worried about him and checked in on him regularly.

"*Caro,* you seem very distant today. Are you sure you're all right?" he asked, trying to get him to open up.

"Yeah, Carlos, I'm fine. I'm just a little tired," Anthony lied. He would allow no one into his pain. To do so would force him to face it head-on, and he was not ready to do that. Anthony looked into the mirror and stared. He didn't recognize the person looking back at him. Yes, there was the same face and the same expressions, but something significant had changed. When he first arrived at NAC, he was an optimistic adolescent with all the wonder and optimism that comes with that. The image of the idealistic young man will never return, he thought. He felt tarnished. His eyes told a different story now.

The sparkle of an innocent young man was gone. In its place was the look of one who has suffered, struggled, and, most importantly, loved. For that love, he was thankful. He truly believed that once touched deeply by love. A person can never be the same. He knew in his heart and eyes; he would always carry that love.

The loss of Miguel in his life was profound, and it made him realize how deeply he needed Kevin. He would not let the same thing happen to him. Kevin understood Anthony's grief but kept it buried within. Neither of them could bring themselves to talk about it. The pain was still so raw. So much of their communication was absent of words. Their compassion for each other was expressed through a look or a touch. The only comfort either of them got was when they slept together. The playfulness of their relationship was replaced by need. Anthony could never seem to get enough of Kevin; he could never be close enough. It was almost as if he was consumed by him. And Kevin buried himself in Anthony's affection. They made love with abandon as their emotional need was transformed into a primal passion for each other. Untamed desire replaced the sweet phrases spoken in Italian. When they were together, the loss of innocence that NAC foisted upon them was kept at bay. They reveled in the love they shared. If only they could remain in the artificial world they had created for one another, all would be well. Outside those four walls, the conflict and disappointment continued to loom large. Their dreams for the future, once brilliant and exciting, were tarnished and uncertain.

Miguel's departure was a turning point for both of them. Kevin no longer sought new sexual encounters. The cat-and-mouse game held no allure for him. During his meaningless liaisons with the other seminarians, the emptiness he felt seemed to engulf him, and he wanted no part of them. A piece of his heart had been ripped apart when Miguel got kicked out. The merry trio had supported and loved each other through every hurdle they encountered at NAC, and now they were missing the third person in their unholy trinity. Only Anthony could fill his need, both sexually and emotionally, and he clung to his dearest friend and lover for fear that he too would be lost.

Anthony manifested his pain in the loss of his own health. He suffered from abdominal pain. During his most stressful weeks at NAC, the dull ache that had been a constant friend flared up into sharp stabs that took hours to subside. He was sure it was because of the emotional rollercoaster he endured over the recent months, but he wouldn't give the faculty the satisfaction of knowing they had gotten to him. He stocked up on antacids and tried to watch his diet. Kevin worried about him constantly, watching as he left the better portion of his meals on the plate. He noticed his weight loss and tried to get him to see a doctor, but Anthony was stubborn and wouldn't hear of it.

Chapter Thirty-Five
A Shocking Revelation

A nthony and his mother had weekly phone appointments on Sunday afternoons. In general, letters had to suffice due to the high expense of overseas phone calls. After their return to New York, the calls were animated as they recounted the incredible visit they had for Easter. Mrs. Rossi could not stop talking about Assisi and the great bells of St. Peter's Basilica. The highlight, of course, was receiving communion from Pope John Paul on Easter Sunday. Late in May, Mrs. Rossi made her regularly scheduled phone call to Anthony, but something was different. After chatting with the rest of the family, her tone changed, and he heard her moving to another room. The clatter of his sibling's banter was more distant.

"Anthony, I have something important to tell you."

"What's going on, mom? You sound so serious. Is everything all right?" Anthony asked.

"Father Joe is in the hospital. He has been there for five days so far," she said.

Anthony's heart skipped a beat, and he took in a sharp breath. "Why, what's wrong with him?" he continued, not waiting for her reply. "Why didn't you call me sooner?"

"We didn't want to worry you. We thought Father Joe would be home by now. Anyway, they still don't know what's wrong with him. It might be pneumonia, but they are not sure. Anthony, your father and I are worried. Nothing they're doing seems to help."

"I don't understand. He has always been so healthy. He's built like a football player."

"Yes, that is why the doctors are so concerned."

"Oh my God, mom. This is horrible news. Can he receive phone calls? Is he all right to talk?"

"I think so, Anthony. I know that he would love to hear from you, even for just a few minutes. Here is the number for the hospital. He is in room 506."

"Thanks. I love you, mom." Anthony placed the phone back on the hook and squeezed his eyes tightly. Then he took a deep breath and rang the receptionist and asked to make the call. Pacing back and forth, he waited by the phone until it rang again. A weak voice answered the line.

"Hello, Uncle Joe?"

"Yes, who is this?" Joe asked.

"It's Anthony from Rome."

"Ah, my favorite nephew. How is life at the Vatican?" Uncle Joe asked.

"It has its challenges, as you can imagine. But more importantly, how are *you*? What's going on with your health?" asked Anthony.

"Oh, you know, I'm getting old," he said, deflecting.

"Seriously, Uncle Joe, you're only forty-eight. What's the story? Do they know what's wrong?"

"Pneumonia, a nasty case. As usual, I'm an overachiever." He laughed a little and launched into a troublesome coughing fit that lasted much longer than it should have. Anthony could sense something was wrong.

"Are you okay? Look, I won't keep you long. I just wanted to see how you were doing."

"Yes, I just need a drink of water. Once I start coughing, it takes forever to calm."

"Okay, but you're getting better, right?"

"I better be. Anthony, you have no idea how good it is to hear your voice. Tell me how you are doing at NAC. I could use the distraction."

"I'm just recovering from mom and dad's visit during Easter. It was amazing, especially receiving communion from the pope."

"What an incredible experience. They are very proud of you, Anthony, and so am I."

"I know, thanks. I'm doing my best to get through the usual struggles here. Enough about me, I'm worried about you," Anthony said.

"Don't worry; I'll be fine. But please pray for me."

"Every day. I'll call you soon. I love you, Uncle Joe."

Once again, he placed the phone on the receiver and stood motionless. None of this made any sense to him. Uncle Joe had never been sick a day in his life. He was athletic and active, and he was the image of strength.

***

When the call ended, Father Joe hung up the phone and closed his eyes. How could he tell Anthony what was really going on? This was just the latest of strange illnesses that he had contracted in the last few months. For a man who had never been sick a day in his adult life, Joe was having trouble making sense of it all. Although he hadn't been officially diagnosed, Joe was afraid that this was the mysterious cancer that he had been reading about. But he pushed that thought far from his mind. *That could never happen to me*, Joe thought. At first, he wasn't sure why he was becoming ill so frequently. He first noticed his constant fatigue before Christmas, then weight-loss, and a cough that just wouldn't go away.

Last week, when he couldn't lift his head from the pillow, his secretary summoned the doctor, who immediately instructed him to get to the hospital. His diagnosis was PCP, pneumonia, which was unusual for a man as healthy as he once was. Dr. Steinburg was one of the best in New York, and he'd been seeing him for nearly twenty years. They had an excellent rapport and got together socially frequently.

His stay at the hospital was difficult. He had been poked and prodded so much that his arms were bruised beyond recognition. After a battery of tests, Steinburg came to his room and closed the door.

"Hey there, Joe. How are you feeling today? Are you breathing any better?" he asked.

"A little, yeah. It's been almost a week with little improvement. What's this all about, Jeff? I never get sick?"

"To be honest with you, I am quite concerned. I need to ask you some delicate questions. Are you up for that?"

"Why all the cloak and dagger? What's this all about?" Steinburg asked.

"Have you been reading the articles in the Times about an obscure type of cancer?"

Panic set in as beads of sweat trickled down his forehead. This was his greatest fear. Working at St. Vincent's Hospital in the village, Dr. Steinburg treated scores of gay men with similar symptoms. He was no longer shocked by the precipitous decline of his patients. Sadly, most of them were young men at their sexual peak. Lying before him was one of his long-time friends. He dreaded giving him this news.

"Yes, I remember that there was some panic about the gay cancer. The evangelicals say it's God's punishment for the gay lifestyle. What does that have to do with me?"

"They don't call it that anymore, Joe. It's AIDS, acquired immunodeficiency syndrome, and it doesn't discriminate regarding who it infects."

"And you think I have it?" he said with his eyes squeezed tight, looking at the doctor.

"Look, Joe, at the moment, we haven't developed a test that can diagnose it. All we can do now is look for symptoms or opportunistic infections."

"I'm not sure I understand. What do you mean by opportunistic infections?"

"What we know about AIDS so far is that it attacks your immune system. It weakens it so much that you can't combat the most common of viruses. For example, the cold that you couldn't seem to get over, a healthy immune system, would have knocked that out long ago. But with you, it turned into pneumonia."

"Is there any cure? Surely, there's something we can do to fight it," Joe said, his desperation showing.

"We don't know enough about it yet, but, no, there is no cure. Unfortunately, you have many of the symptoms and the opportunistic infections that we just don't see in healthy men your age." He paused and let the news sink in. "That's why I need to get a better picture of your lifestyle."

"All right, then, shoot."

"Look, we've never had a conversation like this. I realize this may be awkward for you, but I need you to be completely honest, and remember, this is in the strictest confidence."

"Yes, of course, Jeff," he responded. "Please, go on."

"Joe, have you had sex with men in the last year? I am sorry to ask, but this is important." Joe's eyes widened, and he let out a labored breath.

"I can't believe this is happening to me. My God," he said, covering his face with his hands.

"Joe, this is important. I know you're a priest and having sex with men carries a great deal of judgment. Please be as honest as you can with me. It's our best chance of determining what this is."

Joe took a deep breath. He knew he had to come clean. So many people he ministered to had already died. If he did have AIDS, being completely honest was his only hope for survival.

"Yes, it has only been with one person. He's a priest too. We've been together for years," he confessed.

"How many years, Joe?" Dr. Steinburg pressed.

"More than I can count, over ten years."

"And do you have both oral and anal sex?"

Joe silently stared off into the distance, thinking, *this is a nightmare. How can you expect me to answer that?*

"I'll take that as a yes," the doctor remained unfazed.

"Why is this happening now? It just doesn't make sense," Joe asked.

"We think it might have to do with having multiple sex partners. Are you both monogamous? Have you had sex with other men?"

"No! I have been in love with him for as long as I can remember." Joe replied.

"And how about him? Has he been having sex with anyone else but you?"

"Look, he's younger than I am. I've had my suspicions, I mean, he's always been adventurous. But I always assumed that we were faithful to one another. I can't believe he could betray me like this," Joe said as he covered his face with his hands once again. He winced from the shooting pain from the IV needle as he bent his arm.

"I'm sure you know many people have multiple partners. I realize the Church preaches abstinence, but most of the world is not Catholic, and most gay men I know don't follow that rule."

"It's clear I haven't done a very good job following that rule either. So much for the vow of celibacy. I am so ashamed."

"You and I have known each other for a long time. I can't say that I understand the whole idea of celibacy, but I do know a thing or two about human nature. You had sex, so what? The problem *is* that there's an epidemic out there. You may very well be caught in the middle of it. I'm sorry."

"So, what now?" Joe asked desperately.

"We do more tests, and we treat the pneumonia. Fortunately, you are a robust man and have always taken good care of yourself. Leading a healthy lifestyle may help. And for now, don't engage in any sexual activity."

"Well, I can certainly assure you of that."

"Joe, listen to me. Try not to get down on yourself. Your emotional state can harm your health. Please try to let go of your guilt."

"Who sounds like a priest now?" Joe said bitterly.

"We can only take this one day at a time. Every day we learn more about this damn disease. Let's not give up hope." Dr. Steinburg squeezed his shoulder and left the room. Joe turned his head toward the window as the tears poured from his eyes.

Chapter Thirty-Six
Moving Beyond Shame

Miguel's departure had been more traumatic than anyone had suspected. Being ripped from the seminary without as much as a warning rocked his foundation. He had known that he was on shaky ground after refusing to go through candidacy, but he never suspected that they would kick him out. And the way it all went down was shockingly cruel. They treated him like a criminal, being whisked away in the dark of night. Thinking back on those two days, he seethed with anger. Pouring salt on the wound, they didn't even allow him to say goodbye to Kevin and Anthony. His lifelines throughout that year were kept in the dark. *What would they think when they find my empty room?* He knew they would be shocked and confused, but his emotional trial was just beginning to manifest itself.

Miguel spent months trying to make his peace with himself and NAC. Did he have any regrets? Perhaps, but those were only about leaving his dearest friends behind. He wished he could have protected himself and them from the judgmental eyes of the faculty. He had been naïve to think he could reasonably affect change by leading those seminars on Vatican II. He believed that the faculty would see his passion and dedication to the mission of the Church – that he wasn't merely a malcontent who was bent upon bucking authority.

He wanted to be seen as a leader whose passion for priestly ministry focused on service to those on the margins. His vocation was not about the trappings of clericalism. It was to spread the gospel through social justice. In hindsight, he understood that although his intentions were good and his reasoning solid, the result was the same. He was actively challenging their authority, as well as that of the Vatican. Using Church documents to make his arguments, he was more dangerous than Anthony with his emotional outbursts. Miguel inadvertently dug his own grave at NAC.

In taking an intellectual approach to his distaste for clericalism, he stood directly in opposition to the authorities who could determine his future in the Church. Miguel reflected endlessly about his actions during his last months at NAC. He could have done things differently, but ultimately, he was proud of himself. He never compromised his values and always acted with integrity. That is what his father had taught him from a very young age. If that led to his expulsion, then so be it.

Miguel was content knowing that he was true to himself throughout each hurdle he faced. He clung to this during his time of self-doubt. When he arrived on his parents' doorstep that afternoon, he presented as a broken young man. His dream of the priesthood had been shattered. His very core had been questioned and deemed inconsistent with the Catholic Church. Anticipating the myriad questions he'd received from his parents, his shame washed over him like hot oil. His mother didn't know why her son had appeared at the doorstep, but she could feel his pain. She engulfed her son and drew him into her arms. There were no words necessary – those would come later. At this moment, Miguel needed the unconditional love of his parents.

In the weeks and months that followed, Miguel took his place beside his father at the ranch. The mindless work was balm to his soul. There was no need to overthink – the work was second nature to him. Being connected to the land brought a much-needed perspective to his life.

Out on the pastures, the clerical world of Rome was worlds away. The intensity of each conflict at NAC seemed trivial compared to life in the real world. Miguel gradually made his peace with what had come to pass. He wasn't sure where destiny would lead him, but he knew he'd be able to handle it.

All he needed was time. Eventually, he was able to write a letter to Anthony and Kevin. There was nothing more he wanted than to talk with them about all that had come to pass. Without them, he felt empty and wondered how they were faring. But during the first weeks back home, he did not know what to say. His internal strife took every bit of energy he had left. He waited until enough healing had taken place before he put his pen to the page.

Dear Anthony and Kevin,

I'm sorry not to have been in contact sooner. I have been completely immersed in my own fucked up world – fighting my inner demons, sometimes winning, most times losing. Being suddenly ripped from NAC in such a cold and heartless way tore me to pieces. Not being able to say goodbye to my dearest friends wounded my heart, and I am still waiting for the scars to heal over.

I don't know how much you know about how it all went down, but you've probably surmised that I was viewed as a threat to the established order. O'Connor feared if I were allowed to see you before my departure, it would further poison our class and cause you to question your own vocations. We all know that it's bullshit. But the fact remains that I'm back in Texas trying to put my life back together without the love and support of my two best friends. I miss you.

Life on the ranch has been good for me. Working beside the man I have admired throughout my life has proven to be my saving grace. I'm sure that you can't picture me rounding up cattle and cleaning the barn. But I can honestly say that it has been my salvation. The bitterness that I feel toward NAC and the Church remains barely beneath the surface. But the pain and resentment are not nearly as acute as it was during my first weeks back.

I am not sure what is next for me. I still feel a great desire to serve others, but it's clear that I won't be doing that as a priest. I'm done with the Church. I know that might be challenging to hear, and perhaps my anger will soften as time continues to pass. But I have to find my own way – without the guidance of the Church. I don't know what that means yet. For now, I am content in my routine at the ranch, and I pray I will discover my true purpose in life.

Please take care of yourselves and drop me a line when you get a chance. I'm sure Monsignor O'Connor didn't give you my address. So now you have it. Let me know how you are faring.

I look forward to hearing about the soap opera that is NAC. It'll be easier to take from thousands of miles away.

Love you guys,
Miguel

Comparatively, that was an easy letter to write. Miguel knew he had to connect with Maria, but he was not ready. How could he consider having a romantic relationship with anybody in his present state? In many ways, Miguel was re-writing his story. All he and Maria shared over the last months, his grappling with priesthood versus married life, had changed. He hadn't been the one to decide if the priesthood was for him. NAC had forcefully taken that away from him. Even if he had ended up leaving, it would have been his decision. His hopes and dreams had been thrown up into the air – the pieces were now scattered. During the months since he left NAC, he was slowly beginning to pick them back up while trying to make sense of his life.

Maria was only a junior in college. She was still so young. How could he ask her to take this journey with him? Miguel knew he was still so screwed up, and he needed time alone to figure it all out. He resolved to call her instead. She answered the phone with her usual enthusiasm, and Miguel felt as if his heart was being crushed. After her initial shock, Maria was compassionate and understanding.

"Oh, honey, I am so sorry. I hate them for doing all that to you. How could they be so cruel?" Maria asked.

"To be honest, Maria, I was shocked by it as well," Miguel said. "They wouldn't even let me say goodbye to Kevin and Anthony."

"Bastards! It makes you want to hate the Church, doesn't it?" Maria responded in disbelief.

"Yeah, well – I'm still grappling with that. But I'm a mess, Maria. I don't really know what comes next. I feel completely lost," he confessed.

"I can't even imagine," she said. "Listen, don't worry about me. I mean it. You have enough to worry about. I'll be fine, really – I'm in Paris for God's sake!"

"I want you to know that you transformed my entire experience at NAC, Maria. You were the light that gave me hope. You are what tethered me to the real world, and I am so grateful to you."

"I'm not going anywhere, Miguel. But listen to me, I'm not ready to give up on us. Promise me we will see each other after you've taken some time."

"Are you serious, Maria? Even though my life is in shambles, you still want to see me?"

"Yes, you fool! I love you, and I think you love me. Let's not give even more power to those assholes at NAC. Besides, we owe it to each other to see this through."

"What is it about you that lifts me up like nobody else? You make me want to drop everything and hop on a flight to Paris," Miguel said with a broad smile.

"Well, then, the semester is nearly over, and I had planned to travel around Europe before my return. It seems like perfect timing. When can I expect you, my dear?"

"That would be so selfish, even foolish."

"Miguel, you feel like shit. You've been beating yourself up for two months now. It's time to move on. You have a woman living in Paris, longing to be by your side. Foolish would be to ignore her invitation."

She knew exactly what to say to heal his aching heart. All at once, he felt comforted and hopeful. Why not go for a visit? They would take it one day at a time. Thankfully, there were no critical decisions to be made. He had the ranch and his family. In the end, Miguel knew he would be just fine.

"You must have magical powers, Maria. Why not? I'd love to see you," Miguel said.

He held the phone away from his ear as he heard her squeal with delight. *Perhaps there is a future for Maria and me*, he hoped.

Chapter Thirty-Seven
An Alternate Reality

I t was late June when Anthony was called the rector's office. Out of the blue, Monsignor O'Connor summoned him. Anthony was to report to him immediately. O'Connor greeted him at the door with a solemn expression on his face.

"Monsignor, is something wrong? Your secretary said that it was urgent."

"I'm sorry to have frightened you, Anthony, but yes, we have a dire situation to discuss. Please sit down. Would you like some water?" Monsignor O'Connor said.

"No, no, I'm fine. Please, tell me what's going on."

"Anthony, it's your uncle, Monsignor Joe. He is very ill." He paused and took a deep breath. "Cardinal McGuire called and asked that you return to New York immediately."

"What? But I just spoke with my uncle a couple of weeks ago. He sounded so much better."

"Listen, Anthony, I don't want to alarm you, but the Cardinal said that his condition is quite grave. Your uncle would like to see you before…" his voice trailed off. O'Connor was rarely at a loss for words, but what more could he say. Anthony's uncle was dying, and the air of mystery surrounding his illness had everyone on edge. He looked at Anthony with compassion as he tried to make sense of the news. His eyes brimmed with tears, and he ran his fingers through his hair.

"No, this can't be right. Uncle Joe was fine. There must be some misunderstanding. He's such a strong and healthy man. He can't be that sick."

"I'm sure this is a great shock to you. I wish I had more information for you, Anthony," the Rector said sincerely. Anthony looked up at Monsignor O'Connor with a startled look on his face. *Was he talking to me?* He hadn't heard a word he was saying.

"Anthony, we have booked you on the Saturday flight. That will give you a few days to wrap up your work for the semester and take your remaining finals this week. I realize that this will be very difficult for you, so if you need to talk to any of us on the faculty before your departure, please know that we are here for you."

"Thank you, Monsignor. I just don't know what to say right now," Anthony replied.

"Anthony, I took the liberty of telling Kevin of the situation. He is in the waiting room. I am sure he can help you get everything together. I am so sorry, Anthony." They stood, and he embraced the catatonic young man before he left the office. O'Connor was genuinely concerned for Anthony. Kevin was pacing outside the Rector's office. He knew Anthony would be a wreck.

Except for his parents, his Uncle Joe was the most important person in Anthony's family. What struck him most was the number of blows poor Anthony had received during his first year at NAC. The darkness that both experienced after Miguel's departure had finally lifted, and he was finally starting to come back to his old self. Now, this. As he waited, Kevin toiled over what to say to him. Just then, the door opened. Without uttering a word, Monsignor O'Connor caught his eye and motioned him over to Anthony. It was almost as if he were in a trance. Anthony looked blankly at his friend as he was led down the hall and to his room. They said nothing to each other the entire way. Kevin opened the door and sat beside him on the bed.

"Hey, Anthony, I'm sorry," was all he could manage, but that was all it took. Anthony lifted his head as if seeing him for the first time, then buried his face in the crook of his neck, and he began to cry. They remained in that position for what seemed like hours. Few words were spoken, and that suited them both. Then Kevin pulled his suitcase from the closet and helped him pack.

***

After breakfast, Anthony climbed the stairs to his room. This was it – his ride to Fiumicino airport would pick him up within the hour. His bags were piled by his bed, ready to be lugged down to the porter. Laying on top of his backpack was a book, *Narcissus and Goldmund,* by Hermann Hesse. Kevin had often spoken of its impact on him during his final year at St. Thomas Seminary and quoted it quite often. It was a story of two medieval men in monastic life and their unique bond of friendship. It told of their conflict between the flesh and the spirit. Whenever he and Kevin grappled with the meaning of their relationship, he used a phrase from this book. *Kevin is so incredibly thoughtful,* he thought. He wished he could bring him to New York with him. Anthony cracked the cover and read the inscription in Kevin's unmistakable script:

Anthony,

There are no words to express what I feel.
But, as we have discussed over so many lunches, burgers, and precious Thursdays, this book seems to say so much so well.
"Let me tell you today how much I love you,
How much you have always meant to me;
How rich you have made my life...

I know what love is because of you.
You cannot imagine what that means,
It means a well in the desert,
A blossoming tree in the wilderness,
It is thanks to you that my heart has not dried up,
That a place within me has remained
Open to grace.[1] "

Now & Forever,
Love,
Kevin

Anthony could not hold back the tears any longer. Bringing the book to his bosom, he pressed the precious words to his heart and wept. Anthony did not know what the future held. He didn't know what kind of pain lay ahead during his visit with his dying uncle. The last twelve months had brought so much unexpected anguish. The young seminarian full of wonder and optimism was no longer.

And although the shine had tarnished, he realized that it was through his loss of innocence that his strength was forged, and he was better for it. Kevin was the instrument through which he found his strength. He had guided him through the unfamiliar landscape of seminary life. Through friendships forged and lost, through the struggles of politics and faith, he had become a man.

Kevin challenged him intellectually and gave him the confidence to succeed in his own way. He loved him tenderly and profoundly. It was through Kevin that he was able to survive this tumultuous year.

---

[1] Hesse, H. *Narcissus and Goldmund* (Bantam edition, 1971, p. 306)

Chapter Thirty-Eight
Life Without Anthony

The days after exams were filled with disruptions to the schedule. Many seminarians were packing for their summer vacations, while new men planned for various study programs and travel. The empty halls echoed with loneliness as Kevin went through the motions of his morning ritual. Each day, after he showered and dressed, Kevin took his journal and walked up two flights of stairs to stop by Anthony's empty room. Since the doors were not locked, he quietly slipped in and sat on his bed. There was his silly poster of a chimpanzee reading a newspaper juxtaposed by an image of St. Francis that bore a striking resemblance to Anthony himself. Glancing at all of his stuff gave Kevin comfort, but it also tore at his heart. His entire being ached for Anthony. His gaze landed on the makeshift altar in front of the window. On it was a statue that Kevin had given him for Christmas: Mary's plain wooden image holding out the infant Jesus to the world. There was no detail in the faces, just smooth lines of motion leading out from the carving. He remembered how moved Anthony was to receive it.

"It's like she's giving Christ to the world, giving the perfect love to each of us," Anthony said as he held it in his hands reverently.

"That's what drew me to it as well. It's not your typical pious image of Mary," Kevin added.

"You know, Kevin – this is what you've done for me," Anthony replied.

"What? What do you mean?" Kevin asked.

"The moment you came into my life here at NAC, you offered your love freely, no strings attached. You never expected anything in return, and you love me for who I am, not who you want me to become. I've never experienced anything like that." A tear trickled down Kevin's cheek as he recalled that day. As he wiped it away with the back of his hand, he realized he had to get out of the building.

He ambled down the stairs and out the main gate. He didn't exactly know where he was headed, but it really didn't matter. Kevin took a right at the bottom of the Janiculum and began to walk parallel to the Tiber. Through the tattered neighborhood of Trastevere, Kevin strolled in solitary stillness. It was not the prettiest part of Rome, but the guys considered it to be their neighborhood. Countless times Kevin and his two buddies walked this same path to the Pasquino – the movie house showed films in English. The streets were strewn with litter, and graffiti colored the ancient buildings. A Fiat Cinquecento zipped by him while he was lost in his thoughts. Moving out of the way just in time, he recalled walking three abreast and having to squeeze themselves against a building to prevent from being run over.

Winding in and out of various alleys, he found himself in the main *piazza*. In the center, the medieval fountain stood crowded with young Romans carrying on and socializing. Looking up at the façade of *Santa Maria in Trastevere*, he stopped in his tracks. The colorful mosaic glittered as the sun bounced off of the gold leaf tiles.

The bright reds and blues jumped out at him against the fiery backdrop. Amid his sadness, indescribable beauty shone all around him. Kevin crossed the *piazza* to his favorite cafe, found a table with a view of the beautiful mosaic, and ordered a cappuccino. Now, he was alone, half of his heart an ocean away. Miguel and Anthony were his best friends, who figured prominently in every new experience this past year, and now they were both gone.

Miguel had written several months ago but rarely responded to Kevin's letters. It didn't make sense to either of the guys. He realized Miguel needed time to heal, but why would he abandon his best friends? Kevin wondered if he bore any resentment toward them regarding the gay thing. Miguel had become more vocal as he chided Anthony and Kevin about their displays of affection. After candidacy, it seemed to escalate, but neither of them gave it much thought. They simply resolved to be more careful around Miguel.

Kevin's thoughts returned to Anthony and the aching deep in his heart. What did all this mean without Anthony? How could his life have changed so dramatically in such a short time? At that moment, he knew what he had to do. He realized that the only thing giving meaning to his time at NAC was Anthony. He had to travel to New York to be with Anthony, especially in such a difficult time. Without him by his side, Kevin was empty. He opened his prayer journal and began to write:

It is through my love for others that your grace has penetrated my being. You've entered my heart through the agony of loving, through rejection and loneliness. Because of Anthony, I have learned how to love another person with my entire being. I carry that love in my heart in his absence. And now, I must free myself to move forward – to make my own choices. My passion for Anthony has touched my heart more profoundly than I could possibly understand. It is you, Lord, who, through this love, has reached into my chest and torn out my heart. At times it is unbearable anguish. I cry out in despair. But the sweetness of our love has brought me more joy than I could have ever hoped for. I have never experienced love as profoundly as I have with him. The idea of staying at NAC falls flat. It is void of the love I have only just discovered. During this year, I've grown in love, self-esteem, and have become more of a man – an adult. The games that are played here seem senseless and evil. They dig their way into my peace and disrupt the goodness that you have placed in me.

The road ahead will not be easy. I know there may be great trials and pain. My journey is just beginning. In many ways, it would be easier to continue here at NAC, but I'm not sure that's feasible. My hesitation to change plans has often kept me stagnant. I usually don't move until I receive a shove or a kick. Indeed, Anthony's departure seems to have served that purpose.

I am a scholar, not a sculptor, but in my heart, Anthony's image is carved, and in my mind, what he has taught me has opened new doors of understanding. He has opened the doors to the sacred through his love, and I know I need to be with him. I am not the same person who walked through the doors of NAC back in September. I will never be that person again. After all, I've remained open to grace because I have been loved. My heart has finally been opened up. I've learned that true love is more profound than romance or infatuation. But I've also learned that to love means to let go. Love speaks from the heart, the core of one's being; it is the divine spark in each of us. What I share with Anthony is not a simple love story, nor a sexual escapade. Through our passion, I've been challenged to take risks and to give with my entire being. I have risen to the challenge, and because of that, I can never love less — my love for Anthony transcends the ordinary. It goes beyond words or senses — beyond distance and time. Love is deepened each day that they are together, not physically, but in their hearts. It is the taste of the divine, and it can transcend the mundane. If I stay at NAC, my heart may dry up. No, I must take the next step. I must act with courage and move beyond.

Reading over his words, Kevin felt almost foolish. It was not like him to get so emotional. He smiled and thought it was just another example of how Anthony had transformed him. He remained at the cafe for over an hour. After paying the bill, Kevin retraced his steps toward NAC. Kevin knew what he had to do. He had to be with Anthony.

A plan began to form in his mind. His father had been laid off from TWA but had recently been called back to work. As a family member, Kevin could fly free on standby. Within the week, all the seminarians at NAC would disperse. The older men would return to the states to be with family. But the new men, not allowed to go back to the United States until after they completed their second year, could travel anywhere else in the world. Most of them had plans to vacation somewhere in Europe, others to do service or ministry. Kevin had made plans to fly to Ireland to visit his relatives. He realized that from there, he could easily sneak home to be with Anthony. No one at NAC would ever know.

Chapter Thirty-Nine
A Time for Honesty

It was the last weekend of June when Joe Rossi picked up Anthony from Kennedy Airport. They made feeble attempts at their usual banter, but it fell flat for both of them. They both knew of the reason for his visit, and it weighed heavily on their minds.

During the drive home, his brother told Anthony that his parents didn't know he was coming home. "I didn't tell them. There's been so much bad news about Uncle Joe that I figured they could use a surprise," Anthony explained.

"Good call, Joe. I can't wait to see the look on their faces when I walk into the house." Anthony opened the back door and yelled out, "Mom, dad, I'm home."

He got the desired response. They were in disbelief, saying nothing for a moment. Then his mother jumped up and smothered him with kisses. It was late Saturday evening when he got himself settled, and his jetlag was catching up to him. "Go, Anthony, go to bed. You look exhausted," his father said.

"No, dad, I really have to see Uncle Joe tonight."

"No, Anthony, he's probably resting by now, and you look like shit," Joe added. "Listen to dad and get some rest. You can visit him tomorrow."

Being six hours ahead, he woke up much too early the following morning, and he was out the door before anyone else was awake. He scribbled a quick note to his parents and drove into the city.

The first Mass was just ending when he rang the rectory bell. When the receptionist answered, her initial look of annoyance turned into a bright smile. "Anthony, I can't believe you're here. Aren't you supposed to be in Rome?"

"Yeah, but they let me come back to visit with Monsignor Joe. Is he up yet?" Anthony asked.

"Oh, I'm so sorry, my dear. Monsignor Joe is at his condo in Westchester. It's impossible to rest at the rectory with all that's going on here. Didn't your mother tell you?"

"I just got back last evening, and I left before they woke this morning. I should have checked with my mom first, but I was so eager to see him."

"Come in. You can call Monsignor Joe from the office. At least let him know you're coming. While you're at it, call your parents and tell them about your plans. I'm sure they're worried," she chided him gently. Even though she was scolding him, he loved that she treated him like family.

He got back into the car and drove another hour to Mamaroneck. As he went up the driveway, it occurred to Anthony that he didn't know what to expect. He knew that Uncle Joe had been very ill, but no one would give him any answers. The official diagnosis was cancer, but Anthony suspected it was something else. No one seemed to know what kind of cancer, and there was no mention of radiation or chemotherapy. None of it made much sense.

When Joe answered the door, Anthony was shocked. This formerly robust man looked like a skeleton. His skin hung off his bones as if there were no muscle underneath. His thick silver hair was patchy, and he had dark purple blotches on his skin. Over the last six months, Monsignor

Joe, who was always fit and healthy, had been in the hospital several times. He had come down with pneumonia, followed by severe gastrointestinal issues, and now he seemed to be wasting away. His virile and spirited uncle was reduced to a shell of his previous self.

Just about a year ago, there was talk of a new gay cancer spreading at an alarming pace. Anthony had read that it was called the Gay-Related Immune Deficiency or GRID, and New York was one of the cities with the most documented cases. His year in Rome had kept Anthony blissfully ignorant of the epidemic they now called AIDS. But Father Joe had all the signs of it, including those dark spots on his skin, Kaposi Sarcoma, a rare disease common in people with AIDS.

"I am so glad to see you," was all that Anthony could manage to say to his uncle.

"You are home, *caro* – they let you come home," Joe cried as he broke into a fit of coughing.

"Are you okay? Let me pour you some water."

Anthony sprang into the house and ran to the kitchen. When the coughing subsided, he sat beside him on the couch and took Joe's hand in his.

"I'm so glad you're here, Anthony. I assumed they would keep you in Rome through your second year."

"Well, that was the plan. But last week, I got called to the rector's office informing me of the Cardinal's wishes for my return to New York."

"Thank God, they listened to me," Joe said. "My one request from them was to see you one last time, *caro.*"

"Don't say that, Uncle Joe, please. You're not going anywhere. Remember, we have to celebrate my first Mass together. That was our plan. You can't go changing it now."

"God willing. But, Anthony, I feel life slipping away from me, and it makes me so furious. There is so much more that I want to do."

Anthony was at a loss for words. He had never heard such despair from Uncle Joe, and it frightened him. They spend the next few days watching videos and catching up. But it became clear that Joe was growing weaker.

By the third day, Anthony packed up all of Joe's clothing and medicines and drove him back to his rectory in Manhattan. It was not good for him to be so far away from his doctor and the hospital. Anthony moved into the guest room but ended up sleeping on the couch in Joe's sitting room almost every night. Over the next few days, he spent hours chatting about the trials and tribulations during his first year at the North American College and watching Joe drift in and out of sleep. It was torture, and his heart was broken at the impending loss of his most significant mentor. *What will I do without him?*

On his better days, Monsignor Joe peppered Anthony with questions of his experience in Rome over the last ten months. He was saddened to hear of the conflicts that had arisen in his class. He was also surprised by the extent of the rightward shift of Church leadership.

"So much of my priesthood has been directing this great ship toward the future. The teachings of Vatican two have guided an entire generation toward greater inclusivity and acceptance of all. I can't believe that the pope and his curia would try to nullify all the progress we made," Monsignor Joe lamented.

"It's worse than that, Uncle Joe. You can hardly mention Vatican II without being labeled as subversive. Somehow belief in its teachings has become synonymous with challenging Pope John Paul."

"That can't be true. These are official Church documents," Monsignor Joe replied.

"Sadly, the conservative Catholics are slowly chipping away at them. They want the Church of the old days where priests are held above laypeople. Authority is not to be questioned, especially in areas of sexual morality," Anthony said, hoping to prompt a discussion about his own sexuality with his uncle.

Although they never really spoke of their sexuality, Anthony had suspected that his Uncle Joe was gay. His circle of friends spoke volumes: handsome, fit men, gregarious, and creative. He knew he was stereotyping, but come on, they were all gay, and Anthony felt right at home with them. Given his experiences in Rome, he had no doubt that many priests were sexually active despite the vow of celibacy. It didn't bother him, though. Anthony believed everyone had to form their own moral code, and it was not for anyone to judge. And given his loneliness and need for companionship this past year, he could certainly understand why priests broke that vow.

"If we continue on this path, the Church will become irrelevant. We saw it happening when everyone simply ignored the ban on artificial contraception back in the seventies," Joe said, shaking his head.

"Well, now it seems that they are pushing harder against homosexuality. You wouldn't believe the lectures we got about overt homosexual behavior. Hell, most of the seminarians are gay," Anthony said.

"And most of us ordained priests as well," Joe said as he looked up at Anthony. This was the moment for him to share his story. But he didn't know if he had the strength. Sensing his discomfort, Anthony let him off the hook.

"Who cares whether or not we're gay. It's our own business, and let's face it, we can't choose who we fall in love with," Anthony said.

"Sage words, indeed, *caro*. But sometimes it can come back to haunt us." Anthony reached out and took his uncle's hand. They were quiet for a moment.

"Anthony, I'm not sure how much you've heard about AIDS during your year in Rome. But the epidemic has ravaged the gay population in New York City. There's no test for the disease, but I'm afraid I have many of the symptoms." With tears welled up in his eyes, Anthony placed his head on Joe's chest. His uncle wrapped his arms around his beloved nephew, and they sat in silence. "So, *caro*, tell me about your life, not the goings-on at NAC. Tell me about your friends," Joe said, breaking the silence.

Anthony sat up and looked at his uncle, happy that he had the opportunity to come out to him. He knew he couldn't share this with anyone else in his family.

"Uncle Joe, I have fallen in love with an extraordinary man at NAC. His name is Kevin, and he has been the only thing that has sustained me throughout this awful year. To be honest, I see nothing morally wrong with our relationship and the expression of our love."

"You mean you are in a sexual relationship with him?" Joe asked.

"Yes," Anthony said, his cheeks flushing red. "I believe that it's a matter of conscience. Although I am sinning in the eyes of the Church, I know in my heart that our love is good, and that my actions are morally correct."

"Anthony," Joe said as he cupped his hand under Anthony's chin. "You are fortunate to have found someone who you can trust and who supports you in your times of need. I, on the other hand..."

"Uncle Joe, I don't need to know your life story. Your personal life is none of my business. I just hope that you have the love you need right now."

"I thought I did, Anthony. But as soon as he discovered how ill I had become, he ran scared. He believes that he's next – which is likely true," he confessed.

"That bastard. Have the rest of your priest friends been by to visit?" Anthony asked.

"The rumor mill has taken its toll on all of my friendships. Those who would be supportive are afraid they'll be infected. The others don't want to associate with any priest who might have AIDS. It would taint their precious reputations or halt their climb up the ecclesial ladder. No, *caro*, I find myself in desolate isolation."

"Surely, my mother has been in to visit, and the rest of the family?" he asked.

"At first, but once your father heard the diagnosis, he forbade her to come. He's afraid I'll infect your mom."

"What is wrong with that man? She's your sister, for god's sake!" Anthony had no words, and though he tried to hide it, his eyes were brimming with tears.

"People are terrified of this disease. There's so much they don't know about it," Joe said, being more generous toward his brother-in-law than he felt.

Chapter Forty

A Precipitous Decline

The month of July was precious to both of them. Anthony would cherish the intimacy that developed between him and Uncle Joe and carry it in his heart for the rest of his days. But there were many practical tasks to be handled. Anthony was grateful for the visiting nurse that came each day and for the Gay Men's Health Crisis (GMHC), a volunteer organization that sent a volunteer to check on Joe every day. Often, he would get him laughing or engage him in conversations that might distract him from his pain. But there were times when Joe just needed to complain or express his despair, and the volunteer would hold his hand and listen. During this time, Anthony began his crash course in AIDS education.

Joe's health deteriorated precipitously. He couldn't seem to keep any food down, and Anthony could see him wasting away before his eyes. He was sitting on the couch with Anthony one day when he lost control of his bowls. Joe was mortified, but the pain had him doubled over.

"I think you should call Dr. Steinburg. Something is terribly wrong."

"On it, Uncle Joe. Let me get you to the bathroom first," Anthony said.

"No, no, I can do it. This is disgusting. You'll get it all over you," he objected.

"This is no time to be embarrassed. Let me help you."

Joe leaned on the vanity while Anthony cleaned him up. His dignity all but gone – he began to cry. Anthony, fighting back his tears, kept at his task and got him dressed. He couldn't let himself give in to his emotions. Joe needed him to be strong. He rested Joe's arm over his shoulder and led him out to the car. Dr. Jeff instructed Anthony to bring him directly to the emergency room. Given the scare of the AIDS epidemic, they couldn't be sure that an ambulance or even a taxi would take the call.

Many drivers refused service for fear of contracting the disease. Throughout the drive, Joe moaned in pain. When they arrived, Dr. Steinburg was standing at the entrance and ushered them in without delay. Anthony was left standing in the emergency room, staring at the doors through which the doctors took Joe. The usual chaos raged around him with ambulance sirens and the shouts of demanding patients, but he was oblivious to it all. The image of his hero reduced to complete dependence on others was jarring. How could this be happening? What was he to do now?

It was days before they allowed Anthony to visit with him. When he got to Joe's room, he looked in from a distance to get himself oriented. He didn't want to show any shock or worry on his face when he saw Joe.

From across the hall, he could see Joe's withered body. His cheeks were drawn, and the dark purple blotches checkered his neck and arms seemed more pronounced. Immediately, tears welled in his eyes, and he cried. A nurse spotted him as she walked by and stopped.

"You had better get that out of your system before you go in there. The last thing he needs is to comfort you," she said.

"I know, I'm sorry," Anthony replied.

"No need to be sorry. It's a war zone here. If this didn't shake you to your core, I'd be worried," the nurse said.

"How did this happen so quickly? Why isn't more being done?" Anthony cried.

"Oh, honey, we're doing all we can. But no one really cares what happens to dying gays. We can't even get this disease classified as an epidemic," she said bitterly. "Go on, get in there. Monsignor needs some company. He hasn't gotten many visitors."

Anthony knew that even his parents had only seen him once since he was in the hospital. After seeing his lesions, they knew it wasn't merely cancer. The AIDS epidemic was all over the local news, and they were embarrassed for him and themselves. The extended family couldn't even be persuaded to visit. As soon as they heard what ward he was on, they simply stayed away. Anthony quietly walked into his room.

Joe was in and out of consciousness, and the nurse advised Anthony to keep the visit short. He sat in the chair beside the bed with his breviary in his hands and prayed. Out of the corner of his eye, he saw Uncle Joe turn his head. "You're awake. How are you feeling?"

"Rough around the edges," he responded and chuckled. But that turned into a coughing fit. Once his body settled down again, he squeezed Anthony's hand.

Days turned into weeks, but Anthony never missed a day. He sat by his side to chat, to read him books, and to watch him sleep. He hoped that by sheer will, his Uncle Joe would be healed. Every now and again, Joe would turn to him with a look of gravity and give some sage advice. More often, he would simply say, I love you.

"*Caro,* I don't have much time left, so listen carefully. Only you can decide what is right for you. You have a good heart. Follow the path you believe is right, no matter what anyone says."

"Thank you, Uncle Joe. You have no idea what that means to me," Anthony said.

"I believe I do."

Then he closed his eyes and drifted off into a restless sleep. Anthony pulled out his journal and wrote:

Uncle Joe is slowly dying. I can't bear to watch him suffer but I can't bring myself to leave his side. I am tortured by his suffering, and I want so badly to believe that he will come out of this. But somehow, I know he won't be the same even if he does. I'm so afraid of losing him.

His guidance won't be there, and I don't know what I'll do without it. I made all my important decisions only after I spoke with him. So much of my drive and my strength came from him. He is the priest I always wanted to be. He looked up at Joe through watery eyes, and although his distress was palpable, a wave of gratitude washed over him. Had they had not allowed him to come home this summer, he would have missed out on this precious time with his uncle. During the weeks they had spent together, Anthony came to know Joe more intimately than all the years that came before. He had always been his mentor, but now he was his dearest of friends. Their time together this summer was undoubtedly the greatest gift he could ask for.

Chapter Forty-One
The Proposal

They were sitting on the seatback of a park bench in Washington Square. Greenwich Village was teeming with people basking in the bright sunshine of a July day. The oppressive humidity of New York summers was noticeably absent. The fountain was surrounded by folks sitting on its edge, chatting, or sunning themselves. The magnificent arch that marks the entrance to the park stood proudly against the azure sky. Anthony and Kevin hadn't seen each other in weeks, and this reunion was fraught with uncertainty. Kevin waited in anxious anticipation. The strumming of a guitar caught his attention, and he turned to look. It was a young man with a sweet tenor voice, just like Anthony's. He couldn't wait to see him. He wondered what they should do with their lives now that they were both away from NAC?

Kevin was almost sure that the dream of the priesthood was behind him. He had fallen madly in love with Anthony, and although they had drifted together and apart from each other several times during the last year, he was sure that they were meant to be together. When they realized Miguel had been ousted from NAC in secrecy in March, his perspective upon the entire year changed. These men who were charged with guiding seminarians through the significant process of discernment were totally inept. Kevin now believed them to be evil, concerned with no one else but themselves and their fragile reputations. It was all about following where the winds blew next. It was clear that Church politics governed each and every decision they made. The seminarians were simply pawns in the ecclesial game of chess, and they were the first to be knocked off the board if they didn't conform.

The months after Miguel's departure, Kevin began to understand that he could only rely upon himself concerning his spiritual well-being. The letter Anthony had received in response to his crisis of faith only served to reinforce that fact. He had heard very little from the Archdiocese of Hartford, and that was perfectly fine. As far as he was concerned, he was done with them and the faculty at NAC. Kevin would make decisions and act according to his own conscience. He planned to finish out the year and decide about his future then.

As he sat on the park bench in Washington Square, Kevin observed all the colorful people parading by. A man on a unicycle rode by, and children frolicked in the fountain. There was so much freedom and joy there. No one was concerned with what anybody else thought of their hair or clothing. They didn't care that some men held each other's hands, or women were kissing under a tree. Why should he worry about the Church or what his family thought of him for being gay? This was his life, and he could love anyone he chose. In this case, it was Anthony.

When he looked up from his internal reverie, Anthony was walking toward him, looking absolutely adorable in his lavender Izod polo and shorts. How he missed him over the weeks they were apart. Anthony's departure from Rome after exams was sudden, and they hadn't gotten much time to chat about his uncle's prognosis. He knew Anthony was going through a rough time, and he pledged to be by his side through it all.

"Hey there, cutie," Kevin said as he engulfed Anthony in the warmest of hugs. "I have missed you so much."

Anthony felt like he was home.

"Oh my God, you are a sight for sore eyes. I feel like I've been living a nightmare with no one to talk to about it there. It feels so good to be in your arms again, *amore mio*."

"Don't you worry, I'm here – always. Tell me what's going on," Kevin said to Anthony.

"It's all but certain that my Uncle Joe is dying. Sitting at his bedside during the last few weeks has been brutal," Anthony told Kevin.

"I'm so sorry, Anthony. This makes little sense. I didn't think cancer advanced so quickly."

"Well, it's not exactly cancer," Anthony said. He went on to explain Joe's diagnosis and the severity of the AIDS epidemic in New York.

"Man, it's as if we were on another planet in Rome. How did we miss all this?" Kevin asked.

"I really don't know, but it has put many of our worries into perspective," Anthony responded.

"It certainly does. I still can't believe that I heard nothing about this when I was in Connecticut last year. Do they know how it's transmitted?" Kevin asked, sincerely.

"They're pretty sure it's from sexual activity. But people are panicked, afraid to be near or touch someone with AIDS. Case in point, almost no one from the archdiocese has come to visit. They're a bunch of fucking cowards – hypocrites," Anthony replied.

"Damned bureaucrats. God forbid they show any compassion to the gays," Kevin added.

That it has primarily affected the gay community has everyone running scared. Half of them are afraid they'll catch it, and the others are afraid their ecclesiastic reputations will be tainted by one of their own who has it," Anthony said bitterly.

Anthony filled Kevin in on his uncle and the Church politics that swirled around his situation. Anthony had learned a lot during the weeks he spent in the hospital. He resolved to educate himself about AIDS. There was no talk about the disease in Rome, especially at the NAC, where everyone was entirely self-absorbed. Kevin was visibly shaken by the gravity of the epidemic. Then Anthony placed his hand on Kevin's knee and squeezed.

"So, hey, I'm sorry that I'm such a downer. I really needed to see you. I needed to be with someone who gives me hope. What's going on with you? How did you manage to get home without NAC finding out?" Anthony asked.

"It was easy. I'm in Ireland with my relatives for the summer. Unless I show my face in Hartford, no one will ever know that I flew back to the states."

"You're an evil genius, Kev. Hey, I am so glad that you're here this summer. We need to spend more time together," Anthony said. "Can you stay over tonight?"

"Absolutely! We have some catching up to do," Kevin said with a wink.

"You're terrible. But you're right. I really need some love right now. God, I missed you! I don't know how I've made it through all this without you."

"Yeah, it's been a desert at NAC since you left. I felt completely lost." They were quiet for a moment, gazing over the colorful scene before them. It was such a contrast to the internal strife that burned within. "So, Anthony, there's something I've wanted to talk to you about."

"Uh oh, sounds serious," responding playfully.

"It *is* serious, Anthony. Look, we love each other. That is painfully clear. And given our conflicts with the Church, I don't feel any loyalty to it anymore. I honestly believe that they don't have our best interest at heart."

"I think we both came to that conclusion this year. So, where are you going with this?" Anthony asked.

"I got here pretty early, and I've spent the morning looking at all these wonderful people doing *exactly* as they please – no bishop or rector breathing down their necks, no worries about whether they're doing the right thing. I've seen so many gay couples holding hands and living completely normal lives," Kevin explained.

"Yeah, that's Greenwich Village for you. It's a wonderful place to be," Anthony replied.

"So, why not live here? You and me – let's stop all this priesthood nonsense. We can both get jobs teaching or something. We could rent an apartment and be a couple. Then we can truly begin our lives together. What do you say?" Anthony looked at Kevin and saw his sincerity. This was an honest proposal, and Anthony never dreamed of the possibility. *But why not? Why can't they just be together?* he thought. But then his doubts set in.

"God, that sounds amazing. I can't even imagine what it would be like to simply live our lives together – without having to sneak around." Anthony paused as he let that thought sink in for a moment. "I don't know, Kevin. There is so much uncertainty in my life right now. I am so confused about my vocation and my uncle. I wouldn't even know where to start."

"I hope you're not confused about me. I love you, Anthony. I know you know that, and you love me. We can do this. I know we can," Kevin responded.

"No, I'm not confused about you. You are the love of my life. You are the first man to treat me with unconditional love, and you have always been honest with me. But, Kevin, are you ready to give up your dream of becoming a priest? You've been in the seminary for many more years than me. Can you honestly let that go?"

"Yes, for you, I can. I love you, Anthony. Please give this some serious thought," Kevin pleaded. He had hoped that Anthony would jump at the idea. There had been conversations about the viability of their relationship after ordination. Kevin believed that this was the perfect solution.

"The truth is," Anthony said as he looked out at the fountain, "I am not sure I can let the priesthood go. It's all I ever wanted."

Kevin's heart sank. This was not how he expected their conversation to go. *How could Anthony turn him down like this?*

"But I promise I will think about it," Anthony continued. "I mean, the idea of living here in the Village with you – it's a dream come true. Can you give me a little time? Let me think about it for a while, okay?"

"Take all the time you need, Anthony. But please know that I am right here with you."

Kevin threw his arms around Anthony and kissed him passionately right there in public. It was one of the most freeing feelings he had ever experienced. Anthony was shocked by his bold public display of affection. And a little embarrassed as well. For Kevin, the mere act of kissing Anthony out in the open unleashed his love. Yes, this is what he wanted for his life. He had to make Anthony understand it was right for both.

Anthony and Kevin were in New York or Connecticut for the next several weeks, visiting each other. Since they were stateside, they tried to get in touch with Miguel. They had heard from him occasionally, but several letters went unanswered. Unfortunately, Miguel couldn't meet them in New York.

In the months that followed his departure, Miguel became increasingly resentful of the poisonous atmosphere in the seminary. Although there were many painful experiences at NAC, the most traumatic was when his advisor invaded his room and came onto him. His sexual advances colored Miguel's image of the Church. It was sick with deception and abuse of power. There was little for Miguel to cling to as he struggled with his faith. And although he truly loved his two friends, Miguel needed time away from it all. He knew they would still be there when his head cleared.

Although they found it odd that Miguel dropped off the face of the earth, Anthony and Kevin were wholly absorbed with each other. Spending so much time together, Anthony was coming around to Kevin's proposal. *I could get used to this – being with Kevin for the rest of my life.* He felt at home with him.

The idea of going back to Rome after spending all this time together seemed foolish. It was refreshing to hang out with each other with no one questioning the closeness of their relationship. It seemed so normal. The two of them openly fantasized about their future together – what neighborhood they'd live in and the apartment they'd rent. It was becoming real to him. Anthony had reached a decision. His life with Kevin was a reality, while the priesthood was simply an idea. It was time he let go of his dream of becoming a priest and live what was real. He was indeed in love with Kevin. How could he choose otherwise?

Chapter Forty-Two
Transitions

Anthony had been staying in Joe's suite at the rectory. When Kevin visited, no one even questioned it. Most evenings, the place was empty, so they had total privacy. Anthony turned toward Kevin as he tenderly caressed his face.

"You know – we're totally alone. Everyone's out, and we have our own bedroom," Anthony said.

"It would be a shame to waste such a promising opportunity," Kevin responded with sarcasm.

Then Anthony stood, reached out his hand, and led Kevin to his room. Anthony sat him down on the edge of the bed, lifted Kevin's t-shirt above his head and kissed him. Their kiss was tender and sensual.

Then Anthony turned his attention to Kevin's jeans. He unzipped them and pulled them off. Kevin stood proud in his white briefs, and Anthony smiled, noticing the thin cotton stretched tightly over his hardening penis.

God, he's sexy, Anthony thought.

Anthony lifted off his own t-shirt and knelt down in front of Kevin and reached out to squeeze him. Kevin gasped at his touch, lacing his fingers through Anthony's hair as he pulled his face closer.

Anthony lowered the waistband of Kevin's briefs and ran his tongue along the length of his sex.

"Oh. My. God! Anthony, that feels so good," Kevin said.

"*O mio amore*, you have no idea what I have in store for you," Anthony said, raising his eyebrows suggestively.

There was nothing rushed or furtive about their time together. Each movement, each touch, was intentional and deliberate. Lying together on the spacious bed, Kevin looked down into Anthony's eyes as he pressed into him. Anthony winced.

"Are you okay, Anthony? Am I hurting you?"

"Just... just slow down. Give me time to relax," he said breathlessly. Little by little, Anthony felt Kevin fill his emptiness. Finally, with their chests touching, Kevin nuzzled his face against Anthony's ear.

"I love you, Anthony."

"*Ti amo, mio tesoro*," I love you, my treasure, Anthony whispered. For the first time, they made love without the worry of being discovered, without the shadow of NAC hanging over them. Their bodies joined together ardently and lovingly. Soon their passions flared as they gave in to their emotions and desires. It was the most profound sexual experience either of them had ever had, both energetic and tender. When it was over, with sweat dripping from their brows, they rested in the afterglow, letting their breathing regulate. Then their eyes met.

"Wow!" was all Kevin could manage to say.

"I've never felt anything like that before – never," Anthony said. Later, they laughed at themselves. It was the first time they could make noise while making love.

"No more seminary sex," Kevin said.

"Ha, I had no idea you were so loud," Anthony said, poking his ribs. After they dressed, they lounged in Joe's private sitting room, sipping their favorite liqueur, Baileys Irish Cream. Anthony decided it was time to tell Kevin of his decision to stay, but he was having trouble working up the courage. He had alluded to it during the previous week, so it wouldn't be a big surprise.

"So, I think I've made a decision, Kev."

"And?"

"Let's just do it. I mean, these weeks together have been like a dream. I'm not ready for this to end."

Kevin jumped on top of Anthony and smothered him with kisses. "You won't be sorry, I promise," Kevin said.

"I better not be. This is the craziest decision I've ever made."

Just then, the phone rang. It was the hospital. Monsignor Joe had taken a turn for the worse. Without a moment's hesitation, they hopped into a cab and were on the AIDS ward in no time to spare.

The nurse whom he had met on his first visit was on duty. She looked up as he and Kevin came by her station. She came around to him, put her hand on his shoulder, and said, "Go, spend time with him. Talk to him, tell him everything he means to you. Though he may not respond, your voice will comfort him." She paused as she looked over to Joe. "It won't be long now."

Tears were streaming down Anthony's face. *This is happening way too fast. I can't lose him now*, he thought.

"Hey, Uncle Joe," he said as he took his hand and sat beside him. "It's Anthony. I don't know if you can hear me, but I want to tell you something." Anthony had to choke back his tears. "Uncle Joe, other than my parents, you have been the most important person in my life. You have been with me through every major decision. You have wiped my tears on countless occasions, and you have celebrated so much joy with me. My dream was to be just like you, be the kind of priest you are, and inspire people with your love. You have touched so many hearts over the years. But I think that you have touched mine more profoundly than any other. I love you, Uncle Joe, and I don't know what I'm going to do without you."

Monsignor Joe's breathing had become labored and noisy. Some referred to it as the death rattle. When Anthony heard that, he began to cry in earnest. Kevin looked on helplessly. This was an extraordinarily intimate moment, and he felt almost embarrassed to be a witness to it.

He ached for Anthony but knew he could do nothing to ease his pain. "Go on now, Uncle Joe. Let go. It's okay, you know. He's waiting for you with open arms. God will take away all your pain. Let go. There is no need to hold on to it anymore. Let go. Just know that you are loved. Rest, be at rest. I love you, *caro Zio*."

Time stood still as he listened to Joe's labored breathing. He could tell that his beloved uncle was suffering. *Why is no one here to anoint him – give him the last rites?* Anthony tasted the bitterness he felt toward the priests who had abandoned Joe in his hour of greatest need. Then he knew what he must do. There were no holy oils, so he took a cup of water and blessed it. Dipping his thumb into the water, he then traced the sign of the cross on Monsignor Joe's forehead, saying:

"Depart, dearest Joseph, out of this world;
In the Name of God, the Father Almighty who created you;
In the Name of Jesus Christ who redeemed you;
In the Name of the Holy Spirit, who sanctifies you.
May your rest be this day in peace,
and your dwelling place in the Paradise of God."

At that moment, he felt the power of the priesthood, the significance of being there at the moment of death. It may have been his imagination, but Joe's breathing slowed – he seemed to be at peace. He kissed the spot where he had just anointed him and sat back down. He held his hand and prayed. Not long after, Joe breathed his last breath. There was an eerie calm in the room – a brief moment of peace. Anthony rested his forehead on his uncle's lifeless body, still warm to the touch as silent tears ran down his cheeks.

It was over.

Chapter Forty-Three
Everything Changes

The days leading up to the funeral were a blur. Anthony's mother was beside herself with grief over the loss of her baby brother. The archdiocese handled all the details and the planning, which was a great relief to Anthony and his family. When he read the press release, however, bile rose in his throat. It merely stated:

Beloved pastor Monsignor Joseph Gallo died peacefully after a prolonged battle with cancer. At forty-eight years old, he was taken from us all too soon.

They hadn't even dared to say that his death was because of complications from AIDS. The Cardinal presided at the Mass, and all the priests that neglected to visit him while he was in the hospital were proudly in attendance for the lavish funeral. There were over thirty priests in the processional, and although Anthony was angry with their hypocrisy, he hadn't the energy to express it. His grief was all-consuming. Kevin was there the entire time, standing at a distance — careful not to interfere with the family's grief. He was seething with hatred for these pompous fools who preached God's love but could not show a drop of compassion while Monsignor Joe lay, dying.

The Mass was held at the Church where Joe was a pastor. The pews were packed with mourners, and the overflow had people lining the side aisles and vestibule. When it came time for the first reading, Anthony walked to the ambo. He stood silently for a moment, then took a visibly deep breath and began.

He looked out at the sea of grieving faces, and with a powerful voice, he read from the book of Wisdom:

"The Souls of the just are in the hand of God, and no torment shall touch him."

All of Kevin's composure melted away. He marveled at Anthony's strength, stricken with grief, yet he was proclaiming the word of God with conviction. Kevin was filled with compassion and admiration for the young man who stood before the multitude of mourners.

All at once, he was overcome and began to cry. Anthony stood with his family at the burial site, whose grief intensified at this final ritual. His mother and his aunts wailed as the final prayers were said. The crowd of mourners pressed in on them from every side. The prayers droned on with few paying attention. Holy water was sprinkled on the coffin. Then the Cardinal addressed the family and friends in attendance.

"Dearly beloved, how can we make sense of such a loss? Monsignor Joseph Gallo lived his life in the footsteps of Christ. His life was snuffed out much too soon. We mourn his passing, but look to the future as we celebrate his life. He spent his priesthood serving God's people with an unrelenting passion, so I ask you to pray with me," he paused. "Let us pray that from Monsignor Gallo's family, a call might be answered that someone will fill his shoes and serve as a priest."

Anthony felt every eye focused on him as they physically turned to look at him. Of course, Anthony was that person. He was already studying to be a priest in Rome, no less. Fear gripped Anthony as he felt his own will being ripped away. The ground beneath him crumbled just as his fragile decision to leave the seminary and start a life with Kevin.

All he could see were scores of eyes focused on him. They would never understand his decision to leave. How could he disappoint them? *Perhaps this is God's will? Maybe that final moment when I gave Uncle Joe the last rites was a sign.* All his doubts about leaving the seminary resurfaced. His mother looped her arm into his and sobbed into his chest.

"Monsignor Joe was always so proud of you, Anthony," she whispered. "Thank God you are here to carry on for him."

A steel cage slammed shut around his heart and barred him from making any other choice.

It crushed his dream of a life with Kevin. Anthony squeezed his eyes closed as if to ward off the Cardinal's words. Kevin's face flashed in his mind. How could he lose him after all they'd been through? But at that moment, he knew that there would be no apartment in Greenwich Village, no romantic strolls in the park. He looked directly at the Cardinal, and he let go. He had no choice – it was a *fait accompli*. He would return to Rome in September to complete his studies. Anthony would be ordained a priest.

The moment was not lost on Kevin. He saw the look in Anthony's eyes, anger, then fear, and finally resignation. How did everything change? In just one sentence, the Cardinal tore his true love from his arms. What right did he have to ask that of Anthony? He knew *exactly* what he was doing. Anthony could never live with that guilt. How could it have changed so quickly? He bowed his head and cried bitter tears.

***

August was rapidly drawing to a close with families busy with back-to-school preparations. Kevin knew he had to make a decision. The idea of going back to NAC filled him with dread. And yet, if he wanted to be with Anthony, NAC was the only solution. It would be a return to their original plans. They would continue their relationship throughout their priesthood.

But over the summer, the notion of living an ordinary life outside of the Church took root. He'd grown accustomed to images of him and Anthony getting jobs and living in an apartment together. He was excited about making decisions on his own and leading an ordinary life. Now that he had seriously considered life beyond priesthood, he wasn't willing to let it all go.

After the funeral, Anthony was a zombie. His grief was a darkness that cast a shadow upon his every move. He trudged through his final days in New York with little thought about what lay ahead. Anthony met with the Cardinal regarding his return to NAC, and neither of them mentioned the crisis of faith he wrote about.

He accepted instructions without question and prepared for his journey back to Rome. He and Kevin never spoke about that moment at the burial site, but he was sure that Kevin had surmised its impact. Anthony hadn't seen him in over a week and dreaded their next conversation. He knew he couldn't avoid it any longer and called him. Anthony drove to Connecticut the next day. They were sitting on his parents' back porch, looking out on the vegetable garden. "I'm sorry, Kev. I didn't have any choice."

"I know. I can't imagine what it felt like to have all those eyes focused on you."

"I was crazy with grief; I still am. The Cardinal took me completely by surprise, and you wouldn't believe what my mother said to me. The pressure just kept piling on."

"Listen, I can't say I am happy with your decision, but I understand," Kevin said.

"But can't we just continue the way we are? Come back to Rome with me. I mean, we always wanted to become priests. We wouldn't be much different from most of the priests out there," Anthony asked Kevin one last time.

Kevin stood and walked over to the railing and gazed out. Nothing seemed in focus. What he had to say next would change everything.

"Anthony, I realized something during the time we spent together this summer," Kevin paused – he turned to look directly into Anthony's eyes. "I don't want to live a life in hiding. Kissing you in the middle of Washington Square was one of the best feelings I've ever had. I felt free for the very first time in my life. I'm not sure I can go back into the closet."

"Wait, what are you saying?" Anthony asked with a combination of confusion and panic.

"It means that I don't want to go back to Rome. I can't live a lie any longer."

Anthony looked away – he was dumbfounded. He had never considered life at NAC without Kevin. This was another blow to his already arduous life. He had no idea how to respond. What more was there to say? He felt betrayed, abandoned.

"Anthony, look at me, please," Kevin pleaded. "This doesn't mean I don't love you. It's just that I want something more for us. I know you have to go back there but promise me something. Once the dust settles and the pressures of the Cardinal's words fade, please reconsider our plan. There is no rush. We can continue to talk about our dreams for the future. Let's just give it a few months. Can you do that?"

"Yeah," he mumbled. "I suppose I can. I just can't imagine my life without you," Anthony replied.

"Believe me. I know what you mean."

"So, what will you do?" Anthony asked.

"I'm not sure. I need some time to think. Maybe I'll go to grad school or teach. But I don't want to stay in Connecticut. I need to go to a city where no one knows me. Where I can just be myself."

"Sounds like a dream," Anthony said wistfully.

"A dream that you could still be a part of, Anthony," he said with a sad smile. Anthony bowed his head – he couldn't look at Kevin in the eye.

Chapter Forty-Four
Closure

Anthony was gone. It was Labor Day weekend, and Kevin found himself on the Metro-North Railroad heading into Manhattan. He didn't have any definitive plans, but he knew he had to get out of Connecticut. Taking the subway all the way down to the Christopher St. station, he strolled along, looking into the many shops and bars. It was a perfect late summer day with so many people enjoying the beautiful weather. With no particular destination in mind, he wandered into Washington Square Park. Gazing up at the grand arch, Kevin marveled at its beauty. *New York City is fantastic!* he thought. *I could really see myself living here.*

Absentmindedly, he found himself heading toward the very same park bench where he had proposed to Anthony. His stomach tightened, almost as if he'd been punched in the gut. He took a deep breath and waited for it to pass. Kevin's heart was broken, but he was not.

For the first time in many months, he felt he was in control of his own destiny – making his own decisions. No longer was he beholden to the bishop or the faculty at NAC.

The priesthood that had always been his dream had been tarnished by the deep divisions within the Church. His eyes had been opened to the reality of a tremendously flawed institution. The Church suffered from the sin of humanity just as any secular institution, perhaps more so. The passion with which the hierarchy clung to their power obscured the foundational teachings of love and compassion. Instilled in him from his youth was deep, abiding guilt.

He knew that the world around him considered his homosexuality a disorder – a grave sin. But the ubiquitous presence of gay culture within the Church only highlighted the hypocrisy of its teachings.

How could the Church preach of the evils of the gay lifestyle when so many priests, bishops, and cardinals were gay? How could they judge ordinary people who struggle to find love when they themselves seek solace in the arms of other men?

The Church's teachings were harsh, but he could understand an institution standing by centuries of doctrine. What he couldn't abide was the blatant duplicitousness of her priests. *From this moment on,* he thought, *I will no longer apologize for who I am or who I love. I will be true to myself and to how God made me.*

"Mind if I sit here?" A voice startled Kevin from his thoughts.

"What? Oh, yes, I mean no, please do," Kevin replied.

"You looked a million miles away. Everything alright?"

Kevin looked over, noticing him for the first time. He wore an NYU t-shirt and a pair of shorts. Dark curls spilled onto his forehead, almost obscuring his green eyes.

"Yeah, thanks. Just contemplating the meaning of life and all.".

"Well, as they say, life is not a problem to be solved but a reality to be experienced."

"Did you just quote Kierkegaard?" Kevin asked with wide eyes. *Wow, he's beautiful,* he thought.

"I did indeed. I'm impressed that you knew that. My name is Diego," he said, offering his hand.

"Kevin. I assume you go to NYU?"

"Grad student," Diego said.

"Let me guess, philosophy?"

"Perceptive. How about you, Kevin? Where'd you get your philosophy chops?"

"That was my undergraduate degree. Just finished my first year of grad school in Theology – long story."

"Looks like you have some time on your hands. How about we grab some coffee, and you can tell me that long story of yours?" Diego asked with a sweet smile.

Kevin was startled by how forward this handsome young man was being. This could never have happened if he had stayed in the seminary. Every interaction was cloak and dagger. As enticing as the invitation was, Kevin wasn't ready to jump right into another romance. He needed time to heal.

"Listen, Diego, I'd love to, but I'm just recovering from a tough break-up. I'm just not ready."

"Of course, I completely understand. Coffee is an enormous commitment. You can't just drink it with anyone," Diego said with a smirk.

"Ok, ok, I sound like a complete fool. Sure, why not? But I'm just returning from Rome. There better be someplace that serves a mean cappuccino," Kevin said.

"The plot thickens. My curiosity is more than piqued. Shall we?"

Deep into their conversation, the newly acquainted friends wandered the streets of Greenwich Village until they found a café acceptable to Kevin's high standards. Meeting a new friend didn't remove his sense of loss, but it offered a glimmer of hope.

***

The ride from Fiumicino to NAC was mercifully uneventful. There were no breakdowns on the side of the road and no busload of new seminarians to contend with. Anthony was peacefully alone. The taxi pulled up to the front entrance of NAC. Luggage in hand and his backpack slung over his shoulder, Anthony looked up at the building with a mix of resignation and determination. No bells were tolling, no applause from upperclassmen, no pomp and circumstance. He was no longer a new man. His long and arduous first year was behind him.

Last September, he passed through these doors with gleeful anticipation and an abundance of hope. It was a dream come true. His idealism was only rivaled by his innocence, both of which had waned into sober realism.

He took in a deep breath and passed through the main doors. Just inside, he spotted Carlos with his arms wide open and a warm smile on his face. "*Caro amico*, I've missed you!" he said as he nearly knocked Anthony off his feet with a bearhug to rival all others.

"God, it's good to see you, Carlos. It's been one hell of a summer," Anthony replied.

"I can't even imagine. I am so sorry about your uncle," Carlos said.

"Thanks. I'm still processing everything."

"Of course you are, Anthony. Give yourself time. You must be good to yourself."

"I think I'm going to need a little help with that, Carlos. I have so much to tell you."

"No worries, *caro*. We have all the time in the world. Now let's get you up to your room. I'm sure you're exhausted."

Once in his room, Anthony systematically unpacked and put everything in its proper place. It was Sunday, and the peeling bells announced morning Mass. He stopped and leaned on the windowsill, feeling the warm summer air blow through his hair. Looking down into the courtyard, he saw that the fifty orange trees, representing each of the United States, were loaded with ripe fruit. Their sweetness wafted through the air, tantalizing his senses. All at once, he felt an overpowering feeling of contentment; he knew he was going to be just fine. This was a new beginning for Anthony at NAC, and he knew that whatever came to pass, he was strong enough to cope with it.

He gazed out beyond the courtyard to St. Peter's Basilica in the distance. The view was spectacular. Then he closed his eyes and said a silent prayer of thanksgiving for Uncle Joe, Miguel, and Kevin.

Although they were not here with him, he would always be grateful for their place in his life. Both, in their own way, had taught him how to love and how to receive love. He would carry that lesson in his heart forever.

Although his feelings for Kevin had only deepened throughout the summer, he was committed to giving the priesthood an honest chance. His heart demanded it. He picked up the statue of Mary that Kevin had given him the previous Christmas. The wooden carving was soft under his touch. Then Anthony closed his eyes and pictured Kevin's smiling face. Images from their first year as the new men at NAC flew through his mind. Each of them was like shiny silver as they marched up the steps to the chapel with bells tolling and upperclassmen applauding. A year later, that shine had dulled — the hardship of growth, disappointment, and loss tarnished each of them. But Anthony knew in his heart they would shine once again, perhaps without the idealism of youth, but with the wisdom of lived experience.

Chapter Forty-Five
New Beginnings

Kevin was daydreaming about the last few days spent with Diego. The time they were together in New York was so natural. There was no pretense about being gay or hiding it from the world. And although Kevin wasn't ready to jump into another relationship so soon after Anthony, he quite enjoyed the companionship. Diego was charming and bright, plus he was adorable with his dark brown eyes and smooth skin. He was certainly easy on the eyes. *Perhaps I should see where this might lead—nothing wrong with a little fling, is there?* It had been a long time since he'd slept with anyone but Anthony. Perhaps it was time for him to stop pining over him. He chose to go back to Rome rather than stay with Kevin, and he had to come to terms with the idea that Anthony had moved on. Kevin was startled out of his reverie by the phone ringing in the kitchen. Looking around, he knew no one in his family would run to answer it.

"Hello, Sullivan residence. Who's calling, please?"

"Good morning. This is Mr. Williams from St. Mary's Prep School in New York City. Is Kevin available?"

"Yes, Sir. This is Kevin speaking."

"We received your impressive resumé, and we would like you to come in for an interview," came the response. "We've had an unexpected opening for an ethics teacher."

Kevin was beside himself. It was Labor Day, and the school year would begin in a few days. He had lost hope of finding a teaching position this late in the season. He had sent so many resumés out during the last weeks of August he could barely remember the names of the schools. Kevin hopped on a train first thing Tuesday morning and made his way to the prestigious prep school. Ascending the steps to the main entrance, he felt butterflies in his stomach. If he got this job, his dream of living in Manhattan might actually come true.

Two hours later, Kevin was getting the campus tour as his teaching contract was being prepared. He had only one day to prepare for his classes, but he was so excited he didn't care. St. Mary's Prep was well established in the city and had apartments for faculty. In a single day, he had found a job and a place to live right in the city. He couldn't wait to tell someone. Strangely, the first person he thought of was Diego, not Anthony. Walking to his subway stop, he stole away into a phone booth and dialed Diego's apartment.

"What a wonderful surprise, Kevin! Don't you think it's too soon to be calling every day?" Diego teased.

"Very funny. I guess I couldn't resist your charm. Listen, I have some fantastic news. I'm officially living and working in New York City."

"What? How did that happen? So much for taking things slowly!"

"Hold on there, handsome. This is about me—not us. But it does open some doors, doesn't it?"

"Well, that's really up to you, isn't it?" Diego replied. "But I wouldn't be opposed to walking through those doors with you."

"How poetic, Diego. You certainly have a way with words. Are you free? Can you come see my tiny apartment?"

"I thought you'd never ask."

***

The next few weeks were a whirlwind of change for Kevin. He was immersed in planning lessons for his classes, learning the school's culture, and adjusting to living in the city. He was struck by how much he loved being in front of a classroom. His students were bright and engaged, and he found that these high school kids challenged him more than he expected. He couldn't simply wing it. He had to be well prepared, and if he didn't know the answer to a question, he would let them know he'd look it up. He couldn't take the chance of making anything up. Kevin felt at home in the classroom.

Before he knew it, the first semester was nearly over. One afternoon, he found himself at his desk and penning a letter to Anthony. The words rushed out, unplanned. As much as he loved his job and apartment, he realized he wished Anthony was sharing all these firsts in his life.

Caro Anthony,

How I miss you. I am so sorry not to have written more often. Although I love my teaching position, I am barely keeping my head above water. Luckily, as long as I plan a week or two in advance, I can stay ahead of them. Who would ever have thought that I would be challenged by high school students?

Living in New York City is a strange and wonderful experience. It is a bit lonely at times, but I have made some good friends. I've been seeing a guy from NYU. It's just a casual relationship, but he keeps me from pining over you! You'd like him. He reminds me of you in so many ways. He's playful and calls me out when I get over-analytical. BUT—he is not you.

How goes year two at NAC? It must feel good not to be a new man any longer. How is the new crop of new men? Are they as big a handful as we were?

There is so much more in my heart and mind. But I can barely keep my eyes open. I want you to know that, although I wished you had chosen to remain with me, I understand you had to follow your own path. I continue to pray that our paths will join together someday. Until then, I hold you in my heart.

Ti amo,

Kevin

Kevin hoped Anthony would make a surprise visit to New York for the Christmas holidays, but the possibility seemed less and less likely as the weeks passed. Even still, Kevin was in a good place. He didn't regret his decision to leave his dream of priesthood behind—not for one second. For the first time, he felt like his life was his own. He had no one looking over his shoulder judging his actions. He loved his job and he had a community of friends with whom he could be his true self. And although he wasn't out to his family, his New York crowd all knew he was gay. Kevin felt free to live his life as he saw fit.

***

Back in Rome, Anthony settled into the usual routine of NAC without a hitch. Before long, he was immersed in his studies. Much to his relief, his second year at NAC was delightfully free of drama. It bore no resemblance to the rollercoaster ride of the previous twelve months. Part of that was his choice. Anthony made a conscious effort to distance himself from Church politics or relationship drama.

He missed Kevin with his whole heart and wrote to him often during their initial weeks apart. The first few letters found both of them pouring out their hearts with wishes of being together once again. But as the semester continued, his schedule filled the void that Kevin left. He was thrilled to discover that Kevin had found a job and thoroughly loved life in the city. Anthony felt a pang of jealousy over Kevin's new life and wondered if he had made the right decision by returning to NAC. To his relief, his studies didn't seem as daunting his first year, and he still loved living in Rome. He resolved to explore the city whenever time allowed. There were many undiscovered restaurants at his avail.

One of his most significant sources of joy was his music. He spent a great deal of time with the liturgical choir and let the voices transport him to a world of beauty. The crop of new men yielded some talented singers for the choir, and Anthony soon found himself as the assistant director. That was where he met Drew. He had a lovely baritone voice and was not shy about sharing his talent. Drew was from Indiana and exuded a friendly midwestern charm. Anthony was drawn to him from the first rehearsal.

"Anthony, would you mind reviewing the harmony one more time? I'm having trouble holding it against the melody," Drew asked.

"Not at all, Drew. But you sound great. I think you've got it."

"Thanks, but I feel shaky on it. Do you mind singing it with me?"

"Let's work on it after rehearsal. I've got to teach a couple more songs." Sitting at the piano, Anthony played Drew's harmony.

Without any hesitation, Drew sat on the bench right next to Anthony. Soon they were singing and laughing at mistakes made and savoring the perfect blend of their voices. Sitting so closely on the piano bench, Drew's biceps rubbed against Anthony's, sending tingles down his spine. Anthony enjoyed Drew's not-so-subtle flirting, but didn't respond in kind. He didn't need any new drama in his life. But Anthony reveled in the attention. *Perhaps this will be a good year after all.*

Chapter Forty-Six
A Blast from the Past

Buried in a pile of final term papers, Kevin struggled to keep his eyes open. It was only 9:00 p.m. but it felt like the middle of the night. Kevin enjoyed many aspects of teaching–correcting papers was not one of them. He yawned loudly and rolled his head to stretch his neck muscles.

"Back to Immanuel Kant," he said aloud to his empty apartment.

Just then, the phone rang. It's probably Diego taking a study break, he thought.

"Hello, Diego. Are you trying to distract me from my duties?"

"Finally! Are you never at home?"

"Who is this? Miguel?"

"In the flesh! How the hell are you, my friend?" Miguel asked.

"Where have you been all these months, you bastard? You dropped off the end of the earth," Kevin exclaimed.

"Since leaving NAC, I've been a busy man. There's no time for idle chit-chat," he replied. "Besides, I've had a hell of a time trying to get your number."

"It's great to hear your voice, Miguel. Don't let it go to your head, but I've missed you."

"Same here. What do you say we meet for a drink?"

"Sure! I'll just hop a flight to Texas, and I'll be there in a jiffy!" Kevin joked.

"Or you can just meet me in New York."

"What? Wait, are you coming to the city?"

"No. I'm here—now."

"Get out! Why? How?" Kevin stammered.

"I'm visiting Maria for the holidays. You remember she goes to Fordham, right?"

"Holy shit! That's awesome! So I guess you two are still an item?"

"Yeah. Can you believe it? Who would have thought?"

Thirty minutes later, the two old friends laid eyes on each other for the first time in nine months. They met at Brandy's piano bar on the upper east side. It was quiet enough for them to have a conversation, and it reminded Kevin of the Fiddler's Elbow in Rome.

"Anthony would have loved this place," Miguel remarked.

"No kidding! He would have been at the mic all night."

"What is up with him? Of all of us, I thought he'd be the first to leave NAC."

"That is a very long story. It breaks my heart, but Anthony felt pressured to go back."

"Pressured?" Miguel asked. "What do you mean?"

Kevin filled him in on all that happened after his uncle's funeral. He was careful to leave out the part about being in love and asking Anthony to live with him in New York. But Miguel didn't let him get away with his evasive explanation. Now that they were both out of the seminary, there were no taboo subjects.

"So, the love of your life left you behind to become a priest?"

"What? No, I mean…"

"Come on, Kevin. Drop the pretense. You two were practically hanging off each other back in Rome. I may be straight or bi or whatever, but I'm not blind."

"I have to admit, you were pretty cool about it. But to be honest, neither of us could tell how you'd react if we came out to you. There are very few straight people who know about me."

"Look, I don't care who you sleep with as long as you're being careful. You know what I mean, don't you?"

"Of course, I do, Miguel. This whole AIDS crisis is terrifying. Anyway, I can't tell you how relieved I am to be able to talk to you about it."

"Hey, Kevin, I can't say I understand what it's like, but I'm your friend, and I love you as you are." Miguel pulled Kevin into a bear hug and held him. "I mean that, my friend. Let's not let months go by. We need to foster this friendship."

"There's nothing I'd like more, that is, other than getting Anthony back to New York. But enough about me. What's going on with Maria? Last I heard, you were jet-setting around Europe."

"It's crazy, but I thought my life was destroyed when they threw me out of NAC. They treated me like a criminal. I went back to Texas with my tail between my legs and sulked for weeks. When I finally called Maria to tell her all that had happened, she helped me see it was for the best. It was as if she opened a window and I could breathe again. Spending time with her these last months has given me much-needed perspective on my life. Just being away from the naval-gazing environment of NAC has helped me to feel hopeful."

"So, you guys are pretty serious, aren't you?" Kevin asked.

"We are. She has one more semester at Fordham University. Then she's looking at graduate programs in Austin. I'm pretty sure she'll be moving to Texas."

"Miguel! That is great. Are you thinking about marriage?"

"Too soon for that conversation, but we know that we want to be together. We plan to see this through."

The two dear friends talked for hours into the wee hours of the morning. The barriers that seminary life had put between them came tumbling down. They shared more stories of the months that had passed and all they learned about themselves since. Kevin had never spoken as frankly to anyone about Anthony. He told Miguel of his marriage proposal and how uncertain he was about moving on without Anthony.

"What of this guy, Diego? Do you love him?" Miguel asked.

"Love? I don't know. We're having a good time. He knows about Anthony, and I've been pretty clear I want to keep things light and easy. No drama, no marriage, just fun."

"Like friends with benefits?" Miguel said, his lips curled into a sly smile.

"Not quite," Kevin punched him in the shoulder. "We're dating. Having been a seminarian for so long, you probably don't know what that is."

Their conversation passed through laughter and pain, discussing the meaning of life and their uncertain futures. When the last call rolled around, they walked to the subway and made plans to meet for dinner with Maria the following night. Kevin made his way back to his apartment with a warm feeling in his heart. No one back home could truly understand what they experienced back in Rome. A wave of nostalgia washed over him—he needed to talk to Anthony. He had butterflies in his belly as he dialed.

"Buon giorno, bello!" Kevin said when Anthony got to the phone.

"Kevin? What a great surprise? What are you doing up so late? It must be three in the morning."

"Miguel kept me out way past my bedtime! And he made me drink too much!"

"Oh, he did, did he?" Anthony laughed. "Maria called me for your phone number. I had a feeling he would reach out to you."

"It was so good to see him. But it made me miss you more!"

"I'm a little jealous that you guys had so much fun without me. I miss you too. I wish I could come home for Christmas, but it's just too expensive. Besides, you know we're not allowed to return home until after our second year. Being home last summer was an exception."

"I figured as much. I suppose we'll have to wait until June. That seems so far in the future," Kevin lamented.

"It is. I'm sorry, Kev."

"Not your fault. Listen, I can't stay on too long. This is costing a fortune. I just wanted to hear your voice."

"I'm so glad you called. I love you, Kevin."

Hearing those three words, Kevin was reassured that his feelings were reciprocated. He slept soundly that night, content to have spent time with an old friend and hopeful for a time when he and Anthony would be reunited.

***

After Kevin's phone call, Anthony felt even more guilty about his recent tryst with Drew. *Why didn't I just tell him about Drew? He's been seeing that Diego guy. Why am I so reticent?* Somehow, Anthony felt as if he were cheating on Kevin. It was totally irrational. Kevin had been sleeping with other seminarians during his entire year as a new man. But after last summer, Anthony felt they had crossed a threshold in their relationship. Neither of them wanted to sleep with other guys.

They were in uncharted territory regarding their relationship. Anthony made a commitment to give the priesthood another try. It had been going well for months. While he missed Kevin, his lifelong dream of becoming a priest had resurfaced as a real possibility. Without the drama of his first year in Rome, Anthony genuinely believed he could take a vow of celibacy. He felt right with God and with the Church for the first time in over a year. That was, until his encounter with Drew.

The two of them were inseparable after their first night together, and Anthony was desperate for his companionship. Rarely had Anthony been in the position of being the older, wiser friend. It felt good to have Drew look up to him and seek his advice. However, what came bubbling to the surface was his need for physical intimacy. Making love with Drew was exciting and fulfilling. Together, they were passionate and playful, tender yet lustful. He enjoyed spending time with Drew. Their relationship wasn't as intense or profound as with Kevin. He wasn't in love with Drew, and somehow it was okay.

By the time spring rolled around, he and Drew slept together regularly. They didn't have deep discussions about celibacy or leaving seminary to begin new lives as a couple. Drew wanted nothing more than to become a priest. Remaining celibate never entered Drew's mind. He honestly didn't care. If Anthony brought it up, his response was the same.

"What does celibacy have to do with being a good priest? Nothing! If I can find comfort in a relationship with another priest, so be it. The whole idea of celibacy is an antiquated notion."

Anthony couldn't argue with that. But he wasn't sure he could live a duplicitous life. More and more, he pondered whether he should leave the idea of priesthood behind and join Kevin in New York. A familiar sense of emptiness crept into his heart as he looked toward the future.

Chapter Forty-Seven
An Unexpected Encounter

Barely awake, Anthony made his way down the *Gianicolo* hill in Vatican City. He didn't care that he was late for his morning class at the Gregorian University. All he could think of was that first sip of cappuccino at his favorite café in the *Piazza del Pantheon*, at *Tazza D'Oro*, the Golden Cup. It was arguably the best café in Rome. Crossing the Tiber river, Anthony breathed in the mild June air. His second year in Rome was nearly over, and he couldn't wait to get back to New York to see Kevin. He had to know if there was still a chance for a future together.

It had been a year since the two of them strolled along the Tiber, chatting about what lay ahead for them. Anthony always believed they'd be together. But that all changed when Kevin dropped his bombshell decision. When Kevin informed Anthony that he would not be returning to Rome, he couldn't believe he was done with the whole idea of becoming a priest. And although Anthony continued to question whether that was the right path for himself, he was not ready to let it go. He still wasn't sure. All he knew was that he'd give anything to spend a night with Kevin again.

As he approached the *piazza*, Anthony smiled. He loved Rome at this time of day. The city slowly came alive—shopkeepers lifted the metal gates, washed the rubbish away from their entrances, and the cobblestones shone with the morning sun. He glanced ahead to the tables in front of the *Tazza D'Oro* and did a double-take. *It can't be!* he thought. That guy looks just like Kevin. Anthony was sure he was imagining things. He was fantasizing about seeing Kevin again. Surely, his mind was playing tricks on him.

"*Ciao bello, comé stai?* You're late—I nearly gave up on you," Kevin said as he stood and winked.

"Kevin? What are you doing here?" Anthony asked.

"What? I can't get a cappuccino at our favorite cafe without checking with you first."

Kevin pulled Anthony into a tight embrace, and he was immediately engulfed in Kevin's warmth. When they finally let go, Anthony looked up at him with watery eyes.

"I can't believe you're here. I was just thinking about you, and here you are," Anthony said.

"Perhaps you conjured me up magically. You always had an enchanting quality about you."

"How is this possible? I thought you were teaching. I don't understand," Anthony's patter was incessant.

"Slow down, *caro*. Let's get you a cappuccino, and I'll explain everything. *Va bene?*"

When they finally sat down, Kevin explained he was in Rome for the entire month of June as a chaperone for a group of students. He reminded Anthony that the private school at which he taught had many wealthy families and went on many international trips. Kevin was a logical choice as a chaperon when they planned a study tour to Rome.

"So, here I am. The flight got in at six this morning, and of course, I can't check into the residence until after noontime. I hoped you'd follow our old routine and stop here for a cappuccino," Kevin said.

"Old habits are hard to break. But why didn't you write or call me to tell me you were coming?" Anthony asked. "I could have met you at the airport."

"What, and ruin the surprise? The look on your face was priceless."

"I still can't believe you're here, and for a whole month! I was just plotting my return to New York—dreaming of how we would spend the summer. This is unreal, Kevin."

"Well, now we can plan it together. There's so much to talk about."

"God, I wish I could kiss you right here, right now in the center of the *piazza*," Anthony whispered.

"Hmm, if we were in Washington Square, you could. Like I said, we have a lot to discuss," Kevin responded with the slightest hint of chastising.

"Point taken, *caro mio*. Let's leave that for later. What's your schedule? Are the students here yet?" Anthony asked, evading the topic.

"Not yet, they sent me a few days in advance to get things organized. I am all yours, at least until the weekend."

"OK then! Walk me to class, and we can meet for lunch," Anthony suggested.

"Perfect. Let's go to the *Abbruzzi*. My mouth is watering for their *rigatoni alla carbonara*."

It was as if no time had passed. The two lovers barely stopped for a breath as they made their way to the Gregorian University. Before they knew it, they stood before the massive doors and bid each other goodbye. Kevin was content to have a few hours to reacquaint himself with his former home. Fortunately, he could to drop his luggage at the residence before check-in, so he wandered down the narrow alley toward the Trevi fountain. At that hour of the morning, the tourists had not yet awakened. Kevin found a cozy spot and gazed at the historic monument, and let his mind wander through his memories.

***

The waiter recognized Kevin immediately. He and Anthony had dined at the *Abbruzzi* regularly. Even a year later, they welcomed Kevin as if he were family. *God, I love Italy,* he thought. Kevin took a seat facing the door, sipping a glass of house wine as he eagerly waited for Anthony to get out of class.

His proposal to Anthony last summer seemed like a lifetime ago. Both were studying to be priests, but were madly in love with each other. They had barely made plans for their lives together in New York City when his uncle died. Family pressure and his grief sent Anthony right back to Rome. But Anthony promised he would not give up on their relationship. *I certainly hope he's come to his senses by now. I know he still loves me,* Kevin thought. Having this month together in the place where it all began could not be better. No sooner did the thought cross his mind, but Anthony walked in the door.

"So, here we are again as if you never left," Anthony said.

"Right!? A year has gone by, and it feels like we were never apart. How many times have we sat at this very table wondering about our futures?" asked Kevin.

"More than we can count, and look at us now. We still don't know what the future holds for us," Anthony said, looking into his wine glass.

"Maybe not, Anthony. But now, we're a lot closer to finding out. Don't you think? I mean, can't you feel it?"

"How could I not? You know, I could hardly concentrate during my classes this morning. If finals weren't coming up, I would have skipped them. I couldn't wait to see you."

"I, on the other hand, couldn't wait for a nice bowl of carbonara!" Kevin joked.

"So you miss the pasta more than me? You suck."

"And quite well, I might add," Kevin replied as they burst into a fit of laughter. They were back. It felt like heaven.

They finished their meal and allowed themselves more than a few after-dinner drinks before leaving the restaurant.

"Let's get you to your hotel," Anthony suggested. "It's long past check-in time, and you look like you could use a nap."

"A nap is *NOT* what I need right now," Kevin said, leering at his friend.

"Well, you certainly haven't changed," Anthony said as he laughed. "Let's get out of here before we make a scene."

Once in his room, Kevin turned to Anthony, placed his hands on either side of his face. He looked deeply into his brown eyes. Kevin was buzzed from all the wine, but he knew what he wanted. He had waited for nearly a year for this reunion.

Kevin bent his head down and softly touched his lips to Anthony's— it was electric. Anthony leaned in, pressing his pelvis against Kevin. That was all it took. They shed their clothes with urgency and fell onto the bed, giving in to their hunger. There was nothing romantic about their lovemaking. It was pure animal passion, and they both needed it. Kevin didn't doubt what it meant. All he knew was that he wanted Anthony as much as he ever did. When it was over, sweat beaded on his brow as he turned to him.

"God, I missed this," Kevin exclaimed, catching his breath.

"How long have you been holding that in? Damn, you nearly crushed me there, tiger," Anthony said, snickering.

"There's much more where that came from, *caro*—much more."

Kevin wanted nothing more than to ask Anthony if he had decided about their future. When Anthony returned to Rome the previous August, he promised to consider their relationship. It broke both their hearts to be apart. But Anthony had to give his dream of becoming a priest one more try. The many letters they'd written to one another continued to prove that their hearts remained with each other. Kevin poured his soul into each word he wrote.

Nevertheless, he made sure not to pressure Anthony. He had to come to his decision on his own. Lying beside him on the narrow hotel bed, Kevin grew anxious. His patience was wearing thin. Kevin needed to know if Anthony would return to New York with him. Would Anthony finally accept his proposal? *I've only been here for less than a day.* Kevin thought to himself. *Just wait for the right moment to bring it up.*

Chapter Forty-Eight
Trouble in Paradise

"Hey, Anthony, where have you been slinking off to each evening?" Drew asked. "We've hardly spent any time together this week."

"Yeah, I've meant to tell you. You remember Kevin from my first year here?" Anthony began.

"Do I remember Kevin? What a question," Drew said. "He looms large in everything we do. Why?"

"He's here in Rome with a student group. He surprised me a few days ago at *Tazza D'Oro*. I've been hanging out with him as much as I can while he's here."

"That's incredible. Why haven't you brought him by?" he asked. "I'm dying to meet my predecessor!"

"He's not your predecessor, Drew. You know how I feel about Kevin. To be honest, I wasn't sure how you'd react to him being here, so I've been stalling. He's been wanting to visit since he arrived."

"What do you mean, Anthony? Why would you worry about me? It's not like he's my competition," Drew said.

Anthony looked away and sighed.

"Anthony? What aren't you telling me?"

"Look, you know how much I love him…"

"You're sleeping with him, aren't you?" Drew had started to raise his voice. "What the hell? Where does that leave me?"

"Drew, you know I love you, but we are not planning on spending the rest of our lives together."

"So you sleep with him without even giving me a heads up? Have you been with him every night?"

"I'm sorry, Drew. I know you have big plans for your life, and while we are good together now while were in Rome, we both know it won't last. You'll be going back to Indiana, and I'll be in New York."

"Hold on, are you seriously thinking of giving it all up and leaving Rome? Kevin shows up out of the blue, and you just jump into a new life? What the hell is wrong with you?" Drew said.

"Drew, I have always been honest with you about Kevin. You know he's the love of my life. I'm trying to figure out what that means. Please try to understand."

"You know, you can be a real dick, Anthony. You're so wrapped up in your own feelings that you didn't even give a thought to mine. I can't wait to meet Kevin. This should be great fun."

Drew stormed out of the room and slammed the door.

Anthony's anxiety mounted. His conversation with Drew had not gone well at all. By contrast, the last week with Kevin was like a dream come true. His heart exploded with love for him, and he could think of nothing better than to start a life with Kevin in New York. But a lot had happened during the last nine months in Rome—not the least of which was meeting Drew. As one of the wide-eyed new men, Drew's innocence enchanted Anthony. He reminded Anthony of his first year and wanted nothing more than to protect him from the struggles he experienced. Anthony took Drew under his wing, and the two hit it off from the start. He never meant for it to become physical.

Their romance had begun after the December 8th celebration, just before Christmas. They had both had a great deal to drink. With the holidays so near, emotions simmered just below the surface as they shared their feelings of loneliness. Sitting on the bed, Anthony pulled Drew into a hug.

"Don't worry, Drew. You're not alone here. You've got me—and a lot of other guys who care about you."

Drew nestled his head into the crook of Anthony's neck and kissed him lightly. Anthony felt his pulse quicken—a feeling he hadn't had since his time with Kevin. A pang of guilt scratched at his conscience, but he pushed it deep inside. Drew smelled of soap mingled with an intoxicating musk. He felt his trousers tighten and kissed the top of Drew's head. Slowly, Drew turned his face up and pressed his lips against Anthony's. Feeling Drew's tongue flicking at his lips, Anthony succumbed to his desire.

That night was the first of many. Drew was a font of cool water in the middle of the desert. He breached the void that Kevin had left in Anthony's heart. With roles reversed, Anthony found himself with words of wisdom as Drew complained about perceived injustices or frustrations with the faculty. Smiling to himself, he wondered what Kevin would think if he could see him as the counselor. Although Drew could never take Kevin's place, he carved out a significant corner in Anthony's heart.

With each letter he wrote to Kevin, Anthony longed to share his feeling for his newfound friend. He had no desire to end things with Kevin but wanted to share the joy with his best friend. Though Anthony knew that would be a mistake. How could he tell him he loved another man? Anthony couldn't betray him like that. He loved them both.

He had kept this secret for months, but now Kevin and Drew would meet. Anthony never dreamed a dilemma like this would present itself. But here it was. He had put off Kevin's constant requests to visit the seminary as long as he could. But a week had passed since his arrival, and Anthony had run out of excuses. While Kevin had no clue, Drew knew precisely who he was *AND* how important Kevin was to Anthony. Drew understood that Kevin was a threat. Anthony could only hope Drew would behave. There was no way he wanted Kevin to get hurt.

***

"Feels like the old days, eh *caro*?" Kevin said as he and Anthony entered the main doors of the college.

"Yes and no," Anthony replied. "While you've been gallivanting all over New York City, I've been holding down the fort for the last year. It feels surreal to be walking in here with you again."

"Still, it brings back some great memories. Some bad ones as well, but this will always be the place where you and I met," Kevin said.

Just then, their friend Carlos appeared, and the reunions began to multiply. One by one, his former classmates heard of his return and dropped by Anthony's room to visit. Out came the Baileys Irish Cream, and a party ensued. As the crowd grew, they moved to the roof deck. The view of St. Peter's Basilica and all ancient Rome college's roof was as magnificent as ever. It was the location of many shared moments for Anthony and Kevin. Anthony let go of his worries and enjoyed the spontaneous gathering.

Kevin was lost in the middle of a crowd reveling in his popularity when a handsome fellow with blue eyes and blond hair strode up to him with an outstretched hand.

"Hi Kevin, I'm Drew. I have heard so much about you. It's nice to meet you finally," he said with a twinkle in his eye.

His assumption of familiarity surprised Kevin, but he rolled with it.

"You have, have you? From whom did you hear of me, and what did you learn?" he asked with a disingenuous formality.

"Our mutual *beau*, of course. But don't worry, he spared me the details," Drew said as he winked.

Drew's response took Kevin off balance. Did he say, *beau*? All at once, he understood why Anthony had been so cagey about his visit to the college today. He had a secret—a big one. Kevin felt his stomach wrench but refused to let his discomfort show.

"Oh, that one?" he said with a laugh. "I wouldn't trust Anthony for a second. But I'll say one thing for him. He's got good taste."

He winked, to which Drew gave a sly smile and squeezed Kevin's hand more tightly. Pushing it a little further, he leaned in with a conspiratorial whisper.

"Perhaps, we'll have time to compare notes—or more."

Anthony watched the scene unfold as if in slow motion. This was his worst nightmare, and it didn't look as if Drew was behaving. Their body language said it all. He knew Drew was being flirty and sly. He could see Kevin playing along but buying none of it. Anthony was in trouble. He quickly moved in to access the damage.

"I see you two have met. Kevin, don't believe anything Drew says. He's young, innocent, and prone to exaggeration," Anthony said.

"Hardly innocent," both Kevin and Drew said at once. They caught each other's eyes and laughed. But Kevin was not amused.

Anthony was in damage control. He didn't know exactly what Drew said to him, but he could see that Kevin was upset. And he wasn't sure, but it looked like Drew had a self-satisfied grin on his face. *If I had only warned Kevin, I could have avoided this crisis*, he chastised himself.

One by one, the partiers excused themselves, leaving only Anthony, Kevin, and Drew on the roof. The tension that had blossomed earlier in the evening continued to simmer below the surface. Anthony decided to take the lead.

"Drew, if you don't mind, I'm going to walk Kevin back to his hotel."

"Of course, why don't I come along so you don't have to walk back alone?" Drew offered.

"No, I need to have some time alone with Kevin."

There, he said it. Anthony could not be more direct. He hoped that would let both of them know his feelings. Kevin remained silent as he stared off into the ancient city. Anthony had a lot of explaining to do.

"I have a better idea," said Kevin. "Why don't the three of us go out to dinner?"

"No, Kev. We have to talk, and we need to be alone," Anthony said.

"I don't know." Drew chimed in, "I think it would be great fun for the three of us to spend some time together. Right, Kevin?".

"Absolutely! I'd think you'd jump at the opportunity to spend time with your two men," Kevin said. Anthony could not mistake the edge in his voice.

"A dinner threesome—an unholy trinity of sorts," Drew added.

"Come on, guys. This isn't fair," said Anthony.

It was all but decided as the three men walked out the seminary doors and down the *Janiculum* hill. Anthony's anxiety continued to build. He remained silent while Drew and Kevin chatted animatedly the entire way to the restaurant. They had bonded over their mutual anger with Anthony.

Chapter Forty-Nine
The Future is Now

The restaurant was just on the other side of St. Peter's Square. *Il Mozzicone* served the best *penne all'arrabbiata* in Rome. Kevin gauged how good it was by how much his head sweated when eating the spicy pasta. Kevin chose it, knowing that it was one of their favorite getaway spots. Little did he know that Drew and Anthony dined there often. The waiter greeted all three of them like old friends and seated them at their usual table. The rest of the evening unfolded with Anthony in the crosshairs.

"So, Drew, tell me how you and Anthony came to be a thing?"

"Oh, you know—the usual, over-drinking at one of the many parties, followed by an intimate conversation in his room," Drew explained.

"Wait, let me guess. Then he soothed your worries with a warm embrace, which led to wandering hands, and *violá!*"

"How'd you guess? You must be psychic, Kevin!" Drew exclaimed.

The rest of the evening continued with Anthony on the spit being roasted by his two lovers. *How could I have let this happen?* he thought to himself. Kevin and Drew were merciless. To his surprise, they seemed to be enjoying each other and the torture they were inflicting.

"I bet the two of you have spent endless hours discussing celibacy and how it's not a viable option," Kevin said.

"And how there are so many priests who continue to have relationships throughout their lives," Drew continued.

"Have you talked about the possibility of living your lives together in secret?" Kevin asked.

"We haven't gotten there yet. But I suppose it's just a matter of time."

Anthony was beside himself. There was little he could do to stop them. The train was out of the station, and it was barreling straight at him.

"Yes, Anthony is a sweet talker, isn't he?" Kevin said. "Don't you just love when he gets so animated and passionate about some topic? His eyes light up, and everyone in the room is riveted."

"He's a charmer, all right," Drew said. "But he's high maintenance. His pasta has to be cooked just right, with no grated cheese on top. He's so critical of my music choices and, don't get me started on his incessant flirting."

"Right!? Then he acts so innocently when his conquests take him up on it. 'Oh, it just happened. It didn't mean anything.' He's quite the victim. Has he hooked up with Carlos yet?" Kevin asked.

"Hey, wait just a minute, Kevin," Anthony finally chimed in. "I seem to recall that you were head over heels infatuated with Carlos. I believe there's a bit of projection going on here."

"Fair enough—I did enjoy his ripped abs, and let me tell you, his supple lips drove me to distraction."

"Is that so?" Drew asked. "I just might have to pursue him more aggressively, especially considering that you're back in the picture, Kevin."

"I *am* back in the picture, aren't I?" Kevin said, locking eyes with Anthony. "So, what happens now, *caro*? Who will you choose, Drew or me?"

Anthony let out a heavy sigh and shook his head. At the end of the meal, Anthony asked Drew to give him some time alone with Kevin. Drew graciously agreed. Although he let him have it all evening, Anthony could tell that he was letting go. He looked back to see Drew watching the two of them walking down the *Via del Conciliazione*. Anthony knew Drew would be all right. Whereas he and Kevin hadn't uttered a word since leaving the restaurant.

The silence continued as they walked towards Kevin's hotel. Anthony didn't know how to start the conversation. But he had to break the chilling silence. Dinner with Drew was a disaster.

"Kevin, I'm sorry I didn't warn you about Drew. I meant to tell you about him earlier this week. I just didn't have the courage."

"This week? What about this month, or last, or in any of the letters we wrote to each other?" Kevin said bitterly.

"You're right. I'm a jerk. I should have told you about him. But I didn't want you to think you'd been replaced. No one will ever take your place, Kevin."

"But someone did. I can see the connection between the two of you. He's certainly in love with you. So, I have one question." Kevin stopped walking and turned to face Anthony. "Are you in love with Drew?"

Anthony took in a labored breath. How do I answer this question? If I don't explain myself just right, I could lose him.

"I love him. But I'm not in love with him, Kevin. I'm in love with you."

Kevin looked deeply into his eyes. Anthony hoped Kevin could see that he was earnest.

"So, where does that leave us, Anthony? What does that mean for our future together?"

"I was hoping we could have this conversation when we were both fresh and thinking straight," Anthony responded. "But I guess now is as good as any time."

Instinctually, they aimed for a bench in *Piazza Navona*. Facing the famous fountain of the four rivers, the two lovers let the flowing water lull them into a trance. They had spent many memorable moments in the piazza; they had sorted through many crises on that bench. The significance of this moment was not lost on either of them.

"So, here we are again, my dear Anthony. The time we sat on a park bench, was when you left me for Holy Mother Church. So now what? Are you going to leave me for another man?"

"How can you ask me that, Kevin? Don't you know that you are everything to me? I wanted you to come back to Rome with me, but you decided to stay in New York. I never wanted to do this without you."

"Anthony, do you hear yourself? Last August, I asked you to marry me—not live secret lives together as priests. I know it's more complicated than that, but I don't want you to be a priest. I want you to come back to New York to be with me. Don't you understand that?"

"I do, and I am closer to that decision than ever. This week together has brought our relationship alive again. I love you, Kevin."

"So, then. What about Drew? I honestly don't know how to feel about that. I feel betrayed," Kevin said, choking back his tears.

"Look, I am sorry I didn't tell you, really I am. But you have been with other guys this last year, haven't you?"

"Yes, Anthony. I've dated other guys. The difference is that I told you about them—all of them, and I wasn't in love with any of them. I feel like there is something more between you and Drew."

"I should have told you. I planned on telling you when I got back home, but your surprise visit to Rome changed things."

"If you weren't in love with him, why wouldn't you have written to me about him? You were, *are*, afraid of your own feelings toward him. You forget, I know you better than you know yourself," Kevin said bitterly.

"Perhaps that's true. But let's be fair. I stood by your side throughout your sexual awakening back when we were new men. I lost count of the many conquests you confessed to me. You knew I didn't like it, but you continued to sleep around. Don't throw us away just because the shoe is on the other foot," Anthony said.

"Fair enough. I was a bit of a whore last year," Kevin said with a smirk.

"A bit? Give me a break!"

That broke the tension, and both men erupted in a familiar bout of laughter.

"We are really screwed up, aren't we?" Kevin said.

"Yes, but we already knew that."

They sat for a few minutes in silence. Anthony surreptitiously inched closer to Kevin on the bench. They couldn't hold hands in public, but he needed to feel the warmth of his body against his. Kevin's rigid body relaxed, and they leaned into each other. They both let down their guards, and for the first time that day, they felt connected again.

They stood and made their way along the cobblestone alleys and found themselves at Kevin's hotel. Anthony turned and looked up at Kevin.

"Can I come up?"

"I don't know, Anthony. I have a lot of thinking to do, and we can't seem to keep our hands off each other when we're alone. We have some significant decisions to make, and I have to sort out all that I learned today."

"Kevin, please," he begged. "I need to be alone with you."

Kevin sighed and waved his arm, signaling that Anthony should enter through the lobby doors. Once in his room, Anthony sat on the bed and motioned for Kevin to join him. He took a deep breath, placed his hands on Kevin's knees, and faced him.

"I love you, Kevin. This year apart was torture, especially the first few months when I felt completely alone. I never expected to be in Rome without you. And although I understood that you had to remain in New York, I felt abandoned. We had always planned to be here together. I never dreamed that you'd be the one to leave. When I met Drew, I had someone to take care of. His struggles, his needs, superseded my own. As I took care of him, it took the focus off my loneliness, and my heart began to heal. I never intended to sleep with him. But to be honest, I didn't fight it either. He and I found comfort in each other's arms, and we do love each other. However, that love can never compare to what you and I share. When my heart found yours, it found its home. *You* are my home, Kevin. I've had a year to work through my feelings, to let go of my dream of becoming a priest. Without you, that dream is empty. My *life* is empty. And while there are people I love, like Drew and Carlos, they can never diminish what I feel for you.

"In many ways, I put my feelings for you on hold for the better part of this last year. It was much too painful for me to deal with. I hate that we are fighting right now. But maybe this had to happen for me to truly understand what I must do. Having both of you work me over at dinner revealed my heart. I do love both of you, but that love is not equal. As much as I love Drew, what he and I share doesn't compare to the depth of *our* love. No one can fully understand what you and I experienced as new men last year. You carried me through some of my darkest moments, and with you, I've shared the greatest of love. So, when you ask me who I will choose, there is no question. It is you, Kevin. It's always been you."

***

Washington Square was teeming with people enjoying the late summer evening. A warm breeze caressed their cheeks, and the table had a magnificent view of the park. It was the perfect spot for people-watching. The waiter placed the steaming bowl of spaghetti alla carbonara in front of Anthony. It looked good, but it was nothing like the carbonara he had in Rome.

"What's the matter?" Kevin asked. "Isn't that what you ordered?"

"Yes, it's fine, just not as good as at the *Abbruzzi*."

"Nothing can compare to our Roman restaurants. But this little place is the closest I've found in New York," Kevin said.

"And I love it."

"And I love you, Anthony."

They raised their glasses and toasted.

"Here's to spending the rest of our lives together," said Kevin.

"Here's to *me*—finally getting it through my thick head that you are the most important thing in my life," Anthony added.

And without a worry about who might notice, Anthony leaned over the table and kissed him.

– The End –

More by Mario Dell'Olio

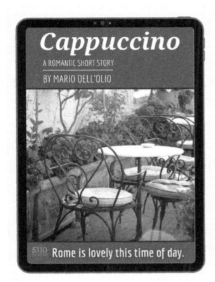

AVAILABLE NOW!

NEW ROMANTIC SHORT STORY

BY MARIO DELL'OLIO
EXCLUSIVELY ON KINDLE

Anthony's second year in Rome is nearly over, and he can't wait to get back to New York to see Kevin. He needs to know if there is still a chance for a future together. All he knew was that he'd give anything to spend a night with Kevin again.

Kevin wants nothing more than to ask Anthony if he had made any decisions about their future. It broke both their hearts to be apart. Kevin needs to know if Anthony will return to New York to be with him. The many letters they'd written to one another continued to prove that their hearts remained with each other... will they be together?

Will Anthony confront his feelings? Will Kevin ask Anthony to move back to New York with him?

You might also like...

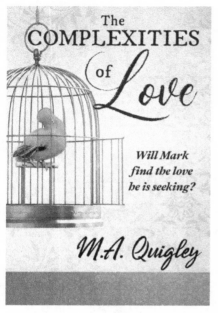

"Intriguing and messily realistic..." – Kirkus Reviews

"Most Anticipated YA LGBTQ Fiction" – Lambda Literary

An Australian teen learns about life, hidden love, and family secrets. Mark Cooney grows up aware that there is something different about him and hopes that his parents will never find out.

Mark's best friend Dave disappeared when he was thirteen and returned ten years later. Mark became more and more vulnerable as they got closer. It came with a price.

Tormented by his inner demons and refusing to be controlled by anyone, Dave reveals a secret that he has kept since childhood, which leads to grave consequences for Mark and his family.

The Complexities of Love **is a coming-of-age story about Mark as he confronts the truth about his family and his identity.** All he yearns for is for Dave to return his love, but will that happen, or will he find someone else?

"**Heartbreaking**... I found myself rooting for Mark to accept himself... and ultimately find true love. — **such a profound novel**." – Mario Dell'Olio, author of New Men: Bonds of Brotherhood

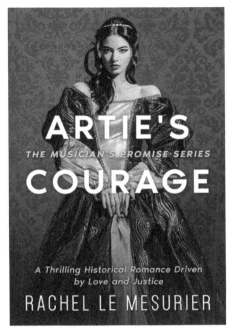

A courageous farm girl's life is changed forever when she falls in love with a charming street musician, opening her eyes to the cruel mistreatment of Mexico's mine workers and compelling her to stand with them against their oppressor — the man she is marrying.

Esperanza lives a charmed life. The daughter of a wealthy landowner, her family is thrilled when she attracts the attentions of the handsome and mysterious Don Raúl, opening the door to a glittering life of opulence for them all.

However, a chance encounter with a charming street musician forces Esperanza to open her eyes to the cruel underworld of Mexico's mistreated working classes, and she begins to doubt everything she ever thought she wanted.

As the people begin to rise up in a bloodthirsty revolution against their oppressors, Esperanza is forced to make choices that she hoped never to face. Esperanza's decisions threaten to tear apart her family, her heart, and the country she loves.

In this brutal world where a few careless words can cost lives, will the price of freedom prove to be more than what she is willing to pay?

Led by strong female characters, *ARTIE'S COURAGE* turns the common damsel in distress trope on its head. Based on real historical events, this thrilling page-turner story of love and courage in the face of adversity follows characters on an emotional journey through laughter, tears, passion, and heartbreak.

YOU MIGHT ALSO LIKE...

CPSIA information can be obtained
at www.ICGtesting.com
Printed in the USA
LVHW031513180522
719025LV00005B/130